THE RED LION

A MEDIEVAL ROMANCE
LIONS OF THE HIGHLANDS SERIES, BOOK ONE

BY KATHRYN LE VEQUE

Kathryn Le Veque Novels

Medieval Romance:

The de Russe Legacy:
The White Lord of Wellesbourne
The Dark One: Dark Knight
Beast
Lord of War: Black Angel
The Falls of Erith
The Iron Knight

The de Lohr Dynasty:
While Angels Slept (Lords of East Anglia)
Rise of the Defender
Steelheart
Spectre of the Sword
Archangel
Unending Love
Shadowmoor
Silversword

Great Lords of le Bec:
Great Protector
To the Lady Born (House of de Royans)

Lords of Eire:
The Darkland (Master Knights of Connaught)
Black Sword
Echoes of Ancient Dreams (time travel)

De Wolfe Pack Series:
The Wolfe
Serpent
Scorpion (Saxon Lords of Hage – Also related to The Questing)
Walls of Babylon
The Lion of the North
Dark Destroyer

Ancient Kings of Anglecynn:
The Whispering Night
Netherworld

Battle Lords of de Velt:
The Dark Lord
Devil's Dominion

Reign of the House of de Winter:
Lespada
Swords and Shields (also related to The Questing, While Angels Slept)

De Reyne Domination:
Guardian of Darkness
The Fallen One (part of Dragonblade Series)

Unrelated characters or family groups:
The Gorgon (Also related to Lords of Thunder)
The Warrior Poet (St. John and de Gare)
Tender is the Knight (House of d'Vant)
Lord of Light
The Questing (related to The Dark Lord, Scorpion)
The Legend (House of Summerlin)

The Dragonblade Series: (Great Marcher Lords of de Lara)
Dragonblade
Island of Glass (House of St. Hever)
The Savage Curtain (Lords of Pembury)

The Fallen One (De Reyne Domination)
Fragments of Grace (House of St. Hever)
Lord of the Shadows
Queen of Lost Stars (House of St. Hever)

Lords of Thunder: The de Shera Brotherhood Trilogy
The Thunder Lord
The Thunder Warrior
The Thunder Knight

Highland Warriors of Munro
The Red Lion

Time Travel Romance: (Saxon Lords of Hage)
The Crusader
Kingdom Come

Contemporary Romance:

Kathlyn Trent/Marcus Burton Series:
Valley of the Shadow
The Eden Factor
Canyon of the Sphinx

The American Heroes Series:
The Lucius Robe
Fires of Autumn
Evenshade
Sea of Dreams
Purgatory

Other Contemporary Romance:
Lady of Heaven
Darkling, I Listen

Multi-author Collections/Anthologies:
With Dreams Only of You (USA Today bestseller)
Sirens of the Northern Seas (Viking romance)
Ever My Love (sequel to With Dreams Only Of You) July 2016

Note: All Kathryn's novels are designed to be read as stand-alones, although many have cross-over characters or cross-over family groups. Novels that are grouped together have related characters or family groups.

Series are clearly marked. All series contain the same characters or family groups except the American Heroes Series, which is an anthology with unrelated characters.

There is NO particular chronological order for any of the novels because they can all be read as stand-alones, even the series.

For more information, find it in **A Reader's Guide to the Medieval World of Le Veque**.

Author's Note

Jamison and Havilland were first introduced in the "Once Upon A Haunted Castle" collection released in September 2016. I wrote a novella for the collection entitled DEEP INTO DARKNESS. I had such a great time writing about Jamison and Havilland that I knew I had to write a "big" book for them – how they met – so here it is in THE RED LION.

Now, let's be clear about this book – it has a highland hero. My first! Jamison is a Highlander to the bone, born and raised in the highlands for the most part. However, not much of this book actually takes place in the highlands, although it is the backdrop for some of the chapters. Most of the action is in Wales. There's a lot of traveling in this book!

Secondly, let's discuss the character names – Havilland's last name is de Llion, which is a hybrid Welsh/Norman name. Family history says that the original family name was something else until the Normans came and it was Normans who gave them the name, for regional identification purposes, that is used in this book. The rub is this – the double "L" in the Welsh language is a sound unnatural to English-speaking folks. It's kind of a hissing sound – the best way to do it is to put your tongue to your teeth as if you are about to pronounce "L", but then blow hard so air hisses out over the sides of your tongue. That's the double "L" sound of Llion!

For our purposes, the name has evolved a bit. The Normans don't like that odd sound, so the way they pronounce the name is more like "duh-lee-OWN". They've Anglicized the Welsh name because, well, they're Normans and that's what they do. They make things to their liking. And Havilland's name is pronounced just like the name of the great star, Olivia de Havilland. No odd Welsh pronunciation there. In fact, the name is an homage to one of the greatest actresses of the Golden Age of Hollywood. Miss Olivia is a tough bird, as is our heroine. When you envision Havilland de Llion, there is a good deal of Miss Olivia in her.

So have fun reading this book and enjoying the variety of characters in it, including the introduction of the next three members of the Lions of the Highlands series – The White Dragon, The Gray Fox, and The Black Falcon. These gentlemen play a significant role in this book and I hope you enjoy them.

Now, go forth and read!

Love,
Kathryn

TABLE OF CONTENTS

Dedication

There are so many people to thank in my life, people who support me in more ways than one.

There is my husband, Rob, who really lives the life of a bachelor while I'm on a deadline but at least he's a good sport about it. He understands a thing or two about living the dream. There are my parents who 'try' not to call me when I'm on a deadline and who are utterly thrilled with this life I lead. There are my children, of course, who couldn't be happier that I do what I do.

And then there is my professional team – my editor who swears at me when I send him a book to edit with two days until the deadline, and my administrative assistant who keeps the Le Veque machine running even when I try to ignore her questions because I'm on that much-mentioned deadline. I adore both Sdcott Moreland and Kris Newberger, and couldn't get along without them. New team member Samantha Williams is really stepping up and helping me with her PA and marketing support.

In a word? I'm blessed, and I don't use that term lightly. But I owe the most to my fabulous readers who make me an author. Without 'you', there is no 'me', so to all of you, thank you from the bottom of my heart!

Dread God

Clan Munro Motto

PROLOGUE

"Do ye see what yer lust

has cost me...?"

August, Year of our Lord 1288
Village of Strathpeffer
Lands of Clan MacKenzie, Scottish Highlands

"YE KNOW I'VE been a-wantin' ye, lass. I never thought I'd be alone wit'ch ye."

A soft giggle filled the stale, urine-smelling air of the barn. "Dunna keep me waitin'," a woman long, dark hair said, lurching forward to capture his lower lip between her two teeth. "I canna promise we will be alone for long."

The man groaned as she nibbled at his lower lip. A hand, rough and calloused, began to pull down the shoulder of her simple shift. He very much wanted the treasures that lay beneath that garment.

"I thought ye said yer brother was a-huntin'," he said, the hand on her shoulder moving to her breast.

"He is – but I dunna know when he'll return!"

The woman gasped as the man pinched her nipple through the fabric. Buried in a pile of dried grass that was shoved back into a corner of a sod-roofed barn, they had as much privacy as they were going to get given the circumstances. Two cows, a calf, three goats, and a smattering of kids watched as the big, auburn-haired Highlander suckled on the woman's neck as he fondled her through her shift.

As the woman moaned and writhed, he managed to get both hands underneath her shift, pulling it up to reveal the unfurling flower between her legs. When he touched her there, she squealed, causing the goats to jump nervously. And when he inserted a dirty, rough finger deep into her woman's core, she grabbed at his hair, pulling his face down to the junction between her legs. The man growled, hungrily, and she moaned as he descended on her, feeding furiously on her flesh. He had waited a very long time for this moment and he was going to taste this shameless piece of female meat if it killed him.

And it just might.

"Eva!"

The shout came from outside the sod structure and the woman started, spurred by the sound of her name. The man's head came up from her groin, his blue eyes narrowed.

"I thought ye said he was a-huntin'!" the man hissed.

The woman nodded wildly even as the man bolted to his feet, struggling to tie up the breeches that had been unfastened and twisted around his thighs.

"He was!" she gasped, quickly attempting to pull down her shift and cover up the breast the man had managed to expose. "Quickly, Robbie! Go from the window!"

Robert Munro was already heading in that direction. The problem was that he was certain that he was too big to slip through the narrow ventilation window built into the sod wall. Still, he had to try. More than that, he was angry to find himself in this situation because he'd brought his brother along to prevent an occurrence such as this.

Why hadn't Jamison warned him?

Infuriated, he raced to the ventilation window and immediately determined that there was no way he could squeeze his bulk through it. The call came again, a concerned brother crying for his sister, and Robert turned swiftly towards the sound only to realize the woman was standing directly behind him. He'd ended up smacking her in the head with his elbow when he turned around, hitting her so hard that he knocked the woman unconscious.

Anger turned to disbelief when he realized what he'd done. He bent down and scooped the woman up, trying to figure out what in the hell he was going to do now. If Eva's brother came in and found him with the man's unconscious sister in his arms, his life would be worth no more than the dirt beneath his feet. In a panic, he caught a glimpse of the ventilation window again and a thought occurred to him – Eva was small enough to fit through it.

Sweet Jesú, he didn't want Connell the Crazed to find him with his sister!

"*Eva!*"

Frantically, Robert pushed Eva right through the ventilation window, hearing her hit the ground softly on the other side. That was all he could do for her, God forgive him. Cast her off like so much rubbish to save his own foolish life. Brushing his hands off, making sure there were no signs of a woman on his body, Robert very casually emerged from the sod barn.

"Are ye lookin' fer yer sister, Connell?" he asked oh-so-casually. "I canna find the lass, either. Did she go tae the town, then?"

Connell MacKenzie's eyes narrowed at Robert Munro, third son of George Munro, chief of Clan Munro. Connell's father, Somerled, was also the head of his clan. George and Somerled weren't exactly allies but they weren't exactly enemies. There was a strained peace between them at the moment. However, that didn't give Robert leave to trespass on MacKenzie lands.

"What are ye doin' here?" Connell demanded. "Ye have no need tae seek out me sister."

Robert held up his hands to show he was no threat. "Me mother has a likin' fer Eva's goat stock," he said, grasping at an excused he'd long planned were it to be needed. "I've come here tae do me mother's biddin', Connell. Me mum wants one of Eva's young male kids."

Connell was still frowning. He wasn't entirely sure he believed the man; that was evident. Standing in the yard of the sod barn, they were ankle-deep in fetid mud as the gentle sea breezes blew in from the east. But the mood that had settled between them was anything but gentle. It was increasingly dark with suspicion. Connell took his eyes from Robert long enough to look around again for his sister.

"I'll not have ye wanderin' the barn," he finally said. "Go stand by the house. I'll find me sister."

Robert complied, or at least pretended to. He needed to get out of there, and quickly, so going to stand by the house wasn't part of that plan. All Connell had to do was walk around the side of the barn and find Eva lying in the mud, unconscious. If that happened, Robert needed to have a head start on the man. Therefore, he had to leave, and leave quickly.

"There's no hurry," Robert said, backing away across the yard. "I'll come back another time. I'll tell me mum she'll have tae wait. Mayhap she will come see Eva herself."

Stop rambling! He silently scolded himself, turning for the fence that enclosed the mucky yard. If Connell wasn't already suspicious enough, mindless chatter would only make it worse.

Robert deftly leapt over the stone fence of the barnyard, praying he could get away cleanly and wondering all the while where Jamison was. It wasn't like the man not to be near, especially in a circumstance like this. Robert had come to see the woman he loved, or at least the woman he thought he loved. He'd been dreaming about her long enough. That brief taste of her flesh had only served to fuel his fire.

"Wait," Connell called after him. "Ye're not a-leavin' yet. I told ye tae go stand by the house."

Robert was still walking as he turned to the man, who was beginning to follow him. "Why?" he asked. "My business is finished here. When ye find yer sister, tell her what I came fer. That way, she'll know when me mum comes tae see her."

"I told ye not tae go."

"I'm not stayin'."

After that, the chase was on.

ଓ

Damn Robbie.

Astride a big, shaggy brown stallion, Jamison Munro was perched on the rise to the north, overlooking the MacKenzie farm where his brother, Robert, had so recently run off to. *A lass*, Robbie had said enthusiastically. *A lass with the beauty of the angels.* Jamison knew the lass and he also knew her brother, and he was quite certain no good could come of Robert's lust.

Eva MacKenzie had an older brother who was called *Sach*, a term in Gaelic that meant madness. Connell the Crazed was not someone Jamison had any desire to defend his brother against but Robert was, after all, his brother, and the man was lusting seriously after a woman who had sampled more than her share of men. Eva was pretty but she wasn't pure. At least, that was the rumor, which was probably why Robert was so determined to have a piece of her. Little Robbie Munro liked women too much and, more than once, Jamison had been forced to protect his brother from irate fathers and uncles and brothers.

Therefore, Jamison felt a good deal of disgust as he gazed down at the MacKenzie stronghold from his position on the crag. He could see the house and the farm for the most part, including the sod-walled barn his brother had disappeared into. The biggest and most intelligent of the four Munro brothers, Jamison was the second son but always found himself in a position of command and control within the family. His father depended on him and his brothers adored him. He was feared and respected by his peers as well as men from other clans, and he was careful with his reputation.

A man's character is all he really has, his father once told him, and Jamison stuck to that belief, which is why he didn't like playing the lookout when Robert engaged in his mischief. Jamison didn't like being put in that position but if he didn't look out for his brother, the man would surely get himself into trouble, or worse. Had it not been for

Jamison on numerous occasions, Robert would have been dead.

Damn Robbie!

And then, he saw it....

Lured from his thoughts of his devilish brother, Jamison caught sight of movement in the distant complex. He suddenly saw a small, female body being tossed from one of the narrow barn windows – or, at least, that was what it looked like. The woman slipped right through and fell heavily to the earth below.

Puzzled, not to mention concerned, Jamison spurred his horse forward, down the rocky green slope, the one that faced the ocean and the glorious morning sunrise. The days of summer were still fairly warm as the season moved into fall and the harsh winter that would soon come, so the ground was stable and not too wet as his horse slid down the incline. He was nearly to the bottom, preparing to urge his horse forward at a gallop, when he heard a cry.

"Eva!"

Jamison knew his brother's voice and that wasn't it. Someone else was calling for that siren of a sister, a lass that lured men to their doom when they came into contact with her brother. So Jamison could only assume that the cry was from Eva's brother. Sending the horse into a gallop, he closed the gap between him and the MacKenzie stronghold. He dismounted and left his horse in a copse of trees as he raced for the big stone wall that surrounded the perimeter. Leaping over the wall, which was no mean feat considering his height and bulk, he headed straight for the woman who'd been tossed from the window. She was just starting to sit up when Jamison came upon her.

"Eva?" he asked, reaching down to help her up. "What has happened?"

Eva had a hand on her forehead. "I dunna know," she said, wincing as she rubbed the bump that was forming. "Robbie and I were... where's Robbie?"

Jamison didn't know but from the sounds of conversation on the other side of the barn, a mumble he could hear, he suspected his brother might not be in the best of positions. Eva was wobbly, having trouble standing, so he picked her up so she wouldn't fall. With the woman in his arms, he rounded the side of the sod barn and walked straight into the scene of Connell chasing Robbie over a rock wall.

"*Stop*!" Jamison boomed. "Connell, *stop*!"

Connell came to an unsteady halt just as he was about to leap over a second rock wall. Robert kept running until a second shout from Jamison stopped him. Robert turned about but Connell was already heading in Jamison's direction, his featured twisted with rage.

"Get yer hands off me sister!" he snarled, reaching out and grabbing Eva by the arm. He yanked, hard, and the woman hit the ground. He dragged her back, several feet, as she tried to get her footing, but his focus was on Jamison. "God's bones… so 'tis ye… 'tis The Red Lion. I never thought it 'twould be ye, Jamison. Ye're the smarter o' the brothers."

Jamison kept his customary cool as he faced off against a fairly angry man. "I will pretend I dinna hear yer slander," he said steadily. "Yer sister has had an accident. I was riding by and saw her in the dirt. She's injured."

Connell turned his attention to his sister, who was struggling to stand. He still had her by the arm. "What is it wich' ye?"

Eva had her had to her forehead where the lump was. "I… I hit me head," she said, still muddled from having been knocked out. "I think Robbie must've hit…." She stopped herself, suddenly realizing what she had just said. Her eyes widened and she looked up at her brother in a panic. "I mean… I must've hit me head somehow!"

Connell wasn't a fool; he'd caught her misstep from the first. He still had her by the arm and he shook her, viciously, until she cried out. "Robbie?" he snapped.

She screamed. "Nae! No' Robbie!"

"Jamison, then!"

"Nae, Connell! *Stop*!"

But Connell wouldn't stop. "Ye've been wit' Robbie," he said as his gaze found Robert, who was still at least two fences over. Far enough away to get a good distance on him if he decided to run. Connell's features twisted with rage as he turned back to Jamison. "That is why ye're here, Munro. Tae cover for yer brother's actions with me sister!"

Jamison could see where this was going. God help him, he could see very quickly where the situation was headed and he did the only thing he could do – try to head off Connell the Crazed from the murderous rage that was about to come forth. Robert might have been a rake, and a foolish one at that, but Jamison wasn't going to condemn his brother before the likes of Connell MacKenzie. He was going to defend him.

"From what I've heard, Robbie's not the only man who's had action with yer sister," he said. He was going to hit and hit hard. "Take the lass back into the house and beat her within an inch o' her life. She lures men to their doom like a siren lures sailors. Get her out of me sight, MacKenzie. Be grateful I'm not beating her instead of ye."

Connell was taken back at the blatant insult. Even Eva yelped in outrage. "Are ye goin' tae let him speak of me like that?" she asked, looking at her brother. "What are ye goin' tae do about it, then?"

Connell's jaw flexed but, surprisingly, he didn't explode. He simply looked at Jamison with an expression that suggested he was torn; the man was, in fact, correct. Even Connell knew his sister had no morals. But, much as Jamison was obliged to protect Robert, he was obliged to protect Eva. The family honor was at stake.

"I'll give ye yer choice," Connell said to Jamison, all but ignoring his sister. "I can fight Robbie or I can fight ye. I'm goin' tae fight one of ye, so ye can make the choice."

It was a challenge and Jamison immediately looked at his brother. He wouldn't refuse such an invitation. He had a sword strapped to his side, held by a leather belt against the rough woolen tunic he wore. Unlike most Scots, however, his tunic didn't go to his knees. It hung just below his buttocks because Jamison preferred to wear breeches.

He'd picked up the habit while fostering in England, far to the south, and he'd never lost the urge to cover up his legs. He felt far more comfortable that way because he didn't particularly like having his manhood exposed. One good tumble and the Family Sword would be unsheathed for all to see. Therefore, when he faced Connell with his *Sassenach* dress and enormous, Spanish-forged broadsword, he looked out of place.

A Highlander without the trappings of the Highlands.

Connell noticed; it wasn't difficult to see. The clans all knew that Jamison Munro wasn't like the rest of them. His father, also a rather widely traveled and educated man, had insisted his sons do the same, but the two younger sons, Robert and Hector, had resisted that wanderlust. They'd never done what the older boys, George and Jamison, had done. George had spent time in France studying with the church while Jamison had fostered with a very fine English family. He'd experienced warfare in four different countries, only to return to Scotland to realize he was different from his kinsmen. Not odd, just... different.

He didn't fit in with them anymore.

Therefore, Connell was a more cautious when facing Jamison. The man knew *Sassenach* tactics, which made him tricky as well as dangerous. He was also as tall as a tree, as big as a stag, as powerful as a mountain, and as unpredictable as the wind. There was nothing wanting about Jamison Munro.

Truthfully, Connell was a bit disappointed that the man had stood right up to his challenge; not that he had expected any differently, but he had hoped – secretly – that Jamison would have thrust Robert at him to atone for what he'd done with, or to, Eva. It was a brother's duty to protect his sister's honor, wasn't it?

By damn, if Jamison isna right – the lass is like a siren who's had one too many a sailor gloss over her ocean, if ye know what I mean....

The reality was that Eva had no honor. Now, she may have very well cost Connell his life because of her open legs and his sense of duty.

Damnable woman!

"This isna yer fight, Jamison," Connell said, trying not to sound as if he was afraid of the man. "Give Robbie yer sword and let him face me like a man."

Jamison shook his head. "Ye gave me a choice of who ye should face," he said. "I chose me."

Connell sighed faintly, knowing that he had, indeed, given the man such a choice. It had been a hasty offer, one he was coming to regret. "Ye canna spend yer whole life defendin' yer brother," he said. "When will Robbie take the burden fer what he's done?"

Jamison unsheathed his sword. "Not today," he said. "Are ye going tae fight me or are ye going tae stand there and yap? I dunna have all day."

By this time, Robert had come back over the rock walls, his feet slapping against the cold, damp earth of the barnyard. "Hold, Jamie," he said. "Ye may as well give me yer sword. Connell intends tae kill one of us and it may as well be me."

He said it with resignation but Jamison didn't look at him. He didn't take his eyes off of Connell.

"Get away with ye," he told Robert. "Go home, Robbie. Ye brought me for protection. Now I'm protecting ye."

Robert was feeling guilty and fearful. He hadn't truly wanted to get Jamison involved with the maniacal Connell, but here they were, preparing to square off against one another. He didn't know what he'd expected when he'd asked Jamison to act the lookout for him when he'd gone to meet with Eva; perhaps he had hoped that nothing would happen at all, that they'd all outrun Connell after he'd had his pleasure and before any real damage was done. Connell was fearsome but he was slow. Knocking Eva in the head and being confronted by Connell wasn't really what Robert had hoped for, but now, here they were.

They were in the soup now, as it were.

"Give me yer sword," Robert said again. "I canna let ye face me folly. I can beat Connell. Do ye doubt me?"

"Aye."

He'd said it with no hesitation and Robert looked at his brother, stricken. "Do ye have so little faith in me skill, then?"

"Aye."

The reply had been quick. Robert was insulted now. He scowled. "Yer words are like an arrow through me heart," he hissed. "Just because men call ye The Red Lion, ye're not the best swordsmen in all of Scotland, ye know. Or did ye think so?"

"Actually, I did."

Robert's mouth popped open in outrage. He looked at Connell. "Do ye hear him?" he demanded, pointing to Jamison. "He'll kill ye just as easily as look at ye. Will ye let him take ye down so easily?"

Connell was listening to the banter, not entirely sure it wasn't some ploy to distract him. "The Red Lion or no', he's not goin' tae take me down," he said, eyeing the brothers. "But… but I dunna want me sister tae see bloodshed. 'Tis not right."

Jamison cocked his head curiously. "Scots women are stronger than we are when it comes tae a fight," he said. "Yer sister has stolen from the wounded in the field. She's cut off a swollen finger tae retrieve a valuable ring and ye know she's done far worse than that. If ye dunna want tae fight me, Connell, then ye take back yer slander against Robbie."

Connell eyed both Jamison and Robert, seeing a way out of this. He was actually feeling rather hopeful. "I'll lower me sword if he lets me smell his breath."

As Jamison looked to his brother, the scowl vanished from Robert's face and his eyebrows lifted in surprise. He suspected why the man wanted to smell his breath – to see if he could smell a whiff of his sister on him. Robert had planted his face squarely betwixt Eva's legs so there was probably little doubt that he had the smell of female flesh on him. He could smell it even now. Would he let Connell smell his lips? Absolutely not. It would be a dead giveaway. With that thought, he shook his head.

"I willna let ye," he said. "I willna let ye close enough to slip a dirk between me ribs. Jamie, give me the damn sword so I can be done with this."

Jamison moved away from his brother, fearful the man would try to make a grab for his weapon and then it would be the two of them battling each other. Holding out a hand to prevent his brother from following him, he lifted his weapon to Connell.

"Ye canna smell his breath," he said. "Make yer move if ye must."

Connell stared at him for a moment, a river of emotions running through his dark eyes. His hope for a peaceful solution to the situation was gone and there was nothing more he could do unless he wanted to look like a coward. Therefore, he unsheathed the dirk at his waistband, a very long and sharp dagger that was nearly as long as a sword itself.

The blade was long and triangular, sharp only on one side. The type of blade was native to the Highlands and the warriors who populated it, and this one was no different with its guardless hilt. The MacKenzie stag was carved into the hilt made out of a stag's horn.

Jamison had seen the dirk before and it was an impressive one. Now, that razor-sharp tip would be aimed for his chest and his broadsword came up. He had the advantage provided that he didn't let Connell get too close to him. The man could cut him badly with a weapon meant for close-quarters combat, but a broadsword such as the one Jamison held could cut a man's head off easily. Therefore, this would be an interesting fight.

They began to square off in the barnyard, circling one another, each man waiting for the other to make the first move. Jamison could hear Eva panting with fear. He didn't even know where Robert was. He couldn't think about that now; all he could think about was the man he was preparing to fight. The battle wasn't long in coming.

Connell charged at Jamison with his blade held high and Jamison deftly avoided the rush. But Connell was on him in an instant, bellowing and shouting, using the dirk in great slashing motions as Jamison deflected them. At this point, he was on the defensive more than anything, waiting for Connell to exhaust himself and then Jamison would put his blade to the man's throat and give him the ultimatum of apologizing to Robert again to save his life.

He was fairly certain that Connell would apologize. He was rash but he wasn't an idiot. And, Robert really *was* having his way with the man's sister so Jamison was, perhaps, not as hard on the man as he could have been. Connell was only defending the vestiges of his sister's honor, something that was long gone. Jamison supposed, in reality, that Connell was really just defending the family pride. So be it. Jamison could hold out until Connell came to his senses.

But those thoughts were cut short when Robert suddenly entered the fight, running at Connell from the side and tackling the man, sending them both to the ground. As Jamison watched in horror, Connell brought that dirk down onto Robert's back, goring him. Robert's screams filled the air and Jamison rushed the pair, broadsword lifted, bringing it down on Connell's neck as the man stabbed Robert a second time. Connell's head was separated neatly from his body before he could stab Robert a third time.

As swiftly as it began, the fight was over, leaving devastation in its wake. None of them had wanted this ending but, in a fit of panic on Jamison's part, that was what it had come to. Eva began screaming at the sight of her brother's decapitated body as Jamison reached down, trying to pull Robert to his feet.

"Robbie," he gasped. "Can ye walk, man?"

Robert was pale and bleeding, blood gushing from the two wounds on his left side. He staggered to his feet as Jamison pulled at him.

"Ye shoulda let me fight him," he said to his brother. "He was goin' tae kill ye, Jamie. Do ye know I couldna live with meself if he did?"

Jamison glanced at Connell's body, the detached head with the sightless eyes staring up into the sky. He swore he saw the mouth move as Eva stood over him and screamed.

"Come on," he hissed at his brother. "We must leave. Now."

Robert grunted, hand to his bloody back. "But Eva…."

"I dunna think she wants tae come with us, Robbie. *Move.*"

Jamison pulled his brother across the barnyard, outside of the rock walls to where his shaggy brown horse was feeding on the wet, green grass in the field beyond. His attention darted about as he looked to see what MacKenzie men the sister's screaming was bringing forth.

"Ye have tae run, Robbie, or we'll soon join Connell in a headless existence," he said, anxiety in his tone. "Move faster."

"I am!"

"Ye lazy bastard, I could crawl faster than ye're movin'!"

They manage to reach the horse as men began pouring out of the MacKenzie stronghold, lured by Eva's screaming. Men were shouting and horses were being gathered. Jamison knew their time was growing extremely limited so he grabbed his brother and literally tossed the man up onto the horse, which was now becoming jumpy and excited with all of the shouting and movement. Jamison vaulted onto the horse behind his bleeding brother and they took off, heading towards the sea and the road that would take them north to Foulis Castle.

Jamison had no idea what he was going to tell his father about the incident but he sincerely hoped he had the chance. He'd rather face his furious father than a herd of rabid MacKenzies with blades. He could hear shouting behind him and knew they were mounting a chase, but he kept focused and held fast to Robert, spurring his heavy-boned horse across the rocky path as they hurled towards the main road that turned for home. If nothing else, Jamison had long learned that cooler heads prevailed. Panic would get him killed and he'd seen many instances of that, so he kept the horse going hard and steady until they finally came to the road that would take them home.

Only when they made the turn north did he dare to look behind him, only to be met by an incoming tide of men on horseback tearing after him. Jamison was fairly certain he could outrun them because he had enough of a lead, but that didn't stop the creeping anxiety. He wasn't so much worried for himself as he was for Robert, who was grunting and bleeding all over the horse. He had no idea just how bad his brother was really hurt but he couldn't stop to analyze it. He had to make it home. Then, if his brother wasn't too badly injured, he planned to beat the man within an inch of his life for doing something so stupid. Not with Eva; he didn't even care about that. But for charging Connell when there had been no need. That had been the stupid part. He'd been forced to kill the man when it hadn't been necessary.

Strangely enough, George Munro the Elder seemed to think that both of his sons were rather stupid when they told him why a hundred MacKenzie warriors were at their gate, trying to tear the place down. They soon came to discover that it wasn't Robert they wanted.

It was Jamison.

ꝏ

The next day

"I HAVE TAE send ye away. I have nae choice."

Jamison was sitting at the great, worn table in his father's feasting hall. It was a big room, with a massive table down the center of the room that had seen many a year and many a man eating at it. Scuffed, with pockmarks in it where dirks had been slammed into the wood, the table was part of the family and had a tendency to bring about fond memories of days gone by when there had been love and laughter and humor.

But not today. Today, the table was part of the judge and jury over Jamison as he sat next to the wounded Robert, listening to their father's decision on how to best handle the MacKenzie anger. Neither man liked what they were hearing, most especially Jamison.

"But why?" he demanded. "Why would ye send me away when ye need me the most? With the MacKenzie intending tae wage war, why would ye send yer best warrior away?"

George looked at his second-born son, a lad he was more proud of than any of the others. That was because Jamison was different than the others – in skill, in character, in everything. George, his eldest, was weak, Robert was a fool, and Hector, the youngest, was still learning. He would be a good warrior when he grew older, but he was far too young.

He idolized Jamison. George the father idolized him, too, which made this decision that much more heart wrenching.

"They want tae wage war because ye killed Connell," George pointed out. "If ye go, their anger will cool, but as long as ye remain, they have something here within Foulis tae fight fer. Dunna ye see? Ye've got tae leave, Jamie, at least until their sense of vengeance is forgotten."

Jamison's red eyebrows lifted. "Until it's forgotten?" he repeated. Then, he shook his head in exasperation. "That could take years, Da. I must go away for years?"

George was a level-headed man and he nodded his head to his son's question. "I would rather have ye alive and away from here than dead and buried in the churchyard," he said sincerely. "That is what this will come tae, Jamie. They want yer head and I willna let them have it. If ye stay, ye bring war upon us and ye'll get us all killed."

Jamison was having a difficult time believing that his presence would instigate an all-out war with the MacKenzies, but on the other hand, Connell had been the clan's heir apparent. He was to become chief upon the death of his father. Frustrated at the turn the situation had taken, Jamison stood up from the table, meandering towards the enormous hearth that was spitting smoke and sparks into the room. The dogs around the fire had been hit more than once with flying embers, forcing them to move out of the firing range. Jamison shoved a big mutt aside as he went to stand by his father.

"Mayhap I should talk tae them," he said quietly. "Men respect my word, Da. Let me apologize for what happened and explain the circumstances. Mayhap they will listen. None of them much liked Connell as it 'twas. A few of them may even thank me for what happened."

George simply shook his head. "They'd kill ye before ye could get a word out of yer mouth," he said, holding up a hand to prevent further argument. "'Tis a matter of pride with them now – ye killed the next chief and whether or not they liked the man isna the issue. Me mind is set, lad. Tonight, ye ride to Alness and from there, take one of me boats south tae Edinburgh. From there, ye'll go south, tae the very south of England. Ye'll go back tae de Lohr."

Lioncross Abbey Castle. That was where Jamison had fostered, where he'd learned his skills, from the best trainers of knights in all of England. In fact, he'd spent several years there before his master, a de Lohr brother, took him to France where they'd faced battle together for a few more years. After they'd returned home, it was the earl himself, Chris de Lohr, who had knighted him and presented him with his golden spurs.

In that respect, Lioncross Abbey was more home to him than his own, but he still didn't want to leave Foulis Castle. It had taken him many years to return here, to come home where his family was. He had been a wanderer, learning something other than the Highland ways as his father had wished it. But now that he was returned, he didn't want to leave. Squaring his broad shoulders, he took a stand against his stubborn father.

"So ye send me away tae make it look as if I fled like a coward?" he asked. "Then every man will say that I ran rather than face the MacKenzie. That is not how I wish tae be remembered. Nay, Da. I willna go."

"Ye will."

A soft, female voice came from the darkened entry of the hall and they turned to see Ainsley Munro make her way into the room. Mother of the four Munro lads, Ainsley had the same red hair that her sons, Jamison and Hector, also bore. She had been a beauty in her day but as of late, her health hadn't been good and her face had developed careworn lines. She shuffled when she walked, wrapped in heavy woolen garments, but her eyes, pale blue, were focused on her big, burly son. There was nothing weak or fragile in that gaze as she bore down on him.

"Ye'll go now," she told Jamison. "I dunna intend tae bury all of me sons and me own husband because of ye. Yer pride isna worth their lives, Jamison. MacKenzie is demandin' satisfaction and if ye're not here, they canna have it. I'll not let ye cost us peace, lad. Ye're goin' tae de Lohr as yer father tells ye and if ye argue wid me, I'll take a stick tae ye."

Jamison knew he was sunk. He could often get the upper hand with his father but never with his mother. She was a woman of an iron all wrapped up in soft skin and delicate health, and she was not to be trifled with. Once her mind was set, there was no changing it. The more he looked at her, the more he realized the situation had already been decided.

He had to go.

Sighing heavily, Jamison turned away from his mother and his father but not before catching sight of Robert sitting at the table. When their eyes met, Robert lowered his gaze, ashamed at what he had caused.

"Ye'd better look away from me," Jamison growled at him. "Do ye see what yer lust has cost? It has cost *me*, Robbie, not ye. Yer lack of control and idiocy will cost me life in more ways than one. Now I go back tae England all because ye had tae taste a woman. Ye're a fool and I'm ashamed tae call ye me brother."

Robert was looking at his hands. The stab wounds in his torso would heal but he wasn't sure his relationship with Jamison ever would after this. He may have ruined everything between them and he felt just as bad as he possibly could about all of it.

"I am sorry, Jamie," he said quietly. "There's nothin' more I can say except I'm sorry. I never meant that ye should take the brunt o' the situation. Ye know that."

Jamison was struggling to control his rage. "Do I?" he demanded. "What did ye think would happen when ye dragged me tae the MacKenzie home so I could watch out for Connell and his men while ye seduced the man's sister? By Christ's Bleeding Soles, I shoulda let them have ye!"

"Enough," Ainsley said quietly as she sat, heavily, at the table. It was cold and damp this day, which made her bones hurt. "Robbie is leavin', too."

Both Jamison and Robert looked at their mother in surprise. "Where am I goin'?" Robert asked anxiously.

Ainsley didn't look at him. Her attention was drawn to her husband, who cleared his throat softly. "Robbie is goin' tae Castle Questing in Northumberland," George said. "Me mother was a Scott and the Scotts are tied tae Castle Questing. He'll be safe there until the MacKenzie blood hunger has blown over. Connell's younger brother, Padraig, is now his father's heir and Padraig is a far more reasonable man. Mayhap, ye'll both be able tae come home by the summer."

Jamison wasn't so sure. By now, he was flustered and frustrated and disappointed. He utterly disagreed with his parents' decision and he was obvious about it. "The memories of the MacKenzies are not so short, Da," he said, doom in his voice. "If I leave now, it will take years tae mend what has been damaged. But if I face them as a man would, then they will know the truth of what has happened. I did nothing wrong."

George wasn't going to argue with him about what he felt was best. He'd already stated his case but Jamison wasn't so apt to run; that was the problem with him. He was brave beyond measure and believed that every situation was negotiable. He had a gift for talk that had given him that confidence. But George shook his head.

"Not this time, Jamie," he muttered. "Ye will leave. I'll send ye word when it 'tis safe tae return."

There was nothing more that Jamison or Robert could say on the matter. It was clear that their parents had decided everything and now it was simply a matter of the execution of the plans – Jamison to the boat that would take him down the coast and away from the rabid MacKenzies and Robert to be spirited away under darkness, taken far south to the borders and the mighty stronghold of Castle Questing. The Lords of de Wolfe held the castle and no Scot would dare move against it. Jamison knew, deep down, that his father was just trying to keep them safe and alive. But he still saw it as fleeing like a coward.

"Very well," Jamison finally muttered. "I'll be back in the summer. I've spent too many years away from home tae want tae stay away any longer."

Ainsley lifted her head, her eyes fixed on her Jamison. He was her shining star, her proudest achievement. She wanted him alive and she didn't care if the means to the end appeared cowardly. All she cared about was the fact that he survived the MacKenzie rage.

"Go, now," she said. "Pack what ye must and go. The boat is a-waitin' for ye even now. Get tae it before the MacKenzies are wise tae what we are doin'."

Jamison knew that. He knew they were watching Foulis so to escape would be tricky, but it could be done. With nothing more to say, he simply went to his mother, kissed her on the forehead, and quit the great hall, heading up the wooden stairs that were more like a ladder than actual stairs to his section of the open second floor where he slept. Only the exterior of Foulis was stone; the interior was completely wooden, making it susceptible to fire. They'd had a few of them in his lifetime.

As he walked, he dragged his hand along the stone wall, thinking how much he was going to miss the place. But he'd done without it for almost twenty years. He supposed a few more months weren't going to break him.

It was with great sadness that Jamison departed at twilight, when a great bank of fog was rolling in from the North Sea, using it to his advantage as he made his way on foot to the town to the north of them, Alness, where one of his father's cogs await. His father often did business with clans across the Firth of Moray, transporting sheep, among other goods, so the man had a fleet of small cogs that he used. It was one of these very simple boats with a single sail that made way as darkness fell, sailing along the coast until the fog lifted and the captain was better able to plot a course.

As dawn began to glow on the horizon, Jamison felt it was a little like a new day was dawning for him as well. He was going back to

England, and back to Lioncross Abbey, back into the hell of English politics that he was so familiar with.

A new day was dawning, indeed.

CHAPTER ONE

Lions of the Highlands

October

T*HEY HAD BEEN waiting for him.*

George Munro the Younger, having studied Religion and Latin and Literature in France at Notre Dame and Sainte-Chapelle, among others, made a weekly pilgrimage to Fortrose Cathedral, one of the oldest churches in all of Scotland. Even though George was slated to be the next chief of Clan Munro, he very much wanted to be a priest, much to his father's displeasure. But the truth was that he was very pious and wished to serve God.

George had tried to learn the ways of the clans, of battles and politics and fighting, but he simply wasn't very good at it. He didn't even say anything when his father betrothed him to a local heiress, the daughter of an ally. But the truth was that he didn't much care about any of it. He didn't want to marry and he didn't want to assume the mantle of his clan. His younger brother, Jamison, would make the perfect clan chief, although Jamison had never expressed any interest in such a thing. George was to be the next chief and Jamison had been very supportive and respectful of that role in life.

George missed Jamison a great deal these days but knew why he'd been forced to go south. With Robert also gone, it was just George and Hector at home dealing with the fallout of Connell's death at the hands of Jamison. George the Elder had tried to placate the MacKenzie, even apologizing for the "mishap" and offering one hundred of his prized cattle to compensate the man. But that wasn't enough for the MacKenzie.

They were out for blood.

George the Elder knew this. So did young Hector, who was much as Jamison had been at that age – cocky, brash, arrogant, and brilliant. Even Ainsley Munro knew it wasn't safe outside of the walls of Foulis Castle these days but the only person who ignored that danger was George the Younger. He knew that the MacKenzie was a threat, in theory, but it wasn't going to stand in the way of him making his weekly pilgrimage to Fortrose. Surely, they wouldn't target a man with no weapons and no interest in war.

Therefore, before dawn on a cold, foggy Friday morning nearly three months after Jamison and Robert had fled Munro lands, George slipped from Foulis Castle on his own and without an escort, and began his twenty-mile trek to Fortrose.

And that's when the MacKenzies had been waiting.

They knew of the heir's weekly pilgrimage; he never varied. On that icy morning, George the Younger never even made it out of his family's territory. The MacKenzies ambushed him when he was just out of sight of the castle, knocking him from his horse and then proceeding to run their horses all over him, killing the man by crushing him. It had been a terrible and painful way to die. When they were sure George was dead, they tied a rope around his feet and dragged him all the way back to Foulis, dumping his battered body within sight of the gate. Because of the fog, the Munro sentries never even saw the body until well into morning when the fog lifted.

Hector was the first one to see his brother's battered corpse. Sickened, he had vomited several times before going to summon his father, who gazed down at his heir without much surprise in his expression. Somehow, he knew it would come to this. He knew the MacKenzies would seek an eye for an eye in the death of Connell but he was still devastated to realize that fear had come to fruition. Shrugging off all offers of help, George the Elder had picked up the crushed, bloodied body of his son and carried the man, all by himself, back into the fold of Foulis Castle.

He wept the entire way.

The days after that were filled with sorrow. George Munro the Younger, also known as Lord Bayne because it was the title held by all firstborn males of the clan chief, was laid to rest in his beloved Fortrose Cathedral in the churchyard where generations of his ancestors were also buried. It was a small mass given the circumstances of George's death, so only the family and close allies were in attendance along with about two hundred armed Munro men in case the MacKenzies tried to attack a gathering of Munros. George the Elder and his wife were well protected by Hector and a huge armed contingent, but they weren't the only men who were armed. The allies had come armed as well.

In this case, there were three particular young men George the Elder had summoned the night of his son's murder. They had brought men and weapons of their own. These three were close friends of Jamison's. They had all fostered together at Lioncross Abbey Castle at the request of Henry III.

These three young men were all soon to be the chief of their own clans upon the death of their fathers but, for now, they were heavily involved in Scotland's politics and in the welfare of their people. When George had sent them all individual missives, informing them of what had happened and asking for them to attend the burial, they had come without question.

Even though the burial of George the Younger had been attended by just a few at the graveside, the clans spread out for mass outside of the churchyard. They gathered in groups under gray skies and cold sea winds as the Munro heir was laid to rest. When the mass was finally over and Ainsley was left weeping over the death of her eldest child, George the Elder approached the three wool-clad young warriors standing off together inside the wall of the churchyard, respectfully observing the burial from a distance.

As George approached, he drank in the sight of Jamison's friends, perhaps the most powerful young men in the north of Scotland and certainly some of the most noble and trusted. They were men determined to make Scotland a better place because in this goal, they understood what some Scots didn't – that if one wanted to live in peace, then one had to learn to work with the English. They weren't going to go away and so long as the Scots continued to resist, there would be continued heartbreak and death.

But that thought had very much to do with English conditioning. That very factor had been the brilliance of King Henry in brokering the transfer of the Highlander sons far to the south so they would learn from the English – and what the lads were taught was a broader view of the world. It taught them that to live in peace, one must understand one's enemy and understand when compromise was called for as opposed to drawing a sword. Those young men, Jamison included, understood that message better than most and petty fights like the one between the MacKenzies and the Munros were foolish and a waste of time in their view. Instead of the clans squabbling, they needed to unite. George the Younger's death had been an utter waste of a life and quite unnecessary in their view.

That was why the sons of the chiefs, known as the Lions of the Highlands, had come to the Fortrose churchyard at George's summoning – to help make tomorrow better for all of them.

George needed their help.

Beaux MacKay was the first man George made eye contact with as he approached the group. A big, burly young man with crown of curly blonde hair, Beaux was a handsome man with a gentle manner about him that belied the deadliness of his sword. He had a dirk he always wore, given to him by his grandfather, and the hilt of it was carved into the head of a dragon. *The White Dragon* was the moniker Beaux had earned because of it. Fair-skinned, gentle-mannered but deadly, the name suited him.

Standing next to Beaux was a tall, sinewy young man with a crown of graying dark hair and a silver beard. His hair had turned color early in his life and the young man was often referred to as The Gray Fox, not simply for his hair color, but also because he was cunning, silent, and swift in battle. Kendrick Sutherland was the only son of his father, chief of Clan Sutherland, and a great ally of the Munros.

Rounding out the three proud warriors was the heir to Clan Ross, Caspian Ross. A fearsome warrior who traveled with a nasty collection of dirks strapped to his body, Caspian was a man to be both feared and respected. He was bulky and muscular, and as strong as an ox. He tended to use his dirks with little provocation. *Talons,* men called them, and coupled with his black hair and dark eyes, Caspian was known to friend and foe alike as The Black Falcon. And this falcon's talons were quite deadly.

Three powerful young warriors soon to head three of the largest clans in the Highlands. Jamison was part of this group even though he hadn't been heir to the Munro until a few days ago. Still, Jamison transcended that position in life; he was *The Red Lion,* the man they considered their leader. He was a great warrior without the trappings of titles because something in Jamison went beyond titles and lands and birthrights. Something in his soul made him a natural leader and men naturally flocked to him.

George knew all this, which is why he had summoned them. They loved Jamison and Jamison would need their help, now more than ever. He was now the Munro heir and with the MacKenzie still out to make trouble for him, George didn't want to take any chances.

"Beaux," George said, relief in his voice as he greeted the young man. Reaching out a hand, he grasped Beaux's hand tightly. "Praise God ye have come. Praise God ye have all come."

George moved to Kendrick and Caspian in turn, shaking their hands and finally hugging Caspian, who was gruff with his affections and squeezed George so hard that the man grunted. Rubbing his ribs, George grinned weakly at the group.

"It has been a very long time since we last met, lads," he said. Then, his smile faded. "I have buried me eldest today. Ye have shared that sorrow wit' me."

Beaux spoke, his voice soft but firm. There was a deadly edge to the quiet tone. "The MacKenzies did this to ye," he said. "But why? Yer missive said nothing about their motives. Why would they do such a thing?"

George sighed heavily. "It started wit' a foolish thing Robbie did," he muttered, both ashamed and sickened by it. "He went tae MacKenzie lands tae seduce Eva MacKenzie and Jamie went with him tae keep him out of trouble, tae keep watch for Connell MacKenzie. Ye know how the brothers protect that girl."

The three young warriors snorted. "Eva MacKenzie," Kendrick grumbled. "The woman has the morals of a bitch in heat. She moans and any man in earshot comes running. So she lured Robbie this time, did she?"

George shrugged. "He was willin'," he admitted. "Connell caught them together and when he stabbed Robbie, Jamison killed him. I sent Jamison south tae Lioncross Abbey and Robbie off tae Northumberland tae get the away from the MacKenzies' anger. But the MacKenzies killed Georgie, instead."

Beaux grunted, hanging his head in disbelief now that the entire story was coming evident, as Kendrick and Caspian looked at each other, knowingly. George the Younger's death wasn't a simple killing. It was clear that it was much more than that. This situation was as bad as they could have imagined.

It was a blood feud.

"'Tis a message tae Jamie," Caspian said quietly. "He took Connell and the MacKenzie took Georgie."

"But they *want* Jamie," Kendrick put in, eyeing both Beaux and Caspian. "Georgie's death is tae lure Jamie home. Ye know that, don't ye?"

George nodded. "I do," he said. "'Tis why I called ye here. Ye must go to Jamie and tell him what has happened. Georgie is dead and now he is me heir. I sent him away tae get him clear of the MacKenzies' rage but it was the wrong thing tae do. He begged me not tae send him away but I thought it was for the best. He thought they would think him a coward, that the Munros are weak. They knew that killin' Georgie would bring him home because I'd have no choice but tae tell him. Now… now they will trap him as they did Georgie."

Beaux shook his head. "They havena sent a trap for him yet," he said firmly. "As long as there be breath in me body, they willna have him. But I agree that he needs tae know what has happened. What about Robbie?"

George shook his head. "As long as he remains in Northumberland, he is safe," he said. "'Tis Jamie the MacKenzie is after, not Robbie."

A soft wailing could suddenly be heard, drifting upon the moist sea breeze, and the four of them looked over to see Ainsley at her son's graveside, now being helped to her feet by a few women. As George watched his wife's grief, his face seemed to age ten years. The lines were deeper, more careworn, becoming the marks of a man who had outlived a child. His heart was heavy with anguish.

"I can weather the loss of Georgie but, God forgive me, I willna weather the loss of Jamie," he hissed as he turned back to the young men around him. "I know he will want tae return home after this and it is me biggest fear – the MacKenzies will be waiting for him and he'll want tae face them. He will feel responsible for Georgie's death and he'll demand vengeance."

Beaux, Kendrick, and Caspian watched George struggle with his grief, not only for one son but really for two. It was a complex situation made more complex by the fact that Jamison would do exactly as his father said he would – he would avenge his brother's death, which meant this feud, this war with the MacKenzies, would become something massive and unmanageable. There were more far-reaching implications than simply a man killing another man because now that incident had resulted in another death. More would come if it wasn't stopped now before it could get out of hand. Otherwise, it could quite possibly divide the Highlands.

Beaux turned to glance at his two companions before looking over his shoulder at the hundreds of Highland warriors standing outside of the churchyard, clad in their wools and tunics, bearing their short-blade swords and dirks. They were fighting men, loyal to the core, and unwilling to surrender until death claimed them.

That was the heart of the Highlander.

"Jamie will return and declare war on the MacKenzies," Beaux said, his gaze lingering on the Highlanders standing beneath the stormy sky. "More than that, he could quite possibly bring Sassenach soldiers with him, de Lohr men and knights, and destroy the MacKenzie completely. If he does that, their allies – the MacRaes, the MacIntoshes, the Mathesons – will rally their men. This will be bigger than we can imagine if Jamison moves tae crush the MacKenzies and punish them for Georgie's murder. I dunna think any of us wants that."

George was already shaking his head fervently. "I do not," he said firmly. "Mayhap with the three of ye, he will see reason. He will understand he canna return and tear the Highlands apart with his vengeance. But there somethin' more ye should know, something that may cast a different light on such things."

The young men were curious. "What 'tis it?" Kendrick asked, interested.

George's gaze moved to the churchyard and the sea beyond, watching as the streams of light through the storm clouds glistened upon the waters. This was the land he loved, the land he lived and died for. The wind whipped around him, tossing his hair about as he pondered his reply.

"Georgie was betrothed tae Agnes MacLennan," he said. "She is a young girl that has seen fourteen summers, but her father has no heir. Only Agnes. Georgie was tae marry the girl next summer to unite our clans but now that Georgie is dead, it is Jamison's duty tae marry the girl and it 'tis a duty he'll not take kindly to."

Beaux's brow furrowed. "MacLennan," he repeated. "They are kin tae the MacKenzies."

George looked the man in the eye. "Aye, they are," he said. "When I made the contract, we were not at odds with the MacKenzies. Now that we are, I intend tae marry Jamison tae the MacLennan lass as soon as he returns. That makes us kin tae the MacKenzies when he marries her. We canna war with kin."

Beaux sighed heavily, glancing at Kendrick and Caspian as he did so. "Ye're correct," he said. "Jamie'll not take kindly tae marrying a bairn, especially since she's kin tae the MacKenzie. 'Twill stoke the flame that feeds his vengeance. 'Twill not stop him if he truly intends tae seek retribution for Georgie's death."

George looked at the three young men, seeing the doubt in their expressions. "I am still the Munro," he said in a voice that discouraged any argument. "Jamison will do as I say. He'll have no choice. As long as there is breath in me body, this situation will be settled as peacefully as it can be because I'll not lose one more son tae a foolish feud. Of that, I vow. Now, go tae Lioncross and tell my son what has become of his family. When ye bring him home, ye will protect him wit' yer lives. The MacKenzies will be watchin' fer him and if they kill him, I'll kill each and every one of ye meself."

No one took offense because it was his passion speaking, not some sense of wicked subversion. George was vastly protective of Jamison but he was also determined to control his son's reaction to the situation when the truth was that he couldn't control it at all. Jamison would do as he felt necessary regardless of what his father wished.

Sense of vengeance aside, the marriage was nearly as undesirable because a marriage to a young heiress in an attempt to end a blood feud was complicated at best. It was a complicated situation in general, but one that needed to be dealt with as soon as possible because the MacKenzies were on the hunt. With George the Younger dead, there was the distinct possibility that the MacKenzie wouldn't stop until George the Elder and Hector and possibly even Ainsley were dead and buried. Then, there would be no stopping Jamison in his quest for vengeance.

The situation was more volatile than they could possibly imagine.

"Aye," Beaux finally said, looking at Kendrick and Caspian, both of whom were nodding in agreement to George's request. "We'll ride tae Lioncross and retrieve yer son. Shall I leave some of me men wit' ye for protection? How many men do ye have, George?"

George almost declined to answer but catching a glimpse of the weeping Ainsley out of the corner of his eye made him reconsider. What they did to George, they could easily do to the rest of them. It was a difficult thing to swallow his pride and admit he needed help, but his wife's safety was of paramount importance.

"A little over two hundred men do I have," he said quietly. "I'll be in yer debt if ye leave a few of yer own."

"I'll leave some of mine, also," Kendrick said. "Me da has more men than he knows what to do with. Ye put them to good use."

"How many?" George asked.

Kendrick turned to point to the groups of Highlanders standing on the moor outside of the churchyard. "I brought one hundred wit' me," he said. "They belong tae ye now."

That bolstered George's numbers significantly and the old man smiled weakly, thanking the young men for their loyalty and friendship, and feeling better than he had in days. The situation had turned out as he'd hoped with the young lions. Everything was not lost, after all.

Now, they would go to Jamison and bring the man home to face the storm that had raged in the wake of his disappearance into England. Even though George wanted Jamison safe, he had to admit that he was pleased with the thought of his son returning home. Shouldering the burden of everything that had happened was nearly too much for the old man to bear. Everything would be resolved when Jamison returned, or so he hoped. He had to hold on to that hope.

The alternative was something he couldn't stomach.

CHAPTER TWO

"Sweet Jesú,

what am I even doing here…."

Four Crosses Castle, the southern Welsh Marches
Four months later

IT WAS A hellish battle.

In pouring down rain and mud up to the knees, the enormous army from Lioncross Abbey had been summoned to quell yet another Welsh uprising. This particular castle had been wrested back and forth between the English and the Welsh for decades. At this particular time, it happened to belong to the English as an outpost for the great de Lohr empire at the northernmost area of de Lohr territory. On a hill overlooking the River Einion, Four Crosses Castle was a very big place with tall walls, no moat, and an enormous gatehouse. It was both imposing and strategic.

The garrison commander, Roald de Llion, a vassal to de Lohr, was part Welsh through his family lineage; but the truth was that he was English to the bone and the Welsh knew that. Therefore, they took issue with the man commanding an English castle on Welsh soil. This latest attack had been one of many in recent months, each one damaging Four Crosses before de Lohr could repair the damage from the previous attack. Little by little, the castle was falling to pieces.

It was all part of the Madog ap Llywelyn's master plan.

Jamison knew that the last of the great Welsh princes was behind all of this as he stood in mud that came to his mid-calf, soaking through his mail and breeches, attaching itself to his pale skin. He could feel the cold, slimy embrace, uncomfortable at best, but he was used to it because it seemed as if he'd been wet and muddy for an eternity. He couldn't remember ever being dry and warm. He was here to prevent this attack from being the last one by the Welsh but, as things were going, that might not be the case. The battle was getting dirtier and uglier by the hour. Reinforcements had come. Chaos was ensuing.

Sweet Jesú, what am I even doing here?

Rain pounded from overhead, hitting Jamison all over his body but he was quite certain most of it was aimed at his head. He wore a *bascinet,* a particular style of helm that was of the latest technology. The House of de Lohr and their war machine was always on the cutting edge of armor and weapons, so Jamison wore a sleek new helm with a visor attached that could actually lift on hinges. The visor was up at this point, water pouring down his face through the ventilation holes, as he and about five hundred de Lohr men were positioned at the gatehouse of Four Crosses. They were the last line of defense between the Welsh and those inside the castle.

The Welsh didn't have the castle, not yet, but with more Welsh coming to reinforce the exhausted, it was only a matter of time. Three days of non-stop bombardment from the Welsh, who were using Scots battle tactics at times, had the castle bottled up as the de Lohr army made a perimeter around the base of the castle walls to hold off the natives. There had been sporadic attacks at the perimeter by the Welsh, trying to weaken the lines, but this was where Jamison had been invaluable. Having the virtue of both English and Highlander training, he recognized the Highlander tactics and was able to help counter them.

It was odd to see the Welsh using tactics from Scotland but it also told Jamison, as well as the high command of the de Lohr army, that these Welsh weren't simply wild savages. Someone in their ranks had training and skill, which made them particularly dangerous. One particular tactic was blatantly Scots – the Welsh, in small groups, would attack part of the perimeter with small, sharp daggers to invite hand-to-hand combat. The English would engage simply to protect themselves but the Welsh would run off to invite a chase.

It was an obvious ruse and many an English soldier had to be called off from following. When that tactic hadn't worked after two days of harassment, the Welsh came back with something new and distracting, another tactic that involved a mounted attack on a light and swift horse. The animal was called a *hobelar* and Jamison had seen such things in Scotland, in raids against other clans and also against the English.

A swift and light mount against heavily-armored warhorses and warriors had seen the English at a disadvantage simply because the horses and men couldn't move as fast. It was meant to throw them off-balance and, at the moment, the Welsh were doing a decent job of that. In fact, he'd just fended off such an attack only minutes earlier, one that had given him a fairly decent gash on his left forearm when a wily Welsh on a wet brown horse had managed to land a lucky strike with a spear tip. Now, he was bleeding and exhausted, refusing to seek treatment for his wound. As he stood in the mud and watched the Welsh disappear into a heavily forested area, he heard someone calling his name.

"Jamie!"

Jamison turned in the direction of the shout, seeing a big knight in rusting armor heading in his direction. The man was only wearing his hauberk, with no helm, and the links of the iron mail were rusting all around his face, rubbing off that red-rust color on his cheeks. The man, handsome and blue-eyed, smiled weakly.

"Be ready, man," he said. "The Welsh have abandoned their horses just beyond the tree line to the south and they are bringing in ladders. Many, many ladders. I think we need to move some of our men into Four Crosses so if we are unable to deter them and the ladders go up, there will be enough men inside to fend them off."

Jamison gazed at his fellow knight and friend; Becket de Lohr was the eldest son of Chris de Lohr, the Earl of Worcester. He had the de Lohr blonde hair and blue eyes, the same toothy smile, and the same military acumen. He was, in a word, brilliant, and Jamison had known the man for many years. They'd virtually grown up together because, unlike the rest of the de Lohr sons, Chris had kept his eldest close to him, training the boy personally, instilling that sense of de Lohr loyalty and honor that was so important to the family.

Having come from a very long line of de Lohr males – from Myles back at the time of the Anarchy, to Christopher the Defender and the right-hand of Richard Coeur d 'Lion, to Curtis the Wise who had been a powerful lord in his own right, and now to Christopher the Second, or Deux as the family called him. Becket was a tribute to all of these great men and had that regal bearing that his bloodlines had given him.

Therefore, Jamison respected him more than most and when Becket told him to be ready, he was immediately on his guard. Those weren't words to be taken lightly in battle.

"Aye," Jamison finally said, glancing back at the castle and the gatehouse that secured double portcullises. "I can take me men and we can reinforce the walls."

Becket nodded, pushing his hauberk back on his fair forehead and leaving rust streaks on his skin. "Be quick about it," he said. "I do not want the Welsh to be upon us with the portcullises open."

Jamison was already moving for the gatehouse. "Have ye spoken to Roald, then?"

Becket shook his head. "I've not seen him since we arrived," he called after him. "Demand him, Jamie – 'tis odd that the man has not been present at his own battle. Tell him what we suspect and demand he open the portcullis to you."

Jamison gave him a wave of his hand, signifying that he understood. At a light jog, no easy feat in heavy mail and pieces of plate, he made his way to the gatehouse and found himself peering through the great iron fangs of the portcullises, straight into the bailey on the other side where dozens of men were gathered, staring back at him with suspicion. Not that he could blame them.

"I'm Munro," he boomed, his voice echoing off the stone underbelly of the gatehouse. "I'm with de Lohr. The Welsh are bringing ladders. I've been ordered tae bring me men inside tae help defend the keep should they mount the walls."

No one answered right away. They shifted about like nervous cattle until one man suddenly appeared at the forefront. A tall soldier, older, in a full coat of dirty mail, his unshaven face peered at Jamison between the slats in the grate.

"Where is de Lohr?" he demanded.

Jamison didn't think the man sounded particularly eager to lift the portcullis. "The Earl of Worcester did not come," he said. "Ye were told that when we arrived. Becket de Lohr is in command. My orders come through him."

The soldier wasn't having any of it. "I would hear the words from de Lohr's mouth, *Gael.*"

Gael was not a particularly pleasant word for a Scotsman. It was considered an insult by many, at least in Jamison's world. He was fairly certain that the soldier had meant it in a derogatory fashion so it was a bit of a struggle for him not to react. Unfortunately, he couldn't quite make good of it.

"He is occupied," he said, his manner cold. "It matters not tae me if the Welsh slit the throats of ye and yer cowardly men, but I've been given an order tae protect ye, so open the damnable portcullis and let me in or I'll scale the walls meself and throttle ye."

"You would not dare."

It wasn't the knight who spoke but a decidedly female voice. Someone was shoving through the crowd of nervous soldiers on the others side of the portcullises. Jamison could see men being pushed around, moved aside, until, finally, the person doing the pushing appeared.

A woman dressed in heavy mail was standing where the weary Four Crosses knight had once stood. She wasn't particularly short, or even tall, but somewhere in between. She had dark hair, dark like a raven's wing, pulled into a sloppy braid that draped over one shoulder and tangled with her mail coat. Dressed as a warrior, she was heavily armed with weapons that had seen some use, but her face....

Frankly, Jamison wasn't quite over staring at that part of her. Through the grime and rain and frowning expression, the woman's face could only be described as exquisite. *Angelic.* In fact, it was quite surprising and Jamison struggled not to come across looking too confused or too besotted with a woman who was looking at him angrily. He shook off whatever spell that lovely face had cast over him, bracing himself against the iron portcullis.

"I was having a conversation with the knight," he told her. "Does the man need a woman tae do his talking for him?"

The soldiers standing around the woman, including the knight, grumbled and shifted, unhappy with the insult. The woman, however, simply lifted her chin at him, cocking a well-shaped eyebrow.

"You will speak to me," she said. "This is *my* castle. You heard St. Clare – we will only open these portcullises if de Lohr tells us to. We take no orders from a Gael."

There was that word again. Jamison didn't like it at all. What he did like, however, was the way the woman's mouth worked and the deep, honeyed voice that poured forth with her lush lips opened. But he didn't like those attributes enough to tolerate her insult. In fact, he had little tolerance for women who did not know their place in the world.

"Then ye're a truly stupid lot and ye deserve tae have the Welsh overrun ye," he said, giving the woman a rather condescending look before turning his head. "I will tell me men tae returned tae Lioncross. Ye dunna deserve our protection."

He turned away completely but didn't move away from the portcullis he was leaning against. He wanted them to see the orders as he gave them to his men, bellowing to them to take their weapons and retreat to the base camp to the east. His men heard the orders and, confused, began to move away from the gatehouse as he had instructed. Clearly, however, they were puzzled and their movements reflected that.

When Jamison was sure his men were heading away, glaring at them when they didn't move fast enough, he turned back to the woman and her soldiers hovering on the other side of the second portcullis. The expressions facing him were considerably less hostile at the thought of the de Lohr army actually leaving. Now, the mood was shifting.

"I wish ye good fortune against the Welsh who, even now, are bringing ladders tae mount the walls," Jamison said rather casually. "They've brought in reinforcements since yesterday so very soon ye'll have a fresh horde of hungry Welshmen climbing the walls and killing everything that moves. If they dunna kill ye, then ye'll wish they had. They've got a man among them that has battle tactics and skill, and that means they'll take their pleasure making ye suffer. So if ye wunna let me and me men in tae help ye fend them off, then ye can face them alone."

The woman was listening to every word he said, her features flushing angrily the more he spoke. By the time he was finished, she grabbed on to the iron portcullis and shoved her face between the bars.

"I would rather take my chances against them than let a barbarian like you into my fortress," she snarled. "You sound like an animal in your foolish manner of speaking. How do I know that you were even sent by de Lohr? How do I know you are not working with the Welsh? They are barbarians just like you are!"

Jamison smiled thinly. "I hope yer fire holds out the first time a Welshman runs his hand up yer shift."

She spoke through clenched teeth. "I will cut his hand off if he tries."

"There may be many hands running up yer shift. Best of luck when that happens, General."

"You do not know me very well."

"And I dunna care tae," he snapped softly. "Ye'd do yer men a favor if ye went inside and scrubbed a floor or two. Leave the fighting tae those who will actually do some good. Clearly, ye dunna have a head for battle because yer decision-making is flawed."

Her lovely face flushed a dull, nasty shade of red. Jamison stood there, waiting for the next volley of insults, when she suddenly began yelling at the men in the gatehouse to raise the portcullises. It was a surprising move and Jamison was rather pleased that his insults had beaten her down to the point where she had obeyed her wishes. Feeling rather superior, he smirked at the woman as if to punctuate his victory.

She glared in return.

The portcullises began to grind open, chains groaning under the substantial weight. Jamison was in the process of calling his men back to the walls when he caught movement out of the corner of his eye. By the time he turned around, he caught the glint of a blade and something moving very quickly down near the ground. It took him a moment to realize the woman had slid underneath the lifting portcullises and was very close to him with a sword in her hand. He barely had a chance to jump back as she took a very swift strike at his head.

Jamison couldn't believe it. She'd actually come quite close to his face with the swing of that blade and he instantly unsheathed his broadsword, a weapon that was far bigger than hers. But she was fast, this one, and she was angry, which made her both determined and slightly reckless. As the de Lohr troops watched with some amusement and, truthfully, some horror, the woman charged Jamison with her small but well-made sword. When he lifted his weapon to fend off her attack, she fell to her knees, sliding in the mud with her momentum, and brought her sword up underneath him. Only Jamison's lightning-fast reflexes prevented her from making contact with his ankles.

It was actually an impressive tactic; she had been aiming for his Achilles' heel. When Jamison realized that she was genuinely trying to hurt him, he took the offensive. He had little choice unless he was prepared to willingly submit to her aggression. The woman was just regaining her feet as he came down upon her, hard, in a broadsword stroke that would have been difficult for a strong man to handle much less a woman. She lifted her sword, preventing he blow from cutting through her midsection, but the power behind the strike was much more forceful than anything she had ever experienced. The blow sent her onto her back and she had to roll out of the way, quick as a flash, to prevent him from seriously injuring her when he brought down a second strike.

Unfortunately for the woman, Jamison didn't give her time to recover. If she was going to try to hurt him, then he was going to disable her before she had the chance. So he went after her in full battle mode, preventing her from gaining her footing, watching her as she rolled and crawled through the mud, now struggling to avoid his blade.

But avoid she did, at least for a few minutes as he clearly tried to kill her, but that grace period soon ended. At one point, the woman's hair became untangled from her mail and as she tried to get away from Jamison, her braid dragged in the mud. Jamison seized on the opportunity and stepped on her hair, bringing her to an instant halt as she screamed in pain. Reaching down a massive hand, he grabbed her by the hair on her scalp, yanking her head back as he brought the sword down, aiming it right for her neck. He stopped short of cutting her head off, however, as the blade rested on her pale, dirty skin.

The fight was over as swiftly as it had begun. Jamison stared down into her face, seeing that her eyes were a deep shade of green, with long dark lashes all around. Her beauty was without compare but he refused to think such thoughts of this woman who had tried to hurt him. He glared at her, his jaw flexing furiously.

"Now," he growled, "ye attacked me and failed. Tell me why I shouldna end yer life right now."

The woman was breathing heavily but, to her credit, there was no fear in her eyes. She gazed back at him with defiance. "I cannot give you a reason," she said, her voice hoarse because he had her head pulled back so far and there was a strain on her neck. "Do as you must."

Jamison didn't want to kill her; he really didn't. He was just trying to scare her because she had been bold and reckless. But he was coming to think that she couldn't be scared. He could see it in her expression, in everything about her. She was brave, this one. A seedling of respect grew.

"Do ye want tae die, then?" he asked.

Something in her eyes flickered, a whisper of fear, perhaps. "Of course not," she said. "But I lost the fight. It is your right to do to me as you will."

His red eyebrows drew together; he couldn't help it. "How would ye know about the rules of engagement?" he asked. "Moreover, why do ye dress as a warrior? Does yer husband allow such things?"

She swallowed, hard. "I am not married."

"Then yer father allows this?"

She didn't respond right away, trying to lower her gaze but unable to for the way he was holding her. "My father has no say in what I do," she said. "This is my home. I defend it as necessary, any *way* I deem necessary."

Jamison was feeling some exasperation. "I told ye I am with de Lohr," he said. "I am here tae help ye. Do ye not understand that, lass?"

Something in her eyes flared as she looked at him. "Do not call me a lass!"

"I would call ye by yer name but I dunna know it."

"And I'll not tell you."

He cocked his head. "Ye have an unruly mouth in the face of a man holding a sword tae yer neck," he said. "Are ye truly so foolish? For certain, that is all I have seen from ye since the beginning."

She sighed, the frown returning to her features. "If you are going to kill me, then get on with it."

Jamison stared at her a moment longer. Then, he swiftly removed his sword and dropped it to the earth. Before the woman could utter a word of protest, he went down on one knee and, still holding on to her hair, put her straight across his thigh. Letting go of her hair, he held her down with that arm across her back as the other arm extended and, without hesitation, proceeded to spank her. His big hand against her backside resounded off of the stone walls. The woman began to howl.

"Beast!" she screamed, fighting and twisting. "How dare you take a hand to me! You will be punished for this – *ouch!*"

Jamison whaled on her buttocks, through the mail coat and through the breeches she was wearing. It probably hurt his hand more than it hurt her backside, but that wasn't the point. She was terribly mannered and it was clear no one had ever disciplined her. He was, therefore, pleased to be the first. It gave him a fiendish satisfaction to do so. He whacked her a few more times before pushing her off his knee, straight into the mud.

"Ye need tae be spanked and spanked often," he scolded as he picked up his sword and her smaller blade where it had fallen. "I dunna know where ye got it intae yer silly head that it 'tis acceptable for a women tae behave as ye did, but ye're a disgrace tae yer sex. Now, get yerself intae the castle and I dunna want tae see yer face again. If I do, I will spank ye as I just did, only harder the next time. Is this in any way unclear?"

The woman pushed herself up out of the mud, staggering to her feet and glaring daggers at Jamison. "I will fight with my men and you cannot stop me," she seethed. "You do not command me."

Jamison wasn't going to argue with her. He took a step in her direction, threateningly, and watched her as she scrambled to get away from him. He did it twice more, herding her back in the direction of the castle. She would jump, keeping away from him, but she wouldn't run. She stood her ground as much as she could, unwilling to let him push her around. They glared at each other, each one testing the mettle of the other – he wouldn't chase after her and she wouldn't run. But she would, wisely, stay out of arm's length.

It was quite a standoff.

With both portcullises open, Jamison's men were starting to filter into the castle as the men from Four Crosses lingered by the gate, watching their lady warrior get a beating from the big Highlander. In fact, Jamison was just taking another step in the lady's direction, hopefully to scare her right back into the castle, when he heard a voice call his name.

"Munro? What in the hell are you doing?"

Jamison turned to see another de Lohr brother ride up. Tobias de Lohr, Becket's younger brother, sat on a wet, foaming charger, gazing down at Jamison as if the man had lost his mind. Jamison could quickly see why – caught, as he was, harassing a woman who was supposed to be their ally. It looked very bad for him and he knew it.

Quickly, he tried to think of a believable excuse but nothing he could come up with sounded plausible. He could have gone for a full confession but, somehow, he thought that might make them all look quite foolish. *The lady attacked me so I spanked her.* No, that wouldn't do. In any case, the truth probably wasn't advisable. Therefore, he simply forced a smile at the younger de Lohr brother.

"The lady and I had a misunderstanding," he said. "All is well now."

Tobias, another blonde and well-built de Lohr son, looked between Jamison and the lady in confusion. His attention finally settled on the woman. "Lady Havilland?" he said. "Are you… well?"

Havilland. So her name had been spoken for the Highlander to hear and she hadn't intended for him to know it, ever. With a sigh of displeasure, Lady Havilland de Llion fixed on Tobias.

"I am very well," she said snappishly. She pointed at Jamison. "Did you tell this… this brute to defend Four Crosses from inside the bailey?"

Tobias nodded. "Indeed," he said. "Those were his orders. What… what are you doing out here? Why are you and your men not inside the castle?"

He was looking at Jamison as he said it. Jamison, realizing he couldn't explain away what had just happened any better than he already had, shook his head in frustration and tossed Havilland her sword, hilt first. He didn't even care that he now knew her name, as beautiful as it was. All he knew was that she had made him look like a fool. He began to walk away.

"We were dancing," he muttered sarcastically as he headed towards the open portcullis, "but she likes tae lead. I willna dance with a woman who leads."

It made no sense to Tobias, who looked at Havilland curiously. Havilland, however, was looking at the massive Scotsman as he slogged through the mud towards the gatehouse of Four Crosses. There was malice in her expression but there was also something more, something that might have been interest but she kept it well guarded. Her gaze lingered on the redheaded warrior.

"*Who* is that man?" she asked. "And why do you have Scotsmen serving in your ranks?"

Tobias turned to glance at the hulking figure of Jamison as the man began shouting orders to his men. "They call him The Red Lion," he said, a hint of awe in his tone. "Have you never heard of the man before?"

"I have not. Should I?"

Tobias shrugged. "His name is Jamison Munro, son of the chief of Clan Munro," he said. "He is a great warrior, fostered and trained with the House of de Lohr. In fact, he is part of a group of Scots that fostered at Lioncross several years ago, placed there by King Henry. Sons of clan chiefs, they were, and they called themselves the Lions of the Highlands. Jamison was their leader. I remember looking up to them, so very much. They are men I both admired and feared in my youth."

Havilland's gaze moved from the big Scotsman near the gatehouse back to Tobias. "Scots fostered at Lioncross?" she repeated. "I had not heard this. They did not stay there, did they?"

Tobias shook his head. "Nay," he said. "When they came of age, they went their separate ways. Jamison was a squire to my Uncle Arthur and when Arthur went to fight in France, Jamison went with him. I think he spent more time there than in England. And the others – there were three more – returned to Scotland, although I have seen them at Lioncross from time to time. My father still considers them his vassals. They were a fearsome pride, the four of them. They scared us young squires and pages to death. Munro, Sutherland, Ross, and Mackay… funny, I've not thought of the Lions of the Highlands in many years."

Havilland's gaze moved from Tobias back to the big Scotsman, now waving an impatient hand at men who weren't moving fast enough. "Were they brutes, then?"

"Nay, simply intimidating young knights."

Havilland cocked her head. "Munro," she muttered thoughtfully. "A chief's son, you said?"

Tobias shook his head. "Indeed," he said. Then, he eyed her curiously. "Clan Munro breeds fearsome warriors, you know. Why was he chasing you? Did you make him angry?"

Havilland turned to look at the young de Lohr brother. She had known him for a few years but she didn't know him well. He had come to Four Crosses on occasion, on business for his father, as had the other de Lohr sons from time to time. A few times, they had even sent de Lohr knights, who were not a part of their family, to conduct business but she had never seen the big Scotsman. She would have remembered. Although she counted herself fortunate in that she'd never encountered him before, in the same breath, she wasn't hard-pressed to admit that the man was rather handsome. His red hair and pale skin was rather beautiful. But it was a thought she hated herself for; any man who would threaten and then spank her was no one she should be wasting her thoughts on.

"How many men are you sending into my bailey?" she asked, changing the subject. "We cannot feed more than a few hundred should we get boxed in."

Tobias shook his head, not unaware that she had shifted the focus. "Jamison has about four or five hundred under his command," he said, glancing over his shoulder towards the south. "The Welsh are moving in with ladders from the south. If they are able to mount the walls, you will be happy to have those men inside and you will be happy to have Jamison in command of them. Where are your sisters, by the way?"

Havilland was already moving back towards the gatehouse. "On the wall," she said, turning to Tobias even as she walked. "Madeline and Amaline have command of the gatehouse and the wall. I have command of the bailey."

Tobias simply shook his head. "I will never understand why your father allows you three women to fight with his men," he said. "He has enough competent men in his army. Where is Roald, by the way?"

Havilland gestured towards the castle. "Inside," she said. "Although he is quite ill. He does not see visitors these days."

"He has been very ill as of late."

"I know."

Tobias didn't push the subject of Roald, which had become a rather odd subject recently, as if the sisters did not wish to discuss him. They would mention he was ill and quickly change the subject, just as Havilland was doing. But that was something for Tobias' father to deal with, not him. He was focused on other things in his life, in particular, the eldest de Llion sister. He thought she was rather special, which brought him back to the subject of her taking up arms.

"Then you will give your father my best wishes for his health," he said, "and tell him that my father thinks it is a travesty that he allows you and your sisters to fight."

Havilland grinned, a very lovely grin on her grimy face. "What does your mother say to that?"

"She smacks him every time he says it."

Havilland burst out laughing before racing back to the gatehouse, unwilling to discuss her father any further. She didn't want the conversation to turn into something she couldn't control. She made it inside just as the de Llion men began to close the fanged iron grates, disappearing into the darkness beyond.

As Tobias headed back to the remaining de Lohr men still maintaining a perimeter around the walls of Four Crosses, his thoughts lingered on the three beautiful de Llion sisters who fought as men because their father had never had any sons.

A travesty, Chris de Lohr had said repeatedly. *A travesty because those three lovely young women would make my sons excellent wives, but no man wants a wife who can best him in a fight.*

Frankly, Tobias didn't care if Havilland could best him or not.

He'd take her, anyway.

CHAPTER THREE

ଓ

"A ghost of a

once-great man...."

ଓ

"WHO WAS HE?" a dark-haired young woman with her hair tied in a knot atop her head demanded. "I saw him strike you! Who is he, I say?"

Havilland had just entered the great hall of Four Crosses, followed closely by two young women who had latched on to her the moment she had entered the bailey. She was frustrated, embarrassed, and the least bit frightened by the news that the Welsh were coming with ladders.

But it was more than that. There were many emotions she was feeling at the moment. She'd come into the great hall, with its smells of dogs and smoke and dirty bodies, with the intention of collecting her thoughts and summoning her father's commanders. They needed to know what was happening. It just so happened that two of those commanders were her own sisters so she grabbed a cup half-filled with old ale, sitting out on the cluttered table, and downed it in one swallow before facing the young women.

"He is a de Lohr knight," she said, trying to brush off the embarrassing subject of having been spanked in public. "The Welsh are approaching with ladders with the intention of mounting the walls. De Lohr wants to put some of his men inside the bailey to help fend them off."

The young women hovered around her, listening intently. "A de Lohr knight?" the one with the knot on top of her head spit in outrage. "But… but I do not understand! Why did he strike you?"

Havilland cocked a dark eyebrow, displeased that her sister wasn't changing the subject. "Did you hear me?" she said. "The Welsh are approaching with ladders. We must summon our commanders and inform them."

The woman with the dark top knot nodded impatiently. "I heard you," she said. "But why did the de Lohr knight strike you, Havi?"

Havilland was quickly coming to realize that she couldn't avoid the subject, much as she wanted to. Madeline, her middle sister, and Amaline, the redheaded youngest, would push until they had answers. It was simply their nature. Therefore, the best she could do was downplay what had happened so she didn't look completely foolish to her sisters. Her pride, a formidable thing, was difficult to get past.

"Did you not see the fight in the gatehouse?" she finally asked. "The arrogant swine… I intended to teach him a lesson."

Both Madeline and Amaline looked at each other in confusion. "Nay," Madeline, the sister with the dark hair, responded. "I only saw it when he knocked your sword away. Then he grabbed you and beat you."

"You should have called for our help, Havi," Amaline insisted. "We could have helped you best the man."

Havilland shook her head. "I am not so sure about *that* man," she said. "Any other man, I would agree, but that one… he is a Highlander. Tobias de Lohr told me that they call him The Red Lion. He is a leader of a pack of Highlanders, sons of clan chiefs, who call themselves the Lions of the Highlands. I can tell you that he is not like the men around here. He is stronger than an ox and more cunning than a fox. I doubt any of our men could have bested him so I suppose there is no shame that he disarmed me."

Madeline and Amaline were looking at their sister in shock and outrage. "And de Lohr let him do this to you?" Madeline demanded. "He let one of his knights beat you?"

Now Havilland was growing uncomfortable, fearful that her sisters would not think so well of her now that she had been bested in a fight. In truth, that had never happened, not ever. Havilland was skilled and fast with a sword, so much so that no man in her father's army had ever beaten her. Of course, deep down, Havilland knew that some of them could have bested her but chose not to because she was Roald's daughter, but that didn't matter. All that mattered was that she had beat them for all to see. But now… now her record was in danger of being tarnished by the damnable de Lohr knight.

"De Lohr didn't 'let' the knight beat me," she said irritably. "I tripped. He disarmed me. It was only through pure luck on his part that he was able to best me. So let us not speak any more of it. I do not wish to discuss it. What we must discuss is the incoming Welsh; that is the most important thing right now. Agreed?"

Madeline was reluctant. "If that is your wish," she said, although she didn't mean it. With a heavy sigh, she shifted her slender body on her leather-clad feet. "Now what? Do you wish for us to summon Papa's commanders?"

Havilland nodded. "Send the servants for them," she said. "I have much to discuss with the two of you before the men arrive."

Amaline glanced over her shoulder, off in the direction of Four Crosses' massive keep. "Should… should I tell Papa what is happening?"

Havilland shook her head. "Why?" she asked, a hint of irony in her tone. "He would not remember, anyway. We would be fortunate if he even knew who you were, Ammie. He does not know any of us these days. He probably does not even realize the castle is under siege."

For the first time since entering the hall, Madeline's tough-as-steel demeanor seemed to weaken. "It is his castle," she said quietly. "Papa will come back to us some day, I am certain. He will be angry if we do not tell him of things that concern his castle. God forbid, what if the castle falls to the Welsh? He will be angry at us for allowing it to happen."

Havilland looked at her middle sister; with sickness in her soul that she couldn't begin to describe. It was melancholy, resignation, and sorrow all rolled into one, which was always the case when discussing their father.

"Papa is never coming back to us," she muttered. "His mind has been eaten away into madness. I do not even consider that man up in Papa's chamber to be my father. I do not know who he is. He is not the man I recognize."

"But he is still Papa," Amaline reminded her softly.

Havilland simply shook her head. "He is a ghost," she murmured, depressed. "A ghost of a once-great man."

No one said anything to that because what Havilland said was essentially true. That was the great secret that Four Crosses Castle guarded so ferociously these days – the madness of Roald de Llion.

Over the past year, Roald had suffered a breakdown of his mind, so much so that the man couldn't remember his own family or even his name. He had a servant who tended him these days, helping him to bathe and eat and dress, but even then, Roald lived in a terrible world, one that saw him weep daily and soil himself. It was a horrid state for the once-proud knight, one the physics could only describe as madness. They had no cure and no suggestions on how to help him, which meant the function of Four Crosses Castle had been left to his only children, three young women.

The three young women who had been raised as men, something that started long before Roald's mind left him. Having no sons, he could not refuse the girls when they wanted to learn to fight like men. Selfishly, he had allowed it. They were tough, these three, but the truth was that they were, indeed, women and had all of the emotions and moods that women had, which made life around Four Crosses volatile at times. Not even Chris de Lohr knew of Roald's state and to preserve the man's pride, the daughters made sure to keep the true condition of their father a secret. As long as Four Crosses remained strong, there was no reason anyone should know.

At the head of the leadership was Havilland, an extraordinarily intelligent young woman. She was the one who made sure her father's secret was guarded and her younger sisters helped to ensure the same. It was a heavy burden for the three but one they felt necessary. The burden also made them closer than most, united as they were, but it also meant they knew each other exceedingly well.

They knew and understood each other's moods, like they did now. Madeline and Amaline wanted to return to the subject of the big Highland warrior but they refrained, knowing any further probing would not be well met. Still, they knew the crime could not go unpunished. They would have to do something about this big red-haired brute and teach him a lesson he'd not soon forget. Having been raised as knights, they fought very well, all of them, their egos fed by men who had willingly fallen to their aggression. It had given them all an inflated sense of pride, something that had been a rude awakening for Havilland.

But Madeline and Amaline hadn't suffered that humiliation yet; even as Havilland spoke of the Welsh and of de Lohr's men entering Four Crosses to bolster their ranks, and even as the Four Crosses commanders were summoned to discuss the situation, the two younger daughters of Roald de Llion were plotting the downfall of one particular Highland warrior. In punishment for their sister's beating, he would soon feel their wrath.

The man would pay.

☙

IT WAS A miserable night.

As predicted, the Welsh came with their crude ladders, leading wave after wave of attack upon the army defending the walls of Four Crosses. As the storm surged and the lightning flashed across the sky, the Welsh were as plentiful as raindrops, all of them pelting the prize of the beaten fortress. The abuse was intense and when some sections of the de Lohr perimeter finally started to weaken, several of the Welsh managed to raise their ladders to the walls. They did it with glee, thinking they had overcome the English, but the truth was that they were heading into a trap.

Jamison and his men were waiting for them.

That's when the battle truly turned desperate and ugly. If Jamison wasn't physically throwing men off of the wall, he was using his broadsword to fend them off. Tremendously strong, he had been able to push several of the ladders away from the wall, sending a dozen men crashing to the wet ground below. But the fallen men occurred on both sides. The wall walk wasn't more than a narrow, wooden fighting platform and, unfortunately, it was crowded with de Lohr men. So, in addition to the ladders crashing down, several de Lohr men had taken the unexpected plunge off the wall walk about fifteen feet to the bailey below. The falls resulted in more than a few injures.

It was dark, too, due to the cloud cover, the only real illumination coming when the lightning flashed. Most of the fighting had been in the dark because the torches wouldn't stay lit in the pounding rain. But there were a few about on the wall, near the gatehouse mostly, as men tried to light their path to prevent them from goring a comrade. That had happened a few times as well. In the darkness, there was confusion.

But there was also great danger.

Jamison had discovered that his first hour upon the wall. In addition to the dark-haired lass he'd tangled with, there seemed to be two more just like her. He'd seen one of them when he'd first mounted the wall walk, a girl with her dark hair knotted up on the top of her head and wearing a heavy mail coat on her skinny body. Jamison could only presume she had seen the beating he'd given the other girl because she had glared at him ferociously. He swore he could feel the shards of steel coming out of her eyes, aimed right at him. Then, she pulled an index finger across her neck in a garroting gesture. He'd simply chuckled.

But the chuckle had been a cover for his heightened sense of protection. Considering how rabidly Havilland had fought, he wasn't taking any chances with the other warrior woman. He found himself watching his back as he positioned himself on the wall, guarding against that steel-glaring lass and also against another woman down in the bailey with wild red hair that made her head look gigantic. She, too, was wishing hate upon him; he could see it in her pale face. Jamison, therefore, knew that the enemy wasn't only outside of the walls of Four Crosses.

It was all around him.

They moved like wraiths, those women, in and out of the shadows of the castle, but Jamison eventually lost track of them as the Welsh mounted the walls and he found himself throwing men over the side. In fact, he forgot about the women completely in the chaos of the fight until shades of dawn began to appear on the eastern horizon and the Welsh attack died down.

From the brutal battle most of the night to the eerie stillness left by their abrupt retreat, Jamison and the beaten, bloodied de Lohr men waited for the next wave of fighting that never came. An hour passed before the de Lohr troops on the perimeter outside the walls began receiving information from their scouts that the Welsh were departing. As great relief swept the weary men of Four Crosses, Jamison was finally able to climb down off the wall.

Exhausted and very thirsty, he managed to make his way to the great hall where the wounded had been taken. He wanted to check on his men. A long stone building with a steeply pitched roof, he entered the hall to see that the wounded had been placed at the far end, away from the entry and the cold, wet weather blowing in. Before he reached the wounded, however, he noticed that there were great, fat bread rolls and ale set out on the big feasting table for the hungry. The lure of food was stronger than his desire to see to his wounded men at the moment and Jamison wolfed down several of the crusty, hard bread rolls, washed down with great gulps of ale.

With a full mouth and a full cup, he finally made his way to the wounded to see how his men were faring. That was one of the things that set Jamison apart from the rest of the commanders; he genuinely cared about his men. He had a connection to them and his men were pleased to see him, assuring him they would be well very soon and praising him for his actions in the battle. Jamison spent a few moments with one man before moving on to the next, and soon he'd spoken with every man under his command. The battle had been fierce and he congratulated his men for their bravery.

He couldn't spend too much time with the wounded, however, knowing that he should return to assess the damages and speak with Becket and Tobias to see what their instructions would be for securing the castle for the eventual departure of the de Lohr army back to Lioncross. So he begged his leave of his men and, with a half-cup of ale still in his hand, returned to the night outside.

The storm had eased, now just a faint mist falling where there had once been rain. It still made for wet and miserable conditions, and Jamison had the gatehouse in his sights, noting that both portcullises were still down which told him that everyone was still remaining vigilant. The Welsh had been known to lay quiet and then come back strong and he, much like the other commanders, weren't entirely certain this lull wasn't a ruse. He was nearly to the ladder leading to the wall walk when something muddy and hard came hurling out of the darkness, hitting him squarely on the neck and shoulder. Mud exploded everywhere.

Mud even landed in his ale. Grunting with disgust and some pain, Jamison put his hand back to the spot where the mud ball had hit him, feeling slimy, wet dirt all over his neck and right shoulder. It was probably all down his back, too, but he couldn't see it and, frankly, he didn't much care. It was there and he was dirtier and more miserable because of it. Angrily, he wiped away what he could and spilled out a goodly portion of his ale to get the mud out of it. He drank the rest, quickly, still tasting some grit from the mud. It was revolting.

With the taste of mud on his lips, he looked around but didn't see anyone who might have been guilty of throwing the mud. Something told him those hateful young women had something to do with it. It was just a hunch he had. He could see that his turn spanking the bold lass at the gatehouse probably wouldn't be the last time he would be beating a woman soundly at Four Crosses Castle. His open palm was ready to spank more should they push him. Turning back for the hall to refill his cup, he was on his guard when a small figure with a sword in hand suddenly appeared in front of him.

Jamison came to a stop, eyeing the small figure in the dim light. She was small and slender, and he thought she might be the skinny lass with the knot on her head he had seen earlier. The figure lifted her sword defensively.

"Now," the figure spoke, decidedly a woman, "you shall receive your punishment, *Gael*. No one beats on my sister and emerges unpunished."

Sister. Now, those hateful stares were starting to make some sense. "Get out of me way, ye foolish wench," he said, his voice low and threatening. "There is no world in which ye would be able tae best me, so get out of me way. I'll not tell ye twice."

The woman swung her sword in a surprisingly controlled movement. "And you'll not threaten me, you brute," she fired back quietly. "You had no right to lay a hand on my sister."

Jamison was weary and snappish, a bad combination. He started to move past the woman, a direct insult, when she rushed at him. Jamison was prepared, however, suspecting she might do something so stupid, so the hand on the hilt of his broadsword unsheathed the weapon and thrust it directly into her path. She met with it, violently, and, much like her sister, did not have the strength to effectively counter such a powerful foe. As she grunted and fought, Jamison drove her back in the direction she had come.

But there was a problem with that; out of the recesses near the wall where it met with another wall, this one encircling the stable yard, Jamison heard a screech cry and the darkness came alive with more swinging swords. The female with the wild red hair was suddenly in their midst, grunting and groaning as she swung her sword at Jamison's head.

Very quickly realizing that these foolish women intended to do him harm on behalf of the beating he gave the woman at the gatehouse, Jamison rapidly summed up the situation and realized there was only one thing he could do – multiple foes called for extreme measures unless he wanted to find himself at the tip of their blades. He had to fight back rather than simply deter them.

He was going to have to get the upper hand.

For as exhausted as he was, he was growing increasingly angry with these childish games. He had just fought off an entire Welsh army and wasn't about to let two small women get the best of him, so he lashed out with his sword hard enough to knock the dark-haired woman's weapon from her grip. He'd hit her hard enough to make her fumble and when she stumbled forward, he reached out and grabbed her arm, spinning her around so her back was against his torso. One big hand went into her hair to control her while the other hand grabbed her wrist, the one still holding her sword. In doing so, he moved headlong into the red-haired woman who had been trying to attack him.

Now, he had woman against woman as he controlled the dark-haired woman like a puppet. As the dark-haired woman screamed in pain, Jamison manipulated her sword hand so he was slashing brutally at the redhead. The redhead, for her part, had gone from supremely aggressive to supremely uncertain as Jamison used the dark-haired woman to attack her.

In fact, she was so caught off guard by the unexpected turn of events and so distressed to see what was happening to the dark-haired woman, that Jamison was able to effectively disarm her. In fact, he'd managed to disarm both women swiftly and now, grabbing both by the hair, dragged his kicking and fighting captives back into the darkened stable yard.

They were a handful, he had to admit, but he was much bigger and much stronger. As they fought against him, he was able to pull them into the nearest empty stall. Filled with damp, dirty straw, his gaze fell upon a leather harness hanging on a peg, a harness that had several loose leather straps.

Seized with an idea, Jamison threw the redhead to the ground, face-first into the dirty straw, and put his foot on her hair, trapping her against the ground. As she fought and screamed and beat at his booted foot, he used his free hand to grab the loose leather straps and proceeded to tie the dark-haired woman to the shoulder-high wall that divided the stalls.

The dark-haired woman was wily, however, and he had to use his weight to trap her against the wooden post as he tied her hands behind her, lashing her to the wood. Her feet were free but any kicking she did managed to hit the redhead on the ground, who was grossly unhappy at being face-first in horse dung. It kept the dark-haired lass' footwork to a minimum as Jamison hauled the redhead to her feet and again using his body weight to hold his prey still, managed to tie the redhead to the dark-haired lass like two pigs on a spit.

Anchored by wooden posts that were meant to withstand the strength of animals, the women had nowhere to go. Jamison tied them very well and very snuggly to the posts. Breathing heavily from his exertion, he stood back to inspect his handiwork.

"There," he said, extremely satisfied with his work. "Ye'll not be breaking loose from that any time soon. It serves ye right, ye foolish wenches. If I can find a whip around here, I'll use it on ye."

The women were so unhappy, and perhaps so embarrassed, that it seemed to him that both of them were trying hard not to weep.

"Do it, then!" the redheaded woman nearly cried. "You are a filthy barbarian of a man and brutalizing women must come easy for you. Find a whip, then! Only a fiend would do such a thing!"

Jamison cocked a lazy eyebrow. "Had ye not attacked me, then ye wouldna find yerself in such a position," he said. Then he leaned forward, condescendingly. "Or did ye not think of that? Did ye truly think ye would best me? Lass, I've spent all night tossing the Welsh out of yer castle. Are ye so arrogant that ye thought ye'd be a match for me?"

The redhead was furious and ashamed; she couldn't even answer the question. Averting her gaze, she looked away and tried not to sob. Meanwhile, the dark-haired woman was staring Jamison down as if she wanted to kill him.

"You are a damnable bastard," she hissed. "You deserved to be punished for what you did to our sister."

Our sister. So the gatehouse lass had two fighting sisters, did she? Jamison actually scratched his head.

"Yer father has *three* daughters that fight as men?" he said, incredulous. "Why on earth does the man allow such a thing?"

The eyes of the dark-haired woman flashed. "For the same reason your father allows you to fight," she snapped. "We are his offspring. It is our duty."

"'Tis a man's duty."

"He had no sons."

Ah... more and more was clear to Jamison now. He was a bright man, able to piece together the situation. "Havilland is yer sister," he said. "Is there just the three of ye?"

The dark-haired lass nodded. "Aye."

"Do ye have names?"

The dark-haired lass regarded him a moment, a calculated gleam in her eye. This one was rather calculated, it seemed to him. "If I tell you, will you untie us?"

He shook his head. "Not unless ye swear ye willna try tae attack me again. We must have an understanding first." He folded his enormous arms across his chest. "Do ye not realize we are on the same side? I am no' the enemy. Ye had no reason tae lift a weapon against me."

The dark-haired lass wasn't repentant in the least. "You beat our sister," she said. "Debts must be paid."

He cocked an eyebrow. "She attacked me first," he said. "I wasna supposed tae defend meself?"

"You must have done something to deserve it."

He threw up his hands. "I did nothing," he assured her. "Yer sister simply likes tae attack men without provocation, 'tis all."

The dark-haired woman didn't reply. She simply kept looking at him, holding his gaze. When Jamison heard movement behind him, it was already too late for him to react. He realized, too late, that the dark-haired lass had been keeping his attention away from his surroundings with her chatter.

That had been his grave mistake.

Thinking himself quite the idiot was the last coherent thought Jamison had before a sharp pain rattled his head and everything went black.

CHAPTER FOUR

"What I do,

I do to keep us all safe...."

"YOU SHOULD NOT have tried to engage him," Havilland hissed as she dragged her sisters towards the keep. "He is crafty and he is brutal. You are lucky I saw him drag you into the stables!"

Madeline was defiant but Amaline was contrite, bordering on tears. "I am sorry, Havi," Amaline sniffed. "Do not be angry with me!"

They were nearing the keep entry, a second-level entry with retractable wooden stairs that led up to it. Those stairs, for the past three days, had been in danger of being destroyed by Four Crosses troops but never closer than they had been the previous night with the Welsh on the walls. Even now, they were a soggy mess, sagging on one side where soldiers, in a panic, had already begun the dismantling. They were fairly dangerous in their current state.

But Havilland didn't pay any attention to the leaning, sagging stairs. As Amaline begged for forgiveness, she came to an abrupt halt and began smacking both Amaline and Madeline in her frustration. Madeline simply threw up her hands to protect herself but Amaline caved in, crying. She let Havilland beat her around the shoulders.

"You should have left well enough alone," Havilland said as she smacked. She really wasn't hurting them; it was more the noise of the slap than anything else. "Do you see what you have done? I had to knock the man out in order to save you both from his wrath. Now he will be looking for all three of us, looking to finish what he has started!"

With that, she stopped smacking and dragged her sisters up the leaning stairs, bracing herself against the side of the keep so they could keep their balance. The entry door was eleven stairs up from the floor of the bailey and she tugged on Madeline, who in turn tugged on Amaline, pulling each other up the stairs like a train of great burdens. Amaline, at the end of the train, continued to weep.

"But he hurt you, Havi," Amaline said, hoping her sister would understand why they had acted as they had. "Would you not punish someone who had hurt us?"

They were at the entry door and Havilland yanked them through. "Nay," she snapped. "I would have let them beat you to death and then I would have danced upon your graves. Do you not understand? You have only made things worse. Now, de Lohr will hear of this behavior and he will wonder what is happening at his garrison. He will wonder why we are attacking his men. He will send Tobias and Becket to investigate. They will want to speak to Papa and know what he intends to do to discipline us for attacking one of his knights. And then what shall we do? They cannot speak to Papa!"

She was shrieking by the time she was finished. Standing in the cold, damp entry to the keep, the sisters faced one another in moody uncertainty. Amaline was wiping her nose while Madeline seemed much more composed. She eyed her older sister without fear of the woman's rage.

"We will fend them off as we always do," Madeline said calmly. "You always become upset over the smallest things, Havi. We will tell them that Papa is ill and is not allowed visitors. It has always worked before."

Havilland faced her dark-haired sister. She and Madeline were quite alike, in fact, not merely with the same dark hair and same delicate face, but also in manner. They were both stubborn and confident, but Havilland, with her long limbs and height advantage, held the edge over her middle sister physically.

And things had become physical between the two more than once, not simply the silly slapping that Havilland had been doing, but an all-out brawl on occasion. That hadn't happened in a while, fortunately, because Roald was no longer in his right mind to break up the fight. Perhaps the girls realized that. They had been forced to grow up quickly in the wake of their father's debilitating mental illness. Perhaps they realized there was no place for their foolish disagreements now. They had a fortress and each other to protect. But even now, as they gazed at each other, Havilland knew it wouldn't take much for Madeline to throw a punch and for her to take her sister's head off in reply.

The fists were beginning to ball already.

"It was you, wasn't it?" Havilland finally asked, her dark green eyes glittering. "You are the one who wanted to challenge him, dragging poor Ammie along with you. It is *always* you, Madeline. You have no sense at all."

Madeline lifted her chin. "You let him beat you," she said, her tone bordering on condescending. "Someone had to teach the *Gael* a lesson."

"I did not ask you to!" Havilland snapped, overlapping her sister's bold statement. Madeline was always pushing her, always overstepping her bounds when she knew full well that Havilland was in charge. Havilland knew her sister didn't like that arrangement because *she* wanted to be in charge and it was a constant battle to maintain her command. Frustrated, she shook her head. "If I need your help, I will ask. If anyone is going to teach the Gael a lesson, it will be me. I am the one he wronged. Now, listen to me and listen well – you will never do anything like that again without my knowledge. One of these days, you are going to do something so foolish that I will not be able to save you. Is that clear, Madeline? And you, Amaline – stop following her. She is going to get you into a goodly amount of trouble someday."

Amaline nodded eagerly, willing to placate her oldest sister, but Madeline was unmoved. She continued to meet her sister's gaze as if she had done nothing wrong.

"At least I am not a coward," she said, baiting Havilland. "At least I fight when there must be fighting."

"What is that supposed to mean?"

"It means that you are content to sit and let the Welsh come to you. The next time they come, we may not be so fortunate."

Jaw ticking, Havilland got in her sister's face in a provocative move. "Tell me more of how I am a coward, Madeline," she said, daring her sister to speak further. "Is it because I will not send out troops to burn their villages and challenge the nearest Welsh outpost?"

"Aye."

"We do not have the men for such ventures. It would be foolish to attack when we know we cannot defeat them!"

Madeline stared at her a moment before shaking her head, averting her gaze. "Ever cautious, Havi."

"Ever foolish, Madeline."

Madeline snorted softly, although there was no humor to the sound. "You sit around and wait for de Lohr to protect us," she said. "You must take the offensive against the Welsh. De Lohr does not live here; *we* do. We should have a say in how we fight the Welsh who continually attack us."

"Mayhap that is true, but I will not do anything foolish to put us all in danger," Havilland countered. "That is the problem with you, Madeline – you have let control of an army consume you. You would step out and do something utterly foolish without thought for the consequences. Well, I will not behave that way. What I do, I do to keep all of us safe. If you do not like the way I run things around here, then you are more than welcome to leave. I will not stop you."

Madeline's dark eyes glittered with rage. "That is an attractive invitation."

"Then I wish you would take it."

"If it would take me far away from you, I might do that."

Havilland stepped back from her sister, glaring daggers at the woman. She had two choices at that moment; continue the argument, which would not end well, or give her sister a command to follow. She chose the latter because Madeline needed to be reminded of who was in command. Havilland found herself having to remind the girl more and more when they had circular arguments like this. Madeline wanted to be the aggressor against the Welsh. Havilland knew they could never sustain such a thing.

It was a bitter argument that was starting to drive them apart.

"You will not leave at the moment," Havilland finally muttered. "You are needed here. Now, you will go to the kitchens and take stock of our provisions to see what we have to feed these additional men. That is our priority. While you do that, Ammie and I will see to the wounded. We had several last I saw. Once you have finished seeing to the provisions, come and find me in the great hall."

Madeline wasn't pleased by the command in the least. "We have servants to tend the provisions."

"And we have servants to steal from us," Havilland snapped. "You must ensure they do not. Go now and do as I say. Food stores are precious and we must make sure to keep track of ours."

Madeline didn't agree with the command in the least, a directive she felt was beneath her. If Madeline wasn't in control of something, then she was unhappy. Inventorying food rations was menial work. It was clear that she wanted to argue more about it but, for some reason, she didn't. She simply turned on her heel and marched from the keep.

Havilland felt some relief that Madeline didn't fight with her about it, but she also felt some wariness about the woman. The truth was that she didn't trust Madeline. The girl had seen seventeen summers upon this earth and thought she knew it all. Madeline believed that she was right and everyone else was wrong. Havilland had, at times, even heard of Madeline trying to summon the support of the men against Havilland's decisions. It was subversion from her own sister.

In fact, had Madeline been a man, Havilland would have thrown her in the vault long ago, or worse. But Madeline was her flesh and blood, born almost two years after Havilland had been born. The sisters had always been close, and very similar, but their father's illness had brought out something in Madeline that Havilland didn't like. There was insurrection in the woman's heart.

If Havilland didn't know better, she would have thought her sister was out to usurp her.

Times like this made her believe that implicitly.

ଓଃ

BECKET WAS TRYING very hard to keep from laughing. "You're sure of this?"

Jamison, pale-faced and with an open gash on the back of his skull, tried to nod his head but it hurt too much. The surgeon that traveled with the de Lohr army had him on a three-legged stool in Becket's dark tent, inspecting the oozing wound as his assistant held up a lit taper so he could better see the mess.

"Aye," Jamison said, his jaw ticking. "That… that *bean olc* tried tae fight me. I took her weapon from her and spanked her. She's fortunate I dinna beat the daylights out o' her. For me mercy, she sent her two sisters tae try and cut me head off."

Becket put a hand over his mouth so Jamison wouldn't see his grin; *evil woman* he'd said in his native tongue. It was indicative of his fury and, more than likely, some embarrassment. Jamison Munro wasn't a man to fall victim to anyone and most especially not to women, so there was damage to the male pride.

Turning back to the small collapsible table in his tent that held his writing implements and maps, Becket was sincerely trying not to laugh at the situation as he picked up the tallow taper on the table and used it to light a second taper, bringing more light into the cold, moist tent. The rain had started up again, the soft patter beating against the roof of the structure.

"So you tied the sisters up when they tried to attack you and then someone hit you over the head and freed them," he said. "I suppose it does not take any great intellect to assume that it was Lady Havilland.

But you must understand that the de Llion sisters have been fighting as men for as long as I can remember, Jamie. These aren't women who simply decided yesterday to masquerade as men. They truly *do* fight as men and Lady Havilland has a good deal of skill. You probably should not have spanked her, which she obviously saw as a great insult."

"Then she shouldna have attacked me."

Becket conceded the point. "I cannot argue with you on that," he said, lifting up a piece of vellum from the table. "That being the case, however, I am afraid we have a bit of a problem. I have been sending missives to my father about the Welsh and their tactics and I have just received a reply from him that involves you. As we noted over the past three days, the Welsh are using Scots tactics. I am afraid it is as we have feared, Jamie – Madog or Madog's sons must have Scots mercenaries among the Welsh near this region of the Marches, teaching them Scots tactics. That brings an entirely new light to these wars. They've brought Scots rebellion to the Welsh Marches and that will complicate things."

Jamison's gaze lingered on the vellum in Becket's hand, holding still as the surgeon began to sew the gash in his scalp. He ignored the pinpricks of pain as he thought on what Becket was referring to – Madog ap Llywelyn, the last prince of Wales to rebel against the English. Madog had picked up where his cousin, Llywelyn ap Gruffudd, had left off a few years before and although Madog hadn't formally announced himself the next Prince of Wales, the Welsh were still rebelling in the south and even more strongly in the north. It was suspected by many English landholders that Madog, the last son of that powerful Welsh royal family, was behind their increasing unrest.

Like now. Even though Jamison had been sent back to England by his father to get him away from a price on his head, his arrival could not have been more welcome. De Lohr had long since suspected that somehow, rebellious Scots had made it into the Welsh ranks and Jamison, with his in-depth knowledge of Scots tactics, had been able to assess that possibility better than most. He sighed slowly, a belated response to Becket's statement.

"Aye," he said as the subject veered away from the three de Llion sisters. "From what I have seen, 'tis a certainty that there are Scots among the Welsh. They used porcupine pike formations on the first day of battle. That is a classic Scots tactic. If I'd seen nothing else during the past three days, that one formation would have told me all I needed tae know."

Becket nodded slowly. "I told my father that very thing after the first day," he said. "Therefore, given that we know there are Scots among the Welsh, he wants you to remain here at Four Crosses in case they are harassed again. I will leave five hundred de Lohr troops with you, but my father wants you to train the Four Crosses men on how to fight back against these Scots tactics. He wants you to train them as you've trained our men over the past few months. If we are facing Scots rebels on the Marches, then my father wants his men prepared."

Jamison grimaced; not because of the surgeon putting black catgut stitches into his scalp but because remaining at Four Crosses Castle was not something he wanted to do. He hated Wales and he hated the Welsh. He particularly hated the three women this castle housed. This was no place for him.

"Are ye serious, Beck?" he asked. "Ye want me tae remain in this castle where those three wild chickens will hound me every move? Ye canna mean it."

Becket was back to fighting off a grin. "I will leave Tobias with you," he said. "I will even leave my cousins Brend and Thad. That is a trio of de Lohr men who can ensure the de Llion sisters do not move against you while you are training their men. But, Jamie… it is my earnest suggestion that you have a meeting with those three and settle whatever differences you may have with them. You need their cooperation and they need yours. This is a very serious matter and they must understand that."

Jamison was growing increasingly frustrated. "Ye're the commander of the de Lohr army," he pointed out. "'Tis ye who must call the meeting with those three and establish the law. I doubt they'll listen tae me, given our introduction, so that order must come from ye."

Becket pondered that suggestion for a moment. "I suppose you are correct," he sighed. "But I must see Roald first and explain what has happened, if I can even get a meeting with the man. He is more elusive than a wraith these days. My father hasn't seen him in almost two years and although his daughters say he is still in command of Four Crosses, something tells me otherwise. The entire situation seems very odd."

Jamison didn't care about Roald de Llion. He most especially didn't care about the man's three wild daughters. He grunted unhappily as the surgeon finished off the next stitch.

"Then what would ye have me do in the meantime?" he asked.

Becket set the vellum in his hand back to the table. "See to moving the de Lohr wounded out of the great hall and get them secured for the return home," he said. "Then you will hand-select your army from the troops returning to Lioncross. We have less than two hundred wounded out of fifteen hundred men, and considering the brutality of the fighting, that is a fairly good ratio. While you are doing that, I will see what I can do about securing a meeting with Roald. And Jamie?"

"Aye?"

"Try to stay clear of those women."

Jamison gave him such a look that Becket couldn't help but laugh at him. There was utter hatred in the blue Scottish depths.

"And just how am I supposed tae do that if ye give me command of Four Crosses?" he wanted to know. "I swear tae ye, Beck, that I will round those women up and throw the lot of them in the vault. I'll not be looking over me shoulder at every turn, waiting for one tae jump from the shadows and slit me throat."

Becket continued to grin. "You are bigger and stronger than they are," he said. "I have faith that you will survive."

"And if I dunna?"

"Then I shall send my condolences to your parents."

That didn't give Jamison any comfort at all. Becket didn't seem to take the threat of those three women seriously but Jamison surely did.

He knew how they could fight and he had to admit that he was impressed. But that admission only made him more defensive.

He wasn't going to make an easy victim.

Jamison remained in the tent while the surgeon finished stitching his scalp, brooding, as Becket went to find Roald de Llion's daughters and presumably arrange a meeting with them. Jamison wasn't looking forward to it in the least but he knew it was necessary if there was to be any chance of peace for the duration of his stay at Four Crosses. He had enough to worry about in the threat of the Welsh without the added burden of danger from within. As he had on the third day of the mighty battle for the castle, he found himself wondering the same thing over and over again –

Sweet Jesú, what am I even doing here?

He just wanted to go home.

But that was not to be, at least not now. The surgeon finished stitching his scalp and swabbed it with alcohol, making it sting like crazy but Jamison didn't flinch. He knew, as did many men, that something in the distilled liquor called *aqua vitae*, also known as spirit water, had a quality in it that would kill poison in a wound. There was a good deal of *aqua vitae* distilled up in Scotland where Jamison came from, a traditional medicinal spirit that was also used non-medicinally and made men quite drunk. His brother, Robert, was one of those who liked to steal it from the local physic.

Robert, he thought unhappily as the memory of his brother came into his head. *This entire situation is all his fault!*

Once the surgeon was finished, Jamison stood up, a bit unsteadily, his hand to the back of his sore head as he made his way from the tent. The rain outside was steady, falling in cold sheets. Jamison was thinking about finding some spirit water of his own to ease his aching head and perhaps even ease the fury in his heart towards those vicious women. Women he would now be forced to work with.

Fleeing back to Scotland and going home was looking better and better to him as he made his way towards the big gatehouse of Four

Crosses. At this point, he'd almost rather face the MacKenzie's fury than deal with three spoiled wenches. What was it he'd told Becket? That he'd throw the lot of them in the vault if given the chance? He still might. He'd do it and de Lohr would never be the wiser. Well, at least not for a while, anyway. The mere thought of those three little witches in the vault brought a smile to his lips.

He'd have the last laugh.

Men were moving in and out of the great hall, seeking shelter from the storm. The light from the open hall door drew him like a beacon in the night. He was tired of being wet and cold, now with a throbbing head to make everything far more unpleasant. His mind began to drift to the possibility of even taking a hot bath, anything to wash away the cold and mud that had become part of his very fabric. He may have been Scots and had spent his fair share of time in snow and cold, but the fact was that he didn't like it. He hated the cold. The glow of the hall drew him in and he entered the belly of the great hall happily, out of the rain and into the stale, smoky warmth.

It was packed with men and servants in the hall, all of them trying to stay out of the rain and cold just as Jamison was. Men were sitting on the floor, near the hearth, on and at the table, and in every corner he could see. They had bread in their hands and in their mouth, famished after days of battle.

Jamison walked among them, pushing aside his irritation with the de Llion women at the sight of his men. He couldn't give them the snappish mood he was feeling. He moved through them, offering a smile or a reassuring word. Such was Jamison's method. Men looked up to him, congratulating him on a battle well fought, but he would turn it around and make it seem like he was simply a lesser part of a bigger strategy. Odd for a man with the arrogance that Jamison had, but he felt, at times, that it was more important to praise his men than seek praise for himself.

There was some laughter and some relief among the men as he moved and he made sure to speak a few words to everyone he recognized. He was making his way over to the wounded, back against the west side of the hall where he'd left them, only now there were far more of them than there had been before. Servants and what physics there were, including the surgeon who had tended him, had their hands full.

Jamison entered the area of the wounded, once again speaking soft words of encouragement to them as he went. There was a particular soldier he wanted to see, a senior sergeant who had taken a tumble from the wall walk in the early part of the siege. Jamison liked the man and had known him for years, a man with eight daughters and one son. After the fall from the wall walk, the soldier couldn't feel his legs and Jamison wanted to see how he was faring. He was nearly to the man, who had been positioned away from the others, when he caught sight of someone beside him, helping to feed him.

Surprise rippled through him when he realized it was Havilland.

CHAPTER FIVE

☙

"I have seen ye fight...."

☙

JAMISON WAS STANDING in front of her.

The man was so big that he filled up her entire field of vision and when Havilland looked up to see the big Scotsman standing there, all she could see was dark bulk. The fire from the hearth was behind him, giving him a surreal silhouette and, to be truthful, Havilland's heart jumped when she realized who it was. Given the size and shape, it could be no one else. A man that size wasn't easy to miss and there was no one else at Four Crosses with that kind of mass. Certainly no one else who radiated such intimidation.

She could feel her palms beginning to sweat.

Sitting on the ground helping feed an injured man because the surgeon had asked her to help, Havilland was in a rather awkward position. It wasn't as if she could run from him or, worse, defend herself if he decided to spank her again. So she simply sat there and looked up at the man, unsure of what to say, wondering if he knew that she had been the one to hit him over the head in the stables. Because the light was behind him, she couldn't even see his features or his expression. Therefore, she did the only safe thing; she simply lowered her gaze and went back to her task without uttering a word.

The soldier she was helping was a de Lohr man, older, and he'd lost the use of his legs after a fall from the battlements. Havilland was spooning beef broth with barley into his mouth when she heard Jamison clear his throat softly behind her.

"I've come tae see how Watcyn is faring," he said quietly. When the soldier looked over at him, the man's face lit up and Jamison came to stand next to him. "Aye, so ye heard me, did ye? Stop being lazy and rise tae yer feet, man. I've need of ye."

Havilland was about to spoon more broth into the man's mouth but he ignored her completely, now focused on Jamison. There was adoration in his expression. It was clear how much he admired the big Scotsman.

"I shall be better in the morning, my lord," he assured Jamison. "A bit of rest is all I need."

Jamison knelt down, his big and bulky presence causing Havilland to pull away. Heat radiated off of his body. His knee, as he took it beside her, came too close, so much so that she visibly recoiled. She didn't want to be that close to him. Or did she? God, she couldn't think with the man so near her.

Why was her heart beating so?

"Aye, a bit of rest is all ye need," Jamison said, patting the old soldier on the shoulder. "I think a bit o' rest is something we all need. It was a fearsome day and ye served admirably. I've come tae tell ye so."

Watcyn's face softened with gratitude, with pride. "We chased the Welsh off, did we not, my lord?"

Jamison nodded confidently. "We did, indeed," he said. "And we shall again should they come back lookin' for a fight. I will expect ye tae be at my side if that happens."

Watcyn nodded his head but he looked rather uncomfortable, uncertain about his condition, embarrassed even. "I will be happy to be at your side when this little trouble with my legs goes away," he said. "I… I am sure I can feel them coming back."

Jamison wasn't sure what to say to that. He happened to glance at Havilland as if she might have some answers but her head was lowered, looking away from him. His gaze lingered on her raven-dark hair for a moment before returning his attention to the soldier.

"I am sure they will," he said quietly.

He couldn't help but eye Havilland again as if his attention was being drawn towards her, unable to look away. He kept hearing Becket's voice in his head; *It is my earnest suggestion that you have a meeting with those three and settle whatever differences you may have.* He'd told Becket that such a meeting would be better coming from him, as the commander, but here was the source of his troubles, right here by his right arm. It was too good of an opportunity to pass up.

Jamison had always been able to negotiate his way out of anything. He had that gift. He was coming to feel foolish that he was hiding behind Becket for something he could do better.

"My lady," he said, his deep voice quiet. "Might I have a word wich' ye?"

Havilland's head shot up, shocked to realize he was looking right at her. She was instantly wary of him. "Aye," she said hesitantly. "You may speak."

Jamison could see the suspicion in her eyes. "Away from Watcyn, if ye will," he said, glancing at the soldier. "I am sure he doesna need tae hear our business."

Havilland was looking at him with increasing apprehension. "I… I cannot leave," she said, feeling like an idiot because she sounded frightened. "The physic does not have enough help. I must stay and help him."

Jamison's gaze lingered on her dark head. From the way she was acting, nervously, she probably thought he wanted to take her outside and beat her again, a far cry from the confident woman he'd met yesterday. Well, perhaps he *had* wanted to take her outside and beat her at one point, but as he gazed at the woman, he noticed again just how beautiful her eyes were. She had a little nose, tinged red from the cold, and her lips were shapely and pale beneath it.

He'd noticed from the beginning how astonishingly beautiful she was and, inevitably, he could feel himself relenting towards her somewhat. He was twice her size and many times more powerful. She *was* just a woman, after all, and he'd come on very strong yesterday at the gatehouse. She had reacted in kind. Perhaps he had, indeed, caused this situation.

Perhaps all of this had been his fault.

"I understand," he said after a moment. "But I must speak with ye. Will ye grant me that privilege?"

Havilland didn't want to. She wanted to tell him to go away and leave her be. But she couldn't quite speak the words. Something about his nearness made her body tremble. *Fear,* she thought with confidence. *Anger.*

... what else could it be?

"Aye," she said, clearly reluctant. "What... what did you have to say?"

Jamison stood up and crooked a finger at her, indicating for her to follow him to the corner of the room, which was just a few feet away. It was in darkness, mostly, and the wounded were crowded all around them, probably too ill or weary to hear what was being said, but he didn't want to have a conversation over Watcyn, especially not for what he needed to say.

Jamison moved, hoping she would follow and, after a moment, she did, although it was with hesitation. He thought she looked as if she waited for him to lash out at her, ever on guard. He didn't really blame her and all the while, he was thinking what he might say to her. He suspected there was only one thing he, in fact, *could* say. He didn't want to spend his time at Four Crosses looking over his shoulder every moment for an attack. For no other reason than that, he wanted to settle their differences.

Make peace.

He was going to have to make the first move.

"I fear that when I came tae the gatehouse yesterday, me mood was foul," he said, sounding as apologetic as he could manage. "I had been three days in the field fighting the Welsh and I fear that I took me exhaustion out on ye and yer men. I am sorry if I caused ye ill-humor. I am sorry ye felt the need tae attack me because of it."

Havilland stared at him. Of all the things she imagined he would say to her at this moment, an apology wasn't among them. In fact, she was shocked. Truly shocked. Her first instinct was to scold him, to agree with everything he'd said, but upon the heels of that thought came ideas far more subtle and endearing.

It was rare for a man to apologize and most especially apologize to a woman. She could hardly believe her ears but those quietly uttered words worked their desired effect – they also softened her stance. Like a fool, she was folding, whether or not she wanted to.

"I suppose you are not entirely to blame," she said reluctantly. "You do not speak like any of the de Lohr knights and I suppose I was not entirely sure you that were not part of the Welsh, trying to coerce us into opening the gatehouse. I supposed I believed it all the more when you were so nasty to my men."

"Nasty?"

"You threatened to throttle them."

He remembered that, clearing his throat awkwardly as he averted his gaze. Then, he snorted, a smile creasing his lips. "I meant it," he said. "But then ye came from the gatehouse tae do the throttling. I barely had time tae protect meself."

Havilland could see that he was grinning. He even glanced at her, the dark blue eyes twinkling. At that moment, she had a most unexpected reaction; her cheeks flushed a dull red and her knees felt strangely weak. It was difficult to breathe for the way he was looking at her.

I am weary, she told herself. *Simply weary. Why else would my knees feel so unsteady?*

But it was more than that, although she had no idea what "more". All she knew was that she couldn't help herself from smiling in return, as if her lips had a mind of their own.

"I was not very successful," she said. "You are a formidable warrior."

Jamison was warming to the conversation in spite of himself. He'd apologized to soften the woman, because everyone knew women were idiots when it came to an apology from a man, but now he found himself genuinely interested in the conversation. She wasn't an unreasonable female and seemingly very sensible, certainly nothing like the woman he had spanked the previous day. She had accepted his apology. Now she was, perhaps, admitting some fault of her own.

It was his turn to be astonished.

"Ye have excellent technique," he said, using flattery to break her down further. "Have ye always fought… well, as a man?"

Havilland thought her face might catch on fire, so warm were her cheeks. She was thankful for the dim lighting in the corner of the hall. "My father had no sons," she said. "I have wielded a sword as long as I can recall."

He was gazing at her most openly, a gesture that was calculated. Jamison knew how to overwhelm a woman with his charm. He'd done it before and was quite good at it. More of that male pride the man had, full enough with it to fill an ocean.

"As I said, ye have excellent technique," he said. Then, he eyed her. "I saw two more women about who also wear mail and bear weapons. Are they relations to ye?"

Havilland felt cornered by the question. She was actually enjoying their conversation until this moment. He'd asked about Madeline and Amaline and because he had apologized for his boorish behavior, she couldn't very well lie to him. In fact, she felt the need to be truthful about the situation. It was rather disheartening because she knew he'd more than likely curse her and walk away once he knew the truth, but she wasn't in the habit of lying to a direct question. Squaring her shoulders, she sighed heavily.

"Aye," she said. "They are my sisters, Madeline and Amaline. I know that they tried to engage you earlier today. They saw you take your hand to me outside of the gatehouse yesterday and thought to seek vengeance against you. Know that I did not tell them to do it. But… but it was I who saved them from you."

Jamison already knew that and he was surprised by the confession. He was also pleased by it. *At least she's honest*, he thought. The seed of respect he had for the woman grew and he found he really wasn't angry about it at all. No matter what he'd told Becket and no matter how much he'd steamed about it, gazing into her honest, somewhat apprehensive face, he found that he just couldn't be angry about it. She had done what he would have, given the same circumstance. Nay, he couldn't fault her at all.

"I know," he said, putting a hand gingerly to the back of his head. "I suspected it was ye. One of yer sisters told me why they'd attacked me. It seems that ever since I've come to Four Crosses, women are intent tae attack me and not in pleasant ways. 'Tis a pity, truthfully."

Havilland wasn't sure what he meant but she was greatly relieved that he didn't seem furious about it. "I do not understand, my lord," she said. "What is a pity?"

He was back to grinning again. "I would have much rather made yer acquaintance over a pitcher of this terrible wine than have lifted me sword tae ye," he said. "But it was me own fault. I shouldna let me fatigue and mood get the better of me. But I will be truthful, m'lady – I was hoping tae find ye today tae address the situation between us because it seems I am to stay on at Four Crosses for a time."

She lifted her eyebrows in mild surprise, although she realized she wasn't much displeased by that thought. "Is that so?"

He nodded. "'Tis," he said. "De Lohr has asked me tae remain and train yer men against the Scots tactics the Welsh seem tae be using. In fact, it is something that de Lohr wished tae discuss wit' yer father. I understand the man is ill."

It was a good deal of information he was delivering and Havilland was trying to stay on an even keel with it. "He is," she said, but she couldn't quite drift on to the subject of her father. She deliberately kept the focus away from him. "You are staying here? With us?"

She sounded rather breathless with the question and Jamison couldn't decide if he was pleased by it or insulted. Was it fear he heard in her voice or excitement? Was it possible this sleek, dark-haired lass found him as attractive as he found her? Suddenly, staying on at Four Crosses didn't quite look so bad.

"Aye," he said, the warmth fading from his eyes. "De Lohr believes ye need me help, especially if the Scots are involved in Madog's rebellions."

Havilland wasn't quite sure what he meant by the Scots being involved. "There were Scots involved in the battle?"

He could see that she wasn't following him. "Did ye spend the entire battle covering the gatehouse?"

"Aye."

"Then ye didna see what was going on beyond the walls?"

She shook her head. "Not really," she admitted. "From where I was, we could only see men fighting and not much more than that."

He nodded thoughtfully, perhaps considering how much he should tell her. He opted for all of it because if he was going to remain here, training men against Scots tactics, he assumed she would be part of that training. The thought, although an odd one, didn't displease him. Women simply weren't trained for battle.

But this one evidently was.

"As I said, the Welsh were using Scots tactics in battle," he said. "Ye say that ye fight as a man, m'lady, but did ye have formal training? Do ye understand the ways of yer enemy?"

Havilland knew she wasn't highly trained; all of her training had come from her father and the knights at Four Crosses. She'd never fostered and she couldn't read or write, so she hadn't studied formally anywhere. It was an embarrassing admission, one she wasn't yet ready to confess to, that she didn't know as much as he did. She had her pride.

"My father and his men have trained me quite adequately," she said, feeling slightly defensive. "I understand Roman and Teutonic tactics as explained to me by my father and even though I have not formally fostered to train as a knight, I can fight as one. You have seen it."

Jamison could see that the question had upset her. Perhaps even embarrassed her. He nodded his head to her statement. "I have seen ye fight," he said. "I told ye that ye have excellent technique. I was askin' if ye knew yer enemy because if ye had seen the battle outside of the walls, ye would have seen the Welsh using Scots formations when approaching the castle. If ye dunna recognize the formations, I intend tae teach ye and yer men. Ye must know how tae counter them."

Havilland couldn't decide if he sounded high and mighty about teaching her or not. He sounded factual, which eased her defensiveness somewhat, but she was still embarrassed. She knew she didn't know as much as he did. But perhaps he was bluffing; perhaps he didn't know anything at all and was simply trying to act superior to her. Quite honestly, she wasn't sure.

"And you are qualified to teach us?" she asked, putting him on the spot. "Please tell me what makes you so qualified to teach us such things?"

Jamison had to hide a grin. He could see she was trying to turn the tables on him to see how much he really did know or if his words were all for show. She was competitive, this one, and she didn't like to be made to feel inferior. He cleared his throat quietly, struggling not to smile.

"I would be happy tae tell ye," he said. "My father is the Munro, chief of Clan Munro, and he himself a very educated and well-traveled man. When I was seven years of age, at the request of yer King Henry, my king, Alexander, sent me and several other lads, all sons of clan chiefs, south tae Lioncross Abbey for fostering. At least, that is what Henry called it, but the truth is that we were hostages. I spent a few years at Lioncross training, learning the ways o' the *Sassenach,* until one of the de Lohr brothers, Arthur, took me as his squire. Arthur was a wanderer and took me all over England, France, and Saxony fighting other men's wars. I spent many years learning the ways of other armies before going back home tae Scotland. I studied under Sir Arthur and the finest men of our time – de Bohun, Bigod, and de Wolfe. Great warriors, all of them. I even spent time at a monastery in Southern France, studying languages and ancient history with the monks because Sir Arthur had an interest in such things. Therefore, m'lady, I am, mayhap, better educated than most men. I believe I am qualified tae teach yer men about tactics."

By the time he was finished, Havilland was looking at him in shock. So great was the tale that she might have thought he was making it up, but for the fact that he didn't seem to be the type. He was quite factual about all of it and even humble about it. Nay, he wasn't making any of it up. She was willing to believe it all.

"You have been to France?" she asked, trying not to sound too awed by it. "Have you been to Paris? I hear the streets are paved in precious stones and gold brick. Is it true?"

He grinned, shaking his head. "Nay, m'lady," he said. "'Tis a dirty place, I think. Never have I met so many angry people than I have in France."

"Mayhap because the English are all over their country."

He laughed softly, revealing big, white teeth with prominent canines. He had quite the dazzling smile, enough to throw Havilland off a bit. All she knew were dirty men, hairy men, and unattractive men. She was surrounded by them. They were all dark and colorless. But here was a big Highlander with his red hair and brilliant smile; he was color in a world that had none, an enigma. Certainly, she was curious about him now and, perhaps, even more than that.

He had her interest.

"I wouldna be surprised if that was the truth," he said. Then, he sobered a bit. "Now that ye know about me, would it be possible tae have a few moments with yer father? I know that Becket needs tae speak with him and I should as well."

Swiftly, they were back on her father again and Havilland was startled at the change of subject, so much so that she couldn't honestly think of a smooth reply. Quickly, she averted her gaze and took a few steps away from him, as if to put safe distance between them. It was a foolish move but, somehow, she felt the need to protect herself from him, brilliant smile and all. She wasn't used to showing interest in any man and had no idea how to appropriately deal with it. That uncertainty made her edgy.

"I… I will ask him," she said. "He has been ill and does not take visitors. I cannot promise anything but I… I will ask."

She continued to move away from him, back to Watcyn, who, by now, was dozing peacefully. Nervously, Havilland picked up the bowl of cool beef broth but by the time she stood up, Jamison was standing next to her again. He was so tall that she barely came up to his sternum and she had to step back, away from him. The man was far too close for comfort.

"I didna mean tae startle ye," Jamison said, his voice quiet. "I only have one more thing tae ask of ye. I would hope there is peace between us now, enough so that I dunna have tae worry about ye leaping from the shadows tae attack me on a daily basis?"

He said it with some humor and, in spite of herself, Havilland gave him a lopsided grin. "You do not have to worry about such things," she said, leaning away from him because he was so close to her. "But make no more threats to throttle my men."

"I willna, I promise."

"Then there should be no trouble."

"And yer sisters? Must I seek peace with them as well?"

Havilland shook her head. "I will speak with them," she said. "Amaline will not be a problem but Madeline…."

"Which one is she?"

"She has dark hair, like me."

He nodded in recognition. "Aye," he said. "The aggressive one. She told me no one would beat her sister and get away with such a thing."

Havilland lifted her eyebrows, half in agreement, half in embarrassment. "That would be Madeline," she said. "I will speak with her but I cannot promise she will back off, at least not right away. If she tries to attack you again, then you have my permission to do what is necessary to defend yourself. But try not to hurt her if you can help it."

Jamison was amused. "Can I spank her, then?"

Havilland's cheeks turned a dull shade of red and she lowered her gaze, but she couldn't quite manage to walk away from him. "If you must," she said, listening to him laugh low in his throat. "Since you seem to like spanking women so much, I would not dare deprive you of the privilege against someone who truly needs it."

His laughter grew. "When she attacks me again, I will remember that."

Havilland fought off a smile. "Confident, aren't you?"

His eyes glimmered at her, fingers of warmth reaching out to touch her, invisible tendrils causing her knees to wobble and her heart to race. "Aye," he said in a soft, deep voice that caused chills to race up her spine. "That I am."

"Of everything?"

"Of that which I know."

"And what do you know?

He flashed that smile at her. "Women."

It was a woefully cheeky statement, as he meant it should be. Havilland turned away then, fearful he would see just how much his laughter and charming presence had disarmed her. She didn't want the man thinking he could use that charm against her when the truth was that he already knew. Damnation… *he already knew!*

Heading away from the wounded and back towards the door that led to the kitchen yard, Havilland couldn't keep the smile off her lips.

The next few days with Jamison Munro were going to be rather interesting.

CHAPTER SIX

"I have lived my entire life in Wales,

but I am not Welsh…."

Four Crosses Castle

BREND DE LOHR and Thad de Lohr were brothers, sons of William de Lohr, who was the Earl of Worcester's youngest brother. There were three elder de Lohr brothers, including the current earl - Chris, Arthur, and William. Arthur, the brother with the wanderlust streak in him that some of the de Lohrs had, never married or had children, so that burden was left to Chris and William, both of whom had two sons.

All of these men were descended from the great Christopher de Lohr, Richard the Lionheart's Defender of the Realm, and Jamison genuinely liked the de Lohr brothers. He had practically grown up with them, although at his thirty years of age, he was slightly older than they were. Becket and Tobias were both younger, but not by much, and Brend and Thad were five and seven years younger than Jamison, respectively. They both had a bit of wild streak in them but they were noble and honest men, and Jamison found a great deal of humor in them. He also found the strength of the de Lohr sword in them as well.

He found himself in command of these men after the de Lohr army took its leave. Three days after the Welsh rebels had finally withdrawn, the training of the de Llion army was in full swing. There were four hundred and eighteen men after the battle, men sworn to Roald de

Llion, and with the additional five hundred de Lohr troops, it made for crowded conditions at the fairly large castle.

There was a stone troop house situated against the outer wall but that could only hold six hundred men at the most, which meant the rest of the men had to find lodgings where they could. The great hall was crowded with soldiers and their possessions as was the entry level to the keep where there was a small solar and a smaller dining hall, now crowded with more men.

Jamison kept the troops out of the small, cramped solar because he needed a place to meet with his knights that didn't have multiple pairs of ears hanging about, listening to everything he said. It was the one place he could get away from the men and since Roald de Llion didn't seem to be apt to show himself, Jamison figured the man wouldn't care if he took over his solar. In fact, he was rather hoping the man *did* care so he would at least present himself. But thus far, de Llion had remained elusive.

So had Havilland. Three days after their conversation in the great hall, the eldest de Llion sister had kept her distance from Jamison – he saw her around the castle, frequently, but she would go the other direction when she saw him, sometimes with a nervous smile to acknowledge him and sometimes not. Sometimes, she would just turn away. When he and his knights gathered de Llion men together in groups to begin training them against the Scots formations, she and her sisters would watch from afar but never join in.

It seemed to Jamison that, in spite of their conversation and his apology, Havilland still wasn't convinced of his sincerity. At least she wasn't attacking him, nor were her sisters, but by the fourth day of his stay at Four Crosses, Jamison thought he should seek Havilland out again. Not only was she missing out on the training he had been asked to give her men, but he had questions about the surrounding area and even the local Welsh lords. There were things he needed to know that he'd hoped to learn from her father but since Roald seemed to be in hiding, he would learn what he needed to know from Havilland. But, deep down, that was just an excuse.

He simply wanted to speak with her again.

Therefore, on a cold February day shortly after sunrise, Jamison went on the hunt for Havilland. She and her sisters seemed to spend a good deal of time in the keep when they weren't on watch, but he'd spent enough time at Four Crosses to know that Havilland was always in the gatehouse in the early mornings. She congregated with the de Llion men there, vigilant at dawn in the entry to the big castle. Even if she was trying to stay away from Jamison, she wasn't shirking her duties.

Jamison and his knights had been sleeping in the solar, crammed into corners and against walls near the hearth that smoldered all night long with great peat slabs burning low and hot. Brend and Thad, who tended to be the messy ones, had their possessions spread out all over the floor, only to be kicked around by Tobias. One time, he kicked Brend's expensive helm through the lancet window, sending it out into the mud of the bailey. Thad had laughed uproariously while Brend and Tobias had thrown a few punches about it. After that, Brend was more careful to store his possessions.

On this particular morning, Jamison had risen with the others, ordering hot water and using a bit of precious soap he'd brought with him to wash his hands and face. The wash was a prelude to shaving, which he carefully did with the edge of his extremely sharp dirk and the help of a small bronze mirror. It didn't cut him too close, still leaving a bit of a pale red stubble on his face.

With a relatively clean-shaven face, he thought his hair looked a bit shaggy, like those great, hairy Highland cows that roamed the moors, so he ended up cutting some length off of the sides while leaving the top longer. He had waves in his hair and he fussed with them, trying to smooth them down or at least make them go in the same direction, but it was to no avail. His hair waved any way it pleased. As he tried to tame the unruly mass, a comb appeared in his face.

"Here," Brend said. "Try this. Who are you grooming yourself for, anyway?"

Jamison took the comb, eyeing the big blonde knight with the dark-as-night brown eyes. "I canna look like an unruly mess me entire life," he said. "And who says I'm grooming meself for anyone?"

"You may not be, but I am," came a voice from across the solar. Thad de Lohr, Brend's ginger-headed brother, was also shaving the stubble from his face. "There are three fine women here, or have you not seen them? They keep themselves hidden away, but I've caught glimpses of them. The eldest one is quite fine. Big breasted, slender of body… aye, she's quite fine."

Before Jamison could speak, Brend replied to his brother's lascivious statement. "How do you know she is big breasted?" he asked. "She wears tunics that hang to her knees. You cannot see her figure through all of that."

Thad, young and hot-blooded, grinned. "Trust me, brother," he said. "I've seen the lass enough to know she has the body of Aphrodite. She's long-limbed, too. Imagine those legs wrapped up around you as you have your way with her. Delicious."

Brend snorted. "Careful what you say," he said. "Tobias has already expressed interest in her. You may have a fight on your hands if you speak that way about her."

Jamison remained out of the conversation until that statement. *So Tobias is interested in Havilland?* He wasn't sure why he should be concerned with such a thing, but he found that he was. Tobias wasn't nearly good enough for a woman of that quality. Nay, he didn't like that thought at all.

"She is out o' his class," he said as he gave his hair a few final strokes with the comb. "A woman like that deserves better than the second son of an earl."

Both Brend and Thad looked at him. "Like a clan chief's son?" Thad teased, his eyes twinkling.

Jamison returned the comb to Brend, standing up from the stool he'd been seated on. "Mayhap," he said evasively. "In any case, remember what I told ye about her and her sisters attacking me. I believe that is why they've been so isolated from what is going on; they are unsure of us. Of me, anyway. So watch yer step with them because they know how to use a sword and ye might come away missing something ye need."

Brend shook his head. "They know us, Jamie," he said. "'Tis you they do not know. Hearing your Scots accent made them panic and try to beat you down like an animal."

Jamison smiled thinly. "Hearing me accent is enough tae soothe the savage beastie in any woman," he said, collecting his big *brecan*, or length of Scottish wool, to swath around his body like a cloak. The temperatures outside were near freezing. "I intend tae seek the lady out this morning and again ask her if we can have a brief meeting with her father. We are four days at this place and still no sign of the commander. 'Tis most irregular and bad of manner."

The humor faded from the two de Lohr brothers. "Becket had to leave without seeing the man," Brend said. "In fact, no one has seen him in over a year. Do you know what I think? I think he is dead and the sisters are afraid to tell us. They are afraid my uncle will take the garrison from them and they will have nowhere to go."

That was the thought that had been rolling around in everyone's mind, Jamison included. He fussed with his cloak. "I have been thinking the very same thing," he said thoughtfully. "I think it's time we all knew what has become of Roald de Llion. I think, mayhap, we should start asking his men what they know. Sooner or later, the truth will be uncovered and I am sure yer uncle willna throw the women out of their home. But if Roald is no longer in command o' the castle, then de Lohr needs tae know."

It was the truth that none of them could dispute. "While you are speaking with her, ask her why there have been no patrols sent out from Four Crosses since the battle," Thad reminded him. "The Welsh could be building up over the next hill and we would not know anything about it until it was too late."

Jamison simply nodded his head, his thoughts now on the lack of patrols and Roald de Llion's absence. It was an increasing mystery that needed to be discovered. As he finished securing his *brecan*, Jamison left the warm, stale solar and proceeded out into the freezing dawn.

The moisture on the ground had turned to ice overnight, creating a thin layer of it on the mud as Jamison headed for the gatehouse. Ice crunched beneath his big leather boots and his breath hung in the air, creating big puffs of fog as he went. As he passed through the bailey, his gaze moved over the gray granite walls of the fortress and the history of the place popped to mind. As told to him by Chris de Lohr himself, Four Crosses Castle, other than being a bone of contention between Welsh and English, had something of a dark and sinister past.

Nearly one hundred years ago, the castle had been part of the de Velt conquest that swept the Marches during that time. Ajax de Velt, a barbaric knight who fed on bloodlust, captured six castles along the Marches and put the occupants of those castles, and anyone resisting him, on stakes. Men and women alike were impaled alive, left to die of exposure and blood loss as de Velt stole their castles.

But twenty years after that, another bloodthirsty warrior came through and did the same thing, stealing the castle from de Velt. That man was a de Llion and the family that still manned the castle were his descendants, Havilland and her sisters included. Given the barbaric and violent history of the castle, Jamison wasn't particularly surprised, in hindsight, that the de Llion women fought as men. Fighting was in their blood.

What these walls have seen, Jamison thought as he neared the gatehouse. If walls could talk, he supposed that Four Crosses would have a great story to tell. He was thinking on that story when he neared the guard room of the gatehouse and, coming around a corner, plowed into someone who was just emerging from the guard room.

Startled, Jamison stepped back, putting his hands out as a purely reflexive action only to see that he had Havilland in his grip. Startled green eyes gazed back at him but when she realized who held her, she pulled away, quickly. He lost his grip and she nearly lost her balance in her haste to step away from him.

"I did not see you," Havilland said, having difficulty meeting his eye.

Jamison had no intention of letting the woman out of his sight now that he'd found her, unexpected as it had been. "No harm done," he said. "Did I hurt ye?"

Havilland's brow furrowed as if the question either offended or confused her; it was difficult to tell. "You did not," she said. Quickly, she averted her gaze and tried to move past him. "If you will excuse me, I have duties to attend to."

Jamison wouldn't let her go so easily. "Wait," he called after her, watching her come to an unsteady halt. "I was coming tae the gatehouse tae speak with ye. Can ye spare me a moment before going about yer tasks?"

Havilland didn't seem too willing. Dressed in heavy woolen breeches, three woolen tunics, and a heavy cloak with a fur collar, her dark hair was braided and pinned to the top of her head. She looked every inch the soldier this morning but Jamison found himself wondering what she'd look like in a fashionable dress. He could only imagine she would be the most exquisitely beautiful woman in all the world.

"I… I suppose I can spare a moment," she said. "But quickly. There is much for me to accomplish today."

Jamison suspected it was a dodge. "Like what?"

She was surprised by the question. "Many things," she said, scrambling to come up with a list of things but then realizing it was none of his affair. "Is that what you wished to speak with me about?"

Jamison shook his head. "Nay," he said. "Have ye broken yer fast yet this morning?"

Havilland nodded. "I have."

Jamison simply wriggled his eyebrows. "I havena," he said, moving towards her and reaching out, taking her by the elbow and politely pulling her with him. "Mayhap ye can spare me a moment or two while

I eat."

It wasn't as if Havilland had a choice. He was pulling her along toward the great hall and, like a dumb animal, she followed. She kept eyeing the hand around her elbow, thinking that it was, perhaps, one of the biggest hands she'd ever seen. But it wasn't the size of it as much as it was the sheer touch; it was as if she could feel his heat through her clothing, a heat that made her knees weak and her heart race. Sensations that were both curious and frightening.

Truth be told, that was why she had been avoiding the man since their conversation in the great hall. He had her attention; she didn't want him to have her attention. She'd never had her attention on a man in her life. Therefore, she thought that if she avoided the man and kept her thoughts off him that she would soon forget whatever infatuation she seemed to have with him. It simply wasn't healthy.

But here she was, being dragged along with him as they headed for the great hall. She didn't want to go into the great hall with him. If she did, then she'd never get over this foolish interest she had in him because she'd be forced to sit and stare at him, drinking in that handsome Scottish mug. Heels dug in, she came to a halt and broke his grip on her elbow.

"Wait," she said. "I do not need to go into the hall whilst you break your fast. You can tell me now what you wish to speak with me about so I may be along my way. What did you wish to say?"

Jamison came to a halt a foot or so away from her, his gaze moving over her in an appraising manner. He could see that she really had no desire to spend any more time with him than necessary and the thought rather shot holes in his male pride. He'd spent his entire life fighting women off but now there was one who evidently had no use for him. Was such a thing even possible?

"Ye can answer a question for me," he said.

"And that is?"

"I thought we had made peace between us," he said. "'Tis clear that isna the case. Will ye tell me what I did tae offend ye again?"

Off guard, Havilland eyed him. "You have done nothing," she said. "I… I am simply busy, 'tis all."

Jamison nodded his head as if he did not believe her. "I see," he said. "Is there anything I can help ye with since ye're so busy?"

She shook her head. "Nay," she replied. "But I would appreciate it if you would come to the point."

He cocked his head. "Ye dunna like speaking wit' me, do ye?"

Now, she looked startled by the blunt question. "I… I do not know what you mean."

He shrugged, averting his gaze in a somewhat resigned manner. "'Tis not tae worry," he said. "I thought after our discussion in the hall… I thought we might be able to speak civilly. Since I have charge of the castle and yer father is the commander, I had hoped tae learn a great deal from ye about many things."

Havilland was curious no matter how much she fought against him. "What things?"

Jamison shrugged, his gaze moving around the vast inner bailey. "I'd hoped tae learn of yer Welsh neighbors," he said, turning on a bit of his natural charm. "I am expected tae lead fighting men but I dunna know much of the area. I was hoping ye could tell me. Do ye have any Welsh neighbors that ye're friendly with? There are things only ye can tell me and since yer father has made himself scarce, then I need tae learn them from ye. Unless ye'll permit me tae speak wit' yer father."

Havilland's gaze lingered on him. He had a point and a very good one. He could learn a lot from her about Four Crosses and the surrounding area, and she certainly had no intention of letting him speak with her father. She supposed there was very much a necessity to speak with someone and that someone needed to be her. Her need to resist him was softening.

With a faint sigh, she lowered her gaze and walked past him, heading for the hall. Jamison, however, didn't move; he just watched her walk away until she suddenly came to a halt and turned to him.

"Well?" she said. "Are you coming? I thought you wanted to break your fast."

Fighting off a victorious grin, Jamison followed.

There were still wounded in the hall, crowded back into a warm corner as the hearth blazed furiously. Dogs slept on the warm stones before the blaze and under the tables as Havilland led Jamison to the end of the big feasting table. The rough surface, old and with splinters, had seen generations of de Llions. Havilland sent one of the servants for food for him before silently indicating for Jamison to sit. He did before she followed suit.

"We have never been particularly friendly with our neighbors," Havilland said, seated on the very end of the table as he sat on the right corner. "Lord Preece is the closest. He lives about a morning's ride away at a place called Elinog. He is not violent against us but he is also not particularly friendly. Years ago, our families were friendlier and I believe Madeline and Amaline still speak with Lord Preece's children, but I do not. He has two sons and a daughter."

"And ye dunna know the sons? Are they men grown or children?"

"Men grown," she replied. "We exist alongside the family but nothing more."

Jamison was listening with interested. "Do ye believe Lord Preece or his sons were part of the Welsh army that attacked Four Crosses?"

Havilland shrugged. "It is possible," she said, "although Lord Preece has never been aggressive against us."

Jamison pondered that. "We believe that those who attacked you are Welsh rebels belonging tae Madog or his sons," he said. "Ye've never known yer neighbors tae be part of these attacks?"

She shook her head. "Not that we have seen," she said. "My father has managed to keep peace with most of our neighbors and even though we are not exactly allies, they do not harass us."

He thought on that information for a moment. "It must seem strange tae live in a land where yer neighbors are of a different breed."

A faint smile creased her lips but it was not one of humor; it was irony. "I have lived in Wales my entire life, but I am not Welsh, nor is my father or sisters," she said. "The Welsh look at Four Crosses as a structure that belongs to them and must be purged of the English that possess it. The attack on us a few days ago was only one in a long line of many. You simply have not been around long enough to see everything we have gone through over the years. Were our neighbors part of that attack? Probably not. But they would not rush to our aid to help us if that was your thought."

Jamison shook his head. "It wasna a thought, in fact," he said. "Ye say the attack was one in a long line of many. De Lohr told me the same thing."

"It is true."

A servant brought a tray with bread, cheese, and a steaming bowl of gruel. Jamison politely offered his food to Havilland first, purely out of courtesy, but when she refused, he plowed into it with gusto.

"Is there a pattern tae these attacks, then?" he asked, mouth full. "Do they come regularly?"

Havilland watched him eat. "Not really," she said, studying the lines of his handsome face and realizing with increasing certainty that her interest in the man had not abated. "We have been bombarded badly over the past few months but there is no real pattern to them. They attack for a few days and damage us just enough. Then they retreat and return again a week or two later."

Jamison took a big drink of his watered wine, smacking his lips. "Have ye sent scouts tae follow them tae see where they go?"

"Not lately," she replied. "We do not have enough men to lose them so easily."

He looked at her. "Have ye lost patrols, then?"

She nodded. "Aye," she said. Then, she exhaled sharply, as if somehow baffled or annoyed. "Since you are asking about recent attacks, I will tell you honestly that I believe we may have a spy within our ranks. Months ago, I was able to send out regular patrols but then the most recent series of attacks happened. I would send out patrols to assess the enemy, but I lost patrol after patrol. It was as if… as if they knew we were coming. I lost eleven men before I finally stopped sending out patrols. Now, we sit here dumb and blind, waiting for the next attack to happen."

Jamison was listening with great interest. Now, they were starting to get somewhere. Random and vicious attacks against a castle made no sense, but now… was there a spy among them? And was there more of a purpose than simply purging the English from Wales?

"What does yer father say tae all of this?" he asked. "From what I understand, he is a seasoned knight. Surely he must have some thoughts about it."

He couldn't help but notice her expression changed drastically when he mentioned her father. She seemed to take on an edgy appearance, unable to look him in the eye.

"I am not entirely sure," she said, averting her gaze. "My father… he has been quite ill, you see, and my sisters and I do our best to keep our worries from him. We fear for his health. He will try to do too much if he knows all that is happening."

She was speaking on her elusive father and Jamison thought to take advantage of it. He could be quite gentle and sympathetic when he wanted to be and he'd never had a lady deny him anything he wanted to know. However, he knew Havilland was different. She didn't seem to think like any of the women he'd known and she certainly didn't act like any he'd known. She was strong and brave and intelligent to a fault. He couldn't imagine she would be easily manipulated. Therefore, he had to treat her very carefully. He liked talking to her and he didn't want to lose the rapport they'd established. He moved forward carefully.

"I am sorry tae hear yer father is so ill," he said quietly. "I can understand that ye wish tae protect him. I had a grandfather years ago, when I was very young, who was ill most o' the time. Me da told me that his father used tae be a great warrior but I only knew him as a sick old man. He had a sickness of the body that affected his mind. He would sneak out at night and return tae the sod home he was born in, which would have been well enough had it not partially collapsed. We would have tae go after him and drag him back home. *Sweet Jesú*, he would scream as if we were killin' him. We'd put him tae bed but he would sneak out again the next night. Sometimes sick men dunna know just how sick they are."

Havilland was watching him as he spoke, feeling herself warm to the conversation. He was telling her something personal about himself and it endeared him to her, just a bit, even though she had no idea that his confession was calculated. She simply thought it was rather sweet that he should tell her.

"My father can be difficult, too," she said. "How long ago did your grandfather pass away?"

"Twelve years," he said. "It seems like ages ago now. What seems tae be yer father's affliction?"

They were back on the subject of her father again. It was a dangerous subject to be on, a slippery slope of secrets that she didn't want to start down. Once down that path, it would be very easy to reveal too much. But the truth was that Jamison was quite easy to speak with. She liked it. Her interest in the man, something she had tried desperately to shake, was now becoming an unbreakable thing because he was difficult to resist. He was kind and handsome and powerful. Still, her last threads of common sense screamed at her.

Do not give away too much!

"His body has simply given out," she said generically. "My father was a very diligent man and an excellent knight. He is old and his body has simply given out."

Jamison was sympathetic. "I understand," he said, "but if ye allow me a few moments of his time, I promise I wouldna overtax him."

Havilland shook her head, looking to her lap. "It is impossible," she said. "He would not want for men to see what he has become. He would be ashamed."

"Is that why ye dunna allow the de Lohr to see him?"

"Aye."

Jamison wasn't entirely sure that she wasn't telling him the complete truth, in fact. For a great knight to be seen as a cripple, or worse, was the worst fate he could imagine. "But *ye* see him," he pointed out gently. "He doesna mind if ye see him?"

She kept her gaze on her lap, thinking of her once-strong father. It hurt her to see what he'd become. "I have to make sure he is taken care of," she said simply.

Jamison could see by her expression that there was something far more troubling about her father than she was letting on. Perhaps the man was, indeed, dead as Thad and Brend had speculated. He was just opening his mouth to reply when a familiar face suddenly entered the hall. Jamison found himself looking at Thad as Thad looked at Havilland.

"Lady Havilland," he said pleasantly. "We have been looking for you. You and your sisters have been scarce as of late."

Havilland looked up at Thad with something that looked like annoyance. She didn't seem all that happy to see him. "We have been busy," she said.

It wasn't much of an answer and Thad grinned that big, toothy de Lohr smile, looking between Havilland and Jamison. "I see that Jamie was able to finally corner you," he said, helping himself to a seat beside Havilland on the bench and causing the woman to scoot a couple of arm length's away from him. "We have been wondering why you do not send out patrols now that the Welsh have retreated. Has Jamie asked you about that yet?"

Jamison spoke before Havilland could. "The lady and I have already covered that," he said, not at all pleased that Thad was interrupting his time with Havilland. "She has explained tae me her reasoning but I think, as of today, we are going tae resume patrols. Will you see tae this, Thad? Random patrols at random hours. The lady has said we are sitting here dumb and blind tae the activities around us. Ye must change that."

Thad cocked his head, seemingly confused. "'Tis as I said, too," he insisted. "The Welsh could be amassing over the next hill but we would not see them until it was too late. Patrols are essential."

Jamison cocked a red eyebrow at him. "Then see tae it."

Thad was coming to sense that he wasn't wanted here but he was resistant to leave. He had shaved and combed much like Jamison had and he wasn't ready to leave Havilland's presence yet. *Big-breasted and long-legged beneath that tunic....*

"I will," Thad said, looking to the food on the table and helping himself to the bread there. "But I have not yet broken my fast. Lady Havilland, would you be so kind as to regale us with stories of life here at Four Crosses as of late? Life when the Welsh were not attacking, of course. What do you and your lovely sisters do to keep yourselves occupied? It has been a long time since last I saw you and I want to know everything."

Jamison rolled his eyes at the question. He knew that now, for certain, Havilland would run off and he could only imagine how she would avoid him the next time he saw her. Nothing was worse than inane conversation. In fact, he didn't even let Havilland answer. He yanked the tray of food out of Thad's reach.

"Find yer own meal," he growled. "And go away. The lady and I are having a conversation that doesna involve ye."

Thad's dark eyes narrowed, seeing that he was clearly being chased way. "If it pertains to the operation of Four Crosses, then I should hear it as well. We all should."

"I told ye tae leave."

"Not until I am ready."

Jamison stood up swiftly, slapping the tabletop as he did and causing Thad to leap out of his seat at the sharp sound and abrupt movement. The young knight was fearful that Jamison was about to reach out and throttle him so he scrambled to get away, tripping over his own feet in the process. He fell to his knees as Havilland burst out laughing, her sweet laughter chiming through the warm, smoky air as Thad, embarrassed and insulted, tried to appear as if he hadn't meant to slip. His mouth was still full of bread as he backed away from the table.

"I am going now," he said to Jamison, "but not because you ordered me, do you hear? I am not going because you told me to!"

Jamison remained on his feet, standing every inch of his considerable height, his dark blue eyes glaring at Thad until the knight made his way from the hall. He meandered a bit as if to prove that Jamison couldn't order him around, but the truth was that he was frightened of Jamison. He'd seen what the man was capable of in battle and he had a temper that was not to be trifled with. By the time he was gone and Jamison sat back down to face Havilland, he looked over to see that she was still laughing. He grinned.

"What's so funny?" he demanded without force.

Havilland shook her head. "Is that how you command your men? By intimidation?"

He wriggled his eyebrows ironically. "It works," he said, watching her as she continued to giggle. He would have said anything just to keep her laughing because he adored the sight of her smile. "It works with the de Lohr brothers, at least, because they are afraid I'm going tae tie them up and beat them with a stick. But me preferred method of control is respect. I'd rather have men obey me because they love me, not because they fear me."

Havilland had stopped giggling by the time he was done. "You and my father have the same philosophy," she said, a glimmer of admiration in her eyes. "He always said a man's respect is worth more than all of the gold in the world."

"'Tis true. If ye dunna have a man's respect, ye have nothing."

Havilland continued to look at him, a far cry from the woman who was trying so hard to get away from him only minutes before. Now, she seemed very interested in speaking with him.

"I saw how you were with your men last night," she said. "It is clear that you have their love and respect. That is difficult to earn which tells me that you have worked hard to attain it."

He shrugged, oddly modest about it. "I have done what I felt was right," he said. "I treat men fairly and honestly. That is more than some men do."

She liked his answer. "Tobias told me that you are known as The Red Lion," she said. "How did you get that name?"

He lifted his big shoulders. "From the color of me hair," he said, watching her smile at the obvious. "And for the fact that in battle, I have been known tae roar. I do what is necessary tae win."

More and more, Havilland realized she was coming to be enamored with him and had no way to stop it. Now, she wasn't sure she wanted to. The interest in him that she had feared had turned into something much greater than she could control.

"You come from a great line of warriors?" she asked.

He nodded. "Me da is the Munro," he said, seeing her curious response to that statement. He grinned. "That means he is the chief o' my clan. I come from a long line of chiefs, of great warriors. It is my destiny tae be as I am, tae be *who* I am. Me mother was born a Sutherland, a very great clan, indeed. I have greatness on both sides of me parentage."

Havilland was swept up in the conversation now. "Will you be chief someday?"

Jamison shook his head. "That honor will go to me brother, George," he said. "I am the second son, but I have lands and a place of me own. Me da gave me a small tower when I was knighted and I have lands that the tower governs. I also have twenty-five warriors that belong tae me, men who serve me da. When I return home, I will go tae me lands and take the men with me."

Havilland didn't much like the sound of him going home. "When are you returning home?"

The warmth from his expression faded. "I dunna know," he said hesitantly. "I… well, the truth is that I killed a man defending me brother and I'm sure the family of the man is out for me blood. That's why me da sent me back tae de Lohr recently, tae escape their wrath. So I dunna know when I can go home, only I hope it is soon."

She sensed wistfulness in his tone. "You miss Scotland?"

He nodded. "I do," he said. "I was away from home for a very long time and only returned last year. I miss the land, me family... I miss everything."

Havilland sat a moment, digesting his words. There was a great deal to ponder in what they were discussing. "I can tell that you love the place of your birth," she said. "I have often wondered what that would be like. I told you that I was born in Wales but I am not Welsh, and that is true. I have always felt like a stranger in the land of my birth. I cannot say I would miss this place if I ever left it."

"Have you ever left it?"

She shook her head. "Never," she said. "I have been as far as Gloucester and that is all. I have never even been to London."

His eyes took on a faint glimmer. "And I have been many places," he said, "but there is nothing so wonderful as being home again. Ye wouldna know that because ye've never been away from home, but ye might miss it if ye had been away for a time."

Havilland shrugged, looking to her lap. "I would like the opportunity to know that for myself."

"Then ye have dreams of traveling, do ye?"

She lifted her shoulders, a weak gesture. "I have always wanted to go to Paris," she said. "Do you recall I asked you about it? That the streets are paved in gold?"

He nodded. "I remember," he said, thinking that he'd take her all over the world if she would only ask him. He was coming to realized he would do almost anything she asked of him. She was a rather defensive young woman but he could see that, below the surface, she was curious and bright and sweet. He liked her sense of humor. *Good Christ*, he could have stared at that smile all day. "If ye want tae travel, then I will make ye a promise – the next time I go tae Paris, I will ask yer father if ye can accompany me. It would be entirely proper, of course, but every young lass should travel and see London and Paris. Ye should meet people and see how the world lives."

Havilland's heart swelled at his words; to travel to London and

Paris had always been her dream, but to travel with someone like Jamison Munro… he was handsome and educated, kind and well-spoken… he was everything a young woman would want. But a man like Jamison would want a fine and elegant woman for a wife, not a female who had lived as a man most of her life. There was no appeal in that. A backwoods, uneducated, scrub of a girl wouldn't make anyone a good wife.

Knowing he made the offer simply to be polite and for no other reason, Havilland held disappointment in her heart for reasons she couldn't begin to understand. For the first time in her life, she wished she was something that she was not –

A lady.

"You are kind," she said, fighting off extreme melancholy. "But I am certain that I am destined to stay at Four Crosses my entire life. I have never believed I would truly ever leave. But I know that some women travel with their husbands when they marry, at least I have heard of such things, so mayhap that is the best I can hope for."

He lifted his shoulders casually. "Are ye the marrying kind, then?"

She grinned, embarrassed. "I suppose I must," she said. "All women must, at some point."

He could see a grand opportunity to push her a little, to see what, exactly, her thoughts were on marriage. With talk of Tobias' interest in her, and even Thad's, he didn't want her attention to turn to them. He wanted to keep it. Was he, in fact, the marrying kind? He didn't even know. He'd never given it much thought. But perhaps with the right woman….

"Ye dunna want tae marry, then?" he asked, sounding concerned. "Even if I promised ye a grand trip tae Paris?"

Her head shot up, her eyes wide on him. "A trip to… *you* would promise me a trip to…?"

He flashed that smile, the one he used to send women's hearts a-flutter. "Ye must marry sometime," he said. "Me da expects many sons and who tae be a better mother tae me sons than a lady warrior. If I have tae bribe ye with a trip tae Paris, then I'll do it."

Havilland's mouth popped open. "You cannot be serious!"

"Why not?"

She was even more astonished. "Because… because you *cannot* be," she said, off-guard and fading fast. "It is most inappropriate to jest on such a serious subject. You do not know me and I do not know you, and this is not an appropriate conversation."

"But why?"

"Because you jest about something quite serious!"

With a heavy sigh, he stood up. As Havilland watched, he removed a very sharp dagger from his belt and put the sharp edge of the blade against his pale wrist. He looked at her, pointedly. "Are ye sure ye willna marry me? I am prepared tae show ye my sincerity but before I bleed all over this table, I must ask ye again."

She wasn't entirely sure he was jesting, but in the same breath she couldn't believe he was serious. She had no idea what to say, a thrill such as she had never known filling her heart. Never in her life had she had any suitors, not ever, so she had no idea how to play the flirting game with this man who was evidently quite adept at it. He was charming and persuasive. But he could very well be toying with her. She simply wasn't sure so the best thing to do, as she struggled to reclaim her composure, was jest right along with him. Then, perhaps, if he wasn't serious, it wouldn't break her heart so much to pretend that she wasn't serious, either.

"Are you really going to cut your wrist?" she asked.

He was firm. "I am."

She stood up and began looking around. "Very well," she said. "But let me find something to stop the bleeding first. I want to be prepared."

His face fell. "So ye'd let me cut meself over ye?"

He said it rather exaggeratedly and she fought off a grin. "Well, of course," she said. "I have never had a man declare his undying love to me. Let me call my sisters so they can watch, also. Can you wait a moment before you do it? It should not take me long to find them."

He scowled. “Ye wicked wench,” he said. “Ye’d let me cut meself tae pieces over ye before ye’d agree tae a marriage between us? I willna cut meself over the likes of ye.”

She was trying very hard not to giggle. “I am sorry,” she said, struggling to keep a straight face. “I know I am terrible. But truly, you do not want to marry someone like me. I am sure you will find a much better candidate someday.”

She was pushing him to see how he would react and he fell right into her trap. Rather than him manipulating her, now she was doing the manipulating. But he didn’t catch on. Frustrated, he shoved the dirk back into its sheath.

“I dunna want another candidate,” he said. Then, he pointed a finger at her. “Mark me words, Havilland de Llion. Ye’ll go tae Paris with me someday if I have tae drag ye every step o’ the way.”

He seemed very serious but she could sense that he wasn’t. For someone who had never flirted with a man in her entire life, she took to it fairly easily. Truthfully, it was easy with him – from their very rough beginnings until this moment, she couldn’t even remember the spanking he’d dealt her. It didn’t even matter. The man she had tried so hard not to be interested in now had her full attention. She hoped he was serious about his intentions – she truly did – but it was far too early to know such things. Until then, she was enjoying the rapport developing between them.

The entry door to the hall swung open, casting light from the morning in their direction and interrupting their conversation. Havilland caught sight of someone familiar entering the hall. It was Madeline, dressed in her mail tunic and strapped down with her weapons, including her small broadsword. Her messy, dark hair was knotted up atop her head as she approached the table, looking at Jamison as if beholding the enemy. She kept her eyes on the man as she approached her sister.

“One of the de Lohr brothers is out there gathering a patrol,” she said to Havilland. “Who ordered this?”

"I did," Jamison replied evenly. "He is gatherin' de Lohr men tae run patrols in the area."

Madeline stiffened. "It is unwise to send out any patrols right now," she said, "or weren't you told that we have lost eleven men to the Welsh in recent months?"

Jamison wasn't entirely sure he liked this girl. She was brash and aggressive, as he'd discovered when she'd confronted him those days ago. She didn't appear to have the ability to ease her rigid manner the way her sister did. Something very arrogant glittered in her dark eyes.

"I was told," he said. "But we need information on the Welsh. We need tae know their movements. Staying inside this fortress will not help us discover what we need tae know."

"It is a risky operation."

"There are risks involved in *any* operation."

Madeline was frustrated that he didn't seem inclined to take her advice. In truth, that infuriated her. She turned to her sister. "Our men should not be involved in anything they do," she said. "In fact, our men should be kept separate from the de Lohr troops."

Jamison wouldn't let her give such terrible guidance. "Hold, lady," he said, his manner growing firm. "'Tis bad advice ye give. Yer men need tae be part of the de Lohr operation because they must learn what I am here tae teach them. Only a fool would isolate their men as ye have done and keep them blind tae what is going on around them. That is a sure sign of a bad commander and if ye keep on that path, ye're going tae kill everyone in this fortress because the Welsh will overrun ye and ye'll not know how tae stop them. Is that what ye want?"

By the time he was finished, Madeline was red in the face, insulted and furious. "We do not need your help," she hissed. "We do not want it."

Before Havilland could stop her sister, Jamison came around the table so their words wouldn't be shouted for all to hear. "Ye have no choice," he said, his voice low and rumbling. "Let me explain things tae ye, lass…."

"You will not address me that way!"

He cut her off, brutally. He'd had enough of her haughtiness and Jamison wasn't a man with great patience for such things.

"Shut yer mouth and listen tae me," he said. "'Tis obvious ye've gone through life thinkin' ye knew everything there is tae know, so let me be the first tae give ye a true education – Four Crosses doesna belong tae ye. It belongs tae de Lohr and the men out there, the men ye think belong tae ye, really belong tae the Earl of Worcester. Nothing about this place is yers so yer grand illusion of being a battle commander is a dream. Nothing but a dream. Ye live here by Worcester's good graces and if he says I must train Four Crosses men tae understand the Welsh threat, then that is what I must do. If ye want to learn, then ye're welcome tae attend me, but if ye want tae continue tae live in ignorance, then go crawl intae a hole somewhere and take yer ignorance with ye. I willna tolerate it. Is that in any way unclear?"

Madeline had never been cut down in such a way and certainly not so harshly. Deeply embarrassed and incredibly furious, she opened her mouth to say something but Havilland grabbed her by the arm and yanked her away from Jamison, pulling her sister from the hall. It was evident that Havilland was trying to prevent a fight because that's where it was headed; Jamison could feel it. Therefore, he maintained eye contact with Madeline for as long as he was able, until Havilland forcibly pulled her through the hall entry.

Then, and only then, did Jamison stand down somewhat, sighing heavily and shaking his head at the arrogant stupidity of the young woman. It was no wonder the Welsh had managed to hit Four Crosses repeatedly with an attitude like that. He wondered if that had been Havilland's attitude, too.

He was hoping that the conversation that just took place at this table had changed that.

Already, he was missing talking to her.

CHAPTER SEVEN

Nights like this drove the cold down to a man's very bones....

WINTER SUNSETS WERE early in the day, with usually no more than seven hours of sunlight in the dead of winter, so by the time night fell, it was cold and foggy and dreary.

Torches were lit upon the battlements and the open gatehouse was heavily protected as the soldiers repairing the damage from the most recent attack wrapped up their work for the day. Sentries with big dogs patrolled the perimeter of the castle, moving through the coming darkness and the fog, making sure that all was well while the gatehouse was open. Men were working quickly to close it and bottle the castle up for the night.

Four Crosses had a postern gate in the kitchen yard, built into the wall. It was a gate used by those who did business with the kitchens and instead of one gate, it was actually two – a fortified iron gate on the outside of the wall, a narrow passageway, and then a fortified gate on the inside of the wall. It was always very carefully watched to ensure no one tried to breach it and there was a path from the postern gate that led to a heavily wooded area and the River Einion. Farmers or servants usually traveled it but as the sun set on this night, someone else was traveling it as well.

She knew the path well, as she was born at the castle. She knew it and the surrounding landscape as well as she knew the lines of her face. But this was different; this was no casual stroll in the fog. There was someone waiting for her at the end of the path and she didn't want to be seen by the sentries on guard on the walls overhead. Even though there was a fog cover, someone might have seen her leave and she didn't want to try to explain that. As she ran along the path, she kept looking over her shoulder, thinking she heard movement behind her. But it was water dripping from the leaves, she was certain.

The path carved out a niche next to the river and the waters flowed beside her as she ran along the trail. It was muddy and cold, but she was heated in her heavy clothing. In fact, her forehead was sweating, but it had more to do with her own apprehension than it had to do with her exertion. She was frightened and she was determined, an odd combination, indeed.

The foliage grew heavier, the thicket of trees dark now that night was falling. She still swore she could hear someone behind her but every time she stopped to look, there was no movement. It was her imagination, she was certain, but she kept her hand on the hilt of her dirk just in case. Certainly, if anyone had seen her, she would do her best to silence them.

Now she was in a heavy cluster of bushes as she moved down the path. The ground was particularly slippery here and she did slip, more than once. The third time, someone reached out from the thicket to grab her. In a panic, she unsheathed her dirk until she saw who it was. Then, relief swept her as a man, darkened by the shadows, kissed her passionately.

"*Fy nghariad*," the man whispered in Welsh against her lips. Then, he switched to her language. "My darling. I have missed you so."

The woman fell into his arms, allowing him to do as he pleased with her. His lips kissed her face, his hands on her head to hold her fast. She whimpered softy as he kissed her, so very glad to be in his arms again.

"I have missed you, also," she breathed as his mouth came close to her lips again and he plunged his tongue into her mouth. He licked her, tasted her, before she pulled away gasping. "Are you well? Were you hurt in the most recent battles?"

The man, dark-haired and dark-eyed, shook his head. "Nay," he said, breathlessly. "Were you, my sweet Madeline?"

Madeline shook her head, also breathless, thrilled to be in her lover's arms again. "Not at all," she whispered. "It is so good to see you. I have missed you desperately."

"As I have missed you."

More hugging and kissing, heated lips upon tender flesh. "So much has happened I do not know where to begin," she said, her voice trembling. "There is much you should know."

He couldn't seem to stop touching her face, running his dirty fingers across her lips. "I have been here every night since the end of the battle, waiting for you," he said. "Why have you not come to me before now?"

Madeline sighed, burying her face in his neck, inhaling deeply of his scent, before pulling back to speak. "I am sorry this is my first opportunity to come," she said. "There are de Lohr troops at the castle now including four knights. The situation is much more complicated now, Evon. You must take great care."

Evon ap Preece smiled at his love. "I have nothing to fear so long as you protect me," he said softly. "As long as you have survived the attacks in whole, I am satisfied."

Madeline smiled tremulously in return, her hands on his shoulders. "As am I," she murmured. "But I do not have much time so I must tell you all that I know."

His brow furrowed. "What do you mean you do not have much time?" he asked, suddenly looking around suspiciously. "Have you been followed?"

Madeline looked around also, just because he was. "Nay," she replied. "But the changing of the guard will come soon and I must be present. I was only able to slip away now because men are growing weary at their posts and I was able to slip by. I will come back tomorrow night and I hope we can spend more time together."

He kissed her again, more deeply this time, before his hands began to roam. "Tell me all you can," he said, fumbling at the belt on her tunic, loosening it. "Tell me while I touch you."

Madeline trembled. "You know I cannot think when you do such things to me."

He laughed, low in his throat. "Try, my darling. *Try*."

Madeline did. She was looking forward to his touch as much as he was; it had been a long time since they had last tasted one another and she missed the way he made her feel. As his cold, dirty hands snaked underneath her heavy tunic and immediately grabbed a small, warm breast, she struggled to think.

"It was de Lohr who helped us fight off the Welsh," she explained as he pulled her tunic over his head and began nursing hungrily at her naked breasts. "He… he left five hundred men behind to reinforce our ranks, including four knights. Three of them are de Lohr sons and of the highest order, but the fourth is a Scotsman. I have never met him before. He is in command and I have heard rumors about him. The men are saying that he is called The Red Lion and that he is the best knight in all of Scotland."

Evon didn't reply right away, as he was too busy suckling her nipples and unfastening her breeches. But he managed to pull his mouth away from her flesh long enough to speak.

"What about him?" he asked as he dragged his tongue over her belly "Tell me what you know."

Madeline was having a terrible time holding a coherent thought as he managed to untie her breeches and pull them down around her thighs. Like a moth to flame, his hand went to her tender woman's core and his fingers began probing her. She gasped as he forced her to stand awkwardly, her legs apart, and thrust his fingers into her.

"He… Sweet Mary, Evon, when you do that to me…." she muttered.

He cut her off. "Tell me, my darling. Tell me what you know."

Madeline was trying to but her eyes were rolling back in her head as he suckled her breasts and thrust his fingers inside of her body. "The Red Lion," she breathed again because she forgot she had told him that already. "He… he is sending out patrols again. He spent all day gathering patrols and speaking to the men about the Scottish tactics that the Welsh are using."

Evon paused in his onslaught, thinking on her words. *Scottish tactics.* Then, his head came out of her tunic and he stood up, looking at her. "He said that?"

"What?"

"That we are using Scots tactics?"

"Aye," Madeline replied, breathless and uncertain. "Are you?"

Evon cocked his head thoughtfully. "Your Red Lion has a sharp eye," he said as he took Madeline by the shoulders and turned her around for the nearest tree, forcing her to bend over and grip the tree to steady herself. "There are Scots mercenaries among us who have been training the men. Their tactics, Madeline… they are far more than the Welsh way of fighting. They are calculated and logical. We lost far less men this time around the way the Scots taught us."

He stood behind her as he spoke, fumbling with his breeches. Quickly, he pulled them down and flipped up her layers of tunics, exposing her slender while buttocks. He bent over her, pressing his manhood against her wet and swollen core, thrusting firmly into her quivering body. Madeline gasped and shifted on her legs, bracing them apart further to allow him better access. She held on to the tree as he began to thrust, his hands on her hips as he held her firmly against him.

Evon's thrusts were quick and brutal, hitting Madeline so hard with his pelvis that more than once, she lost her grip on the tree. She ended up with her head against the tree, repeatedly ramming her head into it as he thrust firmly behind her. The hands on her hips began to slap at her buttocks, harshly enough to cause a sting, but his handprints on her white flesh excited him terribly. He slapped her buttocks as she yelped in pain.

"Tell me more," he breathed, spittle dripping from his lower lip and landing on her buttocks. "What else has your Red Lion said?"

Madeline groaned as his thrusting caused her pleasure-pain. "He… he is sending out patrols again," she reiterated, grunting. "He… is teaching our men to fight the way the Scots fight. If… if you have Scots mercenaries among your men, then they should know this."

"I will tell them," he said as he thrust, feeling his climax coming and slapping her buttocks again. "Are there plans for the English to leave the castle?"

"There… there are no plans of leaving that I know of."

"Then the English are staying?"

"Aye."

"When do the first patrols leave?"

"I do not know… tomorrow, mayhap. Soon."

He withdrew from her woman's core and, using the moisture from her own body, slicked up her second maidenhead, her anus, and pushed into her. Madeline bit her hand to keep from crying out as he continued to make love to her in a most unnatural way. But it was something Evon liked and, being in love with the man since childhood, she permitted it no matter how much it pained her. She belonged to him and always had. It was a dream they had, to rule Four Crosses together.

Madeline was doing all she could to ensure that dream came true.

Evon gave one hard, final thrust and released himself into her body, into the orifice where it was guaranteed no children could be born. He didn't need a bastard from a half-Welsh wench, but what he did need was information for Madog's rebellion. His father, Lord Preece, wasn't part of the rebellion sweeping the country, the dying throes of the last Welsh prince, but Evon was part of that movement and he used Madeline de Llion to gain his information.

Madeline thought it was because he loved her, but the truth was that he was simply using her. He'd tell her everything she wanted to hear simply to make sure she told him everything that was happening at Four Crosses. Madog's men wanted the fortress very badly and Evon was helping in any way he could. It made him an important man in Madog's ranks.

He had his own spy within Four Crosses.

So he hugged Madeline and told her how much he was looking forward to their future together, lying through his teeth as he said it. He questioned her more about the patrols, about the Scotsman they called The Red Lion, and about anything else he could think of that might help his cause. The damage to the walls was being repaired and the army was now reinforced by English troops. That wasn't good news and it was something Madog's men needed to know.

Evon had to rush back to his rebel force but he made sure to elicit a promise from Madeline that she would meet him again tomorrow after the nooning meal, here in their thicket, with more information on what was transpiring at Four Crosses. Now, with the addition of three English knights and their Scottish commander, the situation had changed markedly.

Now, the conquest of Four Crosses might be in jeopardy.

ꟿ

NIGHTS LIKE THIS reminded Jamison of nights on the Highland moors, dark and foggy and wet. The only difference for him was that at his home, one could smell the sea. He couldn't smell it here and he missed it. All he could see were land and rocks and winter-dead hills, as far as the eye could see.

After a long day of training troops on Scots tactics, Jamison had the night watch. He wasn't particularly tired so he relieved Tobias and Thad of the wall and planted himself up by the gatehouse with a big bowl of steaming broth. It was bone broth, from boiled sheep bones, cooked with onions and turnips and carrots and highly seasoned with salt and precious peppercorns. The de Lohr army had brought the salt and pepper with them, and the cook at Four Crosses seemed to have a talent for cooking. So Jamison leaned against the parapet of the gatehouse as the fog settled and the sun set, drinking his bowl of hot broth and feeling warmth in his belly. He remembered thinking during battle that he might never be warm again so the hot soup was comforting.

But he was still cold and damp in spite of the warm broth. He was in layers of wool, his hands with heavy leather gloves on, and he was chilled. Nights like this drove the cold down to a man's very bones and the only thing he could do was to move around to try to chase the chill away.

Nights like this were also very dangerous. Without the ability to see to the horizon, an entire army could sneak up to the castle using the mist as cover and no one would know until the army was upon them, so vigilance was the order of the moment. Jamison began walking the fighting platform, the one that had been repaired in the past few days, encouraging the men on watch to be heedful. This could very well be the night that the Welsh returned.

The men were on edge with the fog, straining to see through it. Torches burned brightly and more were lit, lining the walls to keep away the night. Jamison continued to wander the wall walk, which happened to go most of the way around the castle. It was quite an architectural feat, in truth, because of the size of the walls. But it was quite necessary to keep watch over the countryside surrounding the castle.

Jamison moved past the gatehouse, keeping his attention on the fog outside of the walls but finding his thoughts turning to Havilland. *Havilland.* Even thinking her name made him smile. In truth, he'd thought about her all day, ever since their conversation in the great hall. He liked the way she laughed and her smile… well, the woman's smile made his heart thump as it had never thumped before.

Bringing up the subject of marriage with her had been impetuous and quite possibly reckless, but it had seemed the most natural of things to do. He had jested about it when he realized, in hindsight, he hadn't been jesting at all. But he wanted her to think that he was. He fully expected her to reject any suggestion of marriage and if she thought he was jesting, perhaps he wouldn't look like such a fool. But he was quite certain her refusal would disappoint him greatly.

It might even break his heart.

He had to smile to himself, thinking that he was capable of having a broken heart from a woman he'd only known a few days. But he didn't have to know Havilland more than a few days to know that she was special. She had an innocence about her that was hard to define, yet it was vastly attractive. And she had bravery and intelligence that was unmatched. That was a rare thing, indeed.

As he moved past the gatehouse, his gaze fell on Tobias standing along the parapet, speaking to one of the senior de Lohr sergeants. Thoughts of Havilland and Tobias didn't mix because it brought a recollection of what Brend had said earlier in the day – *Tobias has already expressed interest in Havilland.*

Gazing at Tobias, a man he genuinely liked, Jamison could feel himself becoming territorial. He didn't want any of the de Lohr brothers lusting after a woman he was attracted to, least of all Tobias. He didn't need or want the competition. He briefly considered throwing Tobias over the wall and then telling everyone it was an accident, but that wouldn't work out well in his favor because there were witnesses. Too many of them. He wasn't sure he could throw that many de Lohr men over the wall, too, in order to silence them, so he put the thought of murdering Tobias out of his mind. At least, for the moment.

Tobias, oblivious to Jamison's dangerous thoughts, smiled when he saw Jamison approach. "Jamie," he greeted. "It is nearly time to change the guards to the night watch. The gatehouse has double the capacity of sentries, as you ordered."

Jamison nodded to the efficient knight. "And the postern gate?"

Tobias glanced over his shoulder. "There are Four Crosses men guarding it," he said. "I would not worry. I checked the gate myself a short time ago and it is quite secure."

Jamison grunted. "It is still an entry point should the Welsh decide tae descend upon us this night," he said, looking around at the fog. "Nights like this make me nervous."

Tobias couldn't disagree with him. He, too, looked out to the fog beyond the walls. "It is hard to believe there is an entire land out there, now buried in mist."

"An entire land that could be crawling with Welsh."

Tobias lifted his eyebrows in resignation. "There is naught we can do about it tonight," he said. "We have three patrols scheduled for the morning, each patrol manned by at least one Four Crosses man who is familiar with the area. Let us see what the patrols have to say when they return tomorrow."

Jamison knew that was the truth; there wasn't much more they could do. He turned to continue his walk, slapping Tobias on the shoulder as he went.

"But we still must make it through the night," he said. "Stay vigilant, Tobias. Yer keen eyes may save us."

Tobias took the request seriously. Jamison continued down the wall, his thoughts on the coming night and not Havilland for the moment, but that changed when he saw Havilland's sister, Madeline, in the bailey below. She was heavily dressed against the night, carrying a torch with her as she crossed from the keep into the kitchen yard. Jamison was heading in much the same direction and kept pace with her as she moved.

It was curious to watch the woman move because she acted like she was being hunted. She moved swiftly and kept looking around her as if either searching for something *or* someone. Jamison thought it all rather odd but, then again, Madeline was an odd one to begin with so perhaps it was nothing new with her. Perhaps, that was simply the way she always moved.

Still, he couldn't quite shake the fact that she seemed to be behaving strangely so he continued to parallel her path, casually, moving down the wall as she moved into the kitchen yard. The fighting platform ended by the time it reached the kitchen yard, however. He watched as she slipped into the kitchen yard, discarded the torch, and stopped to speak with the half-dozen men on guard at the postern gate. It was difficult to see what was transpiring through the mist, but he could see the outlines of men and the outline of Madeline as she spoke with them.

He had only been watching a minute or two when the men who had been guarding the gate began heading away from their post. Madeline, however, remained. She simply stood by the gate, like a sentry, as the men made their way out of the kitchen yard and into the bailey.

Vastly confused, Jamison wondered if she intended to guard the gate all by herself. Given the arrogance of the woman, he wouldn't have been surprised, but he didn't approve of that particular situation. That gate needed at least a dozen men on it and he intended to tell her just that. Heading for the nearest ladder that led down to the bailey, he cast a final glance into the kitchen yard in time to see Madeline slip from the postern gate. In the blink of an eye, she opened the gate swiftly and was gone.

Startled, Jamison flew down the ladder and ran into the kitchen yard, hardly believing what he had just seen. Why on earth the lass would leave the safety of the castle was beyond him. Was she out checking the perimeter wall? It was a foolish notion at best and he began to build up a serious rage thinking that Madeline believed she knew better than anyone else on this misty, cold night. Going outside the walls was lunacy at best.

Charging through the narrow tunnel that comprised the postern gate, he emerged into the other side, outside of the walls, expecting to see Madeline walking along the tall, stone perimeter. He was surprised to see that she wasn't there and as far as he could see down the wall, she was nowhere to be found. Greatly puzzled, he turned to the path that led down the side of the slope and into the foliage below. There was a small river down there, he knew, and it took him a moment to realize he caught a glimpse Madeline far below, heading down the path. She disappeared from his line of sight almost as quickly as he saw her and, like a flash, Jamison was after her. He wanted to know where the woman was going.

Into the trees he followed her, deeper and deeper still. Spending the first ten years of his life in the Highlands, he had been taught the art of tracking from his father and grandfather. He knew how to be quiet and unseen. He was excessively good at it and was able to follow Madeline without her knowing.

Wrapped up in his wool *brecan*, he was concealed by the darkness and the trees, and easily blended in. Madeline was far enough ahead of him that she had no idea that someone was behind her although she did stop once or twice to glance behind. Jamison simply froze, shielded by a tree trunk or a bush. Not seeing anything, Madeline would then turn about and keep going.

She headed down by the river path and he followed, moving in stealth. He honestly couldn't imagine where the girl was going. She'd never come across to him like a wanderer so her behavior was most puzzling. Still, he had to see where she was going. It could have been something completely innocent – or it could have been something more than that. What was it Havilland had said to him earlier in the day? *I believe we may have a spy within our ranks.* To be truthful, Jamison hadn't taken her seriously until now. Was it possible there really *was* a spy and was it further possible that the spy was her very own sister?

He was about to find out.

Up ahead in the misty trees, Jamison heard Madeline yelp but she was just as quickly silenced as Jamison heard a male voice. It was faint, but it was definitely male. Then, it hit him – had Madeline snuck out to meet a lover. Seized with the possibility, Jamison lost himself in the vines and leaves and bushes, creeping closer to the voices. They were soft but unmistakable.

Creeping closer still, he ended up on his belly, his head covered by his dark wool *brecan*, peering out from beneath some bushes as Madeline and a tall, slender young man whispered and passionately kissed in the darkness. He could hear bits and pieces of what was being said.

Why did you not come to before now...there is much you should know... tell me now while I touch you.

Jamison didn't want to move, didn't want to chance that he might be seen, but he very much wanted to hear what Madeline had to say. He was trying to ignore the fact that the man was intent on having his way with her as the woman tried to speak.

It was de Lohr who helped us fight off the Welsh... he left five hundred men behind to reinforce our ranks, including four knights... one is a Scotsman... the men are saying that he is called The Red Lion and that he is the best knight in all of Scotland.

Jamison's heart sank. Whoever this man was, Madeline was freely telling him about the situation at Four Crosses. With every kiss or touch from the man, she would tell him more and it was quite clear to Jamison that the man wasn't part of any allied force. If he was, he wouldn't be hiding out here in the trees and meeting with Madeline in secret. She was providing him with intelligence as he put his head beneath her tunic and did things to her that were making her writhe and gasp. *He is seducing her*, Jamison thought, feeling a spark of anger deep in his belly. *And... she is letting him. Fool!*

After that, it grew even more uncomfortable and infuriating for him. The man was all over Madeline, using his mouth and hands to violate her. Madeline continued to stammer out more information as Jamison listened... *he is sending out patrols again... he knows there are Scots among you....*

By the time the man bent her over a tree, dropped his breeches and took her from behind, Jamison had heard enough. He'd even heard a name – *Evon* – a name that was decidedly Welsh. As a logical man, the evidence of this rendezvous was overwhelming – Madeline was evidently the spy that had cost many lives at Four Crosses. There was no other conclusion he could come to.

As he listened to the sounds of lovemaking, Jamison decided to retreat. He wanted to make it back to the castle before her because he had much to discuss with the knights. They needed to know that there was, indeed, a spy in their ranks because now, the situation had changed dangerously. Everything they said and everything they did would make it back to the Welsh rebels who were very much trying to destroy them.

Therefore, they had to plan.

They couldn't let one of their own sink them.

Moving in the dark, the fog, and the wet, Jamison made his way back to Four Crosses Castle.

CHAPTER EIGHT

"You cannot control

the heart that covets...."

"WE CAN DO one of two things," Tobias said. "We can throw Madeline in the vault and stop the bleeding or we can use her to feed the Welsh false information. We can even use her to trap their leaders. Evon, you said? Has anyone heard that name before?"

In the small solar of Four Crosses, Jamison, Tobias, Brend, and Thad huddled around the glowing hearth, mulling over the shocking story that Jamison had just relayed to them. It was disgusting, truly, and there wasn't one man among them not thoroughly disheartened by Madeline's behavior. Given the way she had behaved towards the presence of the de Lohr troops, and most especially to Jamison, no one seemed particularly surprised by it. Now, things were starting to make some sense.

The spy had been revealed.

"She must have been doing it all along," Jamison said. "Four Crosses has been hit hard in the past few months, attacks that have progressively damaged the walls. Lady Havilland mentioned tae me that she thought there was a spy among them, but I'm sure she never thought it was her own sister."

Tobias sighed thoughtfully. The news of Madeline had him disenchanted with all three de Llion sisters. "Then you do not believe Lady

Havilland is in on this treachery?"

Jamison shook his head. "I dunna know her as ye do, but in me conversation with her today, I dinna receive the impression that she might be complicit with what her sister is doing. I canna believe she would be."

Tobias shook his head. "Nor I," he replied firmly. "But I would have never believed Madeline capable of such things, either."

Jamison sat forward, elbows on his knees, head propped up by his hands. He gazed thoughtfully into the fire as the flames danced hypnotically.

"I will proceed on the assumption that Lady Havilland doesna know of her sister's activities," he said, "which means we must tell her. She must know. We need her knowledge of who 'Evon' might be and why Madeline is giving him information. But I'll tell ye something more, something I dinna tell ye at the beginning – the man seduced Madeline as I watched. He did things most of us keep tae the bedchamber, all the while demanding answers from her. She told him everything she could."

The three knights looked a bit startled by the realization. "Madeline?" Tobias repeated, just to be clear they were all speaking about the same woman. "Cold and aggressive Madeline?"

Jamison nodded. "I wouldna believed it had I not see it with me own eyes."

"Then what do we do?" Thad wanted to know, disappointed that one of the three ladies he was lusting after was, in fact, a spy. "I say we throw her in the vault."

Jamison shook his head. "Nay, lad," he said. "I tend tae believe that this is a great opportunity for us, as Tobias has said."

The others looked at him curiously. "Use her to bait the Welsh?" Tobias asked. "Do you have plan?"

Jamison was still looking at the flames. "From what we saw in the days o' battle, there were no more than two thousand Welsh," he said. "A big enough force, tae be sure, but de Lohr can raise five times that amount of men. I say we bring this tae yer father, Tobias, and tell him what we know. Tell him we have a spy that doesna know we are on tae her. We could set up such a trap with de Lohr's numbers that we could seriously damage Madog's southern rebellion. If we destroy most of his men, he'll have no choice but tae retreat back north. And we can use Madeline tae help us and she willna realize she's been used until it 'tis too late."

Tobias liked that plan. "My father will want to hear what we know," he said. "It will make sense to him why there has been so much activity against Four Crosses as of late."

Jamison nodded. "That is what I think," he said. "Meanwhile, I believe we should let Lady Havilland in on what is transpiring. She must know her sister is betraying her so she doesna tell the lass any more than necessary."

"You truly believe Lady Havilland is trustworthy?" Brend asked, not entirely convinced.

But Jamison nodded to the question, without hesitation. "I do," he said. "Trust that I will be prudent when dealing wit' her."

Tobias' gaze lingered on him a moment. "I have known her for longer," he said. "Let me do it."

Jamison could sense something more than simply duty or politeness in that request. *He has interest in her*, he reminded himself. *Perhaps he is trying tae establish his claim*. If that were the case, Jamison would not allow it. If anyone was going to stake a claim with Havilland, it would be him. Here, in the midst of a serious situation, he was worried about a woman, misplaced as that worry was. Still, he couldn't help it.

"Nay," he said. "I appreciate yer offer, but I am in command. It must come from me. Moreover, the lady and I had a long and pleasant conversation earlier today. I believe we have established some trust. It is time tae test that trust or I would be a poor commander, indeed."

Tobias wasn't happy with that answer. He'd heard from Thad that Jamison had been seen in quiet conversation earlier in the day with

Lady Havilland and he didn't want the big Scotsman to assert himself on her before he could. He'd had his eye on the lady for a while and wasn't about to lose her to Jamison.

"Then I will come with you," he said.

Again, Jamison shook his head. "It would appear to her as if we were joining ranks against her," he pointed out. "It will be much easier if I do this alone. If I need yer help, I will ask."

Tobias couldn't argue with him much more than that because then it would look like he was pushing for contact with the lady and not because of the subject at hand. Unhappy, he simply turned away, leaving Brend and Thad and Jamison grouped around the fire.

Jamison could feel Tobias' displeasure at the situation but he wouldn't address it. It would be better if he didn't because once it was in the open that they were interested in the same woman, it would change the dynamics between them. Many a man, and many a command, had been brought down by men's passions. Jamison didn't intend that this should happen to them but if Tobias pushed it, then Jamison would have no choice but to tell him his intentions towards Havilland. Intentions he really didn't even know himself, but he did know one thing for certain – he couldn't let Tobias have her.

Finally, he stood up, loath to move away from the fire but anxious to seek Havilland. "It is very late and Lady Havilland may already be in her bed, but I will seek her out," he said, looking to Tobias, who still had his back turned to him. "Tobias, ye will find Madeline. I dunna know if she has returned tae the castle yet, but find out. Watch her. Once I speak with Lady Havilland, I will find ye. Brend, Thad, ye seek out Lady Amaline. I dunna know if she is in this with Madeline, but we would be wise tae find out. Discover Amaline's current activities and then report tae Tobias. I will seek ye once I have spoken wit' Lady Havilland."

The men had their orders. Tobias left the chamber without so much as acknowledging Jamison, followed by Brend and Thad. Jamison brought up the rear, going to find the nearest servant to ask Lady

Havilland's whereabouts.

The servant, an old Welsh woman who had been at Four Crosses most of her life, pointed up the stairs of the keep, indicating that Havilland was in her chamber on the upper floors. Jamison sent the woman to rouse Havilland and send her to the solar. With the wheels in motion, he retreated back to the warm solar to await her arrival.

Like an idiot, Jamison's first thought upon realizing he would be seeing Havilland again soon was of his appearance. He stole Brend's comb and ran it through his hair, trying to tame his waves, before rubbing a hand over his face and realizing that he probably looked like a grizzled old bear. He had no time for a shave but then he got to smelling himself, and his tunic, and noticed that he smelled like the moldering leaves he had been rolling around in when he had followed Madeline.

Ripping off the *brecan* and the two tunics he had beneath it, he went to his saddlebags to see if he had something less smelly, something that wouldn't drive a woman away, and came across a lightweight tunic that he used when the weather warmed. It wasn't nearly enough against the cold outside but at least it didn't smell of compost, so he put it on and hoped he wouldn't freeze to death. A man with thin blood such as his was a sorry man, indeed.

Jamison was setting aside his smelly clothing when the old servant knocked softly on the door, entering the chamber to tell him that Lady Havilland was on her way. Jamison thanked the old servant and asked the woman to bring them some warmed wine. When the woman fled, he moved to the fire to make sure it was stoked. He wanted Havilland to be comfortable. He spent a good deal of time worrying about her comfort and his appearance, so much so that he didn't even notice when Havilland entered the room. She was halfway to him before he realized she had come.

But the sight of her made his frenzied thoughts calm immediately. In fact, the sight of her alone was enough to bring him peace like he'd never known it, joy that he couldn't describe. It filled him. More than that, it was the first time he'd ever seen her in anything other than tunics and mail; she was wearing a heavy woolen night shift and wore a fur-lined robe over it. Her dark hair was unbound, flowing about her in soft waves down to her buttocks. She looked like an angel.

With a sigh of appreciation, Jamison set the fire poker aside.

"M'lady," he greeted quietly. "I am sorry tae disturb yer sleep, but it seems we have a situation on our hands and I require yer counsel."

Havilland had, indeed, been asleep, perhaps the first good sleep she'd had in weeks. But a message from a servant and the mention of Jamison's name, had her rushing to do his bidding. She didn't know why she should rush, only that he had summoned her and she was compelled to obey him.

"My lord?" she asked with concern. "How may I be of service?"

Jamison indicated one of the two chairs that was situated before the hearth. "Please, sit," he said, sitting down once she took her seat. "As I said, I am sorry tae disturb ye. But this is important."

Havilland was listening with some trepidation. "It must be," she said. "What is it? What has happened?"

Jamison reflected on how he would approach the subject for a brief moment before answering her. He didn't want to be harsh or abrupt, but he couldn't dally. The woman needed a straight answer.

So did he.

"Have ye ever heard the name Evon?" he asked.

Havilland cocked her head, puzzled. "Evon?" she repeated. "Where did you hear that name?"

He kept his manner calm. "I will tell ye in a moment," he said. "Can ye tell me if ye've heard it before?

She nodded without hesitation. "Aye," she said. "Evon Preece is a neighbor."

The name she mentioned caught his attention. "Preece?" he asked. "Lord Preece?"

Havilland nodded. "Aye," she said. "Evon is his eldest son."

The very neighbor she had mentioned earlier and had sworn the man wasn't part of the group that had attacked Four Crosses. Jamison was struggling to sort it all out in his mind. "The son of the man ye said wasna part of the force that attacked us?" he clarified. "Ye know of no other Evon?"

"Nay. Should I?"

Jamison was putting the pieces of the puzzle together and the resulting picture was something he didn't like, not in the least. "I dunna know," he said. "I simply wanted tae know if ye had heard the name."

Havilland nodded, but in the process, she also began to look at him strangely. "What has happened that you would ask such a question?" she asked. "What about Evon Preece?"

Jamison leaned forward in his chair, his elbows resting on his knees. He had eyes only for Havilland. "I will tell ye what I have discovered but first, I must know something more," he said. "I believe ye said that yer sister, Madeline, still spoke tae Preece's children. Do ye know that for certain?"

Havilland was trying to figure out what he might be trying to tell her but it was all still a big mystery. "I do not," she said. "Madeline and I have not spoken of Lord Preece or his children in years. I do know that as a child, she was quite fond of Evon. She pretended she was going to marry him. Why are you asking, my lord? Will you please tell me what is wrong?"

Jamison had no choice but to tell her now. He didn't receive the impression that she was hiding anything or complicit with anything that her sister was doing. Her answers had been open and instantaneous. Therefore, he stuck to his original opinion that she was not in league with Madeline when it came to espionage or betrayal. With that in mind, he knew she was in for a shock and tried to ease the blow.

"I was on the wall tonight, setting the posts before the night watch came on," he said quietly. "I was heading towards the kitchen yard when I saw Madeline. She was making her way tae the kitchen yard, also, and she dinna see me. As I watched from the wall, she sent the guards at the postern gate away and when they left, she slipped through the gate. I followed her, mostly because I was going tae berate her for leavin' the safety o' the fortress, but she led me down a path along the river. She was moving swiftly, m'lady, as if she was in a rush, so I fell in behind her tae see what had her in such a hurry. She never saw me, mind ye. As I watched from the trees, she met up with a man, tall and slender. I heard her call him Evon."

Havilland was listening to him with wide, startled eyes. "Evon Preece!"

He lifted his big shoulders. "'Tis possible," he said. "I only heard her call him Evon. But… there is more. M'lady, as I listened, she told him much of what was happening at Four Crosses. She told him about me, about the de Lohr men, and she told him that I suspect Scotsmen among the Welsh rebels. Everything I have told ye and yer sisters, she told this young man. She even told him that I will be resuming the patrols. I would like tae think the young man is an ally, but something tells me he isna."

Havilland's mouth was hanging open by this point, her expression full of outrage and fear and extreme disappointment. "Sweet *Jesú*," she finally breathed. "Are you sure you heard correctly?"

He nodded, sorrow in his features. "I am," he said gently. "Ye mentioned this morning that ye thought there was a spy in yer midst. I… I think I have found her."

Havilland's hands flew to her mouth, so great her shock. She closed her eyes against the horrible news he was telling her, her heart and mind reeling with disbelief. She was inclined to accuse him of mishearing, of perhaps even lying, but she knew in her heart that he was being truthful. He had no reason to lie about anything. Moreover, everything was coming to make a good deal of sense now – her sister's behavior, her absences now and again that she refused to explain – things that had become before the de Lohr knights had even come to Four Crosses, but a pattern just the same. She always knew that Madeline wanted to be in charge of the castle and her sister constantly challenged her, but for it to go this far… Havilland was sickened. Tears popped to her eyes.

She could hardly believe it.

"Nay, Madeline, *nay*," she hissed, struggling not to weep. "How could she do this? How could she betray us?"

Jamison could see how upset she was. In a gesture of comfort, he put his hand on her arm. It was a gentle touch, but one that set his heart to racing. It was a struggle to stay on task.

"I dunna know," he said softly. "But now isna the time tae ask why. Now is the time tae stop the bleeding she has created before it destroys Four Crosses. The young man she was with pressed her for information repeatedly so I can only assume he is with the Welsh rebels. There would be no other reason for him tae demand information from her. Now, this is where I need yer counsel, m'lady – I need tae know what yer wish is as far as yer sister. We can put her in the vault and stop the leak or we can use her tae our advantage."

Havilland was overcome with everything, wiping at her eyes, trying to follow what he was saying. All she could think of was her sister and how the woman was trying to destroy them all. *Damn her!*

"To… to our advantage?" she repeated. "How?"

Jamison kept his hand on her arm, a comforting gesture. The truth was that he simply wanted to touch her. "By feeding her false information," he said. "It is me intention tae go tae Lioncross and inform the earl what we have discovered. I am going tae suggest that we use yer sister tae feed the rebels false information and set a trap for them. This may work out tae our advantage, m'lady, if we can end these attacks once and for all."

Havilland understood what he was saying and she couldn't disagree. "But my sister?" she wanted to know, anxious. "What becomes of her when this is over? The earl will know she is a spy. Will he execute her?"

Jamison couldn't answer for the earl but the truth was that execution was always the end for a spy. He patted her arm. "I dunna know," he said. "She is a female and 'tis usual tae execute female spies, so I dunna know what will become of her. All I know is that she is risking everyone's life at Four Crosses, including yers and mine, and she must be stopped. Ye must understand that."

Havilland was heartsick. She gazed at the man, watching the fire glisten off of his red hair and she was very much aware that his hand was still on her arm. The simple human touch gave her a world of comfort. She was the strong one, always the strong one, but sometimes she just didn't want to be strong. She wanted someone to hold her and tell her everything would be well, giving her comfort as she so often gave it to others. Looking at Jamison, she wondered what it would be like to be comforted by him, to have his arms around her, to have him tell her that everything would be all right. Her heart, a naïve thing, longed for it.

She wondered if she would ever find out.

"I understand," she said sadly. "But I feel… I feel as if, somehow, this is all my fault."

He cocked his head, concerned. "Why?"

She lifted her shoulders, averting her gaze. "Because I am the eldest," she said simply. "I command Four Crosses. Madeline does not much like that I do because she wants to be in charge. Since my father… since his illness began, she has challenged me repeatedly. She is always trying to countermand my orders or undermine me so, you see, this news you bring is not entirely surprising. I suppose I have been expecting something like this all along."

He squeezed her arm. "Whatever Madeline has done is no reflection on ye," he said. "Never forget – I have seen ye command and I have seen ye fight. Ye have a good head on yer shoulders, m'lady. And ye canna control the heart that covets."

She found some comfort in his words and her eyes came up, fixing on him. He was a very wise man. But in the midst of this serious conversation, of her heartbreak, it seemed strange to her that he continued to address her so formally. She longed to hear her name from his lips.

"Will you do me a small honor, please?" she asked.

"Anything, m'lady. Ye only need ask."

"Will you please call me by my name? It seems strange to be so formal under these serious circumstances."

He grinned, those big white teeth glistening in the firelight. "And if ye call me by mine, I would consider it the greatest honor. Besides… ye'd better become used tae it."

The moment turned from sorrowful to warm with the shift of the conversation. It was something Havilland needed desperately, for the news of Madeline's true colors had made everything in her world seem uncertain at the moment. Jamison, with his wisdom, seemed to be someone that could right it. Perhaps she was looking for light that only he could provide.

"Why must I become used to it?" she asked.

He lifted a red eyebrow. "Because ye canna call yer husband 'my lord'. People would laugh."

She burst out into giggles, her heart feeling giddy and light. "Are we back on that subject again?"

"We never left it."

Her laughter continued, softly. "I told you that you should not jest on such a subject," she said. "What if I take you seriously? I would hold you to it."

"I wish ye would."

Her smile faded, her eyes locking with his. There was something liquid and warm flowing between them now, the same thing that made her knees weak and her heart flutter. It was something intangible yet something immensely powerful and her breath caught in her throat as she gazed into his dark blue depths. Thoughts of Madeline's treachery faded for the moment.

"Are you telling me that you are serious about this?" she breathed.

He nodded, the hand on her arm squeezing again. "Aye," he replied. "I have traveled far and wide, Havilland, but I've never found a woman like ye in all my days. I would be a poorer man the rest of me life if I left this place without ye. Would ye at least consider it?"

Havilland stared at him. It took her several long moments to realize that he was completely serious and when it finally hit her, her eyes widened.

"You are not jesting?" she asked.

He shook his head. "I told ye I wouldna jest on so serious a subject."

She was at a loss, then; giddy, thrilled, but at a total loss. "But… but I am not a fine lady."

"Ye're the finest lady I have yet tae see."

She shook her head. "I did not mean that," she said. "I mean… I meant that I am what you see. I am *all* you see. I do not know how to sew or manage a household. I cannot do anything fine ladies are expected to do."

His other hand came up, gripping her by both arms now as he gazed into her eyes. "And I wouldna have ye any other way," he insisted softly. "Ye're brave and intelligent and sweet. Ye make my heart joyful, Havilland. Tell me that ye'll at least consider me offer."

Havilland didn't know what to say other than the obvious. "I… I will," she said, feeling so excited that she was lightheaded with it. "If you truly want to marry me, then… then I will think on it."

He flashed a grin that nearly made her swoon. "Then ye've made me a very happy man," he said. "I will speak tae yer father right away. Do ye think he'll give his permission? He dinna have someone else in mind for ye, did he?"

Her smile quickly faded. *Oh, God, what to say?* "I…."

"Jamie!"

A hiss came from the solar door and they both turned to see Tobias standing there. His gaze was on Jamison as he motioned to the man. "Come," he said. "I have need of you."

Jamison stood up, taking his hands from Havilland. "What is it?"

Tobias eyed Havilland before returning his gaze to Jamison, obviously trying to wordlessly tell the man that he didn't want to speak freely in front of Havilland. Jamison took the hint. Quickly, he looked at Havilland.

"Go back tae bed," he told her quietly. "I will see ye on the morrow. But if ye see yer sisters, either one of them, tell them nothing about this conversation. All of our lives may depend on it."

Havilland's brow furrowed in concern. "But Amaline knows nothing, I am sure."

Jamison shook his head. "Until we are certain of that, say nothing, please." When she nodded, he winked at her. "I will see ye on the morrow."

With that, he was gone, slipping from the solar after Tobias and leaving Havilland sitting alone, still in a great deal of shock from their conversation. Madeline was a traitor. And now, Havilland had agreed to think about becoming betrothed to Jamison. Was it all really possible? Surely this was a dream. The last she remembered, she had gone to her bedchamber. She had laid upon her bed and fallen asleep. *Aye, that must be it – this is all a dream.* In the real world, Madeline wouldn't be a spy and Jamison wouldn't want to marry her.

... right?

Unable to decide if this was truly a dream, Havilland sat by the fire deep into the night, pondering the turn of events, pondering a life that was about to change forever. Pondering a sister lost and a betrothal gained.

There was someone she needed to talk it over with.

CHAPTER NINE

"They almost did, lass.

Did ye not hear what I said?"

"PAPA? PAPA, CAN you hear me?"

The room at the top of the keep was tiny, filled with a bed and little else. It smelled like rotted food and urine, a smell that permeated the stone and everything around it. A man lay on the bed, wrapped in heavy blankets, while his servant, a man who was mute and blind in one eye, slept in a corner, cramped up against the cold wall with his feet against the hearth.

It was Havilland who had spoken the softly-uttered words to the man on the bed, calling for her father in the darkness. She tiptoed around the sleeping servant's feet and moved closer to the figure moving about in the blankets. She reached out timidly, touching the shoulder.

"Papa?" she whispered again. "'Tis me; 'tis Havi. Are you awake?"

Roald de Llion rolled around on his straw-stuffed bed, finally lifting his head when Havilland spoke his name once more. He looked at her, illuminated by the firelight, and sat up, running his hands nervously through his long, gray hair. It was hair he used to keep neatly trimmed along with a mustache he had been quite proud of. Now, the mustache was overgrown into a long, dirty beard and the hair hadn't seen a cut in over a year. He reached out to Havilland, pulling her into an embrace.

"Precious," he muttered. "My precious."

Havilland let her father squeeze her. He was still quite affectionate in spite of his illness but sometimes his affections became rather inappropriate. Havilland would let him hug her but she would pull away quickly, avoiding the lecherous behavior to follow. "Nay, Papa," she said firmly. "It is Havilland. I am not my mother. Can you see my face? Look at me. I am not your wife."

Roald looked at her but her words didn't really register with him. When he looked at Havilland, he saw his wife, Lady Precious, and in his muddled mind that was all he saw. He couldn't see his eldest daughter, a young woman who had been forced to assume an enormous burden because of his illness. He only saw the past and his long-dead wife.

"Precious," he murmured again.

Havilland tried not to be disheartened but it was inevitable. Every time she came to see her father, she prayed that this would be the time that he emerged from whatever sickness polluted his mind and recognize her. She still prayed that whatever affected him wasn't permanent but every time she saw him, she was disappointed anew to realize that he was just the same. Prayers hadn't healed him and his mind was still as muddled as it had been, growing worse as the weeks and months went on. Every visit with him depressed her more and more. It was difficult to hold out any hope that he would heal at all.

"I do not even know why I come here," Havilland finally murmured, still looking at her father, who was smiling at her. She knew it was because he thought she was her mother. "I come here every day to see you and every day, you think I am my mother. Or you think Madeline is our mother. Papa, Mother is gone. She had been gone for eleven years. Papa, I need you now. Can you understand me? Can you at least try?"

Roald reached out to touch her cheek, muttering his wife's name again. It was nearly all he could say these days. Havilland sighed sharply and took his hand, her expression beseeching.

"Papa, *please*," she said, her throat tight with emotion. "I need you.

The Welsh have been on the attack and now… now I have been told that Madeline is giving information to Evon Preece. You remember him, Papa – he is Lord Preece's son. Madeline is telling him everything about what is happening at Four Crosses and I am afraid he is telling those who are attacking us. I do not know what to do, Papa. If Lord de Lohr is told about Madeline's treachery, he will kill her, but if I let her continue to do as she is, then she will kill *us*. I do not know what to do!"

Roald continued to stare at her, uncomprehending. He touched her cheek again, affectionately, and Havilland pulled away from him, despondent. He didn't understand her. Leaning against the wall, she gazed at him with great sadness, cutting her to the very bone.

"I do not know why I came here," she said again, hoarsely. "There is so much happening and I am afraid, Papa. I do not want to make the wrong decision but my instincts tell me that Madeline must be stopped. She is trying to kill us all and I cannot let her. And de Lohr's commander… Papa, he is a Scotsman. He is strong and intelligent and… and I like him a great deal. If my saying that distresses you, I wish you would say so. I would give anything to hear you berate me for thinking well of another man."

Roald, disinterested in Havilland now that she had pulled away from him, lay back down on the bed and turned his back to her. He was going back to sleep. Havilland watched her father wriggle around on the mattress, getting comfortable, before pulling the coverlet back over him. She snorted ironically.

"Then I am sorry to have disturbed you," she said, going over to the bed and pulling the coverlet up over his shoulder, guarding against the chill of the room. "But I had to come. I had to tell you what is happening. I… I suppose I shall make the decision I feel best, Papa. I have no choice. I will try to do what you would do in this circumstance. I only wish you could tell me so."

Roald let out a snort that sounded more like a snore. Havilland simply patted his shoulder, leaving the dark room and silently closing the door behind her. She threw the bolt on the outside, the one that kept her father from wandering. He had been known to do that. If they wanted to keep his illness a secret, then a wandering fool would surely announce to the world what had become of the once-great knight.

With a few hours left until dawn, Havilland retreated to her bed and in thinking of her father and how very alone she felt in the wake of such a crisis, cried herself to sleep.

☙

JAMISON FELT AS if he hadn't slept in days. Truth was, he'd slept very little in days, little enough so that he was starting to get dark circles beneath his eyes, but it couldn't be helped. The lack of sleep during battle wasn't unusual and the fact that he'd been training men since the battles with the Welsh ended several days ago was enough to keep him active and awake. As morning dawned over a misty landscape, he was already up and moving.

His thoughts were on Havilland. He simply couldn't help it. For the past few days, she had been his first thought in the morning and his last thought at night. Even as he rolled off his pallet and sent a servant for hot water, he was thinking of her. He washed with his precious bit of soap, using a rag, trying to get the compost smell off of his body from the night before. Around him, Brend and Thad were awakening, preparing for the coming day.

Tobias was on watch until dawn. He and Jamison had stayed up most of the night, discussing Madeline de Llion and the situation they found themselves in. When Tobias had plucked Jamison out of the solar the evening before and away from Havilland, it was to tell him that Madeline had returned to the castle and was mingling among the men on the wall, her usual post. She was back as if nothing had happened.

For most of the night, Jamison and Tobias had kept an eye on her until she finally retired a few hours before dawn. That was when Jamison went to bed, also, leaving Tobias to wait out the night.

But the discussion between Jamison and Tobias had been productive. They had decided to send Brend to summon Chris de Lohr to Four Crosses with his army because they were both afraid of what would happen if they left the fortress for the seven-day trip to Lioncross Abbey. Without the senior knights there, they could very well return and find the castle flying ap Llywelyn colors, so they made the decision that it would be unwise to leave.

Frankly, that suited Jamison just fine.

He didn't want to leave, anyway. He didn't want to be away from Havilland and he certainly didn't want to leave Tobias behind with her. That wouldn't do at all. So as the sun rose, turning the mist shades of pale gray, Jamison dressed in two tunics that didn't smell of moldering leaves and his *brecan*, which did smell, unfortunately. He hated smelling like rotten compost with a woman about.

There wasn't much he could do about it because it was so cold outside that he didn't want to be without it, so he had little choice. Jamison and Brend and Thad would have the day watch while Tobias slept. Jamison would inform Brend of his mission back to Lioncross Abbey. It was imperative that the earl come to Four Crosses and bring as many men as he could. When a plan was formulated to trap the Welsh rebels, they wanted to be ready.

Dawn turned into mid-morning and the mist began to burn away, revealing glimpses of bright blue sky above. It was still cold as Four Crosses settled down to a busy day. Brend, having been informed of his mission as he broke his fast, had already departed for Lioncross Abbey, taking the message of what was transpiring at Four Crosses straight to the earl. The damaged wall was almost halfway repaired and sections of the wall walk that had been damaged during the bombardment were also being repaired. Men were fixing the roof of the troop house with more sod they had dug up from the hillside and in the kitchen yard, the cook was boiling a pig. The smell of pork was filling the air and causing men to lick their lips in anticipation.

It was a relatively normal day in a series of days and weeks that had seen few days like this. Jamison was standing at the open gatehouse, deep in discussion with a few Four Crosses men as well as Thad. Four Crosses had no moat, with only the tall outer wall for protection, and Jamison was of the opinion that a moat and earthworks on the exterior of the castle would be excellent for its defenses.

Of course, no alterations of that magnitude could take place without de Lohr's approval but Jamison thought that it was something to discuss with the earl when he arrived. He rather liked planning castle defenses and had an excellent eye for design. Once, he had expressed interested in wanting to be a builder but his father had killed those dreams quickly. No son of George Munro was going to be anything other than a warrior.

Therefore, planning out castle defenses was great fun to him. As Jamison watched some of the men pace off what would have been a decent-sized moat, he caught movement at the gatehouse, turning to see all three de Llion sisters emerging through the gatehouse tunnel.

Jamison's attention was immediately drawn to Havilland. Her long hair was in two braids and she wore a dark green tunic that hung to her knees, baggy leather breeches, and boots that went as high as her ankle. Madeline was beside her, with her hair twisted up in that severe topknot she always wore, while Amaline brought up the rear with her wildly curly red hair.

Jamison didn't move to greet the women. He thought it best to maintain a civil but polite manner with them, especially with the situation with Madeline now. Truthfully, he couldn't even look at her, knowing what her lover had done to her the night before. That skinny, arrogant girl had been used in ways that prostitutes were often not. Big arms folded across his chest, his gaze lingered on the approaching women before casually returning his attention to the project at hand.

"Measure out two feet from the wall and then begin yer measurement o' the moat," he said to the men who were using a length of hemp twine to mark out distances. "It 'twill have tae be at least twelve feet across so men canna easily breach it."

"But why not put it all the way against the wall?" Thad wanted to know. "Why are you leaving ground between the wall and the moat?"

Jamison glanced at him. "Because if we dig too close tae the wall, we could undermine it by weakening the foundation."

"What are you doing?"

Havilland asked the question and Jamison turned to see that she was standing fairly close to him. Madeline stood next to her, arms folded and back straight, while Amaline still stood behind the pair, seemingly uncertain. More than likely, it was because she was still terrified of Jamison from the brutality of their first meeting. But Jamison didn't give any regard to Amaline or Madeline; he smiled politely at Havilland.

"I am thinking on reinforcing the fortress wit' a moat," he said. "It would make her much stronger in the face of the Welsh attacks but the problem is that it would take a long time tae build. Digging all of that dirt doesna come quickly or easily."

Madeline snorted. "A moat," she said, inferring that he was an idiot. "We do not need a moat."

Jamison's gaze lingered on the girl a moment before flicking his hand at the damaged wall under repair. "Ye need something," he said, "because yer walls are not as strong as ye think they are. 'Twas only by God's good graces that the Welsh werena able tae mount the walls. The next time, we mayna be so fortunate."

Madeline wasn't convinced, shrugging her shoulders haughtily. "It seems like a waste of time to me."

"Why?"

She looked at him, rather nastily. She didn't like to be questioned. "Because Four Crosses has stood for many years without a moat and it has survived many attacks," she pointed out. "Do you think we know nothing, *Gael*?"

There was that ugly word again, making another appearance. It was clear that she was challenging him. Havilland, standing next to her sister, cast the woman a threatening glance to shut her up.

"The ground is full of rocks," she said, indicating the obvious nearby as rocks jutted from the earth. "It is not a bad idea but I do not know if it is practical. It would be very difficult work and it would take years. I doubt we could get conscript labor from the area to do it, which means our soldiers would have to do it. That would leave our fortress unprotected."

Jamison thought that was a very intelligent point but, then again, he was seeing the beauty in everything about Havilland these days. He thought she was the smartest woman he knew. "The Welsh serfs wouldna help ye," he said, shaking his head as he looked around at the landscape, at the stark hills and rocks that made up Wales. "The Welsh are barely beyond living out o' caves as it is. Backwards, dirty people who fight and live like animals. Yer work force would come from hired English. I'm sure de Lohr can put his finger on quite a few o' them."

Havilland was watching the men as they measured out the size of a potential moat. "Are you going to suggest he fortify the fortress?"

Jamison was careful in his reply, knowing anything he said would get back to the Welsh rebels through Madeline. He shrugged, turning to watch the men scratch dimensions in the earth. "It was a thought," he said. "I was pondering how tae protect the walls when the next wave of Welsh barbarians come."

He was calling the Welsh names for a reason. He wanted to see if Madeline would react to his slander but he didn't want to look at her to see if he was gaining headway, so he began to walk, pointing out things for Havilland to see.

"The wall could be extended upward," he told her, pointing to the top of the wall. "Right now, without a moat, yer walls are vulnerable tae ladders or war machines. Have ye ever seen any used against ye?"

Havilland was following him, as was everyone else, moving like a herd with Jamison leading. "War machines?" she repeated. "Like trebuchets?"

He nodded. "Those, and mobile fighting platforms," he said. "Ye have enough wood around here tae build any manner of devices tae mount the walls. I'm afeared that the next time the Welsh come, they may do just that and we willna be prepared."

All of it was meant for Madeline's ears. He was making it sound as if they were weakened and uncertain, when the truth was quite the opposite. Thad was following, listening as well, but unlike Jamison, he kept his eyes on Madeline. He wanted to see her reaction.

But Madeline didn't change expression much except to show, increasingly, that she believed Jamison to be a fool. She rolled her eyes repeated to what he said, shifting about on her feet impatiently as her sister listened to what the man had to say. It was clear she had no respect for him or what he was saying, and wished she was anywhere else but standing there listening to him yap. Rude didn't quite encompass her behavior; disrespectful was more like it.

If Jamison noticed Madeline's shifting and sighing and eye rolling, he didn't let on. He kept talking defenses with Havilland, who seemed to be hanging on every word. With such lovely attention, he didn't have time for Madeline's antics but, at one point, he looked up and saw that she was shaking her head. She didn't agree with something he'd said. He zeroed in on her.

"And ye, Madeline?" he said, not even bothering to formally address her. "Ye have something different tae say about all of this?"

Realizing she was in his crosshairs, Madeline's head came up and she looked around her, at all of the attention on her. She struggled not to look as if she'd been caught in her face-making and foolery.

"I… I simply think it is all a great waste of time," she said, lifting her chin defiantly. "Four Crosses has stood for over one hundred years against Welsh attacks. What makes you think you know better than the men who built her?"

It was a semi-valid point and Jamison took it seriously. "Because the men who built it were fighting unorganized tribes, men who had spears and bows and arrows, and little else," he said. "The Welsh who fight today fight with different tactics. They are better trained and better equipped. As they grow as fighters, so must Four Crosses grow as a fortress or she will fall. She came very close tae falling with the last battle, so measures must be taken tae ensure that doesna happen again."

Madeline shook her head. "They will not breach the castle."

"They almost did, lass. Did ye not hear what I said?"

She flamed at the term lass, something she clearly didn't like. "But they did *not*," she emphasized. "We do not have the money or the manpower to make the changes you are suggesting."

Jamison smiled thinly. "'Tis not up tae ye," he said. "Need I remind ye again that this isna yer fortress? It belongs tae de Lohr. If he wants tae improve her, then he will. Ye'll have no say it in."

Madeline was nearing a temper tantrum; her face flushed and her ears turned red. Havilland moved forward, putting herself between her sister and Jamison because she wanted her sister to focus on something else. She was genuinely afraid that Madeline would go mad and challenge Jamison to a fight, something she had been known to do. Jamison would more than likely laugh at her, which would only make things worse. It was imperative to stop the rising anger before it reached the boiling point so she inserted herself between her sister and Jamison, giving her sister a "quiet yourself or die" expression. Madeline saw it but she wasn't over her humiliation yet. As Havilland moved in close to her sister to whisper a few well-chosen words, she caught a glimpse of something on the road to Four Crosses.

A rider. About the time she saw the horse and rider, the sentries on the walls saw it also and the cry began to go up. It was only a solitary man so there was no panic, but there was genuine curiosity. Jamison, seeing the rider approach, motioned to Thad.

"Move the women inside," he said. "Quickly, now."

Amaline was already running for the gatehouse but Havilland and Madeline dug in. They would not be moved or pushed by any man. Jamison watched Thad politely ask them to return to the safety of the fortress but they ignored him. Thad finally looked to Jamison, defeated and silently asking for help, but Jamison just waved the man on. He would have to deal with the two stubborn wenches himself. As the rest of the men who had been following him around turned for the open gatehouse, Jamison went to Havilland.

"'Twould be better if ye went inside until we know this man isna at the head of a bigger army," he said quietly. "I am going inside, also. No need tae meet the man out here in the open."

Havilland looked at him. "I wasn't going to remain out here," she said, "but I did want to see if he had any identifying colors or if I recognized the man."

She was calm, collected, and he appreciated that. This wasn't some flighty woman that scared easily. She had faced battle before, many times, and bore burdens that would have crushed a weaker woman. The seed of respect that had sprouted for her so long ago had grown into a fine, strong sapling. He had immense respect for this lovely woman.

"Very well," he said. If she wasn't going to move right away, then neither was he. Madeline was still standing there, too, but he couldn't have cared less about her. "Ye'll tell me if ye do?"

Havilland nodded, her gaze riveted to the incoming rider. As everyone else moved into the gatehouse, Havilland and Jamison and Madeline stood outside of the structure and waited, watching the rider approach from a southeasterly direction. It was the road that led from Llanfair Caereinion and points south, and that was the direction of the Marches. Therefore. Jamison wasn't too concerned but he was very curious. Closer the rider came until Havilland finally spoke.

"He is English," she said. "See the tack on his horse? The style is English. I do not know who he is."

That was enough to satisfy Jamison. He didn't feel particularly threatened but he kept his hand on the hilt of his dirk, just in case. He stood patiently with the two women, waiting as the rider drew close. Finally, Jamison raised his hand to the man.

"Come no closer," he said. "State yer business."

The rider pulled his frothing horse to a halt. He was dressed in mail, bearing a tunic that Jamison had seen but couldn't bring to mind. It was black with a big red beast on it. The rider tipped his helm back, wiping the sweat on his brow.

"Who am I addressing, my lord?"

Jamison answered without hesitation. "Sir Jamison Munro," he said. "I have command of Four Crosses Castle at this time. Who are ye?"

The rider eyed him curiously. "You are Scots."

"A brilliant statement."

It was sarcastic and the rider lifted his eyebrows apologetically. "I did not mean that the way it sounded, my lord," he said. "Merely an observation. I have been sent by Sir Luc de Lara of Trelystan Castle. He was told there was some trouble here and sent me to discover the truth."

Now, Jamison recognized the English Marcher lord's name. The House of de Lara was very big along the Marches, almost as big as de Lohr. They controlled much of the mid-Marches and were solid de Lohr allies.

"De Lara?" he repeated. "The Lord o' the Trilateral Castles. I know the family. I dinna realize we were so close to Trelystan."

The rider nodded. "It is a two-hour ride at most," he said. "We are to the east of Welshpool."

"And ye were told of trouble here? By whom?"

The rider glanced around the castle, in the obvious stages of repairing damage. "A passing merchant," he replied. "He told Lord de Lara that he had been told of a big battle at Four Crosses Castle. I can see that he was speaking the truth."

Jamison nodded. "Welsh rebels," he said, very conscious of Madeline's presence. "We believe Madog ap Llywelyn's rebellion has made it down this far. That being the case, Trelystan should be vigilant."

The rider nodded. "But the situation has calmed, my lord?"

Jamison lifted his hand to shield his eyes from the glare of the sun, now glinting off of the rider's helm. "It seems tae," he replied. "Will ye not come inside and share our hospitality?"

The rider shook his head. "I've another castle I must visit today," he said. "I have come with a message from Lord de Lara. He says that if you are not too busy in your fight against the Welsh, then he invites you for a festival in honor of his daughter's marriage. The festival begins tomorrow with all manner of games and food, culminating in the marriage of Lady Alis de Lara to Sir Derec le Mon. It will be great fun for the young ladies, my lord."

Jamison lifted his eyebrows. "Then ye've not come offering assistance?"

The rider shook his head. "Nay, my lord," he said. "But I will tell Lord de Lara what I have seen today. If you attend the festival, then you may ask him for assistance personally."

Jamison thought it was rather selfish of a local lord not to offer help against the Welsh, especially another border lord like de Lara. He was powerful. But the man wasn't so selfish that he wasn't beyond inviting his neighbors to a festival on behalf of his daughter's marriage.

Scratching his head curiously, Jamison turned to look at Havilland only to be met by the most hopeful expression on her face. It was full of wistfulness and longing and joy. *She wants to go tae the festival*, he immediately thought. *To hell with the fact that de Lara did not send an offer of assistance; she wants tae go tae the party!*

Jamison glanced at Madeline and noted that, surprisingly, she seemed to have the very same expression on her face. So they think of parties over military assistance? But then he began to think on the world these young women lived in, a world of battles and warfare, of men and of a sick father. It was stark and hopeless. There were no grand opportunities for them to look like, or feel like, women. Offers for something like this party must have been extremely rare, indeed, and Jamison could see that his answer was already decided for him. He knew he couldn't deny Havilland something that clearly meant a great deal to her.

Holding up a hand to beg patience from the messenger, he crooked a finger at Havilland and took her a few feet away for a private discussion that was inevitably joined by Madeline. He wanted to chase the middle sister away, in truth, but he didn't. He simply kept his focus on Havilland and didn't acknowledge Madeline at all.

"I dunna want tae be rude tae de Lara, but I am not entirely certain this is a wise idea," he said, trying to make his case even though he knew they would be attending. "With the Welsh on the attack, I am not sure it is wise tae leave."

Havilland's eyes were lit up with the thought of a party. "But we will not take the entire army with us," she pointed out, "and we will not stay overlong. Just a day or two. Please, my lord? I… I think that I should like to attend. I remember Alis de Lara from when I was a young girl but I've not seen her in years. I should like to wish her well in her marriage."

"And attend a party."

"Well… *yes*."

Jamison twisted his lips wryly, all the while eyeing the woman in disapproval. She simply grinned, flashing him that hopeful smile that melted his heart away. He finally shook his head, defeated before the battle even began.

"Do ye even have anything tae wear?" he wanted to know. "Ye canna go looking like a soldier."

Havilland looked at Madeline, who had a rather eager expression on her face. It was strange to see something on her features that didn't reek of arrogance or impatience. With her features relaxed, now smiling at her sister, she actually looked pretty.

"My mother has an entire wardrobe that has been packed away," Havilland said. "I am sure there is something in the trunk that we can wear."

"Then ye truly want tae go, do ye?"

"Aye."

"Are ye sure?"

"Aye."

Jamison sighed heavily and lifted his shoulders in resignation as he broke away from their huddled group and made his way back to the rider. He lifted his head, his eyes squinting from the sun.

"Very well," he said. "Tell Lord de Lara that we appreciate his invitation and would be honored tae attend. As ye said, 'twill give me an opportunity tae ask the man for assistance."

The messenger nodded. "Excellent, my lord," he said. "I will tell Lord de Lara to expect you. Now, may I water my horse before continuing on my journey?"

Jamison waved the man in through the gatehouse, watching him as he went. But then his focus moved to Havilland who had, with her sister, turned for the gatehouse as well. They were moving faster than the messenger was, excitement at a potential party causing their legs to move quite fast, indeed. Seeing Havilland practically running back into the fortress made him grin.

He still didn't think it was a good idea to leave Four Crosses now. Attending de Lara's party was against his better judgment, but he honestly couldn't deny Havilland something that excited her so. He'd leave Tobias and Thad in command and take only a few men-at-arms with him so the majority of the army would remain behind. They would only stay at Trelystan for two days, perhaps departing tomorrow and then returning the following day. If Havilland complained about the shortness of the visit, he would remind her that she was fortunate, given the circumstances at home, to have gone at all.

And then he'd probably agree to remain as long as she wanted to, anyway.

Idiot….

CHAPTER TEN

"And you belong to us...."

THE TRUNKS THAT stored Lady Precious de Llion's clothing had been difficult to find. Havilland thought they had been stored in her parents' former bedchamber, which now belonged to Madeline and Amaline, but she found out quickly that her sisters had moved the trunks out when they took possession of the chamber.

Therefore, Havilland and her sisters had been forced to retreat to the stables where there was a storage area in the loft that kept many things not needed, or not wanted, around the castle. Precious' trunks were shoved up against the wall where the roof pitched steeply, trunks that the woman had brought with her from her wealthy family when she married Roald, so they were lined with precious aromatic woods that kept out the vermin and bugs. When Havilland and Madeline finally tossed up the lids, their coughs were due to the dust that had settled on the trunks and not the state of the clothing inside.

Like a treasure trove revealed, silks and brocades glimmered in the weak light. There were surcoats, shifts, and belts. Another trunk held shawls and cloaks and shoes. Although Amaline didn't remember her mother very well, Havilland and Madeline did. Havilland even remembered the dress folded up neatly on the top of the stack, a dark blue silk with yellow embroidery. There was some emotion attached to the clothing as Havilland remembered her mother with bittersweet fondness.

Wishing she was still here.

The fashions were old but still quite serviceable. Very carefully, Havilland began taking out the rolled dresses, handing them to Madeline, who would unroll them, shake them out, and turn them over to Amaline. Amaline had the thrill of draping them over her shoulders and arms so they wouldn't touch the straw and dirt of the loft, feeling the soft material against her skin. It was as close to her mother as she had, perhaps, ever been.

Having been informed by Madeline of the invitation, Amaline was more than eager to go, for she was a shy girl by nature and had never truly attended any type of party in her life. The garments that were being pulled forth out of their mother's trunks were beautiful and soft, far different from the breeches and tunics she wore. But, being the younger sister of two older and stronger-personality sisters, she simply did as she was told. They said wear breeches and she did. She'd never really liked fighting as a man, but rather than fight against it, she simply went with the will of the majority. Therefore, the reality of fine dresses thrilled her to death.

Long ago, these garments had been lined with fur at the collars or sleeves, and even embellished with precious jewels and gold to show off the wealth of the House of de Llion, but those adornments had been stripped after Lady Precious died, taken back by Roald for his coffers. As Havilland pulled the garments forth, she could see where the fur had once been or a gold belt; there were remnants of silk stitching left.

"Do you remember Mother, Madeline?" she asked as she lovingly inspected a blue-dyed canvas dress, but a very fine weave and surprisingly soft. "Do you remember her wearing this dress?"

Madeline had a green brocade garment in her hands. She glanced over at the surcoat Havilland was looking at. "Nay," she said. "I do not remember. What I do remember is that she had dark hair, like us. I remember she used to hug us all of the time."

Havilland smiled faintly. "I remember that, too," she said. "I suppose I remember more of her than you would. I was eight when he passed away. You were six years of age and Amaline was only three. Ammie, what do you remember of Mother?"

Amaline had a dress in her hands, the color of yellow roses. "I do not remember much," Amaline said. "I think I remember feelings more than anything. How she made me feel, comforted and safe."

Havilland sighed, leaning back against the trunk. "I always wondered if she would be proud of us," she said. "I still talk to her sometimes, you know. I ask her about things. I ask her even more now that Papa is ill."

Madeline snorted. "Mother is about as apt to answer you as father is these days."

Havilland lifted her eyebrows, a reluctant agreement. "True," she said, returning her attention to the garment in her hand. "I do not know if Mother would have been happy that we were never sent to foster, that Papa kept us here and let us fight as men. He always wanted sons, you know. Mayhap in some way, in the way he raised us, boys are what he ultimately received."

Madeline set the dress in her hand aside and dug into the trunk for something else. "I do not intend to be like this forever," she said. "I want to marry someday and have children, and I will not fight alongside my husband. I will wear dresses all of the time and burn these breeches that we wear; that Papa forced us to wear."

Havilland looked at her sister, thinking on the conversation she'd had with Jamison the night before about Madeline and her Welsh lover. Her prideful sister was trying to kill them all and the more she looked at her, the more her anger and hurt and confusion returned.

Something in Madeline's comment made her think of Madeline's motives for giving information to the Welsh. On the surface, Madeline was cocky and brash, but beneath, she was sensitive and resentful and afraid. Havilland knew her sister well enough to know that all on the surface was not the truth. She found it interesting that Madeline commented on the fact that their father forced them to fight as men.

Perhaps that's where all of this arrogance and resentment started in the first place.

"You feel that Papa forced us to be what we are?" Havilland finally asked.

Madeline nodded firmly. "He always wanted us to fight," she said. "You know that as well as I do, Havi – he gave us swords and taught us to fight. Whenever we spoke of wanting to do the things that women do, because we *are* women, he would tell us how much he wanted us to live in his image. He would tell us how proud he was of us and make us feel as if we would terribly disappoint him if we did not do as he wished."

Havilland knew that. Her feelings were much the same, feelings she had expressed to Jamison. *I am not a fine lady.* It had been a horribly embarrassing admission for her.

"So you are angry at Papa," she said quietly. "You are angry at us all. You show me that every day. Not that I blame you, Madeline. We were never given a choice with Papa. But this is the life we live and we must make the best of it."

Madeline had a dress in her hands and she let it go, letting it fall back onto the stack in the trunk. "I will live my own life," she said defiantly. "Papa is mad. He can no longer tell me how to live. I will do as I wish now."

With a Welsh lover? Havilland bit her tongue. It was so very difficult for her not to fight back but she didn't want to give Madeline any hint that she knew of her treacherous activities. *Sweet Jesú, Madeline! Do you know what you are doing? Do you think to kill us all with your selfishness?*

But no, Havilland couldn't, and wouldn't, say a word. Too many people's lives were dependent upon it. If she thought Madeline's folly had been an innocent mistake, that would have been one thing. She would have said something to her in that case. But she knew Madeline well enough to know that what she was doing was calculated. Selfish, but calculated. Havilland couldn't even pretend to guess what was going through Madeline's mind as she sought to betray her own family.

Perhaps she was finally getting revenge on the father who forced her to dress as a man.

"You have nowhere to go and no one to go to," Havilland said after a moment, not looking at her sister, wondering how she would react to such a statement. "You must remain here with Amaline and me. This is our home and we must protect it."

Madeline's jaw tensed as it so often did when displeased. "I hate this place," she hissed. "It does not belong to me."

"But you belong to *it*. Remember that, Madeline. And you belong to us."

Madeline shook her head, looking at the dresses her sister had dug out. She was feeling sadness and angst and frustration, everything she could possibly feel. "I was born here but that is all," she said. Then, she moved away from her sisters, heading for the ladder that led out of the loft. Havilland watched her go.

"Where are you going?" she asked.

Madeline was already on the ladder. "To the kitchen," she said. "It… it is close to the nooning meal and I am hungry."

"Don't you want to look through more dresses?"

"Nay."

"But we must leave for the party soon!"

Havilland received no answer. She found herself looking at Amaline as Amaline looked rather sadly at the dress in her hands. She knew Amaline wasn't thinking about the dress. The youngest de Llion sister was the sensitive one and Madeline's moods tended to affect her deeply.

"And you, little chick?" Havilland asked softly. "Are you angry at Papa, too?"

Amaline shrugged. "Nay," she said. "He is Papa and we do as he says. But I wish Madeline would not be angry so much. She is very mean sometimes."

Havilland nodded. "She is," she said. "Madeline is… unhappy."

Amaline looked at her sister. "What would make her happy?"

A Welsh lover, perhaps? Havilland thought. But as she looked at her little sister, something more occurred to her. Madeline was heading to the kitchen yard where the postern gate was, the same gate she had left from yesterday to meet her lover. This morning in front of the gatehouse, much had been discussed in Madeline's presence. Havilland had been surprised that Jamison had been so free with his thoughts and information. Now, Madeline had something more to tell her Welsh lover.

Suddenly, she was headed to the kitchen yard.

... the gate!

Putting the dress in her hands aside, Havilland also made her way to the ladder. Amaline watched her go.

"Where are *you* going now?" Amaline asked, concerned.

Havilland didn't want Amaline following her. She pointed to the trunks. "To see if the nooning meal is ready," she said. "I will return. Meanwhile, you will select the three most beautiful dresses of Mother's and bring them up to my chamber. We must see what needs to be done to the dresses so we can wear them. Also, see if there are shoes to go with them. I doubt my boots will go well with a fine silk gown."

Amaline had a task now and she was very good about following through, so Havilland didn't worry about her sister trying to follow her. Amaline was easily distracted. Quickly, Havilland slipped down the ladder and made her way out of the stables, following Madeline's path to the kitchen yard to see if her sister was really there as she said she would be.

Havilland wasn't particularly surprised to discover Madeline wasn't anywhere to be found. When she asked the cook standing over the boiling pig if she had seen Madeline, the woman pointed to the postern gate.

It was as Havilland suspected.

She followed.

ଓ

"DO YOU THINK this is a good idea, Jamie?" Thad asked. "This party, I mean. What if that messenger was really Welsh? What if it is a ploy to drag you away from Four Crosses so the Welsh can attack?"

Standing in the armory of Four Crosses, which was set on the ground level of the northeast tower, Jamison had gone to there to select weapons for the men who would be accompanying him and the de Llion sisters to Trelystan. But Thad, who had been informed that he would be left behind and in command along with Tobias, wasn't so sure this was a good idea. He was following Jamison around now, not at all convinced he would let Jamison leave this place without standing in the man's way. But Jamison only grinned at Thad's concerns.

"Do ye think they are waiting over the hill, watching until me big red head leaves this place?" he asked the young knight. "Ye and Tobias will have command for two days. That isna a long time."

Thad was unhappy. He frowned, watching Jamison inspect a couple of spears. "I am going to wake Tobias up," he said. "He must hear what is happening."

Jamison held up a hand. "Let the man sleep," he said. "He was up all night and has only been sleeping for a few hours at most. Truthfully, I dunna know what ye're upset over. Would ye rather go wit' me?"

Thad nodded almost instantaneous. "Why do *you* get to go to a party with the de Llion sisters?"

Now the truth was out. Thad wanted to go with the women and Jamison began laughing, low in his throat, just enough to irritate Thad. "Why are you laughing?" he demanded.

Jamison shook his head. "Ye hot-blooded little pup," he said. "'Tis not that ye dunna want me tae leave Four Crosses; 'tis simply that I'm leaving and taking the women wit' me."

He continued to laugh as Thad continued to frown. "It is *not* funny."

Jamison put the spears down. "Aye, it 'tis," he said. "Ye ridiculous whelp, I'm leaving ye here and that's the end o' it. Go cry tae someone who cares what ye think."

Thad flinched. "Now you are becoming nasty."

"Not as nasty as I'm going tae be if ye dunna stop whining about this. Me mind is made up."

"Is that so? Let's see what Tobias has to say."

Jamison gave him a wry expression. "I'm in command here, not Tobias. It doesna matter what he thinks. Now, go select about a dozen men tae accompany me tae Trelystan. I want them heavily armed and ready tae depart at dawn."

"I want to be one of those twelve."

"Get about yer task before I beat ye like a rug."

"I am going to tell my uncle about this!"

"I hope ye do."

Thad rolled his eyes petulantly. That made Jamison stomp his big foot in Thad's direction as if threatening to reach out and grab the man. The young knight, always unable to keep from flinching when Jamison did that, bolted out of the armory, heading off to do as he had been told. But he shook a balled fist at Jamison, his last stand to save his pride, and Jamison simply shook his head and brushed him off. Thad was an excellent knight but he was still very young. That youth was great fun to taunt, or at least Jamison thought so, especially when Thad began to whine. With a grin, Jamison was just turning back to the weapons in the armory when he caught sight of Madeline heading away from the stables and in the direction of the kitchen yard.

Jamison faded back into the armory doorway, watching the woman from the shadows. The last he'd heard, the sisters were tracking down their mother's old clothing, hoping to find something serviceable to wear to the de Lara festival. Now, Madeline was out by herself, heading into the kitchen yard. Jamison didn't trust her where the kitchen yard or the postern gate were concerned, not after what he'd seen the day before. Therefore, when she disappeared from sight, he thought very heavily on following her just to see where she was going. He was just about to make his move when he caught sight of Havilland, also heading out of the stables and seemingly following her sister's trail.

Curious, Jamison watched Havilland cross the bailey towards the kitchen yard. She seemed to be on a mission, moving quickly and focused on the kitchens ahead. As soon as she passed from sight, Jamison came out of the shadows and, purely out of curiosity, began to move to the kitchen yards himself.

It wasn't as if he could be stealthy in the broad daylight. His red hair gave him away, a bright splat of color against colorless surroundings, so he casually moved towards the kitchen yards like a man who wasn't tracking two women. He was simply walking. If he ran in to either one of them, he could simply ask them about the clothing and pretend he wasn't following them. He would use the clothing for an excuse. But the truth was that he really wanted to see what the pair was up to.

Passing through the gate into the kitchen yard, he immediately looked around for Havilland or Madeline, preferably both, but he didn't see either of them. Puzzled, as he knew there was nowhere else they could have gone on the trajectory they were traveling, he made his way over to the cook in the middle of the yard.

The round woman, with a red face, was standing over a big pot of boiling pork and beans. Wonderful smells wafted into the air but Jamison had to step back as the wind shifted and steam blew in his face.

"Have ye seen Lady Havilland or Lady Madeline?" he asked the woman.

Brushing stray hair from her face with her wrist, she pointed to the postern gate. "There."

Jamison turned to see what she was indicating. "The gate?"

"Aye." The woman went back to stirring her pot.

"Both of them went through the gate?"

"Aye."

With a sinking feeling, Jamison followed.

CHAPTER ELEVEN

ꝯ

"I am not afraid to die...."

ꝯ

MADELINE WASN'T DIFFICULT to follow.

Trailing her sister away from the castle and down the side of the hill into the foliage near the river, Havilland hung far back as she followed her sister along the water's edge. She could see Madeline up ahead, walking quickly, moving as if she had a purpose. It didn't take a genius to figure out what that purpose was and the more Havilland followed, the more distressed she became.

Sweet Jesú, it's true....

The reality was that Havilland was feeling foolish that she hadn't discovered Madeline's treachery before now. She had suspected everyone else *but* Madeline. But now it was clear that Madeline had been playing her for a fool, evidently wrapped up in some kind of covert operation designed to bring down Four Crosses. In truth, she was playing everyone for a fool, not simply Havilland.

With that understanding, it was difficult for Havilland not to run after Madeline and beat her, berate her for what she had done. Still, there was some small part of her that was hoping this was all a mistake. Perhaps Madeline had simply come out to the forest to collect mushrooms or winter roots. Perhaps she even wanted to hunt. Even now, Havilland was hoping it was something else.

The alternative was heartbreaking.

Quietly, she crept behind her sister, trying to stay low, ducking behind trees as she watched Madeline up ahead. The ground was soaked and icy, and more than once she slipped, trying not to make any noise as she did. Truthfully, she didn't know what she was going to do when she caught up to Madeline. What could she say to a woman who had lowered herself to something despicable and shameful?

Then, momentary self-doubt crept in. Was she to blame for all of this? Had she done something to drive her sister into the life of a traitor? Years of the competition between them had brought them to this point but Havilland couldn't honestly think of anything she would have done differently with Madeline. There wasn't a word or an action she regretted.

Havilland had been able to tolerate her sister's challenges and attempts at undermining, but if Madeline was truly intent on taking her rebellion to an entirely new level, then Havilland would have to do what was necessary in order to protect her people. She knew she wasn't to blame for her sister's behavior.

"*Dyna ferch cyfrwys.*"

A man grabbed her from behind, whispering those words in her ear. Startled, Havilland could feel something sharp against her torso and she immediately started to fight, using an elbow to try to ram the man but he jabbed her with what was most assuredly a dagger and she yelped as it poked through her clothing.

Now in full-blown panic, she began to fight and slap and kick, trying to grab the man by the hair but he had wedged himself in tightly behind her. She wasn't able to get a good grip on him but he, on the other hand, had an excellent grip on her. The two of them fell onto the forest floor, rolling around in the moldering leaves as Madeline, alerted by the sounds, came running.

"Evon!" Madeline cried. "Stop!"

Evon had Havilland pinned, her face in the dirt as he tried to suffocate her. Madeline, seeing that Evon was trying to kill her sister, screamed at him.

"Stop!"

Evon, winded from the fight, let up a bit, enough so that Havilland was able to pull her face out of the dirt. Gasping for air, she tried to hit him again and he came down on her, hard, but this time she was smart enough to turn her head so he couldn't push it into the earth again. Madeline ran over and grasped Evon by the arm, trying to pull him off of Havilland.

"Leave her alone!" Madeline yanked on Evon. "Get off of her!"

Evon wouldn't budge. He had Havilland pinned in a bad way, an arm twisted behind her back and his dagger still in his hand. "She was following you!"

"It is my sister!"

That caused Evon to falter. Curious, he peered down at the woman he had trapped beneath him. "Which one?"

"Havilland!" Havilland grunted, twisting beneath him. "Let me go!"

Evon got a good look at Havilland, or at least as much as he could with all of the dirt and leaves on her face and hair. "Havilland?" he repeated, surprised. "I've not seen Havilland in ten years. God's Bones, she's beautiful. What was she doing following you?"

"She left the castle and I wanted to see where she was going," Havilland answered the question, twisting and grunting beneath him. "'Tis not safe outside of the walls of the castle!"

Evon nodded. "That is a very true statement," he said. Suddenly, he stood up and yanked Havilland to her feet. He'd nearly broken her arm by the way he was twisting her around, now still causing her pain on the same arm as he yanked it. "So you were following your sister, eh? Now it looks like I have an important hostage to take to Madog's men."

Havilland, in pain and angry, was still trying to fight against him. "You are mad," she hissed. "Let me go, you fool."

Evon reached out to push some of her dark hair away, revealing her sweet face and lush lips. He grunted. "She'll make a fine prize," he muttered, looking her over. "In fact, I'll be able to sell her to the highest bidder. Have you been plundered, girl?"

Havilland was increasingly horrified with what she was hearing. "Plundered?" she repeated. "What does that mean?"

Evon had a lazy smile on his face. "Touched," he said. "Has a man touched that silken skin?"

Now she was disgusted as well as horrified. "That is none of your affair," she said. Then, she looked at Madeline. "Where were you going, Madeline? And why is Evon here waiting for you? Answer me!"

Madeline was standing a few feet away, a shocked look on her face. She was completely unlike the arrogant, aggressive girl they had all known. She looked cornered and scared.

"I... I...," she stammered, swallowed, and started again. "It is not like that, Havi. Evon and I love each other. We want to marry."

Disbelief filled Havilland's features. "Marry?" she spat with disgust. "Madeline, what have you done? Why were you meeting Evon in secret?"

As Madeline struggled to come up with an answer, Evon spoke. "Because Madeline believes as I believe," he said. "We believe castles in Wales should be ruled by the Welsh. The English have no place here. Madeline his helping restore our country to us."

Havilland's heart sank. *So she is the spy!* Less panicked and more distraught, Havilland focused on her sister. "Is this true?" she asked hoarsely. "Is that why they have been able to beat us down over the past few months? Because you have been telling them our weaknesses?"

Madeline met her sister's gaze but couldn't seem to bring herself to speak. Everything in her expression rang of shock, now joined by sorrow and defiance. Evon, seeing the distress between the two sisters, answered for her.

"Your father is mad, Havilland," he said. "Madeline has told me everything. A madman is in charge of Four Crosses and now his daughters are trying to defend it. Don't you see? It is time to surrender the fortress to those it belongs to. Four Crosses never belonged to your family, Havilland. It belongs to the Welsh. This is *our* land."

Sweet Jesú, it was true, all of it. The more Evon spoke, the more

Havilland could see the scope of Madeline's betrayal. She had to close her eyes against the knowledge that Madeline had told Evon about their father and the loss of his mind. Now all of the Welsh rebels knew, at least the ones that Evon had managed to tell. The illusion that Havilland had tried to keep up against the English had been shattered by the Welsh. They knew more than the English did now. She couldn't have possibly felt any more betrayed than she did at this moment, knowing Madeline had told the Welsh all of their secrets. There was nothing left now.

Nothing left except Four Crosses.

Havilland wasn't going to give in so easily. It wasn't in her nature. The most difficult thing she ever had to do in her young life was realize her sister wasn't to be trusted anymore. As of this moment, Madeline was the enemy. Had she not been so angry and disgusted, she would have wept over it.

But she had to get herself out of this predicament first. Time for weeping would be later.

"Then it seems we are at an impasse, Evon," Havilland finally said, forcing down her sorrows and her fears. "If you would kindly let go of my arm, I promise not to run or fight. Let us speak as civilized people and not as enemies."

Evon didn't see any reason not to believe her. Besides, he was taller and faster than she was and he was quite certain she couldn't outrun him. Letting go of her, he stepped away as she rubbed at her twisted arm. Evon kept the dagger in his hand, just in case he was forced to throw it at her. He wouldn't miss.

"Now," he said. "What did you wish to speak of? For certain, I am not in a position to negotiate Four Crosses with you. I will have to take you back to my encampment. You can discuss it with my leaders. Once they are finished with you, of course."

It was a lewd comment and he laughed at it but Havilland stared at him without reacting. She couldn't even bring herself to look at Madeline.

"I am not going back to your encampment," she said flatly. "I will return to Four Crosses and you can take this discussion back to your leaders."

Evon cocked his head. "Lady Havilland, you are my prisoner now," he said. "I am sorry if I did not explain that to you sufficiently. You are returning with me to camp."

"I am not."

Evon lost the faint smirk on his face. "I assure you that you will not make it back to Four Crosses alive," he said. "If you try, I will kill you. Then, Madeline will return and tell everyone that you accidentally fell into the river and drown. Your death would put Madeline in command for she tells me that she is second in command only to you. With Madeline in command, it will be a simple thing for her to make the decision to surrender the fortress. Then, when the English have been purged, Madeline and I will command Four Crosses together. Quite a tidy plan, actually."

Havilland looked at Madeline, then. She couldn't help it. She never thought she could hate her own flesh and blood so much.

"Is this true?" she asked. "Is this what you had planned?"

Madeline looked rather miserable. She looked at Evon for support in her reply but Havilland snapped at her.

"Look at me, Madeline de Llion," she said, watching her sister turn to her, warily. So much pain and angst flared up between them, filling the very air with emotion. "I asked you a question. Is this what you had planned? To force the surrender of Four Crosses so that you and Evon could command together?"

Madeline was so very torn. She'd spent so much of the past year resenting her sister and hating her that now that the moment had come for her to truly dominate the woman, she was having a difficult time doing it.

Now, she was second-guessing everything, fearful that Evon truly intended to kill her sister. She didn't know if she should take her sister's side and try to help her get away or take Evon's side and force Havilland to submit.

She made the coward's choice.

"Just surrender the fortress, Havi," she said, feeling resigned even as she said it. "He'll not let you leave until you agree."

Havilland felt as if she'd been stabbed in the gut by Madeline's words. The defeat in her eyes was painful. "He'll not let me leave, anyway," she said. "Did you not hear him? He plans to throw me in the river and say that I drown or he's going to take me back to his camp and sell me to the highest bidder."

Madeline shook her head, looking to Evon. "You won't do those things, will you?" she asked. "If she agrees to surrender the fortress, you will let her go?"

Evon frowned. "Why would I do that?" he said. "Listen to her; she told you what is going to happen to her. Even if she agrees to surrender the fortress now, I cannot let her go."

"Why not?"

"Are you truly so stupid? She will tell everyone that you are a traitor."

Madeline didn't particularly like that idea but she didn't want Havilland murdered because of it. She struggled to summon her courage against the man. "But you do not have to kill her or sell her," she said. "Please. I ask you not to do that. She is my sister and…."

"And *what*?" Evon cut her off rudely. "All I have heard from you is what a terrible commander she is and how unfair it is that she is in command and not you. And now you defend her?"

"Please don't kill her!"

Evon shook his head, turning to look at Havilland as she stood a few feet away. His eyes raked her. "She is very fine," he said. "It is a pity to have to treat her as anything other than a fine lady, but I have no choice. Therefore, I will make the choice yours, Madeline – either I kill her and throw her in the river or I take her back to camp and sell her. What is your choice?"

Madeline was horrified. She looked at Havilland only to be met by her sister's hateful glare. Madeline knew this was her fault, all of it, and her heart began to beat faster. Evon was putting her sister's life in her hands but the truth was that she didn't want to make that decision; she *couldn't* make it. She didn't want the responsibility now that she had it. Always wanting to be in command and hoping to be in command, was far different from actually having the power of the final decision.

Now, the power over Havilland was hers.

"You may as well kill me," Havilland said as Madeline agonized. "I will not allow you to return me to your camp so you may as well kill me. I am not afraid to die."

Evon's gaze lingered on her, standing tall and proud. "I do not expect that you are," he said. "But if that is your choice, so be it. Madeline is too much of a fool to make such a decision but you are not. I respect that. In fact, I…."

Havilland suddenly took off at a dead run, bolting back along the path in the direction of the castle. She was making her break for freedom, for help. She wasn't simply going to stand around and let Evon kill her.

Evon, with a hissed curse, took off after her, closing the gap between them fairly swiftly. He was within several feet of her when someone came flying out of the bramble, hitting him so hard that he went tumbling down the small incline and straight into the icy river below. The man that had hit him was also coming down the incline, charging like a runaway herd of cattle, tearing up trees and bramble, and as Evon came up out of the water, gasping for air, the man pounced on top of him and pushed his head under water.

Evon never stood a chance.

Strength beyond human strength held Evon's head down in the water as Jamison pinned the man on the shallow banks of the river, feeling the fight drain out of him. He'd been lurking in the bushes after following Havilland and Madeline down the narrow foot path. He soon realized that Havilland was in great danger when a man suddenly jumped out of the bushes and grabbed her.

But she'd put up a good fight, as Jamison had expected her to. Still, the man was stronger and tried to kill her. Jamison had been about to break his cover when Madeline had intervened and he watched, astonished, as Madeline and her Welsh lover had confessed everything for Havilland's ears.

As unfortunate as the situation was, Jamison was glad that Havilland heard the entire rotten conspiracy from Madeline's mouth. Or Evon's mouth, as it were. He heard Evon threaten to sell Havilland off to the highest Welsh bidder, something that filled him with rage. He also heard Evon discuss their plans for the future and how Havilland and Madeline's father was mad. *Mad, is he?* He didn't pay much attention to what was being said about Roald, however, because he was more concerned with Havilland's immediate future.

So he bided his time, listening, and waiting for his moment to pounce. When he heard Evon offer Madeline the choice of her sister's fate, he knew he couldn't wait much longer. He knew he had to make his move. His only concern had been making it to Havilland before Evon could, but Havilland had solved his dilemma by running away. Thank God she had run. With that move, he'd had a chance.

He took it.

Now, Evon Preece was dying beneath him, sucking in the icy waters of the River Banwy. On shore, he could hear Madeline screaming but he paid no attention to her, making sure Evon was quite dead before leaving the body in the water and making his way onto the shore. He was winded but not exhausted. He was, however, enraged, and all of that rage was focused on Madeline.

Havilland had hold of her sister by the edge of the water, her arms wrapped around Madeline so the woman wouldn't jump into the water to try and save Evon. Madeline was screaming at the top of her lungs, screaming even more when she saw the body of Evon floating down river with the current.

By the time Jamison climbed onto shore, it took every bit of strength he had not to charge Madeline. She was a woman, after all, and he would never take a hand to a woman no matter what the circumstances. But Madeline was sorely pushing his willpower. Walking up on Havilland and Madeline as they struggled, Jamison reached out a massive hand and grabbed Madeline by the neck, wresting her out of Havilland's grasp and pushing her back against the nearest tree trunk. She was pinned and unable to move.

Panicked, Madeline tried to kick and fight, her instincts as a warrior taking hold, but Jamison held her firm, more firmly still when she struggled. His face was in hers as she tried to dislodge his hand around her neck.

"Listen to me and listen well," he growled. "I stood by and watched while ye let someone threaten tae kill yer sister. Ye made no move tae save her except in yer weak and cowardly way so I'll tell ye now that ye belong tae me. Ye'll no longer be a threat tae Havilland or anyone else at Four Crosses. Those days are over. Ye are my prisoner tae do with as I see fit. Do ye understand?"

Madeline twisted and fought, her hands on his wrists as he held her fast. "You killed him!" she cried. "You killed Evon!"

It wasn't the answer Jamison was looking for. The grip on her neck tightened and he probably would have caused her to pass out had Havilland not laid a hand on his wrist, gently, so that he understood her silent message to ease up. But that was the only mercy she asked for her sister. She didn't speak another word about it. Even so, out of respect to Havilland, he eased his grip.

"I killed a threat tae everyone at Four Crosses," he snarled. "How long have ye been giving him information, Madeline? How long have ye let him use ye to betray yer family?"

Madeline was openly sobbing, all of the arrogance drained out of her. That proud, haughty girl was a shell of her former self. "I love him," she wept. "He loves me!"

Jamison thought she was rather pathetic because he could see that she believed what she was saying. Young, foolish, and having been caught in the biggest mistake of her life, Madeline probably didn't realize just how serious her actions were, even with the threat against her sister's life.

"Ye're a stupid lass," he rumbled. "He loved ye as far as the information ye gave him. When ye were of no more use tae him, I can promise ye that he'd have thrown ye in the river, too. Ye let him use ye and ye nearly let him kill yer sister."

"I would not have let him kill her!" Madeline shouted, spit flying from her lips and landing on his wrist. She was trembling, quaking in his grasp. "You must believe me! I would not have let him do it!"

Jamison jerked her away from the tree, pulling her up to the path with a grip on her arm so tight that nothing short of God's good command could have loosened it. Like a vise, it caused Madeline to gasp in pain as it bit into her tender flesh. But he didn't speak to her again as he began to drag her back up the path towards Four Crosses, towing her behind him as she tried to fight and dig her heels in. The harder she fought, the tighter his grip, until Madeline was all but sobbing from the pain of it.

She would have to atone for her sins and she knew it.

Havilland followed behind her sister and Jamison, heartbroken over the entire incident. Given what she'd just gone through with Madeline and Evon, and given how her sister had behaved, she was, perhaps, more heartbroken to realize that Madeline wouldn't have lifted a finger to help her. *Death or enslavement.* Madeline had been given the choice and rather than try to convince Evon to let Havilland go, Madeline had taken his question at face value as the only options she had.

While Havilland hoped that Madeline would not have chosen death for her, the truth was that she couldn't be sure. She didn't even know her sister anymore, this girl she had grown up with and experienced life and death with. Nay, this wasn't the same Madeline.

That Madeline was dead and gone.

She had to keep telling herself that as Jamison locked Madeline up in the vault of Four Crosses and, even then, as Jamison went to find Tobias and Thad to tell them what had occurred, Havilland sat on the steps leading down to the vault and listened to her sister sob for the rest of the day.

Truth was, she couldn't even summon the will to feel pity for her.

My God, Madeline... what have you become?

CHAPTER TWELVE

"Are ye going tae make me beg, lass…?"

"PREECE'S BODY IS going to be found by someone, at some point," Tobias pointed out. "Will they believe he simply fell into the river and drown or will they think someone killed him?"

It was sunset at Four Crosses as Jamison sat with Tobias and Thad in the great hall, now mostly vacant as servants moved about, preparing for the evening meal. The fire burned hotly in the big hearth and the dogs were spread out over the stones, warming themselves on a cold winter's evening.

Jamison was on his third cup of the average-tasting wine they kept at Four Crosses. The wine had been shipped from France according to the burn marks on the barrels but it was surprisingly mediocre. Jamison had noticed it from the beginning. But it wasn't so mediocre that it couldn't get a man drunk, which was all he was concerned with at the moment. He was a bit woozy but didn't care. He needed something to fortify him after the day he'd experienced.

"He drowned," Jamison said simply. "There is no great mystery tae it. Whoever finds him will think he fell intae the river and drowned."

Tobias shook his head still baffled by the entire situation. "Madeline," he muttered, sipping at his wine. "God's Bones, who knew she was capable of such things?"

"Not me."

"Do the men know? Surely they must have seen you take her to the vault."

Jamison shook his head. "Only a few at the gatehouse saw," he said. "The sergeant in charge has told the men not tae speak of it, tae anyone. He is also personally selecting men tae guard her, men he trusts. That should keep the rumors quiet for a while."

"But the men are going to eventually miss her, Jamie. She is always around."

"When the time comes, we will tell them the truth. But for now, out o' respect tae the family, we should keep it quiet."

Tobias couldn't disagree. His thoughts then shifted from Madeline back to the circumstances Jamison had described by the river's edge and the horrors therein.

"And Havilland," he said after a moment. "Had you not followed her, she would more than likely either be dead or someone's concubine by now. You saved her life."

Jamison didn't want to think about how close he came to losing Havilland but, on the other hand, it was *all* he could think about. The wine wasn't doing much to wipe away that terror. With a heavy sigh, he drained what was left in his cup and moved to pour himself more.

"I canna believe a sister would permit her own flesh and blood tae be threatened so," he said. "But it wasna just Havilland; it was all of us. She put all of us at risk feeding the Welsh information as she did."

Tobias nodded his head. "Agreed," he said. "My father shall know this. I am sure he will want to take Madeline with him when he departs back to Lioncross. I am not entirely sure what kind of punishment he will decide upon, her being a woman, but whatever it is, she will pay for her crimes. Treachery cannot go unpunished."

Jamison knew that. He took another big gulp of his wine. "But there is something more," he said, eyeing Tobias. "I heard Evon say something that may be the answer tae a question we have been asking ourselves since we arrived."

"What question is that?"

Jamison lifted his eyebrows, prefacing some very serious information. "He spoke of Madeline divulging the true sickness o' her father," he said. "Roald de Llion isna sick as we've been told, Tobias. Evon said that he has gone mad."

Tobias looked startled. "Mad?" he repeated in disbelief. "Is that why we have not seen the man for over a year?"

Jamison drank his fourth cup of wine in one swallow, standing up from the table and weaving unsteadily a bit. Wine always went straight to his head. "According tae Madeline, it 'tis," he replied. "And I am going tae discover the truth of it from Lady Havilland. If Roald is mad, then yer father will want tae know when he arrives. It changes things a bit."

Tobias nodded but he put out a hand to prevent Jamison from leaving the table. "Wait," he said. "Lady Havilland is probably averse to seeing you so soon after you put her sister in the vault, so I will go and speak with her. I've hardly had the time to speak with her since the battle ended."

Jamison looked at the man, squarely, thinking that now might be a good time to establish the line with Havilland. He couldn't blame Tobias for being interested in her but he couldn't let it go on. Tobias had to know that Havilland was not as unattached as he would have hoped. Jamison hoped that Tobias would understand and surrender his claim, as a proper gentleman would, but he wasn't so sure. Tobias had that de Lohr aggressiveness in him, something that served him well in battle but was misplaced in a situation such as this.

"There is a reason for that," Jamison said, trying to sound as non-confrontational as possible. "Lady Havilland is spoken for."

Tobias' eyes widened. "She is?" he asked. Then, his features flooded with disbelief. "How is that possible? I have heard nothing about this!"

Jamison tried not to smirk like a man who harbored a great secret. "Because it only just happened," he said. "I've asked Havilland tae be me wife. I would, therefore, appreciate it if ye kept a polite distance from her. She's not tae be trifled with."

Tobias looked him, dumbfounded. "You… you asked for…?"

"Her hand, aye."

It was clear that Tobias had no idea what to say. He stared at Jamison, his features wrought with shock, but the shock soon turned to disappointment and he lowered his gaze.

"I see," he said quietly. "I had no idea you had those thoughts about her, Jamie. Had I known, I would have told you that I had the very same thoughts."

Jamison already knew that but he didn't want to make it seem as if he had known. To do so would have been to insult Tobias. *I knew ye were interested but I wanted tae get tae her first….*

"Ye do?" he said, feigning ignorance. "Ye never told me."

"I know."

"Did she know?"

Tobias shook his head. "Nay," he replied. "I would not have told her. She would have probably spit in my eye. Havilland de Llion is a warrior above all. I do not think she gives credence to womanly emotions."

Jamison wasn't sure what he could say to that so he didn't say anything at all. He could tell that Tobias was upset by the news but, much to the man's credit, he didn't argue about it. He simply acknowledged it. Feeling rather bad that his friend was feeling some disappointment, he slapped a big hand on Tobias' shoulder.

"She does, more than ye think," he replied. "I will go speak wit' her now about her da. I'll let ye know what she tells me."

With that, he turned and walked away but a soft hail from Tobias stopped him. Jamison came to a halt, turning to look at his friend. When Tobias saw that he had his attention, he took a step or two towards him, curiously.

"When you asked Havilland to be your wife, what did she say?" he asked.

So he isna going to go quietly, Jamison thought. "She agreed," he lied.

Tobias simply nodded his head, looking rather like a kicked dog about the whole thing. Jamison felt bad for the man but not badly enough to try and comfort him. That would have been odd. Departing the hall and leaving Tobias to nurse his wounded heart and wounded pride, Jamison headed back to the gatehouse where the vault was, the last place he had seen Havilland.

His thoughts switched to her quickly and easily. She was never far from his thoughts, anyway, so it was easy to open his mind and let her blow in like a breeze, touching everything about him. He drew in a deep, cleansing breath as he crossed the bailey, gazing up into the sky and seeing that the mist was starting to form again as dusk drew near. The smells from the pig the cook had been boiling all day were heavy in the air, making the men hungry, and Jamison found himself wondering what the evening meal would be like with Madeline in the vault and traumatized Havilland and Amaline. Truth be told, he was fairly traumatized himself about the entire thing.

The gatehouse drew near and he disappeared into the small doorway with the stairs that led down to the sublevel below. There were two cells down there, very small, and a big, fatted torch burned heavily in an iron sconce, giving off a good deal of light as he came to the bottom of the steps and looked around. Madeline was still where he'd put her, in the first cell, sleeping heavily on a pile of fresh straw and a blanket someone had given her. He didn't even feel any pity when he looked at her, knowing what she had done. But there was no Havilland down here so he made his way back up the stairs and asked the first soldier he came across if he'd seen Havilland. The sentry pointed in the direction of the stables.

Following the woman's trail, he ended up in the stables that housed several big horses belonging to the knights. He found his own horse there, a shaggy black mount he'd purchased in Edinburgh. Slapping the horse on the arse affectionately, he came to a halt when he heard soft female voices. He looked around but saw no one until he realized they were coming from overhead in the loft. Finding the nearest ladder, he climbed up.

In the corner of the low-ceilinged loft, which was strewn with piles of hay, he could see Havilland and Amaline off in a corner where there seemed to be some kind of storage area. The young women were speaking softly, sitting before a pair of big trunks and rummaging through what looked like clothing. Fabric was everywhere. Jamison came off the ladder and made his way across the loft, nearly bent in half because of the low ceiling. Amaline was the first one to see him and she let out a yelp of surprise, causing Havilland to swiftly turn to him. When she saw that it was Jamison, she gave him a half-smile.

"You startled us, my lord," she said.

He took a knee a few feet away so he was able to straighten out his neck. "My apologies," he said. "I dinna mean tae. I heard yer voices from down below. What are ye doing?"

Havilland pointed to the trunks. "These are our mother's belongings," she said. "She had a great many clothes and we are looking for something serviceable for Alis de Lara's party."

The warm expression faded from Jamison's face, glancing at Amaline before speaking. "Ye still wish tae go?" he asked hesitantly. "After what happened today?"

Havilland looked at Amaline, who was sitting on her bum, looking at a dress in her lap. She sighed faintly. "Ammie knows," she said quietly. "I told her everything. I told her what Madeline did and I told her how you saved me."

Jamison looked at the young woman with the wild red hair. "I see," he said quietly. "'Tis unfortunate what happened with Madeline. I just checked on her. She was sleeping."

Havilland was touched that he would show her sister polite concern no matter what she had done. To her, that spoke of the man's true character, as a merciful captor. "And the men?" she asked. "Do they know what she has done?"

Jamison shook his head. "Only the sergeant in charge of the gatehouse and a few trusted men know," he said. "There is no need tae announce tae the world what Madeline has done. We shall keep the matter private for now."

"What are you going to do with her?" Amaline's head came up, her question directed at Jamison. "Are you going to keep her in the vault?"

It was the first time the young woman had actually spoken to him. Most of the time, she hid from him, frightened like a rabbit. He answered honestly.

"What Madeline has done is a very bad thing," he said. "I am holding her for Lord de Lohr's arrival. 'Tis he who will decide her fate."

"Lord de Lohr is coming?" Havilland asked. "Have you sent for him already?"

Jamison nodded. "Brend rode for Lioncross this morning," he said quietly. "Given what was happening with yer sister, I felt it necessary tae summon the man."

Havilland knew that. She knew her sister was in a huge amount of trouble. Her feelings were still torn, in so many ways. "I understand," she said, looking at the garments in her lap. "What do you think he will do?"

Jamison wouldn't tell her what he really thought. The situation was still too fragile given the upheaval of Madeline's capture. He'd spoken briefly on it yesterday when he first informed her of Madeline's treachery but he didn't want to elaborate, not now. He didn't want to upset her and Amaline more than they already were.

"I dunna know," he said. It was the truth, he really didn't. "But de Lohr is wise man. Trust that he'll do the right thing."

"I hope he keeps her in the vault," Amaline muttered.

Both Jamison and Havilland looked at the youngest sister. "What did you say, Ammie?" Havilland asked.

Amaline's head came up and she looked at her sister, frowning deeply. "I said that I hope he keeps her in the vault," she said. "Madeline is mean and terrible. She yells at me and tries to push me around… and she tries to tell the men not to obey you, Havi. You know that. And now that she has tried to kill you… I do not want her to come out of the vault, not ever. Our lives will be much better if she does not."

It was a surprising statement from a young woman who never voiced her opinion and Havilland felt a good deal of pity for her youngest sister. She knew that Madeline pushed Amaline around quite a bit, ordering her about constantly. She also knew that they were exceptionally close, so she had some doubts about Amaline's desire to keep Madeline in the vault. She couldn't really imagine that she meant it. Still, Havilland's thoughts lingered on the sister who had ruined her life forever.

"Well," she said softly, "I suppose Lord de Lohr will decide what is to be done with her. As much as it pains me to say it, I will not plead for her. I think she would only try to do it again. I do not believe she will ever amend her ways and that is a very sad thing for me to say. She is my sister and I am supposed to support her, but the truth is that she was more than willing to let me die and watch Four Crosses be destroyed. Even if Lord de Lohr were to release her out of pity, I would not want her here. I could never trust her again."

Jamison could see how torn she was about the situation. "I canna say that I blame ye."

"Nor I," Amaline said. She set the garment on her lap back into the trunk and stood up, brushing the hay from her breeches. Her gaze found Jamison, shyly. "Thank you for saving my sister. I never really knew my mother, you see, and Havilland is the closest thing I have to one. Thank you for… well, just thank you."

Quick as a flash, she ran to him, pecked him on the cheek, and scurried from the loft, leaving Jamison watching her go with a grin on his face. When he turned to Havilland, he saw that she was grinning, too.

"She is probably mortified at herself for doing that," Havilland said quietly, watching him chuckle. "It took all of the courage she had."

Jamison shifted so he was sitting on his bum. "Good," he said. "That means she was sincere."

Havilland watched him settled is big body down on the straw. "She is," she said. "Amaline is one of the most honest people you will ever meet, unlike Madeline. But she is also very close to Madeline in spite of what she has said. How I have two sisters so completely different in character, I will never know."

Jamison leaned back on one big arm. "That happens in families," he said. "I have three brothers. Me eldest brother, George, is meek and studious. He is tae take me father's place as chief of our clan someday but he doesna want tae do it. He'd rather be a priest. Then, there is Robbie, who is younger than I am. A greater rascal has never existed. Hector is the youngest and a good deal like me."

Havilland was listening with interest. "You have mentioned George before," she said. "But I've not heard you mention Robbie or Hector."

Jamison grunted. "Because it was Robbie I was defending when I killed a man," he said. "I wasna intending tae forgive him for sending me back intae England but I think I can now."

"Why?"

"Because had I not come, I wouldna met ye."

Havilland grinned, averting her gaze. She had no idea how to respond to him, untried in the ways of courtship as she was, but she was getting a little better at it. She liked it when he flattered her like that.

"Had the Welsh not attacked us, you would never have come to Four Crosses," she said. "I suppose it is strange to be grateful for dangerous situations, but in this case, I… I suppose that I am also glad the Welsh attacked."

He leaned in her direction, flirting openly with her. "Are ye, lass?" he asked. "Does that mean ye've thought more on me marriage proposal?"

She flushed red, unwilling to look at him. "Mayhap."

"And?"

She kept turning her head because he was trying to look her in the face, moving closer and closer. The closer he drew, the more she turned her head away to the point where she had to turn her back on him. But Jamison wouldn't let her. Reaching out, he grabbed her by the shoulders and spun her about, causing her to fall back against the trunk. He was right next to her, his big body against hers, his warmth scorching her tender flesh.

Having never been this close to a man that she felt something for, Havilland was having difficulty breathing. He was big and fleshy, powerful and handsome… and his nearness to her… *Sweet Jesú*, his nearness had her entire body quivering. When a big hand came up to touch her cheek, she thought she might faint dead away.

"And?" he pressed, his voice a husky whisper.

Havilland's heart was pounding against her ribs as she gazed into his eyes. A deep, dark shade of blue that looked like a sapphire she'd seen once. Had he asked her a question? She couldn't even remember what it was.

"Are ye going tae make me beg, lass?"

She was breathless, her mouth dry. "Beg… beg for what?"

"For an answer," he murmured. "Will ye be me wife."

She nodded. She couldn't manage anything more than that. With a grin on his face that nearly made her swoon, Jamison's lips slanted over hers, gently at first, acquainting her with his touch. He wanted this kiss to be careful and sweet and special, a promise of things to come, but the moment he tasted her, he knew this kiss wouldn't be a brief one.

It was going to take all of his strength not to ravage her.

Warmth. Honey. Sweetness. Those were the thoughts rolling through his mind as he touched her, his first impressions. *Sweet Jesú*, he could smell her and it was an intoxicating mixture he'd never smelled before – her own sweet musk mingled with leather and something that smelled fresh, like green leaves. He couldn't quite put his finger on what it was but all he knew was that it excited him beyond reason. It filled him. *She* filled him.

He had to have more.

His hands were on her face, snaking into her hair. He knew he was overwhelming her with his attentions, but he didn't care. All he cared about was satisfying this hunger he seemed to have about her, this inherent need to possess her. He knew he'd pushed her about marriage and he'd very well pushed himself on her in general, but he was a man who knew what he wanted. He was determined to have her even if he had to force her into it.

Somehow, his mouth was moving along her face now, that sweet and beautiful face that had first caught his attention. Her skin was smooth and her lips, those lush and full lips, drove him mad. Her big green eyes with their dark lashes and delicately arched brows, were kissed and kissed again, just because he could. And she was letting him. He could feel her trembling beneath him, little sighs of pleasure feeding his lust. There was so much he could do to her now, in the privacy of the loft.

But so much he wouldn't.

For the first time in his life, Jamison was aware that he wanted to take his time with a woman. He'd experienced a lot of women in his life, the brawny and sexy beast that he was, and he'd looked upon all of them as a conquest of sorts. Some were simply sport to him. But Havilland didn't fall into any of those categories. She was naive and unspoiled, and he liked that about her. He wanted to take his time with her, to teach her what it meant to physically satisfy a man. To satisfy *him*. As his wife, he wanted her to know everything that made his heart race, something she seemed to be able to do with frightening ease.

"Mayhap I shouldna done that," he murmured, his lips against her jaw, gently kissing her, before finally pulling away and looking her in the eye. "But I've been a-wantin' tae do that since nearly the first I met ye."

Breathless and very close to swooning, Havilland struggled to regain her composure. "That… that is not true."

He frowned, gently done. "Why would ye say that?"

She swallowed but there was a glimmer of humor in her eye as she spoke. "The first time you saw me, you spanked me," she said. "And then you threatened to spank me every time you saw me. There is a distinct difference between spanking and kissing."

He grinned, rolling his eyes at their rough beginning. "Aye, now," he said, shrugging as if to defend himself, "there is a distinct difference between kissing and spanking, but in this case, when I said 'spank', I shoulda said 'kiss'."

She smiled because he was. "That is *not* what you meant."

"It 'tis, I tell ye!"

She laughed softly. "You also said I was a disgrace to my sex," she said. "Did you mean that?"

He looked at her, then, a big hand coming up to cup her face. The power from his gaze was intense. "I meant tae say that ye're the most beautiful and brave woman I've ever met," he said in a voice that sent chills up her spine. Gooseflesh popped out on her arms. "I've never in me life met someone as remarkable as ye, so remarkable that I knew I had tae make ye me wife. No one else is worthy of ye, Havilland. Only me."

Oh, the chills that continued to run up her spine as she met his gaze, feeling the heat from the man, feeling his sincerity and his interest. Her breathing still hadn't righted itself, made worse by the expression on his face. When he leaned forward and kissed her again, tenderly, she swore she saw sparks flying before her eyes. Whenever the man touched her, it was as if a fire was igniting somewhere deep in her soul.

"I… I have never had anyone say such things to me," she whispered. "I told you that I am not a fine lady and men seem to want beautiful and refined women. I do not know the first thing about being beautiful and refined. Surely… surely you do not want a wife who dresses in tunics and breeches."

He gave her a half-grin, looking over at the dresses that were strewn about from the open trunks. "Ye would do justice tae any one of those dresses," he told her. "Anything ye wear will look glorious on ye, including tunics and breeches. I'm not marrying yer wardrobe, Havilland – I'm marrying ye, and if ye come tae me in breeches and tunics, then so be it. The real treasure is what is inside the clothes, not the clothes themselves."

Havilland sighed at the sweetness of his words but at the same time, she was shaking her head at him in disbelief. "I cannot believe my lack of wardrobe doesn't concern you," she said. "It is too good to believe. You truly do not care?"

He shrugged. "I want ye tae be happy," he said. "If ye want tae wear dresses like other women, then do it. But dunna do it because ye think I want ye tae."

She looked over at the dresses, too. "I would not," she said "But… but my sisters and I were only recently discussing how it is Papa's doing that we dress as we do and fight as we do. Never having sons, he raised us as sons after my mother passed away. He told us he wanted to be proud of us and fighting at his side was the way to do it, so we did."

He was listening with interest. "But ye made it seem as if this is what ye wanted as well."

Havilland shook her head. "I do not honestly know," she said. "We were all so young when my mother died and Papa set forth to make us his sons. We did it because we were told to, not because we had a choice. Now it has become a way of life. Earlier today, Madeline was telling me how she did not intend to dress this way any longer. She said she wanted a home and husband and family and… well, that will not happen now for her. We were pulling out these dresses to attend Alis de Lara's party but I do not suppose we can go to that now, either."

Jamison didn't think it would be wise, or in the best taste, to leave Four Crosses with everything that had happened. "Ye would feel comfortable going tae a festival with yer sister in the vault, facing an uncertain future?"

Havilland shook her head. "I did not mean it the way it sounded," she said, although she sounded disappointed. "It was simply an observation."

Jamison didn't particularly believe her. He knew she'd had her heart set on going to the celebration. "If I offered tae still escort ye, would ye go?"

Havilland shook her head. "It does not seem right to do that with

Madeline locked away," she said. "It would be difficult for me to enjoy myself. No matter what she has done, she is still my sister. Going to a festival would seem as if we were somehow celebrating her captivity. It would seem irreverent."

He was glad she showed some restraint and common sense given the situation. Havilland was not a silly woman, in any case, and she understood the seriousness of what was going on around them, and no matter how she felt about her sister, going off to a party while Madeline was in the vault would have been an unsavory thing to do. Reaching out, he took her hand, bringing her fingers to his lips for a gentle kiss.

"I am sorry ye'll not be able tae go," he said quietly. "But I am not sorry that I was forced tae act against her. Madeline's situation is of her own doing."

"I know."

He continued to kiss her fingers, calloused and dirty from the fighting life she led, but it didn't matter to him. They were the sweetest fingers he'd ever sampled. But in thinking on the situation with Madeline, he was reminded of something else that had been said during the conversation he'd listened to between Madeline and Havilland and Evon. A small matter of Roald de Llion and his true state of health.

Given the circumstances, Jamison felt he had a right to know the truth. Perhaps this was the moment for it.

"If I ask ye a question, will ye tell me honestly?" he asked quietly.

Havilland was watching him kiss her fingers, fascinated and upswept in her first real taste of affection. "I will always be honest with you."

"Good," he said, eyeing her a moment before continuing. "When ye were speaking with Evon and Madeline, I heard Evon say that Madeline had told him the truth about yer father and that the man was mad. Will you tell me truthfully what yer father's affliction is, Havilland? Why has no one been able tae see the man for over a year?"

The warmth on her features faded as she realized he was asking her a direct question about her father. It caught her off-guard, to be truthful. One moment they were speaking of Madeline and of the festival they would not attend, and in the next moment they were speaking of Roald. Havilland realized that this was a defining moment. At this point, she usually panicked and tried to change the subject, but this time, it would be different. Different because she knew she could no longer continue the charade.

It was time to tell the truth.

There was no way she could lie to Jamison; to do it would be to destroy the fragile trust building between them. But she was so used to being evasive about her father that there was a lie on her lips before she even thought about it. She had to force herself to swallow that lie, to push it aside in favor of an admission she hoped she'd never have to make. But if Jamison had already heard about her father's difficulties from Evon, then there was no use denying what he'd heard. He already knew.

The time for truth had come.

"Come with me," she murmured.

Jamison did. He followed Havilland from the loft, down the ladder and out of the stables. He walked beside her beneath the building mist of the coming night but kept a proper distance, difficult because he wanted very much to hold her hand. So he clasped his big fingers behind his back, holding tightly to his own hands so he wouldn't forget himself and make a grab for her. After that brief taste in the loft, he very much wanted to savor her again.

Many thoughts were rolling through his mind as he followed her, not the least of which was the fact that she was taking him somewhere, presumably in answer to his question about her father. He didn't ask her and she didn't offer, but he had a feeling he was about to meet Roald de Llion, the first person to see the man in well over a year outside of his family. But that anticipation and curiosity was nothing like the reality of it once Havilland took him into the keep and up to a third floor chamber that smelled as if an animal live there.

In that dark and smelly bower, Jamison discovered the truth about the once-great warrior known as Roald de Llion.

CHAPTER THIRTEEN

He very much wanted to give her some joy in life....

"MAD," TOBIAS HISSED. "I would have never have guessed that was why they have been keeping Roald out of sight. Completely mad, you say?"

Jamison nodded his head. "Aye," he replied. "The man thought Havilland was his dead wife. He canna speak anything other than his dead wife's name, apparently. I spent a few minutes with the man tae see his state for meself and believe me when I say that it was enough. 'Tis not a man in that chamber but a vegetable. Roald de Llion, as people knew him, no longer exists."

Tobias was nearly beside himself with astonishment. "And the three sisters have been commanding the fortress for the past two years by themselves? That is nothing short of remarkable."

Again, Jamison nodded. "According tae Havilland, her father started showing signs of his madness a couple of years ago," he said. "As of last year, he could barely communicate so they keep him in a chamber with a servant tae tend his needs. The sisters have been trying tae keep the illusion alive that Roald is still in command. And they've been doing a damn fine job of it."

No one could argue with that. The truth about Roald de Llion was a startling revelation but, in hindsight, not a completely surprising one, at least for the de Lohr knights. They had been dealing with Four Crosses and Roald de Llion far longer than Jamison had been and the man's absence the past year had been a great mystery, as they had mentioned many times. Now, they knew why. Jamison had been able to establish such trust with Havilland that she had told him the shocking truth.

A shocking truth with many far-reaching implications.

It was late in the night now, well after the evening meal and well after everyone had retired for the night. Havilland and Amaline had retired together, sleeping in the same bed to lament what had become of Madeline, leaving Jamison and Tobias and Thad in the solar that had become home to them, discussing what had been a far too eventful day. With Madeline's treachery and now the truth about Roald revealed, there was quite a bit to absorb.

They were still trying to process it.

"My father is going to be very interested in what has happened around here," Tobias said, thinking on how his father would react to the news of his old friend Roald. "Not only does he have a decision to make about Madeline, but now he has to decide what to do with Four Crosses. He cannot leave Havilland in command."

Jamison was sitting in front of the hearth, warming his thin blood. "Nay," he said. "But he can leave me in command when I marry the woman."

Tobias looked at him, quickly, as if he'd forgotten all about the fact that Jamison had proposed marriage to Havilland. There was a flash of disappointment, again, that he quickly quelled, turning instead to fill his wine cup with that cheap French wine. Like a bad dream, the subject had come up again and it wasn't any easier the second time around.

"Is that what marrying her is about?" he asked. "Gaining command of Four Crosses?"

Jamison didn't flare to what could have been construed as an insult. "Ye know me better than that," he said. "This old fortress holds no beauty tae me and certainly not enough tae hunger for the command."

Tobias did, indeed, know better but it was his disillusionment talking. "With no father to ask permission, I suppose you had your way made simple in obtaining the lady's hand," he said, sipping at his wine. "But if Roald is truly mad and Havilland has no other menfolk in her family, I believe the question of marriage should be proposed to my father. She is his vassal, after all."

"Marriage?" Thad, who was stretched out on his bed in the corner, suddenly rolled over. "Lady Havilland and Jamison are getting married?"

Tobias frowned at him. "This does not concern you, little maggot," he said, waving a hand at him. "Roll over and go back to sleep. Let the men talk."

Thad, the youngest cousin of four boys, was used to being bullied but he didn't like it. He was a knight, too, just like they all were and he didn't take kindly to belittling. Tobias wasn't usually so combative, which upset him.

"I am in command here, too," he pointed out. "You needn't get so nasty. I had not heard that Jamison and Lady Havilland were getting married. Is it true?"

"It 'tis," Jamison said before Tobias could reply. He eyed Tobias as he spoke. "I have asked the lady and she has agreed. Tobias, I know ye were sweet on the lass, but she belongs tae me now. I've told ye that. I am trying tae be sympathetic tae yer disappointment but becoming belligerent wit' me will only gain ye me fist tae yer face. Am I making meself clear? And if ye harass Havilland about it, that will bring me wrath twice as fast."

Tobias met Jamison's gaze for a moment, challengingly, as Thad watched the pair with some concern. He could see, clearly, the trouble between Jamison and Tobias, surprising as it was. He never thought a woman would cause hard feelings between the two and given that it was Lady Havilland had him quite surprised. He didn't know why he hadn't sensed any of this before.

"Is there going to be a battle over this?" Thad wanted to know, looking at the glares between Tobias and Jamison. "Tobias, we've all known you were fond of Lady Havilland but you never did a thing about it. You cannot be angry because Jamison did. Besides, if you two go to battle, my money is on Jamison. He will mop the floor with you and toss you out with the water."

Jamison tried not to grin at the comment, turning his face away from an outraged Tobias as Thad laid back down on his bed and rolled over so he was facing the wall. Infuriated, Tobias picked up the nearest object, which happened to be a cup, and threw it at Thad, hitting him in the buttocks. As Thad yelped, rolled over, and threw the cup back at Tobias' head, Jamison stood up.

"Enough," he said, deftly catching the cup in mid-air. "The situation is settled. Madeline is in the vault, Roald de Llion is mad, and Havilland and I shall be wed. Let us put the focus where it should be – on the events o' the day. Much has happened and I feel a good deal of pity for Havilland and Amaline. Their world was shaken today, badly."

Tobias was still riled up, still focused on his petulant cousin and the loss of Havilland. "It could not be helped," he said. "Better we discover Madeline's treachery now than in a day or week or even a month when the Welsh attack us again using her information. And as far as Roald is concerned, they should have told us that long ago.

It was true, but it was a rather blunt statement. Jamison was feeling a bit kinder than Tobias was. "'Tis a terrible thing that Havilland and Amaline have suffered through today," he said. "Discovering their sister tae be a spy was a bloody dirty thing. As if they dunna have enough trouble with the Welsh without Madeline's treachery, like havin' yer heart cut tae shreds. So much sorrow around this place as of late. In fact, I thought today we might have a bit o' light on their situation."

Tobias was pouring himself more wine, spilling it out of the cup in his agitation. "And what was that?"

Jamison shrugged. "As of this morning, the poor lasses thought they would be attendin' a festival," he said. "With everything that has happened, it wouldna be right tae go. But I was thinking…."

Tobias didn't much care what Jamison had been thinking as he drank his wine, but Thad did. "What, Jamie?" he asked.

Jamison rubbed at his stubbled chin. "Well," he said slowly, "'tis a fact that Havilland and her sisters were desperate tae attend Alis de Lara's festival. They pulled out their mother's old trunks tae find something decent tae wear. All women want tae go tae festivals, dunna they? Those three were no different."

Thad shrugged. "And?"

Jamison sat down again, leaning back against the chair. "I watched them this evening during the meal," he said. "Havilland and Amaline looked so… sad. And why shouldna they? A mad father, a sister who tried tae kill all of us… they're too young tae know such heartache. Neither one of them has even attended a festival or even a mass or a party because their father wouldna let them. Havilland told me so. He never let them do anything that young ladies do. So I was thinking… if we canna take them tae a festival, what if we had a festival here?"

Thad sat up, his features alight with the suggestion. "A festival!" he said. "What did you have in mind?"

Jamison shrugged. "We canna have a real festival," he said. "We've no musicians for dancing and we've no entertainment. But we could have games for the ladies tae watch. Contests and the like."

By this time, even Tobias was listening. "Games?" he repeated. "Jamie, the people of Four Crosses are trying to rebuild their castle. The threat of Welsh attacks is hanging over our head, every single day. Madeline de Llion is in the vault as a prisoner and Roald de Llion has been exposed as being mad… and *you* want to have games in the midst of this?"

Jamison knew his suggestion sounded rather foolish and frivolous, but the truth was that he'd been thinking of it for most of the evening, ever since Havilland realized they wouldn't be going to Alis de Lara's festival. He hated to see her so disappointed. The woman had so little happiness in her life and with the event of her sister's capture and the revelation of her father's health, he felt compelled to bring something happy to her. Something to make her smile.

He very much wanted to give her some joy in a life that had been rife with darkness.

"The wall is mostly repaired," he said to Tobias' statement. "The gatehouse is strong; everything about the castle is strong. Tobias, these people have been suffering months of Welsh attacks and terrible threats. For one day, mayhap they'd like tae forget all of that. I'm sure Havilland and Amaline would. So we take the entire east side of the bailey, where the troop house is, and we arrange spectacles – wrestling, hammer-throwing, archery – and we let the men compete and enjoy themselves. And we let Havilland and Amaline dress in their mother's clothing and, for once in their lives, feel like ladies. They can be the queens of their own festival. It would lift their spirits at the very least."

Thad slapped his thigh. "I think it is a perfectly marvelous suggestion," he said. "What is the harm, Tobias? We will be inside the fortress the entire time. And wouldn't you like to beat Jamie at something?"

Tobias was actually quite attracted to the idea but didn't want to show just how much he was. He frowned at Thad before looking to Jamison. "Of course I would like to beat him," he said, "but I think this suggestion is in poor taste."

Jamison knew that but he just couldn't get past the hope of cheering Havilland up. It was all he could think of. "Mayhap," he said. "But it would be a good way for the men tae feel some relaxation and relief as well. It would lift morale."

Thad nodded eagerly. "It would definitely lift morale," he said, looking at his cousin. "What do you say, Tobias? I think this is an excellent idea."

Tobias sighed faintly, looking at Thad and how excited his young cousin was. He knew it would be a good opportunity to lift the men's spirits after some terrible struggles. But he couldn't agree completely, not just yet.

"Mayhap," he said after a moment. "But one thing is certain; no matter if I am victorious against Jamie, and I will be, it seems that he already has the best prize in the house."

He meant Havilland. Jamison gave him a half-grin. He wasn't going to let Tobias beat him down about the situation any longer. The man was going to have to face facts.

"So compete tae carry Amaline's favor," he said. "Do ye know what a thrill ye'd give the girl? She'd remember it the rest o' her life."

Thad completely agreed. "That is true, she would."

Jamison looked to the young knight with a smile on his face before returning his focus to Tobias. "Well?" he said. "What say ye, man?"

Tobias looked at the pair, seeing the enthusiasm in their eyes. Truth be told, he was enthusiastic for it, too. He loved competition and a good game or two, and it was well known he was a sportsman. Tobias had a great competitive streak in him which was why he wasn't so willing to graciously concede defeat with Havilland. In fact, he was coming to think that if he impressed Havilland enough at a sporting event or two, she might reconsider her commitment to Jamison.

It was a hope, anyway.

"Who will organize it?" he asked.

Jamison extended a hand to him. "I was thinking ye would, Tobias. Ye're good at that sort of thing."

That put a new spin on the situation. Tobias would be in charge of the games, which he liked. He could pick the best opponents for himself. What he didn't realize, however, was that Jamison had purposely asked the man to arrange things, hoping that would bring Tobias out of his funk and give him something of a distraction. It worked; Tobias was already focused on what was coming but for different reasons than what Jamison thought.

Tobias was going to try to win himself a wife.

"Then we will start right away," he said. "I will gather some of the off watch soldiers and clear out the bailey by torch light. We should be able to designate an arena and even build a viewing platform for Havilland and Amaline to watch from."

Jamison lifted his eyebrows. "Ye'll start tonight?"

Tobias shrugged. "Why not?" he said. "I have the night watch. I can be doing something else with my time other than watch the mists form over the hills."

"Ye're supposed tae be watching for Welsh."

"I'll have hundreds of pairs of eyes on the wall that can do that while I go about other tasks."

Jamison didn't argue with him. He'd put the man in charge of the games, after all, and if he wanted to get started right away, all the better. Perhaps by morning, they'd have something to show for it and, perhaps in some small way, Havilland might find a bit of joy from it all. At least, that was the hope.

Let the games begin.

CHAPTER FOURTEEN

"We cannot keep the charade up any longer..."

HAVILLAND HAD SLEPT well past dawn.

Buried in the bed her parents used to share, her back pressed against Amaline's back in an attempt to stay warm against the cold winter's night, the two of them had slept relatively heavily given the burdens on their minds from the day's events. Havilland's sleep had been full of dreams, however, dreams of attacks and rivers and redheaded Highlanders. It had been a busy night of dreaming and towards morning, she slept dreamlessly, finally able to relax.

Oddly enough, however, she awoke to sunlight streaming in between the windowsill and a gap in the oiled cloth that covered it. She hadn't seen sunlight in the morning in months, for they were in the dead of winter and the mornings were almost always gloomy. But not this morning; looking around the room, it seemed very bright and the fire had been stoked, which was odd considering she hadn't heard a servant come in. In fact, there were bathing things laid out, like soap and towels and combs. Someone had been busy in this room and she hadn't even been aware.

And then she saw it.

One of her mother's gowns was carefully draped over a cushioned oak chair that her father used to sit on to ease his aching back. It was a big chair, with a pillow on the seat, but she couldn't see the pillow or much of the chair for that matter because of the dresses draped over it. Puzzled, she sat up in bed and rubbed her eyes.

When Havilland finished rubbing her eyes and looked again, the dresses were still there. Her puzzlement grew and she climbed out of bed, careful not to wake her sister, and tiptoed over to the dresses. She recognized them as garments she had seen in her mother's trunks; one was a deep blue *tiretaine*, a very fine woolen fabric, with elaborate gold embroidery around the neckline and at the elbows, and the other one was a dark green brocade that had strips of green-dyed leather finely sewn into the skirt. With the rounded neckline and angel's wing-type sleeves, which were sleeves that draped elegantly from the wrists to the floor, the green dress was particularly lovely.

Baffled, Havilland fingered the dresses, wondering how in the world they had gotten into the room, when she glanced over at a second chair and saw a myriad of cloaks, scarves, and belts thrown onto it. There were even a few pairs of shoes on the floor next to it. Scratching her head, she went over to the second chair and fingered through everything that had been placed on it.

As she mulled over the miraculous appearance of the clothing, the chamber door creaked open and a serving woman appeared, the same serving woman who had tended those in the keep for years. Burdened with a tray of food, she was an older woman who had once served Havilland's mother. When the woman looked up and saw that Havilland was awake, she grinned.

"So you are awake, m'lady," she said. "Good. I was a-feared I was going to have to awaken you."

Havilland eyed the woman strangely. "Why?" she asked. "And where did these clothes come from?"

The serving woman paused to look at the dresses, her expression almost loving. "I remember when your mother wore those garments," she said, her tone wistful. "She was so beautiful in them. I think they should fit you because you are about her size, but Lady Amaline is smaller than you are. I fear I will have to alter the dress a bit to make it wearable for her."

Havilland was still puzzled. "We will not be needing these," she said, looking around. "Where is the clothing I left here last night?"

The serving woman went to set the tray down on the small table that was near the hearth. "I was told to take those breeches away from you," she said. "You are to wear one of those dresses today and you are not to ask any questions. Sir Jamison told me to tell you that."

Havilland's eyebrows lifted. "He did?" she asked. Then, she shook her head firmly. "But… but I cannot wear one of these garments."

"Why not?"

She looked at the dresses almost fearfully. "I… I have no need to," she said. "Bethan, what nonsense is going on? Where is my clothing?"

The serving woman simply grinned and moved away from her, heading towards the door. "Pick which dress you wish to wear and I shall return with warmed water to help you bathe," she said. "Sir Jamison will be coming for you shortly and you will want to be ready."

Now, frustration was joining her puzzlement. Havilland put her hands on her hips. "Ready for *what*?" she said. "Start making sense, woman."

The serving woman giggled. "You will see, my lady," she said as she went through the door. "You will see. Do as you are told and ask no questions. Pick a dress to wear!"

With that, she was gone, the door shutting behind her. Annoyed, Havilland started to follow but quickly realized she was in her night shift and had no other clothing to wear since her breeches and tunic were missing. She wasn't about to go out with only her night shift on so she turned, again, with some fear, back to the dresses that were laid out on the chair.

So Jamison was behind this nonsense? Was he, in fact, forcing her to dress like a woman now? He told her yesterday that he cared not what she wore but that was evidently a lie. He must care very much, indeed, if he was sending dresses up to her chamber for her to wear and stealing her breeches in the meanwhile. It was all greatly confusing and quite hurtful. As she went to pick up the green dress, gingerly, Amaline stirred over on the bed.

"What is happening, Havi?" she questioned as she sat up, yawning. "I heard Bethan."

Havilland looked at her sister, green dress in-hand and distress on her features. She hadn't told Amaline about Jamison's proposal, or anything else about him, and now she was glad. Now she wouldn't be ashamed that the man had said one thing to her and obviously meant another. Perhaps, he never even meant his marriage proposal. Had he been sweet to her just to bend her to his will? Not knowing him well, she couldn't be sure. All she knew was that she was hurt and confused.

"I… I am not sure," she said, tossing the green dress back onto the chair and marching across the chamber. "Bethan brought some food. Eat and I shall return."

Amaline rubbed her eyes sleepily. "But where are you going?"

"I shall return!"

Havilland tossed open the door and passed through, shutting it behind her as she emerged onto a landing. On the second floor of the keep, her chamber was directly across the landing and she threw the door open, charging across the small chamber to the wardrobe on the other side. It was messy, and full of breeches, torn and dirty and otherwise, and a few tunics hanging on pegs.

Havilland sifted through the pile of breeches, finding a woolen pair to wear, before reaching up and lifting a couple of tunics off their pegs. One tunic was fine linen while the other was a heavy wool offering protection against the cold weather. With these garments in hand, she turned around for the door and stopped dead in her tracks. With a gasp, she lost hold of the breeches and they fell to the floor but she didn't bend over to pick them up. She was frozen at the sight of Jamison standing in the doorway.

Eyes riveted to a sleepy-looking but thoroughly delightful Havilland, Jamison smiled at the woman.

"The servant told me ye were awake," he said. "Did ye sleep well?"

Havilland nodded hesitantly. "I think so," she said. "I feel rested."

"Excellent."

"What are you doing here?"

His smile broadened. "Did ye see the clothing I had brought tae ye?"

Havilland struggled with her hurt feelings. "I did."

"The green dress will be most becomin' on ye."

She was under the impression that he was insisting she wear the green dress, soft though that insistence might be. With a lingering glance at him, she bent over and picked up the breeches she had dropped. "I will not be wearing a dress today."

His smile faded. "Ye dunna like that one?" he said. "I can go back to yer mother's trunk and bring back a selection. I thought the green dress matched yer eyes."

She held the tunics and breeches against her like a shield, protecting her against Jamison and the fact he really wanted a wife who dressed like a woman. Never one for great tact, she spoke her mind.

"I thought you said you said you did not care what I wore," she pointed out. "You told me that you would be marrying me and not my wardrobe."

He could sense irritation with her. Perhaps even hurt. It puzzled him. "It is the truth," he said. "Why would ye say that?"

She frowned. "Because you had someone take my clothing from the chamber last night and replace it with those dresses," she said. "Were you lying to me, Jamison? Do you really prefer to see me in dresses and all those words about not caring what I wore were just to soften me?"

Instantly, he could see that his gesture had been misconstrued. Havilland seemed genuinely upset and he quickly sought to ease her.

"Nay," he said firmly. "I meant every word I said. But today… today I have a surprise for ye. Ye were denied a visit tae Alis de Lara's party, so I thought ye might like tae wear a fine dress today because… well, I canna tell ye why. 'Tis a surprise."

Havilland's hurt was quickly soothed because he seemed quite sincere. She believed him. She didn't know why she should, but she did. The man hadn't lied to her since they'd known one another and she was coming to think she had jumped to conclusions. She thought the worst of him and she shouldn't have. In fact, she was the least bit touched by his actions and quite a bit intrigued.

"A surprise?" she asked, dubious yet very interested. "Why can you not tell me?"

He pursed his lips ironically. "If I did, it wouldna be a surprise," he said. "Ye must trust me. Ye must go back into yer chamber and put on the green dress. Or, if ye dunna like it, I will bring ye the entire trunk tae choose from. Will ye do this for me, Havilland? Please?"

Now he was asking in the sweetest way possible and there was no way she could deny him. The man had the ability to turn her to putty quickly, as if she were born to bow to his wishes. With something of a remorseful grin, she lowered the tunic and breeches she had clutched against her chest.

"If you say so," she said. "I… I suppose I can wear the green dress if you like that one."

"'Twill be the most beautiful dress in the world on ye."

Her grin turned genuine as his sweet words took effect. "Are… are you sure this is not your way of telling me that you would rather see me dress as a lady?"

He shook his head, grinning. "If ye dunna believe me, then I will say this – wear what ye wish," he said. "If ye wish tae wear yer breeches, then do. I willna say a word. But I think ye'll want tae wear one of yer mother's gowns today. I think ye'll be glad ye did."

She simply smiled at him, giving a chuckle or two because he was being so very sweet about it. She felt badly that she ever doubted him. But her smile must have been an invitation because Jamison came into the room, when he knew full well that he shouldn't, and cupped her face in his hands to give her the most tender of kisses. Havilland closed her eyes as his lips slanted over hers, feeling the warmth of the man embrace her. She was coming to very much like his kisses. But it was over too soon and he kissed her nose and a cheek before letting her go and heading out of the chamber.

"Hurry and dress," he told her. "I will come for ye in a half an hour."

Havilland, still tasting the man on her lips, nodded a bit unsteadily. He winked at her and left the chamber, and she could hear is boots fading away as he went down the stairs. Once the sounds faded away, she threw the breeches and tunics onto her bed and ran back across the landing, into the chamber she'd slept in the night before.

When she entered, Amaline was on her feet, inspecting the two dresses tossed over the chair. Havilland entered so swiftly that Amaline was startled.

"Where did you go?" she asked.

Havilland ran straight to the chair and snatched the green dress away, spreading it out on the bed to look at the entire garment. "Ammie," she said thoughtfully, avoiding her sister's question altogether, "do you recall yesterday when we were in the loft, looking at these dresses and speaking on how Papa forced us to dress as we do?"

Amaline nodded as she came to stand next to her sister, looking down at the green dress. "Aye," she said. She fingered the garment. "Why are these dresses here?"

Havilland looked at her little sister and thought she might like to tell her about Jamison. After all, she'd told no one and something inside her felt like bursting, to declare her joy to the world. She put her arm around her sister's shoulders.

"Because Sir Jamison had them brought to us," she said. "So very much has happened since he and the de Lohr knights arrived, I hardly know where to start. Ammie… he has asked me to marry him."

Amaline looked at her sister with big eyes. "He has?" she said. "But… but he spanked you! When he first met you, he spanked you!"

Havilland giggled, kissing her sister on the temple. "I know, little chick," she said. Then, she sighed somewhat dramatically. "I do not know how this has happened, only that is has. One moment, he was telling me that I was a disgrace to my sex and the next, he was telling me he wishes to marry me. Ammie, he is not like any other men we have ever known… he is thoughtful and compassionate. I know it is difficult to believe by looking at him, but he is. And when he saved me yesterday from Evon… oh, Ammie, you should have seen him! He was magnificent! There is not a man in the world who can best him in a fight."

By this time, Amaline's mouth was hanging open, shocked to the bone that her serious and duty-minded sister should show attention to a man. It was almost more than she could bear.

"You… you *like* him!" she accused. "Havi, is it true? You like him?"

Havilland nodded, feeling her cheeks flush at the admission. It wasn't as if she was embarrassed about it – it was more the way thoughts of him made her feel. He made her feel all warm and flushed inside.

"It is true," she said, giving her sister a squeeze. "I like him a great deal. And I have decided to accept his marriage proposal."

Amaline's features slacked in shock and, as Havilland watched, turned to distress. "Marriage," she finally breathed. "Oh, Havi… even as you say it, I cannot believe it. You have never expressed interest in marriage at all. When we spoke of it yesterday with Madeline, you never said a word. She spoke of wearing dresses and having children, but you did not say anything about it."

Havilland's giddy excitement took a dousing with Amaline's angst. "Just because I did not speak of it does not mean I was not thinking about it," she said. "Of course, I would like to marry and have children. I simply have not thought any more than that on the subject. But Jamison is offering me a fine marriage with a man I truly admire. I can see nothing wrong with it.

"Except that you will be leaving me," Amaline said, full of sorrow. "With Madeline in the vault and you marrying, I will be left here all alone."

Havilland put her arms around her sister, squeezing her. "I promise

I will not leave you all alone," she said. "You can come with Jamison and me, wherever we go."

"But what will happen to Papa and Four Crosses?"

Havilland's gaze lingered on her younger sister for a moment. "I have a feeling that Lord de Lohr will know of Papa's situation soon enough," she said quietly. "It is time he knows, Ammie. We cannot keep up the charade any longer. With the Welsh on the attack, I will be honest… it is more than I wish to handle alone. I am very tired of handling such terrible problems alone. I do not want to do it anymore."

Amaline knew the burden of command had taken a toll on Havilland since their father had gone completely mad. She had watched her sister go from a relatively carefree maiden to a serious, sometimes sullen young woman. When their father was in command, the situation was much better with the sisters because the responsibility wasn't theirs. But when Roald lost his mind, Havilland had been forced to assume that burden. It had been a great deal for her to handle.

"I know," Amaline said. "I am sorry. I did not mean to be selfish. If you like Jamison, then you should marry him."

"And you will come with us?"

"Aye, of course. But… but what of Madeline?"

Havilland shook her head. "Her place in the vault is of her own doing," she said. "I cannot help her. You cannot help her. I am afraid she is lost to us."

In spite of her declaration the day before that she hoped Madeline was never released, a night of sleep and longing for her sister had changed Amaline's mind somewhat. She and Madeline had always been close in spite of Madeline being mean and manipulative at times. Still, Madeline was their sister, part of their blood. The morning saw Amaline torn on her position about Madeline's imprisonment.

"Will you never speak to her again, then?" she asked quietly.

Havilland shrugged. "I do not know," she said honestly. "She almost let Evon kill me. I am not sure I can forgive her for that."

Amaline understood. But something in her felt a good deal of pity in spite of everything. "I understand," she said, sorrow in her voice. Her gaze trailed off to the dresses on the chair and on the bed, and she hastened to change the subject. Speaking of Madeline was too depressing. "Will you tell me why Sir Jamison brought us these dresses, then?"

Havilland, who still had her sister in an embrace, released the young woman. "I do not know," she said honestly. "He told me that we should put them on and then he had a surprise for us."

Amaline was greatly interested in that. "A surprise?" she asked, the distress from moments before out of her voice. "I wonder what it could be?"

Havilland shrugged. "Unless we put these dresses on, we shall never find out," she said, picking up the green dress. "You help me put this one on and I shall help you put the blue one on."

Amaline was more than eager to help, her depression about Madeline eased by the lure of some manner of a surprise. When Bethan entered the room a few moments later, bearing hot water, the toilette of Havilland and Amaline was in full swing. Having never dressed as women before, it was something of an adventure, but in the end, it was something they very much liked.

Finally, without Roald de Llion convincing them that breeches and tunics were acceptable clothing for young ladies, they were able to experience what they'd never experienced in their life –

The feeling of being a woman for the very first time.

ଓ

JAMISON WAS WAITING on the landing.

Exactly half an hour after leaving Havilland to dress, Jamison had returned. He was without his mail on this day. Instead, he wore a type of traditional Highland dress – over a traditional saffron tunic he wore his *brecan,* woven around his waist to create the traditional great kilt, or *pladjer* – the Gaelic name for the type of dress he was wearing. It was a very Scots style of dress, something Jamison never really wore, but on this occasion, he thought he should. He was proud to wear it, proud for

Havilland to see him in it. This was what she would be marrying into, a clan that was nearly as old as Scotland herself.

On his feet were his heavy boots, something that wasn't particularly Scots but he liked his shoes and didn't want to part with them. He'd washed his face and hands, and he'd even shaved, so when he knocked on Havilland's chamber door, he was ready to face her.

But what he saw when the door opened took his breath away.

Havilland stood before him, dressed in her mother's green dress, laced into the garment so that her breasts looked full and delicious and her slender waist was emphasized. Her dark hair, so soft and lovely, had been plaited into two braids that draped elegantly over her shoulders. Someone who knew something about dressing women had taken a pale green scarf made from *albatross*, a very fine type of fabric, and had wrapped it around her head, like a headband, and wove it into her braids. Jamison swore, at that very moment, that he'd never seen a more beautiful woman in his life.

"M'lady," he said, his voice hoarse with emotion. "Surely the angels are jealous of yer beauty. Ye're the finest woman I've ever had the privilege tae see."

Havilland flushed deeply, hugely flattered and hugely embarrassed. "My thanks," she said. "Bethan helped us dress."

"Bethan?"

Havilland pointed into the chamber to the older serving woman standing over by Amaline. "She used to be my mother's maid."

Jamison nodded to the woman. He had met her during the course of the early morning when he had her bring garments up to Havilland's chamber. "Ye've done her justice," he said to Bethan. Catching sight of Amaline, whose wild red hair had been tamed and put into a hair net, he smiled his approval. "On both ladies. Ye've done a remarkable job."

The old maid waved him off, grinning. "'Tis you I should thank, my lord," she said, finishing with a pin in Amaline's hair. "I have been wanting to tame these young women for years but there has been no one to support my position. Lady Precious' daughters are meant to be young women, not soldiers in the field."

Jamison chuckled at the old woman, chuckling again when Amaline yelped because a pin poked her scalp. But his gaze returned to Havilland, standing beautiful and groomed before him. He couldn't take his eyes off of her.

"Well?" he asked, a twinkle in his eye. "How does it feel?"

"How does what feel?"

"Looking the way you were always meant to look."

Havilland grinned, pulling nervously at the scarf on her head. "It seems very strange," she admitted. "I saw myself in the bronze mirror and I am the exact image of my mother."

"Then yer mother was a beautiful woman."

"Aye, she was," she said. Then, her gaze moved down his body, realizing he wasn't wearing any breeches. He had his cloak all wrapped around his torso and legs and she peered strangely at his clothing. "What are you wearing?"

Jamison looked down at himself. "This is what the Highlanders wear, lass," he told her. "Ye see this long stretch of fabric? 'Tis called a *brecan*. The way I have it doubled up and wrapped around me legs is called a *pladjer*. And the big tunic ye see beneath it is traditional, too. It goes down tae me knees. We dress this way for comfort and warmth. 'Tis the proud dress o' a Scotsman."

Havilland was looking at it all quite closely. "I have seen you wear this woolen fabric as a cloak," she said. "But I have never seen it used for a skirt before."

He grinned. "If ye tell a Scotsmen he is wearin' a skirt, then ye'd better be prepared tae defend yer words," he said, watching her grin. "'Tis no skirt, lass. 'Tis a Scotsman's traditional clothing and we wear it proudly."

She looked up at him. "But you wear breeches and tunics like the English," she said. "Why do you not dress like your kinsmen all of the time?"

He shrugged. "'Tis a personal choice for me," he said. "I am more comfortable with me legs covered."

It was a simple explanation but it made sense. Jamison continued to stand there, grinning like a fool at Havilland because once the discussion about his clothing was finished, the focus was back on her and her dress. She looked so vastly uncomfortable that he found it humorous. But he knew it was purely out of ignorance on her part. If the woman realized the scope of even half of her beauty, she wouldn't be embarrassed at all. She was embarrassed because all of this was so new and uncertain to her. But she wouldn't be embarrassed long, he hoped. May new things were coming to her today and he hoped she would find all of it thrilling.

"There," Bethan shoved the last pin into Amaline's hair, swatting the girl on the backside when she whined and pulled away. "The ladies are ready, my lord."

"Excellent," Jamison said. Then, he held out an elbow to Havilland, who looked at it dumbly. She had no idea what to do with it. "M'lady, when a man offers ye his arm, he means tae escort ye."

"Escort me where?"

"Take me elbow, ye insufferable wench."

He said it so comically that Havilland snorted at him and clutched his elbow. "Very well, then," she said. "What about Amaline? Will she take your elbow, too?"

He nodded. "Of course, she will," he said. "Once we quit the keep, I'll have ye both on me arms and I'll be the most envied man at Four Crosses."

Amaline was still fussing with the stabbing pins in her scalp as she followed Jamison and Havilland from the chamber. Jamison preceded them down the stairs that led to the entry level of the keep. Sunlight streamed in from the open door and from a pair of ventilation windows high over the entry, illuminating the entryway with soft white light. As Jamison came off of the bottom step into the entry, holding out a hand to help Havilland down as she cautiously held her skirts up to her knees, she finally came off the steps and clutched his hand, looking at him rather strangely.

"Where are you taking us?" she asked.

"Ye'll see," he said coyly.

Her eyes narrowed. "Something seems very strange with you."

He simply grinned at her and opened the door.

Stepping out onto the top of the stairs that led down into the bailey, Havilland and Amaline were faced with Thad and Tobias, down in the bailey before them, both of them dressed to the hilt in armor and weapons. They were dressed for battle. A group of soldiers stood around them, forming a circle, and Havilland was immediately concerned that something terrible was taking place. That is, until Tobias saw the ladies emerge from the keep. Both he and Thad turned to them, bowing deeply.

"Lady Havilland," Tobias said loudly, "and Lady Amaline. We have prepared for you this day an amazing spectacle of games and mock battles. You ladies shall preside over the games as our queens. The first contest will be me against my foolish cousin to see who will have the honor of bearing Lady Amaline's favor for the remainder of the games. Be prepared to be amazed by my skill as I beat my cousin into the ground."

Havilland and Amaline were greatly awed and greatly confused. They had no idea what was going on. A festival? *Here?* When they turned to Jamison for clarification, he could see a thousand questions in their eyes. His gaze was gentle upon Havilland as he spoke.

"Ye couldna travel tae Alis de Lara's festival," he said simply. "We thought tae bring the festival tae ye."

Havilland's eyes widened. "Bring it to *me*?" she gasped, looking at Thad and Tobias again as they collected their weapons in preparation for the fight. "You… you did…?"

She couldn't even finish her sentence, completely overwhelmed by what she was seeing. Jamison took her hand, gently, and tucked it into his elbow.

"Today, we bring some joy and adventure tae Four Crosses," he said quietly. "Havi, I know it has been a terrible few days for ye. Hell, 'tis been a terrible few years. Yesterday, when you asked tae attend Alis de Lara's party, I'd never seen ye so excited. Ye've lived such a plain and brutal life that any mention of something beautiful and frivolous had ye glowing. But Madeline's imprisonment and the truth of yer father's condition took that joy out of ye. I couldna stand tae see that happen. Ye may think this is in poor taste because of Madeline being in the vault, or because of the situation in general, but for one day I didna think it was too much tae ask tae try and bring happiness into yer heart again. It's only for a day, love. For one day, I want ye tae pretend there is no sorrow in yer life and no uncertainty. For today, pretend there is nothin' but joy. That is what I want tae bring tae ye."

Havilland stared at him and he could see the emotions running through her head. Her wide-eyed gaze told him everything – the shock, the disbelief, and the thrill. She was overwhelmed. As he watched, her eyes grew misty and she began to blink rapidly as if to stave off the tears that threatened. She looked out over the bailey where she could see that a few other things were going on as well. There seemed to be something that looked like a fenced-off arena over by the troop house and men were milling about, still working on things. After a moment, she shook her head in wonder.

"You did all of this for me?" she whispered.

Jamison nodded faintly. "All for ye."

Havilland was genuinely speechless and struggling not to tear up. "No one has ever done anything for me," she said hoarsely. "Certainly never anything like this. A… real festival?"

"Better than any festival Alis de Lara would put on," he said arrogantly. But she seemed so taken aback by the entire thing that he was worried he might have offended her. "I am sorry if ye think this is in poor taste because of current circumstances, but…."

She cut him off, shaking her head. "Nay," she said quickly. "'Tis not that at all. 'Tis simply that… that I have never even attended a festival before. I have never had anyone be so kind to me like this. I do not know what to say to you except that I am deeply touched that you would go to the trouble."

He patted the hand clutching his elbow. "'Twas no trouble at all," he assured her. "This is as much for the men as it 'tis for ye. They need something tae boost their morale, also. Months of fighting can take its toll. If men are tae keep up the fight, sometimes they need some happiness and hope tae help them along."

It made perfect sense to Havilland, who clutched his elbow tightly as Tobias and Thad launched a vicious attack against each other. Sparks flew and men grunted as an exciting battle ensured in the bailey, right at the feet of Havilland and Amaline. They were the queens, watching men battle or their favor.

It was a welcome battle, indeed.

CHAPTER FIFTEEN

"I do not believe you...."

UNFORTUNATELY, THINGS DID not go well for Tobias.

Thad, an excellent knight in his own right, pulled a few tricks on his cousin in the midst of their combat that sent Tobias to the ground, enough so that Thad was able to pin him and be declared the victor by a host of gleeful soldiers. Therefore, it was Thad who had the privilege of carrying Amaline's favor, which turned out to be a hairpin because she had nothing else to give him.

Securing the iron pin on the collar of the linen tunic beneath his armor, Thad victoriously escorted Amaline over to the makeshift arena they had built over by the troop house, leaving Jamison to escort Havilland and Tobias to nurse his wounded pride. Certainly, it hadn't been the glorious victory Tobias had expected.

But he had organized the games so he threw himself into his task, which at this point involved an archery competition they had set up in the arena. Including him and Jamison and Thad, Tobias had hand-selected several de Lohr men he knew were good archers and a few Four Crosses men who had come recommended to him as excellent archers. At the edge of the arena, there were two gambling tables set up and men going mad placing bets on the competitors. Already, money was changing hands at an alarming rate and the mood of the castle on this bright winter's morning was electrified with excitement in complete contrast to the sullen, suspicious, and beaten mood that had filled the men and the castle for months on end.

Because of this, the knights were realizing, more and more, that Jamison had been correct in his decision to have a day of morale boosting. It wasn't simply about giving joy to two young ladies who had known little; this was about lifting the spirits of the entire castle. The men were happier already, alive with the excitement of the coming games, and as the two ladies and their escorts reached the makeshift arena, the noise was already loud with men excitedly shouting as competitors began to take the field for the archery competition.

Increasingly, Havilland and Amaline seemed to be overcoming their shock at the unexpected festival and were coming to the realization that Jamison and his men had done a massive amount of work overnight. After the surprise wore away, the glee began to take hold and by the time Jamison and Thad lifted the ladies up onto the viewing platform that the men had constructed during the night, both women were smiling a great deal, thrilled at the spectacle. But no one was smiling more than Havilland was.

And all of her smiling was aimed at Jamison.

Once he lifted her to sit on one of the two chairs that had been placed on the viewing platform, she didn't want to let him go. He was sweet and attentive, asking if she wanted a cushion, and then sending someone to fetch old Bethan to stand with the ladies and be a chaperone with them while he wasn't able to stand at her side. It was utterly unnecessary to have the old servant as a chaperone to women who could easily handle a weapon, but in the civilized world, it was the proper thing to do. Jamison was being very thoughtful and kind, more than anything Havilland had ever experienced. If she had any doubts about the man and his feelings for her, his actions of the morning had dashed them.

And her feeling for him were true, as well.

Therefore, when Bethan arrived and was heaved up to the platform by two soldiers, Jamison turned to leave but Havilland grabbed his hand and wouldn't let him go.

"Why do you leave?" she asked anxiously.

He smiled at her, pointing to the arena with the hand she didn't have a viselike grip on. "I am going tae compete," he said. "I know that Scotsmen aren't known for their archery skills, but lest ye forget, I trained in England. I can handle a bow better than most."

Havilland turned to look at the arena, too, seeing how they had set up a row of targets by using the troop house for a backstop. The targets were of wood, cut square although they were of varying sizes, hastily done, and all of them held up by a wooden frame. Right in the center of the target was a circle made from lime mortar, the same mortar they were using to rebuild the walls of Four Crosses. It was a neatly-formed circle, white, that also gave off a strange glow-like quality because of the minerals in the lime. The targets were very easy to see across the arena floor.

"Very well," she said, letting go of his hand. "Best of luck to you. I… I will be cheering for you."

He smiled at her. "And I will hear ye," he said. "But ye must give me a token for luck. I dunna have one."

In a panic, she began looking around on her body, trying to see if there was a spare piece of cloth from the dress that he could have. But there was nothing. She had no idea what to give him when she suddenly caught a flash of a blade. As she watched, Jamison unsheathed one of his dirks and used the razor-sharp blade to cut the end off of the scarf that ran through her hair. It was just a couple of inches, but it was enough for him. With a grin, he lifted it to his nose, smelling it, before tucking it into his belt.

"That'll do," he said quietly, his eyes glimmering at her. "Now, watch the games. I think ye will enjoy them."

Havilland smiled at him, watching him as he deftly leapt off the platform and headed out into the field. In fact, she had eyes only for him as he moved to a crowd of men at the edge of the arena and pulled forth a bow from one of the de Lohr soldiers. There were plenty of yew-branch bows from the armory but the ammunition for them was rather scarce, so they had handed out what ammunition they had to the competitors to be reused. Jamison, inspecting the bow he was to use, was taller than even the tallest man, his red hair glistening in the weak winter sun. He was all she could see.

Adoring. That's the only way Havilland could explain her feelings about him at the moment because she had no context on anything greater. She'd never loved a man nor had she ever been in love. But watching Jamison made her feel like smiling. What he had done for her today, arranging this festival in her honor simply because he couldn't stand to see her so disappointed, went beyond anything she had ever imagined. She thought, quite possibly, that she could grow to love this man. Wasn't that what adoration was, anyway? Anyone who would do such marvelous things for her was surely worthy of her love.

"Havi?"

Amaline was tugging on her sleeve, distracting her from thoughts of Jamison. Havilland turned to her youngest sister to see distress on the girl's face. She was instantly concerned.

"What is it?" she asked.

Amaline was distressed, indeed. "Bethan has asked where Madeline is," she whispered. "What do I tell her?"

Havilland glanced at the old woman, standing on the other side of Amaline, watching the activity on the field. "What did you tell her?" she asked quietly.

Amaline almost glanced at Bethan, too, but stopped herself. She didn't want to make it obvious that she was talking about the woman. "I told her that I had not seen her yet today," she said. "It is the truth. I have not seen her today."

Havilland knew it wouldn't be the first time someone asked about Madeline today. As much as she and Amaline were, Madeline was an important and visible figure at Four Crosses. Her absence would be obvious and they simply couldn't pretend as if she did not exist. As much as thoughts of this festival were meant to buoy her, now thoughts of Madeline were dragging her down.

With a fresh day dawning, her anger towards her sister was just as strong as it ever was but there was also a sense of extreme hurt and disappointment that Madeline would so easily betray them. Now, the anger was starting to gain some momentum and she struggled to put it aside for she didn't want to ruin this special day and everything Jamison had worked hard for. She refused to let Madeline ruin this day.

"You told her what you could," she said after a moment, her gaze on Jamison as he moved to his spot in the arena, which happened to be almost directly in front of her. "If anyone asks, we will simply say that she did not wish to be part of this day."

Amaline nodded, watching the men take position in front of the platform. There was Thad and Tobias and then Jamison in front of them, and then a host of other soldiers down the line, all of them with their bows, facing the targets across the arena. Amaline didn't say anything more about Madeline but she was surely thinking about her middle sister. In fact, as the first round of arrows flew to their targets and the crowd cheered, including Havilland, Amaline found her attention pulled to the gatehouse and the vault beneath it.

Now, she couldn't stop thinking of her sister. *Oh, Madeline... did you really do what they say you did?* In truth, she had been wondering that from the start. Was it possible there had been a miscommunication or a misunderstanding? Madeline was bossy and aggressive, and Amaline had meant it last night when she said she hoped that Madeline would stay in the vault forever. But morning had seen Amaline's stance wavering. She was afraid for her sister, afraid of what Lord de Lohr would do to her. Weren't spies executed? Was it possible that Madeline would be put to death? The more Amaline thought about that, the more fearful she became.

Perhaps she needed to hear from Madeline's lips what really happened. Perhaps she needed to make her own judgement about her sister and not rely on Havilland and Jamison, the only two people who had witnessed Madeline's treachery. Not that she believed they would lie to her, but perhaps there was another explanation. Somehow, Amaline didn't truly believe that there was, because she was sure that Madeline was capable of what she had been accused of, but something inside of her demanded to speak with Madeline.

She had to hear from Madeline's own lips about her treachery.

Lost in her thoughts of turmoil, Amaline stood up from her chair and Havilland immediately put her hand on Amaline's arm.

"Where are you going, Ammie?" she asked.

Flustered, confused, and upset, Amaline struggled to come up with an excuse that Havilland would believe. She knew if she told her where she was really going, Havilland would deny her. Therefore, she lied.

"I… I must use the privy," she said. "I will hurry back."

Havilland had no reason not to believe her so she smiled at her sister and watched the girl leap off the platform, losing herself in the crowd of men that was standing around the arena.

But that was as far as her attention for Amaline went. As her sister went off to relieve herself, Havilland turned back to watch Jamison take a second shot at the archery target and hit it dead center. The men cheered and she clapped loudly, proud of the man as she had never been proud of anything in her life. She'd never known what it was to be proud of someone who had shown her such affection, such attention.

Having never had to protect her heart before, the only thing Havilland could do was give it over freely. Jamison, in her eyes, had proven himself. Perhaps they'd had a rough start, but Jamison had more than made up for it. The Scotsman known as The Red Lion had done the impossible… he had won her heart.

So Havilland watched as Jamison continued to hit the center of the target as other men were eliminated. She had cheered louder and louder with each win until, finally, he was matched against Tobias for the victory. When it was just the two knights, the bets were flying fast and furious, and men were betting heavily on Jamison. He and Tobias drew straw lengths to see who would go first and it was Tobias, so Jamison stood back graciously and watched as Tobias set himself up for the first round. There would be three total and the man closest to the center target, or within the center target, would win.

Jamison leaned against the platform as Tobias lined up his first shot, turning to wink at Havilland more than once. She smiled openly at him, so openly that the men watching the exchange were beginning to whisper. Many of the soldiers at Four Crosses had watched Havilland and her sisters grow up so to realize she was fond of a de Lohr knight sent gossip spreading through the groups of men like a wildfire. Not only was Madeline missing, as many had noticed and commented on, but now Havilland was evidently sweet on the big Highlander. Already, the day was quite eventful.

Tobias launched his arrow and hit the target, but not dead center. Jamison collected his bow and arrow, planted his big feet, and fired off an arrow that hit dead center in the middle of the target. Tobias, not to be outdone, launched his second arrow and was slightly off center. Jamison shot his second arrow and hit his first one, splintering it. The crowd went mad.

Inflamed, Tobias launched his third arrow and hit the center mark again, but at the edge of it. Jamison, with a grin on his face, launched his last arrow and landed it slightly below his other two, but still nearly dead-on center. The man that Tobias had appointed the marshal of the games declared Jamison the obvious winner and men cheered in response. Once again, Tobias emerged the loser and his mood was growing more foul by the moment. What he had viewed as a chance to win Havilland away from Jamison was turning into an embarrassment for him.

Jamison wasn't oblivious to Tobias' shame but he had no idea what was truly behind it. After being declared the winner, he didn't rejoice or shout his triumph for all to hear, but rather made his way over to the platform where Havilland was sitting. She was sitting straight in her chair, watching him eagerly as he approached. With a grin, he leapt up onto the platform, took her hand, and kissed it.

"Yer favor brought me luck," he said. "Ye have me thanks."

Havilland smiled up at him, her handsome victor. "You have a good deal of skill with a bow," she said. "I wish I could have competed, too."

His smile faded. "Are ye not enjoying yerself watching the games?"

She nodded quickly. "I am," she assured him. "But… well, it seems strange to be sitting here and not participating."

He chuckled. "Fine ladies dunna usually participate in men's games," he said. "They watch from the lists and cheer on their men."

She wriggled her eyebrows in an ironic gesture. "I suppose that is something I must become accustomed to," she said. "What will you be doing next?"

Jamison looked out at the arena where men were removing the archery targets and gathering the arrows that had fallen or were loose. He could also see, at the far end, that the marshal and his helpers were bringing out a length of hemp rope.

"The hammer throw," he told her. "I've been throwin' hammers since I was a wee lad. I will destroy these English who think they can best me."

He said it rather dramatically and Havilland laughed softly. "I look forward to it."

He turned to look at her, grinning because she was. "Of course ye do," he said, "because I shall triumph again. Where is yer sister? She will want to see me triumph as well."

Havilland looked around. "She had some business to attend to," she said, politely phrasing the nature of her sister's absence. "She will return soon."

Jamison simply nodded, looking over to the edge of the arena where the men were gathering to begin the hammer throw. Tobias had confiscated all of the blacksmith's hammers for this event and there were six of them, long-handled hammers with heavy iron heads. Jamison gave Havilland's hand a squeeze before releasing it.

"On tae the next event," he told her, fingering the favor that was still in his belt. "Ye've brought me fortune, m'lady. I expect ye will bring me more."

Havilland could only smile in return. In fact, it seemed that she had been doing an awful lot of smiling at the man. She couldn't seem to do anything else. As she opened her mouth to reply, a shout to Jamison stopped her. Both she and Jamison turned to see one of the gatehouse sentries coming towards them. Jamison was immediately fixed on the man.

"What is it?" he asked.

The sentry had to push through a group of men in order to reach Jamison. "Riders, my lord," he said. "The commander on watch has asked me to summon you and Sir Tobias."

Jamison forgot about the hammer toss for the moment. He was already moving in the direction of the gatehouse. "How many riders?" he asked.

"Three, my lord."

Jamison frowned. "That is not a great number," he said. "I see no reason tae panic. Can ye make out any colors or standards?"

The sentry nodded. "The commander on watch says to tell you that the men are wearing what you are."

Puzzled, Jamison cocked his head. "What is that?"

The soldier pointed at his *brecan*. "That."

Jamison was running for the gatehouse without another word.

CB

IT HAD BEEN a simple matter for Amaline to enter the gatehouse and descend the stairs leading to the vault because the direction of the entry faced the bailey even though the cells themselves were underneath the gatehouse. Therefore, she could avoid the men inside the gatehouse for the most part. More than that, the sentries on duty seemed to be watching incoming riders. She had heard their shouts and had seen their interest, and she had used it to her advantage. With them occupied, it was nothing at all for Amaline to slip down the narrow, slippery stairs into the vault that smelled like earth and rot.

The vault of Four Crosses was a very large hole that had been carved out in the earth of Wales, a hole big enough for two tiny cells and little more. The floors weren't even; they tended to slope and the ground was slippery and unstable in places. Water ran down the eastern wall and pooled in a green puddle.

A single iron sconce had been hammered into that wall, holding a fatted torch that billowed up thick black smoke into the low ceiling. The air down here was bad, anyway, and the smoke didn't help.

Amaline was frightened to be down there, frightened of what she'd find. The torch didn't light the area very well and she stood at the base of the stairs for a moment, her eyes growing accustomed to the light. Gradually, the cells became clear and she could see a figure in the cell closest to her, lying on a pile of fresh straw with a couple of heavy blankets over it. The figure had its back turned to the door but knowing it was Madeline, Amaline rushed up to the iron bars.

"Madeline?" she whispered loudly.

The figure jerked and suddenly sat up. Amaline found herself looking into Madeline's red-rimmed eyes. When Madeline saw her youngest sister, she rushed to the iron grate and grasped Amaline's hands.

"Ammie!" she gasped. "You have come to me!"

Amaline nodded uncertainly. "Aye… I wanted to see you."

Madeline squeezed her hands, hard. "Oh, Ammie, I am so frightened!"

Amaline peered curiously at her sister; the woman had never uttered that word in her life – *frightened*. She didn't even know Madeline knew what it meant to be frightened. Greatly puzzled, and a bit wary, she pulled her hands away from Madeline so the woman couldn't grab her through the bars. She was squeezing so hard she was hurting her.

"Havi told me what you did," Amaline said, distressed. "How could you do it, Madeline? You have told the Welsh all about us and now they will destroy us!"

Madeline was cold, hungry, and terrified. "What is happening?" she asked, not directly denying what Amaline had said. "No one has told me anything. What are they going to do?"

Amaline wasn't foolish; she realized Madeline didn't address her accusations. "Lord de Lohr is coming," she said. "He will decide your punishment."

Madeline's eyes widened. "Who told you that?" she hissed. "Jamison? Havilland?"

Amaline nodded. "Jamison has sent for Lord de Lohr," she said. Then, she frowned. "How could you almost let Havilland be killed? How could you do such a thing?"

Madeline could see that her younger sister hadn't come to the vault to comfort her. She had come to berate her. Miserable, Madeline turned away from the iron bars and threw herself onto the hay pile.

"Go away, Ammie," she said. "If you have only come here to scold me, just go away."

"But what you did was wrong!"

Madeline lifted her shoulders. "Mayhap to you it was wrong," she said. "But to me… I loved him, Ammie. I would do anything for the man I loved and now he is dead. Jamison Munro murdered him!"

Amaline was outraged at the accusation. "But he was defending Havilland!"

Madeline had always been the manipulative type, especially with her younger sister. Amaline had been most pliable at times. Madeline didn't want to face de Lohr justice; she wanted her freedom before Lord de Lohr arrived. She wanted to run to those Welsh rebels who had meant so much to Evon, men who were a part of his culture and blood, including his brother, Morys. Morys Preece had been at the head of the Welsh attacks on Four Crosses, at least according to Evon, and Madeline was sure that Morys would want to know what really happened to Evon. *Her love.*

God, she missed him.

"I knew they would lie to you," she muttered. "What did they tell you, Ammie? That Evon attacked Havilland? That he tried to kill her? It is not the truth, I tell you. I will tell you what happened – Evon Preece and I were in love. We wanted to marry. Because he is Welsh, I had to meet him in secret, whenever I could. Havilland followed me to one such meeting and brought Jamison with her, to call me a traitor when I am not. I only wanted to meet my love. As I watched, Jamison attacked Evon and broke his neck, throwing his body in the river. That is the truth, Ammie. I knew they would not tell you the truth of it to cover up for the murder that Jamison committed, but it is the truth just the same. Jamison killed the man I loved and he is trying to put all of the blame on me."

Amaline was greatly confused. "Jamison saw you with him before yesterday," she said. "He saw you with him two days ago and he heard you tell Evon about things you should not have told him. You were telling him what was happening here at Four Crosses so that the Welsh would know what our weaknesses were."

Madeline was shocked at the news that Jamison had evidently seen her with Evon before. Yesterday was not the first time. Startled at the realization, she burst into tears.

"It is not true!" she said. "I met him because I loved him and I knew I would not be allowed to see him freely because he is Welsh. Ammie, do you know what will happen when Lord de Lohr comes? He will take me back to Lioncross Abbey and he will execute me. He will kill me! I do not want to die, Ammie! You must help me!"

She was sobbing by the time she was finished, playing on Amaline's tender senses. But Amaline resisted, although it was difficult. Madeline never cried so the woman's tears had her off-guard. In fact, she'd never seen Madeline behave this way at all. It was like watching another person. Amaline had no idea what to do or who to believe now, yet her instincts told her that Havilland wouldn't lie to her.

But Madeline would.

"I do not want to help you," Amaline finally said. "Why would I help you? What would you do? Run back to the Welsh and tell them all about us? You are a traitor!"

Madeline could see her tears hadn't worked, but in truth, the tears were real. She was terrified of her fate. "Please, Ammie," she rolled off of the hay pile, on her knees as she gripped the iron bars. "I do not want to die. Do you know what happens when they execute people? They will force me to my knees and a man with an ax will take my head off. Look at my neck; look at it! He will slice through it and my head will roll!"

Amaline was greatly distressed by the thought. She backed away from the iron grate as Madeline held on to it, using it to support her in her grief. "You must be punished," Amaline said. "You tried to kill us all, Madeline. You are the enemy!"

Madeline shook her head. "My only crime was to fall in love with a Welshman," she said. "Please, Ammie… please help me. If… if you release me, I swear I will run away and never come back. At least give me a chance at life. I have only seen seventeen years! I want to grow old and have children. I promise I will run away and never return if you release me from this cell. Please, Ammie… do not let de Lohr cut my head off!"

Amaline was standing back against the walls of the vault now, watching her sister beg. She'd never seen such a thing before. It was as if her entire world was turning upside down today – seeing behavior from Madeline she'd never seen before, and also seeing Havilland in a gown as she was smitten with a knight. So many changes for the young woman to stomach. At fourteen years of age, she was far too young to bear it gracefully. As Madeline wept at the thought of her impending death, tears came to Amaline's eyes.

"What you did was not right," she said hoarsely. "You are not even sorry that you almost let someone kill Havi."

Madeline could see that throwing herself on her sister's mercy and telling her what she wanted to hear might be her only chance of escape. She had been hoping all night that Amaline would make an appearance because if there was anyone she could manipulate to do her bidding, it was Amaline. Her younger sister was her only hope and she was trying her hardest to convince the girl to help her. Surprisingly, Amaline wasn't bending. Madeline closed her eyes, weeping.

"I would not have let him kill her," she said. "He threatened, but I would not have let him. You must believe me."

"Tell me you are sorry!"

"I am sorry!"

The words were shouted at each other, so much so that Amaline quickly looked up the stairwell to see if anyone had heard them. Sounds were greatly muffled in the earthen prison. When Amaline was certain they had not attracted any attention, she returned her focus to Madeline.

The woman was bent over, on her knees, still clutching the rusting iron bars that imprisoned her. Amaline watched her, so terribly torn. She didn't want Madeline's head to be cut off, but she wasn't sure she could forgive the woman for what she'd done. She wasn't even sure she could believe her when she said she would run away and never return. Amaline's entire world was in turmoil and she didn't know where to turn. Tears filled her eyes as she looked at Madeline.

"Tell me again," she whispered.

Madeline sobbed openly. "I am sorry," she said. "Please, Ammie… forgive me."

Amaline stared at her. There was something in Madeline's tone that was false as false could be. She'd known her sister too long to think otherwise. Sick to her stomach with indecision, she had to go with her instincts.

"I do not believe you."

With that, Amaline ran back up the stairs, trying not to trip over her skirt, listening to Madeline's screams as she went. There was great pain and suffering in that vault, something Amaline was trying to escape but she couldn't quite manage it.

By the time she hit the top of the stairs, she was openly weeping, too.

CHAPTER SIXTEEN

"I shall have ye and no other...."

"GREAT BLEEDING JESUS! 'Tis that big red beast in the flesh!"

Standing in the gatehouse of Four Crosses and facing the road that led up to the castle, Jamison heard the familiar exclamation from a distance and he knew, even at length, who the three riders were. If he'd been blindfolded and knew nothing about their physical characteristics, he still would have known that voice anywhere. A man he'd lived with, and fought with, and faced death with. He knew him like a brother. Nay; *more* than a brother. The man was part of his soul.

The White Dragon was in his midst.

"Beaux MacKay!" he bellowed. "Is it possible ye've dragged yer ugly arse all the way tae Wales?"

He could hear laughter, laughter he recognized, and he grinned from ear to ear, shaking his head as if in extreme disapproval. "By all the saints," he muttered in disbelief. Then, he lifted his voice. "Dunna tell me ye brought yer sisters wit' ye. Is it truly Kendrick and Caspian I hear?"

The three riders spurred their shaggy horses forward, galloping the rest of the way up the road and closing the gap to the gatehouse in short order. Rocks flicked up from the excited horses, pelting Jamison in the bare legs as he made his way to the three riders. He pushed aside big, frothing horse heads, coming to the first man who had dismounted and throwing his arms around him. It was an embrace of gratitude and of joy. It was an embrace that satisfied him to his very bones. Jamison finally released the man, grasping the familiar face in his hands.

"My God," he breathed, drinking in the sight. "It 'tis ye, Beaux. Am I dreaming?"

Beaux shook his head, smiling into a face he'd not seen in a very long time. "Nay," he said. "Ye're not dreaming. But it's been too long, Jamie. How long since we last saw ye?"

Jamison shook his head. "At least four years," he said. "I last saw ye at Lioncross four years past. It was Christmas and I'd just come home from France with Arthur."

Beaux remembered that Christmas and the heavy snows of it, making it particularly memorable. But before he could reply, however, Kendrick and Caspian made their way to Jamison, hugging him in turn, reveling in the joy of being reunited with their old friend. Jamison still had his hands on Kendrick and Caspian, looking at the pair in shock.

"I canna believe it," he said. "The three of ye here. Are ye sure this isna a dream?"

Caspian slapped him softly on the cheek. "'Tis no dream, lad."

Jamison chuckled. "I dunna even know where tae start," he said. "Why are ye here? How did ye find me?"

Beaux slapped him on the shoulder, tugging him away from Kendrick and Caspian. "Take us inside, feed us, and we shall tell ye," he said. "It has been a very long journey."

Jamison was already moving towards the gatehouse. "Where did ye come from?"

"Home."

That gave Jamison some pause. For some reason, a warning bell went off in his head and now the joy of their appearance was starting to turn into something else, something darker. He struggled against the sense of foreboding that filled him.

"Then it took ye months at the very least in this weather," he said, endeavoring to remain calm. "Why did ye come?"

"Inside, man. We'll tell ye everything."

"Ye'll tell me now."

It was clear that Jamison wanted answers before he settled his guests. Their appearance was not only surprising, it was concerning. There was no earthly reason for the men to be here unless it was a serious matter and Beaux knew he had to tell Jamison something before the man grew less friendly and more demanding. Already, his manner was changing as they tried to avoid his questions.

"We went tae Lioncross," Beaux finally said. "Lord de Lohr told us ye were here at Four Crosses. There's much tae tell ye, Jamie."

That didn't clear up any of Jamison's confusion. In fact, it only made it worse and, suddenly, he was seized by panic. He came to a halt just shy of the gatehouse, facing Beaux.

"Tell me what?" he wanted to know. "*Sweet Jesú*… is it me da? Is he well?"

Beaux could see the distress in Jamison's face and he hastened to reassure him. "Yer da is well and healthy," he said quickly. "But… tae be truthful, all is not well at home, Jamie. Let us go inside and speak o' it."

Jamison wouldn't budge. Now that the truth behind their shocking visit was coming out, he wanted to hear all of it at that very moment. He didn't want to wait until they were comfortable and plied with wine. He was selfish in that he wanted to know immediately. In truth, even as his mind went wild with possibilities, he already knew what it was about. His gut told him so.

MacKenzie.

"What has happened?" he demanded quietly.

Beaux was exhausted; he and Kendrick and Caspian had been traveling for, quite literally, four months. With the winter season, the roads had been difficult and the weather had been atrocious. What should have taken them several weeks had taken much longer, but they had persevered. They had made a promise to George Munro and they would not go back on that vow. So here they were, finally facing

Jamison, and the man wanted answers. With a sigh, Beaux began to loosen his heavy leather gloves.

"Are ye sure ye want tae here it now?" he said. "It would be much easier for all of us over some mulled wine and a good fire."

Jamison swallowed hard; they could all see it. "I would appreciate it if ye could tell me now, Beaux. Ye dinna come here tae see me pretty face. Something is amiss, something so terrible that it has ye traveling hundreds of miles in the dead of winter. Tell me what has happened."

Beaux removed a glove and scratched his head. "Then I'll come out wit' it," he said, looking Jamison in the eye. "There's no easy way tae tell ye, Jamie. Georgie is dead. Yer da sent us tae give ye the news."

Jamison's features rippled with surprise and then, just as quickly, with grief, but to his credit, that was his only reaction. He steeled himself admirably. "What happened tae him?"

Beaux glanced at Kendrick and Caspian, as if the men would help him carefully phrase the answer, but Kendrick spoke because Beaux seemed hesitant to.

"The MacKenzies murdered him," Kendrick said, his voice low and deep. He was a truthful man to a fault. "They lay in wait for him, Jamie. Georgie was going tae church and they ambushed him. Trampled him with their horses and dragged his body back tae Foulis for yer parents tae see."

That drew a reaction from Jamison; his cheeks reddened and he rocked back as if he'd been physically struck. He stared at Kendrick in horror. "Oh, God...," he gasped. "They killed Georgie."

"Aye, they killed him," Kendrick said. "Yer da told us that ye killed Connell whilst defending Robbie. Ye know the MacKenzies killed Georgie tae send a message tae ye, Jamie – this is tae lure ye home. Ye fled and they want ye tae come home tae face them."

Jamison felt as if he'd been hit in the chest. He was having a difficult time breathing. All he could think of was his pious older brother, a tall and rather meek character whose only goal in life was to become a priest. He hated fighting and politics. He wanted to live in peace. To have met such a violent end sickened Jamison so badly that the more he thought of it, the more nauseous he became. It was little time before he became violently ill and ended up vomited the contents of his stomach into the grass at the side of the road. He could feel a hand on his back, meant to give him comfort and support, but there was no comfort to be had. He knew the truth.

He had killed his brother.

"*Sweet Jesú*," he breathed, still bent over. "I killed him. As I live and breathe, I killed Georgie. Tae get tae me, they killed him."

Beaux was standing next to him, his big hand on Jamison's back. "Ye know that's not true," he said quietly. "Yer da said that Georgie wouldna listen tae him. Yer da tried tae tell him not tae leave the safety of home, but Georgie left and the MacKenzies found him. Had Georgie listened, he would be alive"

"Had Robbie not lusted after Eva MacKenzie, none of this would have happened!" Jamison suddenly roared as he stood up, wiping his mouth. He was pasty-white as he faced off against his friends, his closest brothers. "I leave for home today. If the MacKenzies want me, then I willna disappoint them."

Beaux and Kendrick were shaking their head at him. "Jamie…." Kendrick said dubiously. "Ye canna…."

"If they want me, I am coming!"

He was already moving, staggering back to the gatehouse, but Beaux and Kendrick put their hands on him, preventing him from continuing. He was half-mad with grief and anger, speaking before thinking, which was exactly as his father had feared. It was Caspian who pushed between Beaux and Kendrick, his intense gaze on Jamison. He was the most serious of the three, a deadly man with a deadly manner.

"Listen tae me," he said, his hand on Jamison's face. "Yer dad sent us tae prevent ye from doing this. Ye'll return, but it will be well-planned. Ye're not going tae walk into their open arms, Jamie. Yer father canna bury another son, and especially not ye. Are ye listenin'? Now, take us inside and feed us, for the love of God, before we collapse.

Let us calmly speak of this. If ye're going tae face the MacKenzie, then ye need tae think it through and we will help ye. Whatever ye decide, we'll be there. Agreed?"

Jamison gazed into the face of his friend, one of the wisest men he knew, and he struggled to control his rage. After a moment, he nodded his head, unsteadily, taking big, deep breaths in an effort to calm himself.

"Aye," he finally muttered. "Agreed. But poor Georgie…."

Caspian slapped him lightly on the cheek. "Not a-now," he said. "Let us go inside first. Just breathe, Jamie. We'll help ye think this through."

They forced him to walk, all three of them, forcibly escorting him through the gatehouse where a host of de Lohr and Four Crosses soldiers were watching the four men with a great deal of curiosity and concern. It was clear that these men had told Jamison something quite devastating because he had vomited and raged all in a short span of time, so clearly, something was greatly amiss.

Once inside the bailey, however, it came apparent to Beaux and Kendrick and Caspian that things were not normal. From what they heard from de Lohr, Four Crosses had been under siege and suffering a great deal of trouble, but the bailey didn't look that way at all. It looked as if some kind of events were happening because there looked to be an arena near the troop house with archery targets and other things going on. It was, truthfully, difficult to tell but it looked to them like something of a party. This didn't look like a beaten castle. Curious, Beaux pointed to the arena.

"What goes on here, Jamie?" he asked.

Jamison, still pale with rage and grief, turned a disinterested eye to the activities. "A festival tae build morale," he said. "Four Crosses has suffered a good deal of warfare over the past several months and we thought tae…."

He stopped, coming to a halt and gazing off towards the arena. His three friends looked, too, simply to see what he was looking at. It was then that the men saw a woman in a green dress emerge from the crowd and head in their direction. But it wasn't just any woman; full-breasted and long of torso, she drew closer and they could see just how beautiful she was. A stunning beauty, in fact, and it was clear that Jamison's attention was on her.

When the woman saw that the attention was on her, she smiled hesitantly as she drew near. Although she looked at the three men she didn't recognize, her focus was mainly on Jamison. In fact, she peered rather closely at him.

"Jamison?" she asked, her voice sweet and deep. "Is everything well? Why did you leave? You know they will not start the hammer throw without you."

Jamison looked at Havilland, sick and torn. He'd never wanted to be held more in his life at the moment, held by her and comforted. God, he needed it badly, but pride kept him from collapsing against her. He knew his friends wouldn't think poorly of him if he did, but he didn't want the men of Four Crosses to see him. He'd already put on too much of a display as it was.

"Lady Havilland," he said, indicating the men standing around him. "I would like tae introduce ye tae men who are closer tae me than brothers. Sir Beaux MacKay, Sir Kendrick Sutherland, and Sir Caspian Ross. Lads, this is Lady Havilland de Llion, eldest daughter of Sir Roald de Llion, commander of Four Crosses Castle."

Havilland dipped her head politely at the men in turn. She would have tried to curtsy but she'd never really done anything like that in her life and she was certain that she would topple herself, so nodding her head had to suffice. But as Jamison introduced them, a recollection occurred to Havilland, one of the very first conversations she'd ever had about Jamison back when they had first met. Tobias had told her about Jamison and his three companions who used to terrorize the young squires and pages at Lioncross Abbey, back in the days when these men were young and in training. Munro, Sutherland, Ross, and MacKay, Tobias had said. It occurred to Havilland that she was looking at the very men he had spoken of.

"The Lions of the Highlands," she murmured, looking over the four of them. Looking at them, tall men with big muscles and an untamed look about them, she could utterly see why they earned that name. "I was told about you but I had no idea you were coming to Four Crosses. To what do we owe the honor of your visit?"

The four men chuckled to varying degrees. "So our reputation precedes us, does it?" Beaux asked, looking at Jamison. "What did ye tell her?"

Jamison shook his head, looking rather surprised. "I never told her about the Lions," he said, looking at her curiously. "Someone else must have."

Havilland nodded. "Tobias did," she said. "Back on the very first day we met. Do you recall? I tried to kill you and you spanked me. Then Tobias told me about you and your Highland brothers. He told me that the four of you were the most powerful clan sons in all the Highlands."

Kendrick and Caspian puffed up, taking pride in a reputation that had obviously spread, but Beaux was looking at the lady with a shocked expression. "You tried to kill Jamie?" he clarified.

Havilland chuckled softly, eyeing Jamison, who was also grinning in spite of himself. "I tried," she said. "It was a confusing day, in the midst of a battle. I mistook him for the enemy."

It wasn't exactly the truth but Jamison allowed her that small little lie, perhaps to save her pride. Perhaps it was to save his. In any case, the more he looked at her, the more proud and pleased with the woman he felt.

Introducing her to his friends had been a monumental moment for him because as he'd done it, he'd experienced feelings he'd never felt before. He was announcing to the world that she belonged to him and that made him feel whole, complete. This beautiful woman whom he wanted to marry so badly, whom he was coming to depend on. Reaching out, he took Havilland's hand and tucked it into the crook of his elbow, a decidedly possessive gesture. He faced his friends.

"Ye should know that I have asked Havilland tae be me wife," he said, looking at the woman who was smiling openly at him. "Any woman who would attack me with a sword is a brave woman, indeed. She impressed me so much that I had no choice but tae marry her."

He expected congratulations. What he received was a myriad of blank and, in Kendrick's case, shocked expressions. As if they didn't understand what he had just said. But as he looked at the three, it began to occur to him that these weren't expressions of shock. They were expressions of dismay. He frowned.

"Have ye nothing tae say tae that?" he said. "I am telling ye that I have asked this woman tae marry me and she has agreed. Ye have agreed, have ye not?"

He looked at Havilland when he asked the question and she nodded, smiling, completely oblivious to the meaning of the expressions on the others. Not knowing them, she had no idea that the lack of a congratulatory word wasn't normal.

"I did agree, although I doubt you would have let me refuse, in any case," she said, jesting with him. "I do not suppose you would have let me think on it."

"Never."

She giggled and Jamison grinned, but he was concerned that his friends had said nothing about his impending marriage. In fact, they were now looking at each other in confusion and Jamison was rather hurt by their response. Hurt turned into disappointment and a little bit of anger.

"Still no word of happiness?" he said, facing Beaux. "Why not? Because she's not Scots? I dinna think that sort of thing mattered tae ye, Beaux. Ye, of all people."

Beaux quickly shook his head, seeing that Jamison was offended by their restraint. "'Tis not that at all, Jamie," he said hesitantly. "What we told ye outside the gatehouse… there is more tae the story. We shouldna speak of it in front of the lady."

Jamison frowned, completely puzzled. "And why not?" he wanted to know. "She is tae be me wife. I will keep no secrets from her."

Havilland, coming to sense that there was something odd and even depressing afoot, put her hand on Jamison's arm. "'Tis all right," she assured him. "I… I will go back to the arena and watch the hammer throw while you speak to your friends. Shall I tell them you will not be participating?"

Jamison was growing more inflamed by the moment. He held fast to her, not letting her leave, while he faced Beaux. He believed his friends were discriminating against her and he was deeply disappointed.

"Ye will tell me why ye havena congratulated me on me impending marriage," he said, "but know if ye say one bad thing about Lady Havilland, ye'll not like me reaction. I wouldna think ye small enough tae denounce her for the country she was born in, Beaux."

Beaux found himself on the defensive. "I told ye 'tis not that at all," he insisted. "I dunna care if the lass is from Wales. It makes no difference tae me. All I care for is yer happiness and if ye say she is the lass o' yer dreams, then I'm happy for ye. But…."

Jamison's eyebrows flew up. "But *what*?" he demanded.

Beaux sighed heavily, looking at Kendrick and Caspian, once again, for silent support in what needed to be said. Jamison wasn't making it easy in the least and they didn't want to speak of this in front of the woman he'd just introduced as his betrothed, but he wasn't giving them much choice.

"Please, Jamie," he begged one last time. "In private, if ye will."

"Tell me now. I'll not hide anything from her."

Beaux rolled his eyes, perturbed at the stubborn stance, when Caspian finally spoke up. "Jamie, it has nothing tae do with yer lass," he said. "She's a beautiful woman and ye deserve yer happiness. But with Georgie's passing, that means ye're now the heir, and with that role comes responsibilities."

Jamison eyed Caspian. "I realize that," he said, offended that they evidently thought he didn't know his role. "I know me responsibilities."

Caspian shook his head. He lowered his voice, hoping that would stress what sensitive information he was about to speak. "George was betrothed tae Agnes MacLennan," he said. "Did ye know that?"

"Of course I did."

"Then know that yer da expects ye tae fulfill that contract," Caspian said, watching Jamison's eyes widened. "The MacLennans are kin tae the MacKenzies. Yer da hopes tae end the blood feud by marrying ye tae young Agnes. The MacKenzies willna fight against their kin; they never have."

Jamison's mouth popped open. "I canna marry that bairn," he said in disbelief. "I have me own bride tae marry."

Caspian shook his head. "As the heir, 'tis yer duty tae marry Georgie's bride," he said. "Ye canna break the contract."

"I dunna care about the contract!"

"It 'twill cost lives if ye dunna marry her."

That brought Jamison to a stop. He stood like stone, staring at Caspian as if incapable of moving. In truth, he was afraid to – afraid to breathe, afraid to move, afraid of what would happen if he did. It wasn't even the fact that his father expected him to marry George's betrothed; he should have realized that. He should have realized it before now but he was still reeling over his brother's death and the greater implications of that event hadn't occurred to him.

But now… dear God, now the full impact was upon him and he was having difficulty processing it all. As the Munro heir, he was expected to marry an ally. He was starting to feel sick again.

"Did me da tell ye that is what he expects from me?" he asked, his voice strained.

Caspian nodded. "He did," he said. "'Tis yer duty tae fulfill, Jamie. I'm sorry."

Jamison exhaled sharply, as if all of the breath had been driven out of his body. One giant, unseen fist to the gut and he couldn't breathe any longer. But he tried; he forced himself to breathe – *in and out. In and out.* Only then did he turn to look at Havilland, who was standing beside him with a queer expression on her face. She was looking up at him, her eyes a bottomless pool of emotion and confusion.

Jamison didn't even know what to say to her. In hindsight, now he realized why Beaux and Kendrick and Caspian wanted to tell him all of this in private. But he hadn't listened. He thought they'd held some kind of prejudice against Havilland and it had angered him. Now, he was feeling as distraught as he possibly could, searching for something to say to Havilland, who had heard everything. But she spoke before he could.

"Your brother is dead?" she asked.

Jamison realized his throat was tight with emotion. "Aye," he replied. "That is why they have come, tae tell me of me brother's death and tae inform me that I am now me da's heir."

Havilland continued to gaze at him, processing the situation, absorbing what she had been told. "I… I am so sorry to hear that," she said quietly. "How did he die?"

Jamison went to grasp her hands, to hold on to her tightly, but she yanked them away, unwilling to let him touch her. He felt like vomiting again.

"I told ye I had come tae de Lohr because I killed a man," he said, his voice hoarse. "Do ye remember?"

"I do."

"His family killed Georgie."

Now, a good deal was coming clear to Havilland and she began to tremble, realizing that the situation was serious, indeed. These three men hadn't simply come to Four Crosses to visit; they had come with a purpose. A life-changing purpose. At this moment, Havilland could suddenly see everything slipping away, the joy she had known, the new emotions she had experienced. All of it was slipping away.

Her life, as she had hoped for it to be, was slipping away forever.

"What does that mean?" she asked, her lower lip quivering. "Are you going back to Scotland?'"

"Aye."

"To marry your brother's betrothed?"

He had never felt so much pain in his life, distress and grief stabbing at him from all directions. "Nay," he said. "I willna do it. "Tis ye I… Havi, 'tis ye I adore. I shall have ye and no other."

"But your father wants you to marry your brother's betrothed."

"I willna do it!"

"You will defy your father, then? For the trouble it would cause your clan, you would do that?"

"I would!"

"For me?"

"For ye."

Havilland wasn't sure she could believe him. She had heard what Caspian had said, how he had stressed that Jamison had no choice. That meant there would be no marriage between her and Jamison because, as clan chief, it would be his duty to marry to strengthen the clan. She knew that much. She understood how marriages in this age worked. Marriage was meant for political strengthening, not for love.

Love.

God, she loved him. But she couldn't have him. She knew that even as she looked at him; something in his expression said that he knew it, too.

It was over.

"You heard your friend," she said, voice quivering as she backed away from him. "Your father hopes to end a blood feud by you marrying your brother's betrothed. It is your duty now. You can go back to Scotland and forget about the knight's daughter you once thought you fancied. I am not a fine lady, anyway. These clothes… they do not belong to me. They do not suit me. I will get along as I have before, as I always have before. You needn't worry about me, Jamison. Just… go home."

With that, she turned on her heel and ran off, so fast that the green skirt was hiked up around her knees, blowing behind her in a rush. Jamison took off after her but she was faster, so fast that she made it into the keep before he did. He was calling her name, yelling after her, begging her to stop, but she wouldn't listen. Havilland reached her chamber and slammed the door, throwing the iron bolt so he couldn't come in. Then, she stumbled to a corner of the chamber and collapsed, hands over her ears, as Jamison stood at the door and banged on it, begging her to open it.

Havilland remained in her corner and wept.

CHAPTER SEVENTEEN

"There will never be anyone else.

Only you…."

EVERYONE WAS CRYING.

The banging on Havilland's door had gone on all afternoon as Amaline had kept to her chamber, the door locked, sobbing over Madeline and over the situation in general. Since fleeing Madeline's cell earlier in the day she had come to her chamber, making herself scarce. In the meantime, however, something terrible had happened and Jamison had done something to upset Havilland, so much so that her sister had been locked in her chamber since morning, weeping steadily as Jamison begged her to open the door.

Amaline couldn't really hear what was being said but she thought it was something about another woman. He was supposed to marry someone else. Or wasn't he? Amaline wasn't entirely sure; all she knew was that Havilland was hysterical because Jamison had some involvement with another woman.

He'd lied to her.

That concerned Amaline deeply. She didn't dare go out onto the landing where Jamison was banging on Havilland's door, begging her to open it. She was frightened of all of the shouting and pleading and weeping. But as the afternoon progressed and Jamison begged so much that his voice grew hoarse, all Amaline could think about was the fact that he'd evidently lied to her sister. The same man who had called Madeline a traitor was now evidently a liar himself. At least, that was the way it seemed to Amaline.

And with that realization, her doubts about Madeline grew. Perhaps her sister really *was* innocent. Perhaps she hadn't done any of those things he said she'd done. How could any of them believe Jamison when he said Madeline was a traitor if he had, in fact, lied to Havilland about wanting to marry her? And now Madeline was waiting for Lord de Lohr to arrive to cut her head off because of what Jamison accused her of.

Was it true?

Did she really spy for the Welsh?

The more time passed, the more uncertain of the situation Amaline became. Indecision gripped her. She wept about it, prayed about it, and peered out of her window at the gatehouse, at the door with the steps that led down to the vault. Madeline was down there, awaiting her sentence because of what a man had said. Until just a few days ago, they hadn't even known who Jamison Munro was. Now, he'd thrown Madeline in the vault and had bewitched Havilland. He'd done terrible things, in Amaline's mind.

He'd torn them all apart.

Perhaps Madeline's only chance would be to run for safety, to flee Four Crosses as she had said she would. Now it wasn't sounding like such a terrible idea. Confused and frightened, Amaline didn't want to be guilty of allowing her sister to be executed if Jamison had lied about her. She wouldn't be able to live with herself if that happened. Perhaps she should free Madeline and let her run off, never to return as she had promised. Perhaps that was the only way to save Madeline's life.

By the time sunset neared, Amaline had all but convinced herself that Jamison had lied and that Madeline was innocent. Listening to the man plead with Havilland all afternoon had fed that doubt, forcing her into a decision she wasn't entirely certain about. But decide she had; she would set Madeline free because she didn't want her sister's head to be cut off. Jamison Munro was not to be trusted. With those thoughts in mind, she pulled a dark, heavy cloak off of the peg on the wall and timidly opened the chamber door.

The landing was dark outside but she could immediately see a massive body sitting against Havilland's door. Her eyes met with Jamison's in the dimness and he simply looked at her. His face was pale, his eyes red-rimmed, but after a moment, he smiled weakly at her.

"I dinna know ye were in yer chamber," he said, his voice so hoarse that he could barely speak. "I am sorry for the noise."

Amaline didn't reply. Nervously, she scooted down the stairs and away from him as he sat in the landing, beaten and muddled. She continued out of the keep, out into the dusk of night, seeing that there were men still in the arena with some kind of object they were running after. She didn't even know what they were doing, but evidently, the day's games were still going on. She was sorry she didn't even get to see any of them, but that could not be helped. Off to her left was the great hall and the kitchen yard, and straight ahead was the gatehouse.

Ever vigilant, she clutched the cloak against her as she kept an eye out for the de Lohr knights, thinking they must surely be somewhere nearby. Even as she neared the gatehouse, she had yet to see them and wondered if they might be in the great hall. She could see a good deal of smoke coming from the chimney, which meant someone was stoking the hearth against the coming winter evening. Perhaps the knights were in there, warming themselves after a busy day.

The temperature outside was dropping, causing Amaline's breath to hang in the air, heavy with moisture, as she made it to the entry to the gatehouse. There were soldiers about as men took their posts for the coming night and she could hear a sergeant, somewhere, yelling. Dogs barked. Looking around nervously, she was about to enter the stairwell leading down to the vault when it occurred to her that the cells were locked and the keys were usually with the sergeant who commanded the gatehouse.

She had to get those keys.

With the heavy cloak still clutched against her, she knew she had to come up with a plan for getting those keys. She wasn't very good at planning, hence forgetting about the locked cell in the first place. Havilland and Madeline were the ones that usually did all of the planning. She simply followed along. But now, she was having to come up with a scheme to break her sister out of the vault and she struggled not to become overwhelmed by it. What could she possible do to get the keys from the sergeant?

What could she do?

So she stood there, apprehensively, as men walked past her, men heading to their posts or just being relieved of them. Men over at the makeshift arena were just finishing up their games and were beginning to clear out, heading for the troop house. Amaline watched them for a moment, her gaze falling on the archery targets from earlier in the day. Now, they were a pile of broken wood near the troop house, having served their purpose. Looking at the big pile of wood pieces, an idea suddenly occurred to her.

Formulating a plan, she quickly made her way over to the pile of wood and picked up a fairly heavy piece, something she could use to hit someone with. *Right in the head, hard enough to knock him out!* Quickly, she draped the cloak over her arm to cover up the hand holding the wood. It was all nicely concealed. Now armed, and feeling much more confident than she had moments earlier, she went to find the sergeant in charge of the gatehouse.

Now, she had a plan.

The man wasn't difficult to find. He was standing just inside the gatehouse near the guard's room because the room was very warm and men were packed inside. When she politely asked him to please admit her to Madeline's cell, the man shook his head and pointed to the wall, explaining that Sir Thad had the keys. Thad, the knight who had carried Amaline's favor for games she had never even seen. Feeling embarrassed, and very anxious, she went to find Thad.

It took her some time to locate the young knight. He was on the northern part of the wall, watching the mist roll in, and she called to him, yelling two or three times until he actually heard her. Quickly, he came to her bidding which only increased her apprehension considering what she was about to do. He smiled at her as he slid down the ladder.

"Lady Amaline," he said. "You ran off this morning and I did not see you at all after that. I hope all is well?"

She nodded, ashamed and nervous. "I… I was not feeling well," she said. "I am sorry I deserted you. Did… did you win any of the games?"

Thad nodded. "I won the hammer toss," he said proudly, "but I only won that because Jamison left and Tobias throws like an old woman. He is angry at me now for besting him."

"Oh," Amaline said, her eyes darting around the bailey. "Where is he?"

Thad was smiling at her, seeing that she appeared nervous but he thought it was because she was simply nervous to talk to a fine, handsome knight, of which he was one. He took it as a compliment.

"He is in the great hall with our visitors," he said. "Did you see them?"

"See who?"

"Our visitors," he said again. "The Lions of the Highlands have come back to England. They came to pay Jamison a visit. Evidently, there is trouble at home and Jamison's father has sent for him."

That bit of news caught Amaline by surprise. Was that why Havilland was so upset? Because Jamison had been summoned back to Scotland? Her confusion grew.

"I… I did not see any visitors," she said. "But Jamison is in the keep. Havilland is weeping and she will not speak to him. He is sitting outside of her door."

Thad lost some of his humor then. "I know," he said. "There is more to it than that, poor man. I am not entirely sure he can straighten things out."

"What things?"

Thad eyed the girl, realizing he'd probably said too much. It wasn't his business, anyway, what was happening with Jamison. He didn't want to start rumors. Therefore, he forced a smile again.

"It does not matter," he said, brushing off her question. "Now, did you wish to speak with me, my lady?"

Amaline was still thinking about Jamison being summoned back to Scotland, forcing herself to push that thought aside with Thad's question. "Aye," she nodded. "I want to see Madeline and the gate sergeant says that you have the keys."

Thad lost his smile again. "I am not sure she is allowed visitors, my lady," he said. "Let me ask Jamison before I consent."

Amaline shook her head quickly. "He is outside of Havilland's room, yelling at her to open her door," she said. "I do not think he would take kindly to your question. Please… I just want to give my sister this cloak, as it is very cold. Won't you please let me in to see her? I will only stay a minute."

Thad eyed her, considering her point. It was true that Jamison might not take kindly to being interrupted when all of the knights knew he was in the middle of a serious personal crisis. Beaux MacKay had told both Tobias and Thad what had transpired earlier in the day and how Jamison had forced them to divulge George Munro's desire that Jamison should marry his dead brother's betrothed. It wouldn't have been so bad had Jamison not forced them to say it in front of Havilland, who understandably reacted poorly to the news. Now, Jamison was dealing with a goodly amount of turmoil while Beaux, Kendrick, Caspian, and Tobias sat in the great hall and drank, waiting for Jamison to emerge from the keep.

But that might take a long time. Certainly, Jamison didn't need to be bothered with something like this if all Amaline wanted to do was give her sister a cloak. Thad didn't see any harm in it. Looking into the young woman's eager face, he relented.

"Very well," he said. "Come along."

Amaline did. Heart pounding, clutching the piece of wood in her hand, she walked alongside Thad to the gatehouse, purposely falling back behind him as he went down the stairs first. She didn't know when she'd have another chance to catch him off guard as she could now, for he certainly couldn't see her pull out the piece of wood as she came down the stairs behind him. If she was going to do this, now was the time.

She summoned her courage, her stomach in knots at the thought of failure. She couldn't fail! They were almost to the bottom when Amaline lifted the wood and cracked Thad over the head, so hard that he fell down the last two steps and landed in a heap, still as stone. Rushing upon him, she rolled the unconscious knight over onto his back and searched him, finally coming up with the ring of iron keys in the pocket of his tunic. Grabbing the keys, she rushed to the cell where Madeline was just starting to wake up.

Exhausted, Madeline had slept on and off for most of the day, as there was little else to do in the nearly pitch-black cell. She had been dead asleep when she'd been awoken by a grunt and what sounded like a fall. Suddenly, Amaline was opening her cell and when Madeline realized this, she scrambled to her feet, rubbing her eyes in disbelief.

"Ammie!" she gasped. "What have you done?"

Amaline didn't have time for any questions. "Quickly," she said, thrusting the cloak at her. "Put this on and go. Go through the postern gate and leave. You promised you would never come back here!"

Astonished, Madeline took the cloak, still a bit groggy from sleep and having no real idea what had just happened. She looked at her sister, her eyes wide.

"But… but why?" she said. "Why would you…?"

Amaline was terrified they would be found out or that Thad would soon regain consciousness. She yanked her sister by the arm, pulling her from the cell.

"Put the cloak on," she told her again, snappish. "Get out of here, do you hear? I have given you your freedom and if you do not leave now, it will more than likely cost me mine if we are discovered. Go,

Madeline! Do not ask questions, just go!"

Madeline didn't have to be told twice. With shaking hands, she pulled on the cloak, a heavy dark thing, pulling on the hood so no one could see her face. She went to hug Amaline but her sister stood back, unwilling to be embraced. She was fearful and uncertain, and in truth, angry. Angry at the entire situation. She simply wanted Madeline gone.

"Ammie," Madeline's features softened with sorrow when Amaline rejected her embrace. "Thank you for doing this. Thank you for saving my life. But what will you tell Havi and Jamison? They will punish you when they discover you have released me."

Amaline yanked her sister towards the stairs. "Since when do you care about me?" she asked. "You only care about yourself or else you would not have asked me to do this."

Madeline took the first step but she didn't leave; she looked at her sister seriously. "Then why are you helping me?"

Amaline sighed heavily, shaking her head. "I am not sure," she said honestly. "Mayhap… mayhap I do not want to see your head cut off. Mayhap Jamison is lying and you really have done nothing wrong. Or mayhap you are lying and I am a fool. I do not know! Simply go and never come back!"

Madeline didn't know what to say. Perhaps there was nothing really to say. Amaline was risking her own freedom to help her escape and she didn't take that lightly. She began to feel guilty for it but not guilty enough to go back into her cell. She was free and she intended to stay free.

"Thank you, Ammie," she whispered. "I shall not forget this."

Amaline didn't say anything. She simply watched her sister run up the stairs, bound by the cloak, and disappear into the coming night. Amaline thought her escape would be rather easy considering that, out of respect to Havilland, Jamison hadn't told many of the soldiers about Madeline's imprisonment. That would be his undoing.

Madeline would be able to slip by men who would recognize her but think nothing was amiss. Still, the fact remained that Thad would know Amaline had set her sister free. He would tell Jamison and she would be punished, now for her own particular brand of treachery.

Amaline had to think of a believable explanation.

When Thad finally regained consciousness a short while later, it was to Amaline's concerned face. She was patting his cheeks, trying to wake him. When he looked around, groggily asking for an explanation, Amaline proceeded to inform him that he had slipped on the stairs and knocked himself out, and when she used his keys to open the cell to provide Madeline with the cloak, her sister had overpowered her and run away.

Amaline made a good show of being quite upset about the whole thing, but deep down, Thad didn't believe her. He was fairly certain it had all been quite planned and he had the bump on the back of his head to prove it.

଼

"IF WE LEAVE this week, we should make it back tae Foulis by late spring," Kendrick said. "I'd like tae spend more than a few days here but we must return as soon as we can. There is no knowing what has happened in our absence."

He was speaking to Beaux and Tobias as Caspian, exhausted beyond all reason, was sleeping with his head down on the table. In fact, all three Scotsmen were exhausted but Caspian was the only one who had succumbed to sleep. The others were fighting it, awaiting Jamison's return to the hall. There was still a great deal to discuss.

But there was a sense of disappointment, too. Disappointment that Jamison's happiness with Lady Havilland had been so cruelly damaged. Of course, Jamison was to blame for that, not allowing his father's message to be delivered in private, but it didn't matter now. Lady Havilland was heartbroken and Jamison right along with her. Beaux had been trying to figure out how to make it all well again, to ease both Jamison and Havilland, but it simply wasn't possible. Jamison was to marry Agnes MacLennan and there wasn't anything anyone could do about it.

If they wanted to end the blood feud, it had to be that way.

Beaux kept rolling that over and over in his mind; *it has to be this way. It must be this way.* He seriously wondered if Jamison was going to obey his father's wishes in this. He would risk a continued feud by not marrying Agnes. Would his life-long happiness be worth pleasing his father? Beaux had known Jamison a very long time and the man was stubborn. He also knew very much what he wanted in life and if he wanted Lady Havilland that badly, Beaux could easily see him defying George for the privilege of calling that beautiful woman his wife.

Some things were worth fighting for.

As Beaux pondered Jamison's wants and desires, Tobias was pondering something completely different. He'd been near the arena, preparing the coming games, when he'd seen Jamison and the three Scotsmen come through the gatehouse. He'd seen Havilland go to meet them and he also saw her run off with Jamison on her heels. Only then had he left his men at the arena to go and see what had happened, being informed by Beaux of the reason for their visit to Four Crosses.

Tobias was a horrible person in that he was glad they'd come.

Glad that they'd come with news that Jamison was now heir to Clan Munro and that he was expected to marry his dead brother's betrothed. The mention of the betrothal had almost been an afterthought following news of Georgie's death and the feud with the MacKenzies, but to Tobias, it was the most important thing he'd heard. *Jamison is betrothed to another!* Finally, now he had his chance with Havilland. He would swear to Jamison he would take very good care of her and make all sorts of promises to the man for the care and keep of Havilland, but the truth was that he was ecstatic over the news. Ecstatic and struggling not to show it. So he pretended, as he sat at the feasting table with the others, that he was as distressed as everyone else. He put on a good show of it.

Finally, something on this day had gone his way.

"I never met Georgie Munro," he said, pouring himself and

Kendrick more hot wine. "What was the man like?"

Beaux, having had four cups of wine already, was feeling the alcohol. Half-lidded, he answered. "He wanted tae be a priest," he said. "The man was kind and quiet. He wasna suited for the life as a Clan Chief. Everyone knew it so there may be some who think his death a blessing. Now, Jamison will assume control and he will be the best chief in the Highlands. With him, there will be no question of the Munro Clan's strength."

Tobias pretended to ponder that but his next question was calculated. "And the woman he is to marry?" he asked. "What about her clan?"

Beaux was feeling just as bad as he possibly could about that. He simply shook his head, imbibing of more wine, as Kendrick spoke.

"She's the heiress tae Clan MacLennan," he said; the man was bloody well drunk with the amount of hot wine he'd consumed. "She's a tiny little lass, barely fourteen years of age, with a pale face and pale hair. She's been sickly most o' her life but she's the only child of Amos MacLennan, a rightly powerful man who commands thousands. Moreover, the MacLennans are a rich lot. More sheep and wool than they know what tae do with. When Jamie marries Agnes, he'll be rich beyond his wildest dreams."

Tobias listened seriously, but inside, he was dancing a gleeful dance. Still, he kept up the pretense of being sorry on Jamison and Havilland's behalf. "And if he marries Havilland, he will get nothing," he said. "Oh, 'tis true that she is a beauty. No doubt about it. She is bright and compassionate. But her father is not a wealthy man. In fact, he's quite mad. Did Jamison tell you that? We only found out yesterday. Havilland's father, Roald de Llion, has been mad for over a year and Havilland and her sisters have been keeping the secret. So if Jamison marries her, he inherits a madman for his wife's father and a castle that does not even belong to the de Llion family. It belongs to my father."

By the time he was finished, Beaux and Kendrick were looking at him in various stages of disbelief. It occurred to them both that Tobias knew Four Crosses and, more than likely, the history between Jamison and Havilland. Clearly, he had divulged a great deal already.

"Lady Havilland has kept her father's madness from her liege?" Beaux said, somewhat incredulous.

Tobias nodded. "She did," he said. "But that is not the worst of it; at nearly the same time we were told of Roald's madness, we discovered that Lady Havilland's sister, Lady Madeline, had been feeding information to the Welsh. Did my father tell you that Four Crosses has been repeatedly attacked over the past several months? It has, you know. Now we find out that there was a spy in our midst – Lady Havilland's own sister."

He was trying to make it seem as if this was a terrible place, with terrible people, and Jamison would be well rid of them by not marrying Havilland. It was a calculated statement. Now that he'd thrown out such terrible information for them to digest, he went back to his wine, watching Beaux and Kendrick out of the corner of his eye, pleased to see that the men were quite shocked by the news.

"A spy," Beaux finally hissed. "And Jamie discovered this, did he?"

Tobias smacked his lips of the tasteless red wine. "He did," he said. "He stumbled upon her as she met her lover. Now the girl is in the vault, awaiting my father's arrival to bring her to justice."

Beaux shook his head, distressed with all he was hearing. "And Jamie has had tae manage all of this?" he said. "How could this happen? Who is in command of the castle wit' the father mad as he is? For a lass tae become a spy… that is a disgrace tae any commander. How could he not have known?"

Tobias shrugged. "It is quite simple how this happened, actually," he said. "Lady Havilland and her sisters were in command of the fortress. You see, they were raised as warriors. Their father, having no sons, raised the girls to fight. When Jamison and Havilland first met, she attacked him with a sword. It was a serious battle until he subdued her. She is a lady warrior."

Now, Beaux's shock increased. His half-lidded eyes lifted a bit. "She fights?"

"And very well."

Beaux looked at Kendrick, who simply lifted his shoulders. "If Jamie marries her, she'll need tae fight," he said. "It may be a blessing."

That wasn't what Tobias was driving at. He didn't want them to think that a marriage between Jamison and Havilland would be a good thing at all.

"If she marries him, then she will be in a strange world, fighting people who will want to kill her simply because she married him," he pointed out. "That is a difficult life to commit anyone to. Nay, for Jamison to marry one of his kind is all for the best. Lady Havilland should remain here and marry someone who will keep her and her family linked to Four Crosses and to the House of de Lohr. That is the life she knows, after all. She will be happier in time. Besides… she has only really known Jamison a week. How can you know your feelings for someone in just a week?"

Beaux and Kendrick pondered what they'd been told, thinking that Tobias made some sense in the matter. They were both caught up in the emotion of it, for Jamison's sake, and Tobias didn't seem to have that handicap. Perhaps the man was right. In any case, it was a sad situation. As Kendrick stood up and leaned over the table, over to a tray of cold meat that a servant had brought earlier, they heard commotion at the entry to the hall and they turned to see Thad staggering in with his hand to the back of his head. The other hand was dragging Amaline behind him.

Amaline was fighting and kicking at him, trying to break free, and it was a scene that brought Tobias, Beaux, and Kendrick to their feet. Tobias was the first one to move away from the table, heading for Thad.

"What goes on here?" he demanded, pointing to Amaline. "Let that girl go."

Thad was pale. His head was killing him and the blow to the back had split his scalp. "I will not," he said. "She hit me over the head and stole the keys to the vault, whereupon she released her sister. Madeline is gone."

Tobias' eyes widened as he looked at Amaline. "You did *this*?"

Amaline was weeping and frightened. "I did not let her go purposely," she sobbed. "I opened the door to give her a cloak and she escaped."

Thad didn't believe her in the least. Frustrated and injured, he looked at his cousin. "She asked me to go to the vault to let her in so she could bring Madeline a cloak," he said. "I took the stairs before her and she came up behind me and hit me on the head. While I was unconscious, she stole the keys and released Madeline."

Tobias was outraged. "How long ago?"

Thad looked at Amaline, giving her a yank to elicit a response. "You heard him," he said. "How long ago did she leave?"

Amaline squealed when he yanked on her again. "I do not know!" she said. "Five or ten minutes. I do not know!"

By this time, all three Highlanders were on their feet, listening to everything. "She canna have gotten very far," Beaux said, a sense of urgency in his tone. "Was she on foot?"

Thad looked at Amaline and, fearful he was going to yank at her again, she spoke. "I do not know," she said. "She ran out of the vault but I did not see where she went."

Tobias was genuinely upset. "She could have walked right out of the gatehouse for all we know," he muttered, glancing at Beaux. "Jamison did not tell the men of her capture out of respect for the family. He thought to handle the matter quietly. Therefore, only a very limited number of men knew she was in the vault. The rank and file, guarding the gatehouse, would not have known."

Thad still had his hand to the back of his head. "Didn't Jamison say he had followed Madeline from the postern gate?" he said. "I seem to recall that he found her by the river."

Tobias nodded. "That would, indeed, mean she took the postern gate," he said. Then, he hissed. "Damnation… she has probably taken it again and has lost herself in the forest along the river. We will never find her in all of that."

"Do we try?" Thad asked. "She cannot get very far on foot and we can send out mounted men to cast a net."

Tobias shook his head. "But in what direction?" he wanted to know. "North? East? South? Where?"

"The longer ye debate this, the further away she gets," Beaux put in. "Mount as many men as ye can and send them out in all directions."

Tobias turned to him. "I cannot risk sending out gangs of men, not when the Welsh have taken every opportunity to attack us," he said. "Sending them out and opening them up to possible organized attacks is not smart. Moreover, it would leave us low on manpower. I dare not risk it."

Beaux could see his point. He didn't agree with it, but he could see it. "I would suggest ye tell Jamison what is happening and let him decide," he said. "He is still in command of Four Crosses, is he not?"

Tobias was loath to agree, given that he had felt all along that he should be in command, so it was Thad who answered. "He is," he said. "He must know."

"I'll go," Beaux volunteered. He eyed Thad. "Ye need tae turn the lass over tae yer cousin and have a physic look at yer skull."

Thad sighed heavily. He wasn't feeling at all well. "Agreed," he said. He thrust Amaline at Tobias. "Lock her up where her sister was. That is the least she deserves. I am off to join the wounded."

He was indicating the far end of the hall that still had a few wounded there left over from the battle several days ago. Most were recuperating but some weren't. The de Lohr surgeon had taken his wounded and retreated back to Lioncross with the army but there was still an old physic left who tended the people of Four Crosses. It was that man Thad sought out as Tobias, unhappy that he has been relegated to tending Amaline, pulled the girl along with him as he headed out of the hall.

As the de Lohr knights parted ways, Beaux turned to Kendrick. "I'll go find Jamie," he said. "This place is an utter madhouse, it 'tis. I would say the sooner we leave, the better. I dunna want tae linger at this place and wait for the next terrible thing tae happen. Spies? Attacks?

Madmen? We need tae save Jamie from this place."

Kendrick couldn't disagree. "Aye," he said. "See if ye can persuade him tae leave on the morrow."

Beaux nodded. "I'll try."

Leaving Kendrick with the still sleeping Caspian in the great hall, Beaux exited the hall out into the coming night. It was very cold and the sun, at this point, was mostly down. Off to his left, he could see Tobias dragging the crying girl to the gatehouse, the one who had freed her sister from the vault. Beaux could only surmise that was another sister to Lady Havilland given the conversation he'd just heard.

More and more, he was coming to think this entire castle was a madhouse. After what Tobias had told them, there was a far greater picture here than he could have imagined. Perhaps coming here might have saved Jamison from becoming entrenched in the madness if he had married Lady Havilland. A warrior woman who lied to protect a mad father... a sister who had betrayed them... now another sister who had released the treacherous sister... aye, this place was a madhouse. Better get out of this place and be well rid of it.

So he headed to the keep, knowing that Jamison was still there because they could still hear him bellowing every so often. Surely, it was difficult for the man to lose a woman he believed he wanted to marry, but Beaux was convinced that getting him out of Four Crosses was the best thing for him. The keep loomed ahead now, a big and squat thing, three stories tall, and Beaux disappeared into the bowels of it.

It was very dark inside now with the sunset. He could see a couple of rooms on the entry level and he peered into each room, in succession, trying to see if Jamison was in any one of them. One was a solar, a cold and dark and cluttered place, and the second room looked to be more of a dining chamber of sorts. He didn't see anyone around so he took the narrow spiral stairs, as dark as pitch, up to the floor above and immediately came into contact with a body seated on the landing. In fact, he almost tripped over the boots. Eyes adjusting to the darkness, he caught sight of red hair.

"Jamie?" he whispered.

The boots shifted. "I'm here."

Jamison had yelled so much that he had no voice left. He spoke in barely above a whisper. Beaux came off the stairs and went to him, nearly tripping again before kneeling down beside him. He sighed faintly, putting his hand on the wavy red hair.

"'Tis not the way ye expected yer day tae end, is it?" he quipped softly.

Jamison shook his head, weakly. "Nay," he muttered. "Why did ye have tae come, Beaux? Why could ye not have simply left me alone?"

Beaux lowered himself onto the floor next to him. "Because yer da asked it of me," he said. "Because ye're closer than a brother tae me and the MacKenzies are out for yer blood. I came tae help ye, Jamie, but I know I dunna seem like it."

Jamison exhaled, low and slow. "I know ye did," he said. "But I have been sitting here thinkin'… if it means I am tae lose Havilland, then I willna go home. Ye can tell me da that ye couldna find me."

Beaux shook his head. "He would insist we look again," he said. "We would have tae look until we found ye. Ye know that."

"Then tell him I'm dead."

Beaux looked at him in the darkness, seeing his profile in the weak light. "Do ye know what that would do tae yer da?"

"Do ye know what losing Havilland is doing tae me?"

Beaux didn't want to be unkind. He knew that men in love were strange creatures. But he never thought he'd see Jamison succumb to a romance so quickly. It was true that Lady Havilland was a stunning creature, but he was sure that Jamison's infatuation with the woman was simply that – an infatuation. It couldn't be love.

… could it?

"Are ye telling me that yer da means less tae ye than a woman ye've only known a few days?" Beaux said. "Think, Jamison. There are hundreds o' people depending on ye, people that are rejoicing in the fact that ye're coming home tae lead them. Are all of those people worth less than yer Lady Havilland?"

Jamison wouldn't look at him. "I know me duty," he said. "I know what is expected. No one knows duty more than I do. But when do I get what I want? If I want tae marry a woman I adore, why can I not do it? Why must I think of others before meself?"

Beaux could see the distress in the man's eyes as he spoke. "Look at me," he said. When Jamison didn't move, he commanded it. "Jamie, *look* at me. Look at me and tell me ye love this woman enough that ye're willin' tae give up everything for her."

Jamison turned to him, then. "I'm willing tae give up everything for her."

"And ye're willing tae let Robbie become Clan Chief when yer da passes on? Because he will be yer da's heir; not Hector. Hector will have tae take commands from Robbie."

That brought a reaction. Jamison looked away, refusing to meet Beaux's eye. "Robbie is a fool."

"I know he is. But if we return tae Foulis Castle and tell yer da that ye're dead, Robbie becomes his heir. Is that what ye want?"

Jamison was staring off into the darkness, unwilling or unable to answer. "I willna leave this place without Havilland," he said, his voice barely above a whisper. "I've made a decision, Beaux – no matter me duty tae me clan, and no matter if it will result in the destruction of an alliance, I willna return home without marrying Havilland first. If it is a choice between peace and me own heart, I will choose me heart. I've never had tae make that choice before."

Beaux wasn't thrilled with hearing that statement but he didn't argue. Out of respect to Jamison, he wouldn't argue, whether or not he agreed.

"What if she willna marry ye?" he asked softly. "She's kept ye outside her door all day long. Ye canna force the lass tae marry ye no matter how badly ye want tae."

Jamison shrugged, weakly. "She has tae come out sometime," he said, turning to look at Beaux with a weary smile on his face. "When she does, I will be here."

There wasn't much more Beaux could say to that. Shifting his bulk, he leaned back against the wall, next to Jamison. For a moment, he pondered the situation and what had brought them to this point. He also pondered the original reason for him coming to Jamison. That had yet to be brought up.

"There's something more ye should know," he said. "While ye've been up here trying tae reason with yer lady, one sister has released the other from the vault."

Jamison's head snapped to him, his face glazed with shock. "Amaline released Madeline?"

Beaux nodded. "I dunna know the name o' the one who did the releasing, but she beat Thad over the head, stole his keys, and released yer prisoner. I think ye need tae go see tae yer command, Jamie. Things are happening while ye're up here in the keep."

Jamison was stunned by the information. "But Amaline was in her chamber all day," he said, pointing to the chamber across the landing. "I saw her emerge about a half hour ago. She dinna say a word tae me. She simply fled down the stairs."

Beaux glanced over at the door Jamison was indicating. "Mayhap she was in her chamber, plotting her sister's release," he said. "In any case, yer spy is gone now."

"Where is Amaline?"

"Thad was able tae capture that one. Tobias took her tae the vault."

It was a shocking set of circumstances he was describing, enough to cause Jamison to think of something other than his wounded heart. Beaux was correct; while he was up here screaming at Havilland, his command was in turmoil. He looked at Beaux for a moment longer before lurching to his feet. He began to bang on Havilland's door again.

"Havi," he tried to yell with his hoarse voice. "Amaline has released Madeline from the vault. I need tae speak with ye!"

Truth was, he didn't expect any real reaction from Havilland. She would probably think it was a trick. But they both heard the bolt on the other side of the door thrown and, suddenly, the panel yanked open. Havilland appeared in the doorway.

"You had better not be lying just to force me to open the door," she seethed. "If you are lying, I swear that I will…."

Jamison cut her off. "I wouldna lie just tae force ye tae open the door," he snapped back. "Or did ye not know that at any point, I coulda simply kicked the door in if I really wanted tae? Did that occur tae ye, now?"

Havilland was pale and drawn, just like Jamison was. They both looked as if they'd seen better days, the weight of emotions having taken their toll in both their manners and appearances. Havilland glared at Jamison as if the man was her worst enemy, unwilling to answer his question about kicking the door down. She didn't see a need to address it. But she did see the need to address the situation with her sister.

"Amaline would not have done such a thing," she said, eyeing Beaux, wondering what the man was doing there. "You heard her yesterday. She wanted you to keep Madeline locked up. She would not have released her."

"She did, my lady," Beaux said because Jamison was simply standing there, staring at the woman. "She hit Thad de Lohr over the head, stole his keys, and released yer sister. Thad has the bump on his head tae prove it."

Havilland's eyes widened and, very quickly, her features washed with distress. "Nay," she breathed, looking at Jamison as she spoke. "It is not possible. Why… why would she do it? She was terrified of Madeline!"

Jamison shook his head. "Who is tae say why the lass acted foolishly?" he said. "What matters is that she has released Madeline and Tobias has taken her tae the vault. Now she is in the same cell as her sister was."

That bit of information changed Havilland's manner drastically. Her jaw hardened and her eyes narrowed. "You will release her," she hissed. "She does not belong there!"

Jamison was on edge and didn't take kindly to Havilland's tone or attitude. He was unbalanced and emotional, a bad combination. "She released a traitor, m'lady," he said rather formally. "Unless I can find Madeline, Amaline will stand trial for her treachery. Now, where would Madeline go?"

Havilland was outraged beyond reason. Jaw ticking furiously, she tried to push between Jamison and Beaux, more than likely heading to the gatehouse where Amaline was being held, but Jamison grabbed her by the arm to stop her. The moment he did so, he had a fight on his hands – infuriated and terrified, Havilland brought up a hand to strike him, which he deftly blocked. He grabbed both of her hands and she still tried to fight him, bringing up a knee to ram him in the torso, but he spun her around and trapped her in his enormous embrace. Like a cat in a snare, she was caught… and battling every step of the way.

"Stop fighting me," he growled. "Tell me where Madeline would've gone. We must find her."

"Let me go!" Havilland demanded, still struggling. "I must go to Amaline!"

"Not until ye tell me where Madeline might've gone."

It was a battle of wills, of emotions, and of strength. Jamison had her on the strength but she was an even match in the other two categories. Having spent the past several hours in her chamber, weeping until she became sick, Havilland was shattered in so many ways. She didn't want Jamison to touch her yet his arms around her undid her. It was an embrace she would never know again, his powerful body against hers.

Truth was, she couldn't fight him any longer. Physically, anyway. She didn't want to hurt him, this man she adored so deeply. She finally hung her head as her struggles died down, trying very hard not to cry.

"I do not know where Madeline would have gone," she said. "I am sure wherever it is, she escaped through the postern gate. It seems to be her favorite access point and one that is not as carefully guarded as the gatehouse. It would have been easy for her."

Jamison could feel her relax in his arms, her warmth and softness clutched against him. "But beyond that, ye dunna know?" he asked, his voice considerably less harsh.

She shook her head. "I cannot guess," she said. "Elinog, the Preece home, is about ten miles to the east. It is possible she may have gone there, but I do not know for certain."

Jamison was satisfied, certain that she didn't know any more. Lifting his head, he nodded at Beaux, who had been watching the entire exchange rather warily. He could see so much power and passion between the two and it was astonishing that so much emotion could develop in just a few short days. But it was clear that there was much feeling there. He felt like he was intruding on an intimate moment as he watched, so when Jamison finally gave him the nod telling him to proceed, he left gladly.

He didn't want to intrude anymore.

Jamison watched Beaux as the man disappeared down the stairs. He heard him as he shut the door to the keep, the hollow echo reverberating off of the stone walls. But he continued to stand there, holding Havilland tightly. At this point, he had no intention of letter her go.

Ever.

"I am sorry that Amaline must be held, but ye understand that she has released her sister, who was me prisoner," he said, his voice scratchy and soft. "What she did was wrong, Havi."

Havilland was quickly growing distraught, not about her sisters as much as over the fact that Jamison was holding her quite closely. She could feel him wedged up behind her, his big body so incredibly comforting and inviting. But she couldn't let herself feel that comfort; it was a charade, a phantom of a love that might have been. There was too much pain in allowing herself to feel it, even one last time.

"Please let me go," she whispered.

His response was to tighten up his hold. "I willna," he murmured, his lips by the side of her head. "I will never let ye go. Havilland, I… I love ye. I havena had the courage tae tell ye before now because I dinna know what I was feelin'. I knew I adored ye – and I told ye so – but now I know that I love ye with all of me heart. I willna let ye go. Ye're going tae become me wife and we will return tae Scotland where…."

"Jamison, *stop*!" she gasped. The tears were starting to come now. "We cannot marry. I heard what your friends told you. You have no choice in the matter. You must fulfill your brother's betrothal and to pretend otherwise is selfish. You know you cannot marry me yet you pretend as if you still have a choice. Do you not know what you are doing to me with your refusal to face the truth? You are killing me!"

He didn't say anything for a moment. He continued to hold her tightly, his mouth next to her head. Softly, gently, he kissed her hair. Havilland felt him and the tears came in torrents, painful weeping as he was utterly and completely breaking her heart. She went limp, trying to force him to release her, then stiffening and trying to pull herself out his arms. No matter which way she went, he held her fast. His kisses against her head continued, even when she tried to move her head away from him.

At one point, she leaned her head so far away from him that he had full access to her tender neck, which he took full advantage of. He latched on to her flesh, suckling her, biting her, as she moaned and wept and tried to pull away from him.

"Jamison, please stop," she begged through her tears. "Please… you are destroying me."

He wouldn't release her, his mouth still latched on to her neck. "Tell me ye love me, Havi."

"Stop… *please*!"

"Tell me ye love me."

"I will not!"

"Tell me so I may live on it the rest of me life."

She burst out in a fresh round of sobs. "I love you," she whispered, utterly and completely miserable. "I have never loved anything in my life like I love you. And I hate you for asking me. I hate you for forcing me to tell you!"

The only sound after that was her loud weeping, so painful that tears stung Jamison's eyes. He couldn't believe he was going to lose her. That wasn't what he wanted; it wasn't in his plan. His plan was to marry Havilland and return home to rule his clan, but increasingly, he kept remembering Beaux's words… *ye canna force the lass tae marry ye no matter how badly ye want tae.* Was it actually possible that Havilland would stand her ground, that she wouldn't succumb to his wishes? He couldn't stomach the thought. He was starting to panic, just a little.

"Ye dunna hate me," he crooned, kissing any flesh his lips could come into contact with. "But I would like tae know why ye dunna believe me when I say I will marry ye against the wishes of me da. I will happily accept the consequences of me actions. For ye, I would do anything."

Havilland struggled to gain control of her weeping. "Because… because marriage is not something to be based on emotion," she said, sniffling. "Marriages are to strengthen bonds and gain allies. If you marry me, what will happen? Your father will be disappointed and your clan will hate you. They will hate me. Do you think that is fair to either of us, Jamison? And what of our children? Will they be hated, too?"

She had some valid concerns but he was certain he could convince her otherwise. "If I marry ye, Clan MacLennan will find another husband for their daughter," he said. "I am not the only man in northern Scotland tae marry and they'll forget about me soon enough. But the MacKenzie will not and neither will I – what I did tae Connell MacKenzie, I did tae save me brother. What they did tae Georgie was revenge. Now it is my turn tae seek vengeance and I shall, but knowing I have ye by me side…knowing I have the most beautiful, most adoring wife a man could have… that will see me through, Havi. I will be invincible."

Havilland had calmed by now, at least sufficiently enough to think the situation through. She was seeing it from a far different angle than he was and as much as it broke her heart, she knew she was seeing it clearly. God, it was killing her, but it was the only way.

She had to make him understand.

Gently, she was able to pull from his embrace, facing him in the dim light of the landing. Her face was still wet with tears and she wiped at her eyes, struggling with everything she had to compose herself. It was important that she say what she needed to say without breaking down. For both of their sakes, she had to do it.

"Shall I tell you what will really happen?" she asked softly. "Because of me, you will fall out of favor with your father as well as your clan. By not marrying the MacLennan girl, you will make an enemy out of that clan as well. And this MacKenzie that you must face...Jamison, if you marry the MacLennan girl, you will not have to face him. Your friends have said so. But if you marry me, you will have to face him. Do you think for one minute I could live with the knowledge that you were forced to do this because of me? Do you think for one minute I could live with the knowledge that I had killed you? I know there is the possibility that you will survive, but there is equal possibility that you will not. I would rather have you alive and married to another than dead and married to me. I do not want to be your widow. Jamison, you must return home and marry this girl and find peace with your clan and the MacKenzies. I love you enough to know that I must let you go. If you loved me enough, you would know that, also. Are you really so eager to die with me as your wife?"

He stared at her, the look on his face something she would never forget. He actually took a step back, an expression of horror and realization beyond anything he'd ever experienced before.

"If ye loved me enough, then ye'd want tae be with me no matter the opposition we would face," he said softly.

Havilland resisted the urge to touch his face, as if the mere gesture could force the man to understand what she was saying. "I love you enough to know that if you marry me, we would never know peace," she murmured. "Is that truly how you want our marriage to be?"

"I dunna care so long as we are together."

He was being stubborn which was weakening her resolve. But she couldn't give in to it, not now. The tears were threatening again but she had to be strong. She had to get through this.

"And I would rather have you alive," she said huskily. "You said that you love me."

"I do."

She stepped forward, then, putting her hands on his face, forcing him to look at her. "You said you would do anything for me."

"I will. Ye know I will."

She forced a smile. "Then go home and marry that girl," she said. "I will be all right. I will continue on here at Four Crosses and I will remember you as the only man I will ever love. There will never be anyone else. Only you. But I will not marry you. All of the begging in the world will not convince me to do it. It is my wish that you go home and do what you were born to do. Become the leader for your clan that I know you can be."

His face darkened. "Havi, dunna…."

"You said you would do anything for me. I am asking you to do this for me."

Pain swept his features. "Ye canna mean it."

"I do. With all that I am, I do. Please, Jamison… go. Do this for me."

His lower lip began to tremble and he stepped back, away from her. "I canna."

"You promised you would do anything for me. This is what I want."

He didn't want to do it. God help him, he didn't want to do it. He couldn't. But she had made her wishes clear. He could feel his throat tightening up, tears of great sorrow threatening, but before he could speak, she suddenly threw herself forward and kissed him. It was a powerful kiss, one of great feeling and emotion. Instinctively, his arms went around her, holding her closer than he'd ever held anything in his life. He knew that this was his last chance to touch her, to taste her, and he wasn't going to waste it. When she tried to pull away, he wouldn't let her. He put a hand on the back of her head and held her mouth to his.

He wasn't going to let this moment end.

Jamison's lips devoured hers, suckling them, before moving to her cheek and chin. Havilland had started to weep now, her composure shattering. She pushed at him now, trying to push him away, trying to separate them, but he wouldn't allow it. His mouth was on her neck, her shoulder, and he suddenly turned around, bracing her against the wall so she couldn't get away from him easily. Now, he had her trapped and he intended to take advantage of that.

His mouth slanted over hers once more, his tongue invading her sweet orifice, as the hand that was behind her head went to her shoulder and pulled the collar of her dress down. She was fairly well cinched up with the ties on the back of the garment but he yanked hard, loosening the stays, listening to her gasp with shock and uncertainty. So many emotions were swirling between them, too many to grasp. When he bit down on her shoulder, a love bite that saw him sinking his big teeth into her flesh, she cried out softly, wanting more.

Havilland had stopped trying to push Jamison away. For the moment, she had surrendered. Back against the wall as he overwhelmed her with his size, she simply wept softly as he pulled the collar of her dress down far enough that he exposed the tops of her breasts. She had such beautiful breasts. He suckled and kissed them, his hands on her neck, her shoulders, finally cupping her breasts as he nibbled on them. When he gave another good yank and exposed her left nipple, she stiffened. He could feel her. But the moment his mouth claimed her taut, warm nipple, her body seemed to collapse against him.

Jamison wasn't thinking any further, at that point, than his need for her – his need to touch her, to taste her, to claim her. He kept pulling her dress down, exposing both breasts in the process and losing himself in their softness. He wasn't feeding his lust as much as he was feeding his soul. Gorging himself on her flesh fed something in him that went beyond passion. It was bonding, emotional at the deepest level. It was expressing his feelings for her more than his words ever could.

And Havilland was letting him express himself in his own way. Her arms were around his head as he nursed against her breasts, holding him to her, experiencing the intimacy. It was overwhelming in its power, the beauty of the strength of love as only they could experience it. Jamison was quite certain that he was going to take the woman, here and now, but the moment he snaked a big hand under her skirt and touched the warm flesh of her thigh, it seemed to frighten her.

It was as if Havilland suddenly realized they shouldn't be doing this. Perhaps she didn't want to do it, knowing she would be branded for life to a man she could never have. Whatever the reason, she abruptly yanked from his grasped and stumbled away. Before Jamison could reclaim her, she fled into her chamber, slamming the door and bolting it.

Jamison was left on the landing, struggling to catch his breath, knowing instinctively that the slamming door was symbolic in so many ways. She was slamming it on him and shutting him out. He knew, without question, that the door would never open again. All of the begging in the world wouldn't change it. He knew that now, no matter how much he wanted otherwise.

It was finished.

Heartbroken, tears fell from his eyes. He didn't try to wipe them away. He went to her door but didn't say a word. He put his hand on it and kissed the wood as if to kiss her one more time. It was a closing kiss, symbolic much as the slamming door had been.

His heart was in that chamber, behind that closed door, never to be reclaimed again.

CHAPTER EIGHTEEN

"You may never have this chance again!"

HE'D SAID SOMETHING about Mynydd Tywyll.

Dark Mountain. Madeline could recall that Evon once spoke of Dark Mountain and the swamps beneath it, spongy and wet areas that were heavily wooded. When he came to visit, he always smelled of compost, a scent so well suited to the swamps. It was a perfect place to hide in, truly, especially for rebels who were trying to stay clear of the English armies moving to and from Four Crosses.

Mynydd Tywyll was a few miles to the southwest of Four Crosses and that was where Madeline was heading. It was growing dark and the mists were rolling in from the east, but the mist was scattered, like patches of clouds, so every so often, the moon would peek out and illuminate the landscape so she could see where she was going.

Madeline was on foot but that didn't matter to her. With her slender build, she had always been able to run faster and farther than anyone else. She had stamina. The heavy cloak that Amaline had brought her slowed her down a little but she was warm in it. Moreover, it helped keep her concealed from the two patrols she had seen from Four Crosses, men with torches who had been looking for her.

But she'd hidden away from them, camouflaged in the trees, and sticking to the myriad of small steams that ran in this area so her trail couldn't be followed. Fortunately, she knew the land, having been raised here, so she knew how to make her way to Dark Mountain. In fact, she could smell it before she actually saw it, that heavy moist smell of compost. She followed her nose.

Once she reached the swamps, she wasn't exactly sure where to look. The Welsh rebels were here, somewhere. She would find them. It was night and, surely, the cooking fires were going, which would provide her a trail to follow because the canopy was so heavy that it was difficult to see. It was eerie, too, with shadows lurking in the night, creatures waiting to jump out and eat her.

Madeline wasn't normally the spooky type but this was different. She was traipsing through a swamp in the dead of night, listening to the sounds of the darkness, hunting for people who may or may not be here. There was really no way of knowing.

She could only pray.

An hour passed. Then two. She lost track of time as she went. The night was deepening and, in spite of the heavy cloak and clothing she wore, she was growing cold because her feet were wet from slogging through freezing water. She was hungry, too, having not eaten since the morning. But she pushed aside her hunger, desperate to find the men she hoped were somewhere near, men whom Evon had fought with. Men determined to free Wales from English rule.

Evon. The man's spirit drove her onward, feeding her sense of determination. It also fed her sense of vengeance against Jamison Munro. Killing Evon had ruined the life she'd hoped to have with the man she loved. Her loyalty had always been to Evon more than it had ever been to her sisters and her father. With Roald mad and unable to command, Madeline was convinced that Four Crosses needed a man at the helm. Evon was to be that man and she was to be at his side. They had planned it that way. It was what she had wanted.

Not strangely, Madeline didn't consider her sisters' fate in all of this, nor even her father's. She assumed that the Welsh would simply let them walk free, as they were of no value to them. Only the castle was. That was what they wanted so very badly.

And that was what she had intended to deliver.

She still intended to deliver it. *Jamison Munro…* that was how she would deliver the fortress to rebels who had been trying to claim it for quite some time. Evon's death would feed their frenzy against the English and, in particular, against Jamison for the murder of one of their own. She would personally lead the charge, bringing down the only home she had ever known and seeing the man who had murdered Evon punished for his deeds. She would point the Welsh right at the redheaded Highlander to ensure the man was targeted.

For Evon, she would help them destroy Jamison Munro.

But in order for any of that to happen, she had to find the Welsh first. She prayed that Evon's clue had been correct and that the rebels, for the most part, were really in the swamps of the Dark Mountain. Even if she just found a few here, it would be enough for her to tell her story and to rally them around Evon's death.

Three hours after entering the swamps, of struggling through the darkness, she made it around to the east side of the mountain base. She was tired of looking in the darkness and without any cooking smells to follow, she wasn't even entirely sure anybody was here. Therefore, she began to call out, softly at first but then with increasing volume. She was fairly certain she was too deep in the swamps for any Four Crosses patrols to hear her. More than that, she was also certain that she was lost in the swamps until morning came and she had some light to see by. There wasn't much more she could do than start calling for help, hoping the Welsh were nearby as Evon had suggested.

She could only go on that faith.

"Cyfarchion?" she called out. *Hello?* Knowing the Welsh language, since she had been born in the country, she called out again, in Welsh. "Is anyone there?"

She was met by silence. Not that she believed they would suddenly jump forth at her first cry, but she had hoped. Cold and admittedly frightened, she found a rotted stump to sit on and she sat there, crying out into the darkness, calling for anyone who might be able to hear.

Her calls went on into the night. Madeline truly had no idea how long she had been sitting there, calling out into the inky blackness, seeing only brief moments of light as the moon emerged from the spotty mists. Somewhere, she heard a bird cry, a night bird looking for prey, and the trees were alive overhead with things moving about in them. She kept her hood on, praying something wouldn't fall down on top of her or, worse, mistake her for something to eat.

Discouraged, she eventually stopped calling out, thinking that she either wasn't close enough for anyone to hear her or there simply weren't any Welsh in earshot. So, she sat there, knowing it would be foolish to try to find her way out of the swamps in the dead of the night. She resigned herself to finding a place to sleep for a few hours. At least until the sun came up. After that, she would have to rethink her strategy. But, at the moment, she was too tired to do that. Tired and disheartened, she was just standing up from the stump to go in search of a dry patch of ground when someone grabbed her from behind.

A hand went across her face, covering her nose and mouth, as another arm went across her torso and began to drag her off. Terrified, Madeline began to fight back, as that was her instinct. She kicked and swung her fists, managing to dislodge the hand that was covering her face. Then she began to scream.

"Evon!" she yelled, hoping that the name might mean something to whomever was attacking her. "I am here because of Evon!"

More dragging and more fighting went on until she began to hear voices around her. She kept repeating Evon's name, over and over, hoping that would be the key to her release. Much to her relief, her hopes were soon realized as whoever had been dragging her suddenly dropped her to the ground. As she fell forward, someone grabbed her wrist and yanked her upward, so she was on her knees, facing a myriad of dark forms in the blackness. There were many of them. Frightened, Madeline spoke Evon's name again.

"I am here because of Evon!" she said in Welsh. "Do you know Evon?"

Someone crouched down in front of her, getting right in her face. Madeline found herself looking at a pair of glittering eyes in the darkness.

"Who are you?" he asked in the Welsh language.

Madeline wasn't entirely sure she wanted to tell them right away. "I have come because of Evon Preece," she said. "Do you know him?"

The man's gaze lingered on her. "Where is he?"

Madeline felt a glimmer of hope. At least they were acknowledging that they knew him. "Please," she said. "It is very important that I speak with his brother. My name is Madeline de Llion."

That brought a reaction from nearly everyone standing about. The man who had been interrogating her suddenly yanked off her hood, trying to see her in the darkness in a more complete picture. But there was very little light, so all he could really see was an outline of her features. Soon afterward, he pulled off his own hood. Dark, dirty hair stood on end, silhouetted in the very weak light.

"'Tis Madeline, is it?" the man said, growing agitated. "*Where* is Evon?"

Madeline was coming to suspect that she had found Evon's cell of rebels. She looked around, wanting very badly to speak further but fearful to do so until relationships were established. She didn't want to give the information to the wrong person.

"Where is Morys?" she asked. "I will only speak with his brother."

The man who had been questioning her was in her face again, aggressively, trying to see her clearly in the darkness. "How do I know you are really Madeline?" he demanded.

Madeline tried not to appear frightened because the man was very threatening. "I *am* Madeline," she insisted. They were all quite wary of her presence and she hastened to assure them she was no threat. "I *am* Madeline de Llion. I am from Four Crosses Castle. My father is Roald and my sisters are Havilland and Amaline. Evon and I have known each other for many years and we were to be married. If you know Evon, then you know this is true. Please… I am who I say I am and I have not brought a horde of English to kill you. I am quite alone."

The man who had been interrogating her nodded. "That, we know," he said condescendingly. "We would not have let you come this far had you been followed."

"Then why do you not believe me?" she asked, desperate.

The man scratched is head, eyeing her. He took a deep breath, forcing himself to calm. Madeline couldn't really see him but she could hear him. "Why did you come here?" he asked again. "Tell me where my brother is. I grow weary of asking."

Madeline was coming to think they might do something terrible if she didn't answer their question. But she was resolute in that she wanted to speak with Evon's brother.

"I will only tell Evon's brother," she said, sounding frightened.

The man sighed heavily. "I *am* his brother, foolish chit," he said, annoyed. "*Where* is he?"

Madeline tried to get a good look at him in the darkness. She had met the man, many years ago when she and her family had come across the Preece family in a nearby town, but she honestly would not have remembered what Morys looked like. Therefore, she had to take his word for it. Moreover, she had to tell him everything if he was going to understand the true extent of why she had come and the fact that she was a fugitive from her own people now because of it. There was much to tell.

"You know that Evon and I have been meeting regularly, do you not?" she asked. When she could see Morys' head bob, she continued quickly before he became too angry with her for not answering his question. "I have tried to help Evon any way I can. We were in love, you see, and he promised me that when the Welsh claimed Four Crosses, that he would marry me and we would rule it together. So I helped him any way I could. We would meet regularly next to the river that flows near Four Crosses. Two days ago, I went to meet him there but I was followed by my sister. Evon captured her and there was a terrible fight because… because a knight from the fortress had also followed me and this knight… Morys, he murdered Evon as I watched. He drowned him in the river."

Morys didn't say anything for a moment but Madeline could hear people shuffling about all around her, hissing to one another, whispering in the darkness. She looked around, trying to see who was all around her, but the blackness made it impossible. She returned her attention to Morys, feeling the tension rise.

"You saw this?" Morys finally asked, his voice oddly tight.

Madeline nodded her head. "Aye."

"The *Saesneg* killed him?"

From out of the darkness, a man spoke Welsh but with an oddly heavy Gaelic accent. "She may be lying," he growled before Madeline could respond. "Dunna trust her."

Scots, Madeline thought. She knew that because Jamison Munro had that very same accent. But more than the accent, it was the words spoken and she was both fearful and defensive.

"I am *not* lying," she insisted angrily. After that, no one seemed to be saying much more and she was starting to feel desperate. "Think what you will of me, that I am English and therefore your enemy, but I assure you it is not true. My deeds were discovered when the knight murdered your brother and I was thrown in the vault. My own sister helped me to escape so that I could come and tell you what has happened. If you truly want Four Crosses and if you truly want revenge against those who killed your brother, then I will help you. I want to punish the man who killed Evon, too!"

More hissing in the darkness as the Welsh discussed what they had been told but, thus far, no one had really reacted to the news of Evon's death. Madeline sensed shock but not much more than that. She could see Morys in the darkness as he hung his head and that was an indication that at least Morys was grieving the loss, but she didn't get a huge sense of anger out of those around her. Anger of the death, a need for vengeance. It made her angry. She had risked herself for these people who seemed so apathetic to the death of one of their own?

"Listen to me," she said, facing the group of figures, like phantoms as they clustered around her. "You must strike now. The castle is not quite repaired from the last attack and the number of soldiers is far less than it has been. When de Lohr left after the last battle, he took most of his men with him. What he left behind were five hundred Englishmen and three knights, including the man who murdered Evon. Do you not want to seek vengeance for his death?"

Morys lifted his head. He wiped at his cheeks, his tears hidden by the darkness. "Of course we do," he said. "And we shall. But it would be foolish to attack now. Our numbers are depleted by men who have returned home, farmers for the coming spring planting. It would take time to reclaim our numbers, but reclaim we shall. My brother's death shall not be in vain, I swear it."

Madeline looked around, seeing the dark shapes of men listening to what she was saying. "You do not understand," she said. "If you do not strike very soon, de Lohr will have returned. The earl himself is coming and there is no knowing how many troops he will bring with him. Once he comes, hope will be lost. Do you hear? You may never have this chance again!"

Morys eyed the girl in the dim light; he knew about her. Evon had explained that she was aggressive and foolish. She was also young and spoilt, demanding in her ways. Morys had helped lead this southern rebellion for months now and wasn't about to let this stupid girl rush him or his men into something they were not ready for.

"Do you not think I want to act?" he demanded, his tone hazardous. "Do you not think that Evon's death does not cut me like a knife? He was my brother, my heart, and now you tell me that he has been murdered. Of course, I want vengeance. But I have less than half of the men I had before and many others have gone home for the winter. They are tired of being cold and without victory. I do not have an adequate strike force against Four Crosses any longer."

Madeline would not be stopped. She thought he sounded like a coward. "Then recruit one," she said. "There are towns all over the area where you can recruit patriotic Welsh. Recruit men to help you for if you do not, de Lohr will arrive with his army and the time to act will be over. Moreover, the knight who killed him may be gone. I want that bastard to pay for what he did to Evon. I want him to die!"

Morys was far more levelheaded than Madeline was. He wasn't foolish enough to rush Four Crosses as she was trying to force him to do. She was English and the enemy, no matter what Evon had thought of her, which, truthfully, wasn't much. He'd only used her for information. No matter what she thought, any feelings from his brother were not reciprocated.

In fact, the more he listened to her, the more suspicious he became. She seemed awfully eager to push his men into attacking Four Crosses, something that made him vastly uncomfortable. Reaching out, he grabbed her by the arm.

"They will all pay," he said, his fingers biting into her flesh. "But you are too eager to be brave with my men. Is it possible you have set a trap for them at Four Crosses and that my brother isn't really dead, simply a captive of the *Saesneg* forces?"

Madeline looked at him, shocked. "Nay!" she gasped. "I would never do that! You must trust me when I tell you that Evon is dead and the knight responsible for it is at Four Crosses!"

Morys didn't like the way she was behaving; she was shifty and pushy. He yanked on her angrily. "I do not know if I believe you," he said. "I do not even know if you are truly Madeline. You could be someone the *Saesneg* has sent to trick us."

He was hurting her arm and she winced. "I swear to you that I am telling the truth," she said. "Evon died for this cause that he believed in. I only wish to help you, to believe in the same things he believed in!"

Morys scrutinized her; since Evon had not returned to camp in a couple of days, he was willing to believe that something had happened because it wasn't like his brother to stay away. Evon was very rooted to the encampment and to the Welsh dedication to clear the English lords out of Wales. Still, Morys was torn.

Gazing into her frightened face, he was willing to believe that some of what she said was true. Perhaps the time *was* right to hit Four Crosses again before it was fully repaired. They'd been doing that for months now and he agreed with that strategy. But he wasn't entirely sure that the overlord of Four Crosses, the Earl of Worcester, was on his way to the castle. In the spirit of prudence, however, he couldn't discount it, either. If they wanted to make one last drive on Four Crosses, while it was still vulnerable, then perhaps the time was, indeed, now.

But that would mean sending men to gather the army that had largely disbanded and that would take a little time. Recruiting from the towns wasn't a bad idea, either. He was willing to send men out to do that. But what he wasn't willing to do was listen to a *Saesneg* chit order him around, a woman who had betrayed her own people.

There was no respect or loyalty to her, but in a sense, she had helped him make a decision – they did, indeed, have to move against Four Crosses one last time and, most especially, if Evon was truly dead. The man deserved to be vindicated so that his death would not be in vain. Moreover, they had to move swiftly – if Four Crosses was as weakened as the woman said it was, then they could only wait a few days at most. They would have to gather what men they could and fight.

And this treacherous girl deserved her reward for helping them. Brutally, Morys yanked Madeline into the trees where his men were lurking.

"You can help my men, then," he said, tossing her so roughly that she fell to the ground only to be swooped upon by the men in the trees. Morys showed no reaction as she screamed. Instead, he lifted his voice to his men. "Take her back to camp and sell her to the highest bidder. I will split the money with whoever makes the bargain!"

The men cheered as Madeline screamed again, hardly believing what she was hearing. Dear God, wasn't this what Evon had threatened to do to Havilland? Was it really possible that this terrible fate had now become her own? She kicked and twisted, fighting against the men's hands that grabbed her, but they had overwhelmed her. There were just too many of them.

"You cannot do this!" she cried. "I was to be your brother's wife! You cannot do this, I say!"

Morys looked at the treacherous girl, not an ounce of compassion in his heart. "Evon already has a wife," he told her emotionlessly. "I do not know what he told you, but whatever it was, he only said it to get information from you. Now you can face your fate as a traitor to your own people."

Morys would remember Madeline's horrified face for the rest of his life as she was pulled into the black trees.

Her screams, however, would haunt his dreams for eternity.

CHAPTER NINETEEN

"This is yer choice, Havilland,

not mine...."

FOUR LONG DAYS.

Four days since Jamison and Havilland had their final discussion, since they'd shared that last passionate encounter. Four days since Havilland had spoken more than one or two words to him. Four days since he'd last experienced a taste of her, the feel of her.

Four long days ago, his life had ended.

Standing on the battlements of Four Crosses as the sun rose through the mist, Jamison couldn't remember when he'd slept last. He thought he might have for an hour or two the evening before, but other than that, he couldn't really remember. Sleep brought dreams of Havilland and he couldn't do that to himself, awakening with a feeling of emptiness more vast that the sky itself, endless in its pain and brutal in its longing. Sleep was not his friend these days even though he desperately needed it.

So he stood in the mist, wrapped in his *brecan*, inhaling the scents that the morning often brought – the smell of smoke from the cooking fires and the smell of the dampness over the land that had settled overnight. It was still bitterly cold, now in the dead of winter. Even though spring would come next month, it didn't seem like it. For now, everything was frozen and dead.

Just like his heart.

As he stood there and gazed out over the land beyond the walls of Four Crosses, he heard some chatter behind him in the bailey and turned to see that the mounted patrols were ready to depart. The mist had been so dense the past few days that they had to wait until there was some light before sending out yet another patrol in an ineffective search for Madeline de Llion and also for any signs of Welsh movements. For four days since Madeline's departure, they'd seen no sign of either. It was as if both had vanished.

But Jamison knew they hadn't. He knew the Welsh were still out there. As for Madeline, he couldn't honestly guess what had happened to her and, to be frank, he didn't care. Perhaps he should have, but he didn't. Amaline was still in the vault, Havilland wouldn't speak to him, and he was coming to think that his time here needed to end. He had a father that was expecting him home and a clan in turmoil. Four days after the news of his new role in Clan Munro, Jamison was coming to think that Beaux and Kendrick and Caspian had been correct.

He needed to go home.

Watching the patrol below as a few Four Crosses soldiers conversed with Tobias, he was coming to the conclusion that he wasn't needed here any longer. Tobias and Thad were capable commanders and Jamison really wasn't needed. Beaux and Kendrick and Caspian were performing small duties around the castle, working with the men, helping with the change of shifts, but the truth was that they wanted to go home, too, but they wouldn't leave without Jamison. They were waiting for him to come around and realize there was no sense in remaining in Wales. There was nothing left for him now, not with the loss of Havilland. Although none of them had said anything to that regard, he knew what their thoughts were. They were trying to be considerate of his broken heart.

A heart that would never heal.

And remaining at Four Crosses would assure that it would never heal. He was reminded of too much here and everywhere he looked, he saw Havilland. She was back in her breeches and tunics these days, handling the gatehouse like she always had, as she had when he'd first met her. In fact, as he stood at the wall overlooking the patrol preparing to leave, Havilland emerged from the keep, dressed in heavy tunics and a cloak. Her dark hair was pulled into a sloppy braid at her shoulder, the same way she had looked the first time he'd ever seen her, only this time his reaction to her was decidedly different. The first time he'd met her, there had been suspicion and animosity. Now, when he looked at her, he felt as if his guts were being ripped out.

He had to turn away from her, unwilling to see her looking up at him. He dreaded the moment their eyes met because looking into her eyes stripped him of all of his control. So he turned back to the wall, looking over the mist that was slowly lifting and knowing that this would be the last morning he would see at Four Crosses Castle.

He knew it was time to go home. He couldn't take this another day.

Leaving the wall, he deftly slid down the ladder into the bailey, glancing once more at the patrol that was preparing to leave but deliberately avoiding looking at Havilland, who was standing next to Tobias at this point. Instead of looking at her and tearing himself up over it, Jamison gave himself a task to focus on and that task involved finding Beaux or Kendrick or Caspian. They were around, for he'd seen them before the sun was up near the great hall, but he didn't know where they had gone after that. He found himself wandering into the stable yard, looking for them, and was rewarded with a sighting of Kendrick as the man tended his horse at the far end of the yard.

Jamison approached Kendrick as the man cleaned out the muck in his horse's hooves. Kendrick happened to glance over and see Jamison approach and he dropped the horse's leg to the ground, standing straight to meet him.

"Jamie," he greeted. "Did ye get any sleep last night?"

Jamison came to a halt next to the big brown horse. "Nay," he said, running a practiced eye over the beast. He didn't particularly want to speak on his lack of sleep so he changed the subject. "This horse looks much like the one ye had several years ago, one yer da gave ye. I seem tae remember that it was a temperamental animal."

Kendrick grinned, slapping the horse on the rump. "He was," he said. "This is one of his offspring, but the horse inherited his mother's good manner, thankfully."

Jamison nodded, running a hand along the horse's back and noticing that it looked as if Kendrick was preparing the animal. "Are ye going somewhere?"

Kendrick moved to the other side of the horse and lifted a hoof, cleaning it out. "I thought I'd go with a patrol this morning," he said. "I've always had a gift for tracking. I thought I'd see if I couldna find a trail or two left by the Welsh."

Jamison stood there a moment, watching the man scrape the hoof. "Dunna go too far," he said quietly. "We should leave for home today."

Kendrick's head came up. "Today?" he repeated, surprised. "What has brought ye tae that decision?"

Jamison was still looking at the horse, unable to look his friend in the eye. After a moment, he swallowed hard, as if struggling to bring forth the words. "Because I canna stand being here any longer," he said. "There is no reason for me tae stay. I am needed at home and the longer I stay here… I'm simply making a fool o' meself, Ken. It is time tae leave."

Kendrick leaned on the back of the horse, his expression serious. "Are ye sure, lad?" he asked softly. "We dunna want tae force ye tae leave if ye aren't ready."

Jamison shook his head. "Ye aren't forcin' me tae go, although ye should," he said. "I've never been one tae be a fool, Ken, but I have been. And I canna stand another day o' it. I canna look at her any longer and know I canna speak tae her. I canna stand another night o' eating in the hall and not being able tae sit wit' her. I must go. For me own sanity, I must."

Kendrick nodded faintly, feeling sorrow for his friend. For the past four days, he and Beaux and Caspian had all felt Jamison's sorrow. It had been a painful thing to watch but they all knew that Jamison would have to be the one to recognize the situation and make the decision to go. They weren't sure how long it would take but, now, Kendrick had the answer. The longer Jamison remained, the more painful the situation was becoming.

"If ye're sure," he said quietly. "When do ye want tae leave?"

"This morning. As soon as I can gather me things."

Kendrick could see he meant it. "I'll find the others," he said. "We'll meet ye here in the stable yard and go as soon as ye're ready."

Jamison simply turned away, heading back out of the stable yard, feeling a sense of grief as well as a sense of relief. He would be heading home and, hopefully, in the time it took to get there, he could clear his head of the love he'd lost. He never knew he could hurt so much but in making the decision to finally leave, his anguish was somehow intensified.

No longer would he be seeing Havilland around the castle. No longer would he be able to look at her, to feast his eyes on her when he knew she wasn't looking. God, it wasn't healthy. It wasn't healthy for him in the least. Therefore, he knew he'd made the right decision and he tried not to be miserable about it.

Heading into the keep, he made his way into the solar that also served as a bedchamber. His area was neat, as was Tobias', but Thad had managed to throw his possessions everywhere again. It looked as if an animal was living in his corner. Chuckling at the messy knight, it was the first thing in four days that had brought a smile to his lips. But as he began packing his possessions, his thoughts began to turn to Tobias.

Truthfully, he'd thought about the man periodically over the past few days, knowing that Tobias was probably more than happy with the events that had taken place. To his credit, however, he'd said nothing about Havilland, or the loss thereof. He'd kept his conversations civil and on other subjects, but Jamison knew that the man must have been pleased. Jamison respected him for not showing it.

But the fact remained that there was to be no wedding between Jamison and Havilland, which left the way open for Tobias. Would Havilland keep her vow to never marry? With Roald de Llion unable to command the fortress, logic and customs would dictate that a man needed to. Jamison had once suggested it would be him, but not now. Now, perhaps, it would be Tobias or even Becket. Would Havilland be forced into changing her mind out of necessity? Jamison wondered. But he couldn't dwell on it. To do so would surely gut him. To think of Tobias touching her as only he should have… nay, he couldn't think of that at all.

Quickly, he packed his possessions, which wouldn't have taken long in any case considering he didn't have very much. He changed out of his *brecan* and into his tunic and mail, looking every inch the serious and powerful English knight, and packed everything away into his saddlebags. Collecting his broadsword, he left the solar without a hind glance.

Jamison went immediately to the stable yard to make sure his horse was saddled. The young grooms who worked the stables were happy to bring forth the hairy black steed he'd purchased in Edinburgh. As he set his saddlebags in the stall, to be added to the horse once he'd been saddled, Jamison thought it best to let Tobias and Thad in on his plans. He didn't want to make it seem like he was leaving because of a broken heart but rather because his father had summoned him home, which was true. He would save his pride and use that as his reason for leaving even though everyone knew otherwise. Before he sought out the de Lohr knights, however, there was something more he needed to do.

The mist was lifting as the day brightened. Jamison crossed the bailey and headed towards the gatehouse, ignoring the knots in his stomach as he knew Havilland would be there. The patrol had just left, both big portcullises lifted to allow them to depart, and as Jamison entered the gatehouse, it was with a purpose in mind. He was searching for the sergeant in charge and he found the man just inside the guard room, speaking to a pair of sentries. Jamison quietly requested the keys to the vault, which the man provided without hesitation. Keys in hand, Jamison headed down to the hole beneath the gatehouse.

Down the dark, slippery stairs he went, rather relieved he hadn't seen Havilland in his quest to obtain the keys to the vault. But that relief was dashed when he came down the stairs and saw Havilland standing in front of her sister's cell. In fact, she was holding Amaline through the iron grate, clutching the girl as Amaline wept softly. Jamison could hear it.

He paused at the bottom of the steps, hesitantly, but the women had heard him coming. The chamber was so small that sound carried greatly and Havilland turned to see Jamison standing there. Their eyes met and Jamison felt that familiar stabbing pain he was coming to associate with her, unable to speak with her, unable to touch her. So he did what he had done as of late; he simply looked through her and moved to the cell. But she was standing in front of the lock and he motioned to her to move away.

"Stand away, m'lady," he said quietly.

Havilland did, standing back and watching him curiously as he opened the cell. Amaline, too, was standing back, watching as Jamison swung the door open. She was shivering, red-eyed, but she didn't try to rush the door to break free. She simply stood there, waiting. When Jamison made a sweeping motion with his hand, inviting her to leave the cell, she looked at him dumbly.

"Ye are free tae leave, m'lady," he said, his voice dull.

Astonished, Amaline looked at him like he wasn't making any sense. Jamison didn't bother to explain; he'd done all of the speaking he intended to. He was almost back to the stairs when a soft voice stopped him.

"What is the meaning of this, Jamison?" Havilland asked, an expression of earnest surprise on her face. "Are you truly releasing her?"

Jamison paused, but he couldn't look at her. His guts were in knots and he simply couldn't bring himself to do it. He didn't trust himself.

"Aye," he said. "She's free tae go. No one really knows what she did, save the knights, so I wouldna tell anyone if I were ye. Not even de Lohr when he comes, although ye'll have tae explain Madeline's escape somehow. Tobias and Thad know, but I doubt they'll tell him if ye ask them not tae."

He took the first two steps in another attempt to leave but she stopped him again. "Wait," she said, rushing up to him, standing next to him. "Why would you do this? I thought you said… you said she would have to atone for what she's done?"

Jamison knew what he said. But all of that seemed so foolish right now. He didn't even care any longer. Havilland was standing right next to him and it took all of his strength not to look at her. He was afraid of what would happen if he did.

"She's spent four days in this hellish hole," he muttered. "That's enough tae scare her intae never doing anything so foolish again, I'd wager."

He started to move again and Havilland reached out, putting a hand on his arm. "Thank you," she said softly, sincerely. "Thank you for your mercy, Jamison. I shall not forget it."

Her hand on his arm was like a brand, searing through his mail and causing him more pain than he ever thought possible. It was like torture. He couldn't even manage to speak. Without another word, he turned to continue up into the gatehouse beyond but came to a halt. There was one last thing he had to say.

"I wish ye would," he said, not looking at her. "I wish ye would forget everything. I'm leavin' this morning and that should make it easier for ye."

She didn't move her hand. In fact, she clutched him. "Truly?" she whispered. "You are leaving today?"

"Aye."

"Will you not look at me when you speak."

"Nay."

"Why not?"

He was struggling not to become agitated. "Because I canna," he whispered harshly. "This is *yer* choice, Havilland, not mine. Ye will allow me tae deal with this in me own way."

Havilland didn't release him. "You know it was not an easy choice," she whispered tightly. "If you think this situation is not killing me, also, then you would be wrong."

He did what he swore he wouldn't do; he looked at her, just in time to see her big eyes flooded with tears. It was too much for him and he yanked his arm away from her.

"I must go," he muttered.

With that, he was gone, moving out into the deepening morning, feeling as if he'd just left a major portion of his soul behind in that vault. He tossed the keys to the nearest soldier and continued on, making his way back to the stables and feeling almost a panic to leave. He couldn't stand the sight of the castle any longer, reminding of a life he'd hoped for but could never have. He had to get out of there, so much so that he was already mounted by the time Kendrick returned with Beaux and Caspian. Seeing that Jamison was ready to leave, and anxiously so, they hurried to saddle their horses and collect their belongings.

They didn't want to keep him waiting.

But in truth, there was a short wait while they collected their possessions and the entire time, Jamison was terrified that Havilland was going to come into the stable yard and try to turn his departure into a some kind of horrific farewell. That wasn't something he could adequately deal with, knowing that his resolve to go home was hanging on by a thread. Havilland had the power to cut that thread and then he'd be lost, unable to make a decision as pain overwhelmed him. He'd said all he needed to say in the vault and he found himself praying that she wouldn't come.

Praying that she would.

He was shattered when she didn't.

As Jamison agonized over his departure, Tobias and Thad came to the stable yard to bid their farewells. Having been alerted by Beaux about the imminent departure and knowing what Jamison was going home to face, they were heartfelt in their farewells. Thad was far more sorrowful to see Jamison leave while Tobias stood back, watching the four Scotsmen load their horses without much emotion at all. He did promise to tell his father what had happened with George the Younger and explain why Jamison had to return home. He assured Jamison that the earl would understand.

Not a word was spoken between Jamison and Tobias about Havilland. There was no need, to be truthful, and Jamison was relieved when Beaux and Kendrick and Caspian were finally ready to depart. He wanted to get the hell out of there. Bidding Tobias and Thad farewell, the four Scotsmen proceeded through the bailey and passed through the gatehouse as the soldiers on duty watched them with varied degrees of curiosity.

No one really seemed to know why Jamison was leaving with the men who had arrived four days earlier, but it was clear that Tobias and Thad knew. They followed the riders out of the gatehouse, coming to a stop at the threshold and allowing them to continue on. Thad waved, Tobias didn't, but Jamison didn't see any of it.

He was riding at the head of the group, keeping his focus straight ahead and slowly dying inside. *This is all for the best*, he kept telling himself. The time had come to put Four Crosses behind him and turn his focus to where it belonged – far to the north at Foulis Castle. As the new heir to Clan Munro, Jamison was an important man now.

And the MacKenzies were waiting for him.

The horses plodded along the road and the mist was burning off rapidly. Patches of blue sky could be seen overhead. It was a bright, new day and Jamison tried to look at it as such. A new day, a new life ahead.

A life without Havilland.

Against his better judgement, he turned to catch one last glimpse of the castle. He wasn't sure why; perhaps, he really had no reason at all other than he simply wanted to remember the look of it. But as his gaze moved over the battlements, he caught sight of a lone woman with a dark braid standing alone on the section towards the north.

It was Havilland.

His heart took a hit. Jamison's gaze lingered on her a moment, knowing that this was her way of saying goodbye. They wouldn't speak to one another, for it was too painful. But her appearance on the wall was her way of making sure he knew she was seeing him off in her own way. Perhaps, in the only way either of them could handle at the moment. All he knew was that he missed her more than words could express.

Looking at her on the battlements, she looked so lost and lonely, much the way he felt. *Lost and lonely.* When she lifted her hand to wave, he couldn't help but lift his hand in return.

Godspeed, my love.

It was a moment that Jamison would remember for the rest of his life.

CHAPTER TWENTY

"'Twill be a mighty sight, Jamie...."

Later that day
The Raven Inn, Welshpool

KENDRICK'S BIG, BEAUTIFUL stallion had turned up lame later that day, forcing the men to seek shelter for the night in a local inn much sooner than they had expected while Kendrick and Caspian went to find a horse that could continue the travel. While the two men were down the street at the nearest livery, Jamison and Beaux secured two rooms at the inn and settled in to wait for Kendrick and Caspian to return.

They hadn't gotten very far in their travels for the day but Kendrick's horse hadn't been able to go on. Therefore, they had some unexpected leisure time on their hands. Jamison and Beaux sat in the common room of the inn, somewhat deserted because of the time of day, and shared a meal, more food that Jamison had eaten in the past several days. It was surprisingly plentiful, a lamb stew and hearty, crusty dark bread with butter, and Jamison stuffed himself.

It wasn't that he felt he was starving but his big body was beginning to slow down from lack of food, so he stuffed himself as Beaux kept up a running conversation about some games he had attended the previous year in the Highlands where men were throwing stones at each other. He laughed about it, listing the men who had been knocked silly or injured by the stone-throwing game, and Jamison grinned weakly now and again. He knew that Beaux was trying very hard to distract him from his sorrow and he was grateful for it.

"I'd like tae put Robbie in the midst o' that game," he said to Beaux. "I'd throw stones at him until I buried him."

Beaux snorted, his belly full from a huge bowl of stew and a cup of hot wine in hand. "Yer da said that Robbie is in Northumberland now."

Jamison nodded. "He's gone tae Castle Questing," he said. "Me grandmother was a Scott and that clan is tied tae the de Wolfes. And we're all related tae the House of de Wolfe through her, so that's why me da sent Robbie tae Castle Questing. William de Wolfe is still alive, ye know. The great Wolfe o' the Border lives still."

Beaux puffed out his cheeks in disbelief. "The man must be as old as Methuselah by now."

Jamison nodded. "Old enough," he said. "The man has a host of sons and grandsons tae his name but the last I heard, he still rules the castle."

"He's a legend. 'Tis his right."

They drank a toast to William de Wolfe with Jamison downing half of his cup in one swallow. With his full belly and two and a half cups of hot wine in his veins, he had to admit that he was feeling exceptionally sleepy. Days of no sleep were finally catching up to him and the more he tried to fight it off, the wearier he became.

He finally excused himself and dragged his big body up the squeaky wooden stairs of the inn to one of the rooms they had rented for the night. Throwing himself onto the bigger of the two beds in the chamber, he was asleep before his head hit the pillow.

The next thing he was aware of, someone was shaking him awake.

"Jamie!"

It was Beaux, hissing his name. Jamison struggled to open his eyes, seeing that the room was completely cold and dark, meaning it was well into night. Having no idea how long he'd been asleep, he rolled over onto his back, seeing Beaux in the dark room as the man bent over him.

Jamison rubbed his eyes and sat up.

"I'm awake," he said, yawning. "What's happened?"

Beaux knelt down next to the bed. "Trouble, I think," he muttered. "Are ye awake enough tae understand me?"

"Aye."

Beaux wasn't entirely sure but he continued anyway. "Then listen closely," he said. "A man came into the inn a little while ago, a Scotsman. I dinna think much of it but Ken and Caspian are returned, and this Scotsman heard us speaking. He came tae the table and wanted tae know where we were from. He's a McCulloch, from the borders. Ye know the McCullochs are a fightin' bunch."

Jamison wiped a hand over his weary face. "A clan of madmen," he said. "What's he doin' so far from home?"

Beaux nodded. "We asked him that," he said. "He told us that he'd been hired away for a task. When we asked what it was, he asked us if we wanted tae help with the Welsh fight against the English."

Jamison was halfway through a yawn when he suddenly stopped, peering intently at Beaux. "Welsh fight against the English?" he repeated. He didn't like the sound of that. "Did he say more than that?"

Beaux lifted an eyebrow, an ominous gesture. "We bought him some wine and with the wine came truth," he said. "The man is mixed in with Madog ap Llywelyn's rebellion and he's in the south tae fight against the English lords on Welsh soil. Jamie, he's recruiting for the fight against the castles in the south. Four Crosses is one o' them."

Jamison's eyes widened as shock bolted through him. "*Sweet Jesú*," he breathed. "Did he tell ye this?"

Beaux nodded. "He says that he is recruiting men tae move on the weakened castle of Four Crosses," he said. "He says he has information that the castle is right for conquest with damaged walls and few soldiers, and he wants us tae join him. He's sure we hate the English as much as he does."

Jamison was already on his feet, looking for his tunic in the darkness. "Damaged walls and few soldiers," he hissed. "Only someone who had been inside the castle would know that."

"That was me thought as well," Beaux said, handing him the tunic he was looking for. He dared to speak what they were both thinking. "The de Llion sister must've made it tae the rebels when she escaped."

"I dunna doubt that, not in the least."

"She's told them everything she knows."

The mere thought was sickening to Jamison although it shouldn't have been. He shouldn't have cared, of course, but he did. Even if his body was away from the castle, his heart was still there. Still with Havilland.

Already, he was terrified for her.

"Then I must speak tae this McCulloch," he said. "I must find out what he knows."

Beaux put a hand on his arm. "I knew ye'd want tae," he said, "but take heed – ye must be calm in yer questions. Ye mustna let him know ye've been at Four Crosses fightin' wit' the English. He believes we hate the *Sassenach* as much as he does. Ye'll get further that way. The man bears a great deal o' hatred."

Jamison was completely lucid by this point, listening to Beaux's advice seriously. "If they are planning on attacking again, then we must get word tae Four Crosses," he said. "With the castle the way it 'tis now, before the earl and his troops arrive, the Welsh will have a good chance of overrunning it."

"If there are enough o' them."

Jamison simply nodded, his mind working furiously. This was a very unexpected bit of news and even as he pulled the tunic over his head and sat down to pull his boots on, his thoughts were whirling with what he'd been told. No matter if he wanted to get away from Four Crosses, he wouldn't be able to. He had to help.

"I'm a-wonderin', Beaux," he said thoughtfully, "that if the man has come tae this inn tae recruit for the Welsh, he canna be the only one. There must be more men spread out in different towns looking for men tae help take up the fight."

Beaux lifted his eyebrows. "There could be a hundred o' them, spread out."

"They could be recruiting thousands."

"My thoughts as well."

That was a terrifying concept. Thousands of Welsh being recruited as Four Crosses sat there, still somewhat damaged and vulnerable. Jamison stood up again, running his fingers through his hair to smooth it down, his mind ahead on what was to come.

"Then let's go talk tae the man," he said quietly.

With steely resolve, the pair headed downstairs into the common room, which was now packed with people since nightfall. A haze of smoke hung over the room from a hearth that was working too hard to provide warmth to the cold. So many people filled the room now that it was difficult to move through the masses. How Jamison had never heard all of this noise, he wasn't sure. It was a testament to just how weary he was.

Over near windows, covered with heavy shutters and also draped with an oil cloth to keep out the cold, Kendrick and Caspian were sitting with another man who seemed quite animated from the way he was waving his hands around. *Typical Scots*, Jamison thought. The Scots he knew often used their hands to talk, passionate in their manner. As he and Beaux came upon the table, Kendrick and Caspian caught sight of them. Caspian reached over and yanked a couple of stools away from the nearest table to provide them with somewhere to sit.

The Scotsman, seeing that Beaux had returned with an enormous red-haired man, grinned up at the pair.

"*Ooch*," he said, looking Jamison up and down. "Did ye bring a giant wid' ye, then?"

Beaux pulled up a stool and sat, as did Jamison. Jamison wedged himself in between Kendrick and Caspian because there wasn't room anywhere else. Also, he wanted to keep a distance from the Scotsman should the urge to throttle the man strike him.

"This is the next chief of one o' the biggest clans in the Highlands," Beaux said. "I wanted him tae hear that ye're recruiting men tae fight wit' the Welsh. Is there money involved, then?"

The Scotsman shrugged, his eyes lingering on Jamison, purely impressed with the man's size. "I could pay ye," he agreed. "I have somethin' of value I could give ye. But ye can also have what ye can take from the castle should we breech it."

"Four Crosses?" Jamison confirmed.

The Scotsman nodded. "Yer friend told ye?"

"He did."

"What's yer name, Man Mountain?"

"What's *yers*?"

The Scotsman grinned, showing deeply yellowed teeth. "Horace McCulloch," he said proudly. "I've been tellin' yer friends that me brother and I have been wid' the Welsh for about a year now. They hired us tae train their men because most Welsh are wild fighters, not givin' tae anything organized. Most of Madog's men are tae the north, but some of us are in the south. Madog wants the *Sassenach* lairds out of Wales and they're as thick as fleas down in the south."

Jamison could hardly believe what he was hearing, especially so early in the conversation. The speculating on the Scots having schooled the Welsh in Scots tactics was being proven in the most unexpected of places. The theory of Scots among the Welsh had been a very big question, indeed, in the early days after the most recent battle at Four Crosses and now he was discovering he'd been correct all along. Scots had very much been present, mercenaries for hire.

It was an astonishing realization.

"They are, indeed," Jamison replied. "We've been seein' them everywhere during the course o' our travels along the Marches."

Horace shook his head in disgust, gulping sloppily of his drink and evidently forgetting that he'd received no answer as to Jamison's name. "Everywhere," he agreed. "I'm told the lot o' ye are comin' from France."

So that was the backstory Horace had been given by Beaux and Kendrick and Caspian. It was something Jamison was happy to confirm. "More fighting there," he said. "They hate the *Sassenach*, too."

Horace snorted. "We have a chance tae take back a castle that has belonged tae the English for years," he said. "Madog's men are very interested it – they want tae use it as a base against the English along the Marches, so 'tis an important location for them."

Even more information was pouring forth out of the drunk man's lips. Shocked, Jamison didn't dare look at his friends. He kept his focus on Horace.

"I see," he said. "Where is the castle?"

"About a half-day's ride from here."

Jamison was pleased to increasingly throw the man off of their trail, their true purpose for being in Wales. He was cunning, playing ignorant.

"Do ye have more men, then?" he asked. "Did ye come alone?"

Horace nodded. "I've sent the men I've been able tae gather on tae the Welsh, who are just south of Caereinion," he said. "But I'm not a leader. 'Tis some of Madog's men and then some men who live locally are leadin' the fight. Most o' the rebel army went home for one reason or another, so I was sent tae recruit men tae fight again. Men I'll have tae train again, the lazy bastards."

He was drunkenly rambling now, spouting off about things that didn't make much sense. Jamison decided to look at his friends, then, who were all gazing back him with fairly emotionless demeanors. It was clear that they were looking to him to make any decisions since he was so deeply involved in the situation. Jamison knew what Horace had already been told, which made it easy for him to build on. He looked at Beaux.

"Well?" he said. "Can we spare some time tae destroy the Sassenach?"

Beaux grinned. "Always."

Jamison looked back at Horace. "How soon do ye need us?"

Horace was thrilled. "Now," he said, slamming his cup on the table and splashing what was left of it onto the old tabletop. He lowered his voice. "I've been four days lookin' for men but I canna look no longer. The plans are set tae charge Four Crosses soon and they'll be a-wantin' ye. We can leave this place at first light and head to Caereinion."

Jamison nodded, pondering what the evening had brought, pondering what was to come. *A return to Four Crosses*, he thought ominously. But the fact remained that they needed to send word to the castle about their discovery. It would be simple enough to send Caspian or Kendrick, and they could tell Horace that the men had deserted the cause. That part of the plan would have to be executed fairly soon if the Welsh were planning on moving on Four Crosses as fast as Horace said they were going to. Beyond that, Jamison thought on what Horace had just said. He didn't want to make it seem like they were too eager to go with him, fearful it might look suspicious.

"But ye have tae make it worth me while," he said. "If we help ye, what do we get from it?"

Horace's dark eyes glittered at him. "I have somethin' for ye," he said. "I was going tae keep it for meself, but I'll give it tae ye. It'll make yer night worthwhile, anyway."

He stumbled from his chair, staggering across the dirt floor of the common room and into a ground-floor doorway. He passed through it, disappearing from view, and Jamison turned to the men at the table.

"What more has he told ye about this?" he hissed quickly, afraid that Horace would return all too soon. "Anything else about the strength of the Welsh? How many men he was able tae recruit?"

Caspian and Kendrick shook their heads. "Nothing," Caspian said. "He has been very vague about strengths which either means he doesna want tae brag or he has very little at all."

Beaux snorted. "Since when does a Scotsman not want tae brag?" he whispered loudly. "I'd wager tae say he hardly has anyone."

"But a force is gatherin' against Four crosses," Jamison said. "Even if the three of ye dunna want tae go with me, I must go and see the size of the force and send a message tae Four Crosses."

Beaux shook his head. "If ye go, we go wit' ye," he said firmly. "Ye know that, Jamie. We'd not leave ye alone with that drunken Scotsmen and a gang of wild Welshmen. Ye might get yerself intae trouble."

He was grinning as he said it, causing Jamison to put a hand on his shoulder and give him a good shake. "Ye bastard," Jamison growled, feigning irritation. But he soon sobered, looking at the others. "Then we do this together?"

Caspian and Kendrick nodded. "Together," they said in unison. Kendrick continued. "Ye're going tae need help if ye're going tae do what I think ye're going tae do."

"What is that?" Jamison asked.

The humor faded from Kendrick's face. "Save Four Crosses."

It was the truth. They all knew it. There had never been any question as to what Jamison was going to do with this information or how he was going to react. With a heavy sigh, Jamison dropped his hand from Beaux's shoulder.

"This could get ugly, lads," he said. "Are ye sure ye want tae risk it?"

Caspian's eyes narrowed. "'Tis the Welsh that are takin' the risk," he said. "The four o' us in battle again… 'twill be a mighty sight, Jamie."

Jamison smiled faintly at his friend, thinking on the potential of facing a battle together, united. Each man was a powerful knight in his own right, something the Welsh would soon find out. But there was much planning to do beforehand, something they would have to find some private time to speak about. They couldn't do it here where others might hear. Already, their discussion was risky.

Therefore, they turned back to their wine and, in the case of Kendrick and Caspian, the food they had been eating. There had been a meal spread out on the table when Horace had approached them. Jamison was just pouring himself the last of the cooling wine in the pitcher when Horace finally emerged from the door he had recently disappeared into.

Jamison happened to look up, seeing that Horace was motioning to him frantically. Curious, he stood up but Beaux stopped him.

"Wait," he said. "I'm a-goin' wit' ye. Ye'll not go alone with that snake."

Jamison patted him on the shoulder. "The day I canna handle a man like that is the day I surrender me sword for a weaving loom and a skirt," he said. "Let me see what the fool wants."

Beaux and Kendrick and Caspian watched him cross the floor, each man suspicious of Horace's motives, but Jamison was confident. One hand to Horace's neck and he could easily snap it, so he wasn't worried. He followed Horace back through the doorway into what was a dark, narrow corridor with two doors off of it. The floors leaned, throwing Jamison off balance a bit. Horace went to the last door and put his hand on the latch.

"I'm done wid' it," he said. "Ye can have it from now on. Consider it payment for yer services against the English."

Jamison frowned. "Have what?"

Horace's reply was to open the door. He pushed it open, revealing a small chamber beyond with a small hearth, glowing, a tiny bed, and a chair. But there was something on the chair. Peering closely at it through the darkness, he could see that it was a small figure. *A woman.* He could see long, dark hair but not much else because the woman was gagged and tied to the chair. She was sitting in the shadows. His frown turned into a scowl.

"What is this?" he hissed. "A beaten wench?"

At the sound of his voice, the woman seemed to rouse. Her head came up and when her eyes met with Jamison's, they widened. *His* widened. It took Jamison a split-second to realize he was looking at Madeline.

Sweet Jesú… Madeline de Llion had finally been found.

Gagged and bound, Madeline began to squeal and Horace slammed the door in Jamison's face. In fact, he nearly hit him in the nose in his haste, which thoroughly upset Jamison. More than that, he was horrified by what he had just seen. It was a struggle not to react to it. He didn't want to show too much emotion, fearful that Horace might wonder why he was so agitated and he didn't want to give anything away, not at this stage.

But inside, he was reeling.

"Keep her quiet," Horace whispered loudly. "She's a noisy one. She'll wake the whole place if ye dunna keep her gagged."

Jamison's heart was pounding against his ribs as he struggled to stay on an even keel. "Where… where did ye find her?"

Horace's dark eyes twinkled in a sickening fashion. "I bought her," he said. "The wench is English. She is the one who told us about Four Crosses. I bought her but I will give her tae ye. I've had me fill of her. She's a bit skinny for me tastes but ye may think otherwise. She might be prettier if she cleans up a bit, but know that she'll take ye in any hole ye want tae put it in. She makes up for whatever she lacks in appearance that way."

He winked lasciviously and the urge to throttle the man swept Jamison. But he kept his fists clenched behind his back. Still, dark and dirty hatred filled his mind, knowing what the man had done to Madeline.

"So ye treat her like an animal," he said, his voice tight with rage.

But Horace didn't sense the rage. He was thinking about the food waiting for him back in the common room. "She *is* an animal," he said, moving away from the door. "Have yer fill of her, Man Mountain. Let yer friends have a little when ye're done."

He fled before Jamison could say another word, heading out to the common room where there were more things of interest for him. Jamison immediately opened the door to the small chamber, shutting the door quietly behind him and bolting it. He went straight to Madeline, kneeling down beside the chair and reaching out to remove her gag.

"If I remove the gag, ye canna make a sound, Madeline," he whispered urgently. "Do ye understand?"

Madeline had started to cry, weeping through the gag. She was saturating it with saliva and tears. Jamison had his hand on the cloth, fingering the knot it had been tied into behind her head, but he hadn't removed it yet. He wanted to make sure she understood to remain quiet.

"Madeline, please," he said softly. "I'll remove this for ye but ye must promise me ye'll not cry out. If ye do, I'll have tae put it back again. Do ye understand, lass?"

Lass. He'd called her that before and it had inflamed her. Much as she used to call him *Gael* and it inflamed him. Words both of them had hated, meant to taunt one another in days past. But she didn't seem to react to the term she'd professed to hate and, taking a chance that she wouldn't scream, he untied the gag and removed it. Spitting, sputtering, she began to cry deep, heart-wrenching sobs.

"I'm sorry," she shrieked softly. "I'm sorry, I'm sorry. Please help me, Jamison. Please."

He felt a huge amount of pity for her. This girl who had betrayed her own family and who had been nasty and aggressive the entire time he had known her now looked like a lost child. No more arrogance, no more aggression. It was a pathetic sight.

Looking her over, Jamison could see that she was badly bruised. Her face was bruised, both ears purple, and her nose had a bump in the middle of it, dried blood around one nostril. Gently, he untied her bound wrists before lifting his hands and cupping her face, turning her from side to side to get a better look at the damage. It was extensive. He could only imagine how badly her body was abused. It made him ill to think on it.

"Ye needn't worry now," he said softly. "No one will lift a hand tae ye again, I swear it. Are… are ye hurt bad elsewhere?"

She simply nodded, hanging her head in shame even as he tried to inspect the damage. "I ran away," she sobbed, talking quickly and fearfully. "Amaline released me because I forced her to. I was afraid of having my head cut off by Lord de Lohr. Then I ran to find Evon's men because… because you killed Evon. I wanted to make them hate you,

Jamison. I truly did."

He knew all of that. "Better men than those rebels hate me," he said, trying to make light of it. "And I killed Evon because he was going tae kill yer sister. I couldna let that happen."

Madeline nodded. "I know," she sniffed, eyeing Jamison as he tilted her head to get a look at the bruising on her neck. "But… I loved him. I thought Evon and I were going to be married. He promised me that we would marry as soon as Four Crosses was captured and that we would command the fortress together. He told me… he told me he loved me, too. He told me so many things and, like a fool, I believed him. Do you know what I discovered? That he already had a wife. His brother told me that Evon had been married for two years!"

She was weeping again, ashamed and so very sorry for her actions, but Jamison couldn't bring himself feel complete and utter sympathy for her. Her actions and the results were of her own doing and from what he'd seen, she had been very cold-blooded in the way in which she had defended her sister from Evon. That wasn't something he could really forgive, not with Havilland involved.

But no matter how he felt about the girl, it didn't stop him from feeling pity for her in the way she had been treated by the Welsh. She was battered, bruised, and abused, and purely out of respect for Havilland, he would tend to her. He had a feeling Havilland would have wanted him to. No matter what the woman had done, she was still Havilland's sister. What he did, he did for the woman he loved and for no other reason than that.

"Life brings about difficult lessons at times," he said simply. There wasn't much more to say to the very harsh lesson she had learned. "I'm going tae get some hot water and wash away some of this blood. I'll send for a physic as well."

In a panic, she reached out and grasped him with her bloodied fingers. "Nay," she breathed. "Please do not leave me! He will come back!"

He patted her hands. "Not tae worry," he said. "Bolt the door from the inside and only open it for me. Meanwhile, pull yerself over to the fire and get warm. Have ye eaten?"

She shook her head unsteadily. "Nay," she said. "I… I cannot remember when last I ate."

He gently removed her hands from his arm, pulling her over to the hearth and pushing her down so she was sitting on the warm stone in front of it. "Stay there," he said, "and for pity's sake, dunna leave this room. I will return as soon as I can. Do ye understand?"

Madeline nodded her head, her battered body shivering and twitching. "Aye," she said. He was just lifting the door latch when she called out to him again. "What are you doing here, Jamison? Why aren't you back home with Havi?"

He paused, looking at her. He didn't want to tell her everything; it wasn't her business, anyway. "Listen tae me," he said, changing the subject. "The man that brought ye here – Horace – believes me tae be a Welsh ally, so ye mustna say anything tae the contrary. Is that clear? If he doesna believe that, it could go badly for all of us."

Madeline nodded solemnly. "I will not tell him anything, I swear it."

Jamison looked at her pointedly. "Not tae say I dunna believe ye, but ye're not known for yer trustworthiness. When I say dunna tell him, I mean it."

Madeline lowered her gaze, looking like a scolded dog. "I will not," she said again. "I… I just want to go home. I should not have done what I did… I was stupid. Do you think Havi will let me come home?"

He just looked at her. "I am trying tae ensure ye have a home tae return tae," he said. "For the time being, ye're going tae remain here and stay safe. I have some things tae do."

"But…!"

"I willna argue with ye," he cut her off. "'Tis best this way, Madeline. I dunna want tae worry about ye, so ye'll stay here for a time. Now, I'll return with water and food. Bolt the door when I leave."

With that, he was gone and Madeline stiffly stood up, moving to the door and bolting it just like he'd told her. She stood there for a moment, hardly believing that he had found her, the one man she'd hated so desperately. It didn't make any sense as to why he was here in an inn, some nameless structure in some dirty Welsh town. She didn't even know where she was, to be truthful. She'd spent the past four days living such a hellish existence that being saved by Jamison Munro was surely a miracle from God. The very man she'd hated so much for killing Evon was, in fact, her savior. There was great irony in that.

And great relief.

Aye, Madeline was sorry for what she'd done, feeling foolish and idiotic that Evon had taken such advantage of her. She'd let him. She'd been led by her foolish heart. But no longer. After seeing what the Welsh were capable of over the past four days, she was coming to see Four Crosses and her family through new eyes. Perhaps it had taken a fall of this magnitude for her to realize just how wrong she'd been.

She wasn't sure if Havilland would ever forgive her, but she'd spend the rest of her life trying to make it up to her.

God had already given her one miracle. Perhaps with time, He'd give her another.

CHAPTER TWENTY-ONE

"A man like Jamison Munro…

he does not belong to himself…."

Four Crosses Castle

SIX LONG DAYS.

That was how long Jamison had been gone, nearly the same number of days she had known him. Havilland had tried hard to settle back into her routine, now with just Amaline to keep her company and Tobias and Thad, who had gone out of their way to be kind to her. It made her uncomfortable, these knights she'd known for years now suddenly more polite than usual. Tobias had even taken to pouring her wine for her at the meal the night before, which made her vastly uneasy. He'd sat next to her, too. He hadn't said much to her but his manner had been… solicitous. It appeared that he was paying close attention to her. She didn't like it in the least. After she was finished with her meal, she'd retreated to her chamber and bolted the door.

She didn't want to have to deal with knights who were trying to be kind to her.

This morning had seen the day dawn without mist, a bright blue sky above hinting at the spring to come. The ground was cold but not frozen as it had been as of late and the rain that had pounded them for the past few weeks also seemed to have vanished. In all, it turned out to be a beautiful day that she'd not had anyone to share with.

She'd never felt more alone in her life.

Odd how a man she'd known such a short time could become such a part of her. She'd tried so hard to convince herself that sending him away had been the right thing for them both, but the more time passed, the more her stance on that opinion was wavering. Jamison was heading north to marry his child bride and she would never see him again. She'd resigned herself to that. But the pain of his departure, instead of easing, had only intensified. By the second day after his leaving, she was seriously considering going after him and begging him to forgive her.

But she held her ground, knowing that her decision to send him away had been the correct one. She forced herself to focus on her duties, on managing the gatehouse and on visiting her father who seemed to be sleeping a good deal these days. He didn't look well, either, she thought, so she had his servant take him out to the kitchen yard that morning to stretch his legs, moving in an area where not many people would notice him. With a cloak over his body and a hood on his head, he was fairly inconspicuous.

Havilland kept an eye on her father and his servant as they plodded around the kitchen yard, finally sending him back inside after several minutes because it was cold outside and she didn't want him to catch a chill. She helped usher the man into the house, making sure he was tended before turning her attention back to the castle at large.

As she headed back towards the gatehouse, she could see Amaline up on the wall, red hair wild and free, dressed in her usual tunic and boots. Even though Amaline was going through her regular routine as well, there was something different about her, something subdued and lost. Havilland watched her sister for a few moments, thinking that, perhaps, the young woman was feeling what she was feeling, as well.

Nothing was the same any longer.

And that included the gatehouse and Havilland's regular duties. The gatehouse was the first place she had ever met Jamison so the structure had some memories for her to that regard. Memories of a man who wasn't afraid to stand up to her, who hadn't been afraid to spank her. What had been an embarrassing incident was now something that brought a smile to her lips.

The Red Lion hadn't been afraid of a half-English girl who fancied herself a warrior.

Even though she'd been heading for the gatehouse, she felt a sudden aversion to it at the moment. The vault below and the structure itself weren't welcoming to her. She kept seeing a redheaded Highlander reflected in those gray granite stones. The ladder leading up to the wall was to her left and she veered towards it, taking the ladder to the wall walk above, finding more solace. Here, she could look out over the landscape and dream of things that would never be.

For now, it was the best she could hope for.

"It will be a clear night tonight."

A male voice came from behind and she turned to see Tobias. He'd come up behind her and she'd never even heard him. When their eyes met, he smiled weakly.

"We should have a full moon tonight," he said, pointing to the sky. "It has been difficult to see the sky these past weeks with the mists so heavy, but it remains clear. It should be a beautiful, well-lit night."

Havilland nodded, glancing up the sky. The sun was dipping down on the horizon as it prepared to set for the night. "It will be clear and very cold," she said. "When the sky is clear, the temperature is always quite cold."

Tobias nodded. He was still looking up at the sky. "Cold enough that the mortar on the repaired section of wall is not curing as it should," he said. "Too cold and too much moisture for it to set properly."

Havilland looked at him with concern. "I had not been told that," she said. "That is a very large section of wall to be weakened."

He nodded. "I know," he said. "But at least there is no snow. In fact, it is odd how there does not seem to be any snow on the ground in spite of the month. Has there been any snow this season?"

Havilland nodded. "There was a bit around Christmastide," she said. "But there hasn't been any since. Last year, we had snow until the last of March."

Tobias pretended to shiver. "I do not like snow well enough to tolerate that," he said. "I was in London around this time last year and there wasn't any snow. I like that much better."

Talk of London interested her. "When were you in London?" she asked.

He leaned against the parapet, his attention moving to the landscape beyond. "My mother's family has a great house in London," he said. "I went there for the season."

Havilland leaned against the stones, too. "I have never been to London," she said. "I hear it is a very big city."

Tobias looked at her. "It is quite large," he agreed. "And there is nothing quite like it at Christmastide. There is a festiveness about because there are many celebrations going on to commemorate the birth of the Christ child. If you will allow, mayhap I will take you there someday. You can stay in my mother's family's home. It is a massive place. You have never seen anything so big."

She looked at him, sharply, thinking that the invitation sounded more than just something that would be part of polite conversation. Just like last night, he was pouring her more wine and generally acting attentive. She didn't like it.

"I do not think so," she said, looking away. "I think that I shall remain at Four Crosses for the rest of my life. I have no great desire to leave."

It was a lie but she wanted to throw him off her scent. She wasn't interested in him, in any fashion. But Tobias wouldn't be so easily discouraged.

"When my father gets here, things will change," he told her confidently. "With your father's mental state, obviously, there must be a man in command of the castle. I am certain he will not throw you and your family out of the castle, but if you want to remain, you will have to have some role in the new command structure."

Havilland didn't like that statement at all. "My sisters and I commanded Four Crosses quite ably for the past year," she said. "I see no need to change."

Tobias shrugged. "You did admirably, considering you are women," he said. "But Four Crosses is an important outpost and it must be commanded by someone who has been better trained and educated. You are a fine warrior, my lady, but surely you agree that a man must be in charge."

She sighed faintly, vastly displeased with the conversation. "Who?" she asked. "You?"

He nodded. "Possibly," he said. "My brother, Becket, might end up here, also. It is hard to say. But the point is that if you want to remain here and have a functional part, then changes will probably have to be made."

"*What* changes?" she asked suspiciously.

Tobias wasn't a fool; he could hear the displeasure in her voice. He'd been trying to warm her to him since Jamison's departure in order to press forward with his suit, but he was sensing that six days was not enough time for that. He was impatient, however. He wanted the chance to marry the woman before Jamison changed his mind and came back for her. At this point, he wasn't much concerned how Jamison was feeling or how Havilland was feeling. He was only concerned with himself.

"That is for my father to say," he said after a moment. "But you must understand that whatever he decides, it will be for the best."

Havilland's gaze lingered on him for a moment before turning away. "When will your father come?" she asked. "Jamison sent for him many days ago."

Tobias nodded. "I know," he said. "But you must allow that, in this weather, it took Brend at least four days to reach Lioncross Abbey, possibly more. Then he has to tell my father what is happening and my father will muster his troops. Things like this do not happen overnight.

It has not yet been two weeks since Brend left but rest assured, my father will come."

Havilland was looking at the road leading from the gatehouse, perhaps imagining the last time she saw Jamison as he rode from the castle. It reminded her of the last day she saw him and of the deeds he did before he left.

"And my sisters?" she asked. "What will you tell him about Madeline?"

Tobias looked at her. "I thought you would tell me what you wanted me to tell him."

"Then you will not tell him the truth?"

Tobias shrugged. "The truth is that she ran off and we have not seen her," he said. "Isn't that the truth?"

Havilland nodded, starting to soften towards him a little. "That is true," she said. "And Amaline…."

"Amaline has no idea where Madeline is."

"Nay, she does not, but…."

"There is nothing more to tell him about Amaline," he said, cutting her off. "Truthfully, Havilland, what will we tell him? That Madeline was spying and Amaline released her sister from the vault so she could run straight to the Welsh? The situation is already over. Madeline is already back with the Welsh and they already know what they know. Telling my father how they know it will not change things. I simply see no need to incriminate Amaline for her sister's actions. There is no point."

Havilland sighed heavily, greatly relieved by the conversation. She had yet to speak to Tobias about the situation since Jamison left and was pleased to see that Tobias wasn't willing to implicate Madeline or Amaline at this point. It eased her attitude towards him, just a little.

"Amaline is very sorry for what she did," she said. "She is young and easily manipulated. She understands what she did is wrong. Keeping her in the vault for those few days terrified her so I doubt she will do anything so stupid ever again."

Tobias lifted his eyebrows. "Let us hope not," he said. "And you? How are you faring after Madeline and Amaline's little adventures?"

Havilland shrugged. "I am well," she said, lying through her teeth. "There is nothing I can do about anything, in any case. We must go on."

Tobias' gaze lingered on her for a moment. When he finally spoke, it was hesitantly. "Havilland, I will not pretend that I do not know about you and Jamison," he said quietly. "He told me that you two were to marry and from what I gather now with all that has happened, that will not take place. I just wanted to say that I admire Jamison a great deal. He is a great man. I am sorry if you are hurt by his return to Scotland, but you must understand that a man like Jamison Munro… he does not belong to himself. That is to say, he belongs to his clan. To Scotland. He was never his own man, able to make his own decisions, no matter what he told you."

Havilland was embarrassed to speak of such things to Tobias. She was terribly uncomfortable with the subject. "He… he will make a great chief," she said, now suddenly uneasy to speak to Tobias. She didn't want to elaborate on what he'd said, fearful she might break down. "If you will excuse me, I must see to the gatehouse."

She was fumbling for a reason to leave, heading towards the ladder that led down to the bailey, but Tobias stopped her.

"Havilland, wait," he said quickly. "I am sorry. I did not mean to chase you away and I am aware this is none of my concern, but I just wanted you to know that I am my own man. I can make my own decisions. So when the time comes for you, when you are ready to consider such things… remember that."

So, he'd spelled it out. He was, in fact, interested in her. But Havilland wasn't interested in him. She couldn't even think of such things. In fact, she was angry at him for even bringing it up.

"I will never again consider such things," she told him sternly. "Tobias, I consider you a friend but nothing more. I do not wish to ever discuss this again."

Tobias could see that she was agitated and it was his fault, he knew. He'd been too soon after Jamison's departure with making his feelings known. Struggling to make up for his clumsy attempt, both he and Havilland were distracted by a sudden commotion at the gatehouse.

They could hear men calling to each other and the sounds of the iron chains as they lifted the portcullises. Curious, Havilland quickly descended the ladder with Tobias right behind her. They made their way into the gatehouse just as a patrol was returning.

But this was no ordinary return. The patrol was riding at high speed, hitting the gatehouse so fast that men had to jump out of the way. The leader of the patrol was yelling for the portcullises to be lowered, frantic in his manner, and Havilland and Tobias ran to the man as he pulled his frothing steed to a halt. Tobias grabbed the reins of the excited animal as Havilland narrowly avoided being stepped on by the beast.

"What is it, Cynfric?" she called to the man. "What has happened?"

The soldier was an older man, quite winded and red in the face. He dismounted his horse, nearly falling in his haste.

"Welsh, my lady," he said, pointing to the east. "We saw them as we were making our rounds; hundreds of them in the trees to the east, making ladders and God knows what else. They were building and building."

Stunned, Havilland's mouth flew open. "And we are just now seeing them?" she asked, exasperated. "Are they so close?"

Cynfric nodded. "They were not there at dawn when we went out," he told her. "They are about a mile to the east, near the River Banwy. The must have come up the river's path from the south, using the trees as cover."

Havilland could feel that familiar sense of fear grip her, the same sense of fear and excitement she experienced every time a Welsh attack was imminent. *Now, it comes*, she thought grimly.

"Did they see you?" she asked.

The soldier nodded. "They chased us as far as the rise just to the east and then they left off," he said. "I suppose they wanted us to warn you."

Havilland looked at Tobias. "Because they have nothing to fear," she said, apprehension in her voice. "They are building ladders with hundreds of men. You said it was to be a full moon tonight, did you not?"

Tobias was calmer than she was, at least on the outside. "Aye," he replied. "They know that the mist will not come tonight, either, and they are going to use it to their advantage."

"Attack when the moon rises?"

"That would be my guess."

It was a familiar strategy, used by armies for thousands of years. By the moonlight, the land would be as bright as day and much could be seen. Havilland had been through this drill many times but she found herself sorely wishing Jamison was here. The last time the Welsh attacked the walls, he stood on the fighting platforms and threw men back over the walls, pushing down entire ladders all by himself. He had been a sight to behold in battle. Aye, they were going to sorely miss him on this night. In fact, she was starting to feel the least bit panicky about it. She turned back to the soldier.

"Take your mounts back to the stables and tell the grooms what is coming," she said. "Have them soak the wood and cover the hay. And have them move the horses to the kitchen yard."

The soldier nodded and was off, running with the rest of his patrol back to the stables to begin helping with the livestock. As the man ran off, Tobias turned to Havilland.

"If you will ensure the keep and hall are secured, I will find Thad and we will secure the walls and the gatehouse," he said. "I will send Amaline to you when I see her."

Havilland nodded, turning towards the keep. It helped keep her panic at bay to think of the tasks that lay ahead of her. She had to secure her father, the keep, and then move to the hall where there were still a few wounded from the last battle they had faced, men who were slow to recover. Tonight would see those men joined by many others, freshly wounded fighting off yet another Welsh attack. She knew this moment would come but she had hoped it wouldn't come too soon. If ever they needed help against an attack, tonight would be it.

Fighting down an impending sense of doom, she went about her duties, praying she would live to see the sun rise.

Jamison... where are you?

CHAPTER TWENTY-TWO

"I hope that is the last thing
ye remember…."

JAMISON HAD BEEN on the other side of a Welsh attack, fighting against what he'd considered unorganized and untrained men. Now, he was with the enemy he had thought so little of and he had to admit that it was quite interesting to watch.

They weren't unorganized or untrained. More than that, he'd come late to a battle that had started just after sunset, when the moon rose full and bright in the sky. By the time he and his friends had arrived, the attack on Four Crosses was already in motion. Beneath a brilliant white moon nestled in a sky of black silk and diamonds, the castle was lit up as if someone had turned a million candles onto it.

But it was more than the moonlight creating illumination. There were far more Welsh than Jamison had expected and many of them were carrying torches. At the gatehouse, men had piled wood against the first of the two portcullises and a massive bonfire lit up the night, a fire intended to weaken the old iron so the Welsh could push through. Then there would be a second portcullis to soften and weaken, but with the amount of wood they'd cut down from a neighboring forest, they had the fuel.

Jamison was worried about it the moment he arrived.

It was difficult to drink everything in and not be alarmed by it. All he could think of was Havilland within those walls, fighting for her life. Dressed in tunics, breeches, and heavy mail as well as his helm, Jamison stood with Beaux and Caspian and Kendrick, watching as a giant battering ram on wheels was rolled out from the forest where the Welsh had built the ladders and cut down all of the firewood. Conscripts rolled the battering ram down the road on unsteady wheels, heading for the gatehouse with the bonfire. Soon enough, the iron would weaken to the point where they could use the ram to bend and damage the iron.

It was truly a sight to see.

"I had no idea they were so organized," Caspian hissed, watching the castle and the fires with concern. "Battering rams? Fires tae burn the portcullis? And look at the ladders – Jamie, they're all over the walls. Surely they have breached the castle by now."

That was Jamison's thought as well as he looked over the chaos. And it was truly frenzied, something far worse than the battle he'd participated in those weeks ago. There were Welsh everywhere.

"This is hell," he muttered. "In the last battle against Four Crosses, it was raining so heavily there could be no fires. This night has seen Welsh tactics change dramatically."

The four of them watched as more men with ladders moved past them. Jamison, in particular, watched the ladders move towards the castle, wondering if a man who mounted that ladder would be the one to kill Havilland. He knew he simply couldn't stand by and wait for that to happen, waiting for Havilland to end up on the end of a sword, or worse. Beaux interrupted those gloomy thoughts.

"There are more than hundreds of men here," he said. "Horace said he'd only recruited a few hundred but there are thousands here. Where did all o' these men come from?"

Jamison shook his head. "They must have combed the entire country for them," he said, looking around. "We must find a ladder and gain access immediately. Four Crosses will need all the help they can get in the face of this madness."

The others wholeheartedly agreed. "Let me move the horses tae an area away from this where we can recover them after the battle," Kendrick said. "I dunna want tae leave me new horse for the Welsh tae collect when they realize I've fought agin' them."

Jamison waved the man on. "Do it," he said. "We'll head tae the north side o' the castle and find a ladder there. Come when ye finish."

"I will."

"Hurry, lad. There's no time tae waste."

The men split off, losing themselves in the hundreds and hundreds of men that were moving towards the castle, swarming on it like flies. So many men that it was difficult to comprehend. Jamison, Beaux, and Caspian found themselves running for the castle but realizing, as they drew close, that Four Crosses had archers on the battlements that were sailing projectiles into the men below. Given that Jamison knew how much ammunition Four Crosses had for their archers, he was fairly certain they would run out of arrows soon.

But arrows were flying in both directions, sailing from the castle but also into it. Those arrows, if possible, would be reused. Still, Jamison and Beaux and Caspian couldn't get too close to the castle at this point without cover from the great wooden shields that had been made by the Welsh to protect their own archers on the ground.

To get the archers close enough, the Welsh had to move within striking range, so they'd constructed big shields of woven tree branches and held in place by soldiers to allow the archers to hide behind them. The Welsh could move up very close to the castle holding those shields and they had, so the Welsh archers, some of the best in the world, could sail their spiny arrows into Four Crosses at close range. The ground next to the walls was littered with Four Crosses men who had fallen from the battlements, pierced by Welsh arrows.

While Jamison tucked up behind one of shields so he could get close enough to get to some of the ladders propped up on the walls, Beaux found shelter behind another big shield but they both lost sight of Caspian. Jamison couldn't worry about Caspian, however, as the man was quite seasoned, and with arrows flying all around, he was only concerned for himself at the moment. In fact, he moved forward and took hold of one of those massive shields, usually a job for two men, and held it aloft, moving ever closer to the walls.

But he couldn't get close enough because now the inhabitants of Four Crosses were starting to pour boiling water down upon their attackers. Four Crosses had two wells, both of them plentiful, so boiling the water and pouring it down on the Welsh could go on for quite some time. It was an effective strategy. Hot water dumped from above would quickly saturate the men below and scald them, not hot enough to do any serious damage but certain enough to hurt and burn.

Better still, the Four Crosses defenders were dropping fairly big rocks on people's heads and the ground near the gatehouse was scattered with men with head injuries. They were putting up an excellent fight and Jamison knew that somewhere behind those walls, Havilland was part of it. He had never been more proud of the woman.

And more terrified for her.

As he tried to make another push forward to get to a ladder, he heard someone call out from behind but he didn't know it was for him until an archer tugged on his tunic. Only then did he turn to see that the great battering ram had made it up the road and was nearing the gatehouse.

Horace was helping about a dozen men push the battering ram but he was trying to get Jamison's attention. When Jamison finally looked at the man, Horace motioned at him to come close. Frustrated to be diverted from what he'd been trying to accomplish, Jamison turned the shield over to the men he'd stolen it from and dashed back to Horace, trying to stay clear of the flying arrows.

"What do ye want?" he demanded.

Horace motioned him to a push bar right in front of him, one of the many that the men were using to push the battering ram. "We need yer strength, man," he said. "Help us push this beast forward. The fire has been burnin' long enou' that the iron should be soft."

Jamison ducked under the shielding presence of the battering ram, peering out from it to gain a good look at the gatehouse. "How long has the fire been burnin'?"

Horace had come to the Four Crosses with Jamison and the others but they'd lost sight of them once they had arrived. Now, here he was, leading the charge with the battering ram. He grunted and pushed as he answered Jamison's question.

"I'm told they started the fire several hours ago," he said. "Long enou' tae soften the iron. And I'm told that a section of the damaged wall tae the south has collapsed, so men are already inside. We need tae break down the portcullis tae help those inside. We'll have this fortress in Welsh hands my mornin'!"

Jamison tried not to react to the news. *The south wall has collapsed.* That was the wall they had been rebuilding, the one that had suffered some damage in previous attacks. Now it was down again and men were inside the castle. That was all Jamison needed to hear.

He broke away from pushing the battering ram, dodging arrow as he made his way around to the south side of the fortress where he did, indeed, see that a damaged section of wall had given way. There were ladders near it and as he watched, men were climbing inside, pushing aside more stones and causing more damage to the wall.

Jamison struggled not to let panic overtake him. All he could think of was getting to Havilland, of protecting her, and he fought his way through several Welshmen to reach the base of one of the ladders. It was an unsteady piece of construction but he didn't care. He didn't even know if it would hold his weight as he began to climb, straining up the ladder, pushing one Welshman out of the way who wasn't climbing fast enough. The man went hurling to the ground as Jamison continued on, straining to reach that gap where men were gaining access to the castle.

But the ladder he was on, ultimately, wasn't strong enough to hold his weight. It was creaking and groaning, finally cracking, and once he reached the gap, the entire ladder gave way and he found himself hanging by his fingertips against broken stone. He nearly lost his grip but he struggled against it, grabbing at the stone and meeting with the soft mortar that had allowed it to fail.

Finally, he had enough of a grip to heave himself over to the ten-foot drop to the bailey on the other side. Carefully, he lowered himself down, dangling by his fingertips again before letting himself fall to the ground. Once he hit the dirty, he stumbled a bit. He was just managing to regain his balance when someone hit him squarely in the back of the head with a plank of wood. His helm flew off and he fell like a stone.

Dazed, Jamison ended up on his back but through his clouded vision, he could see something swinging at him again. He rolled out of the way, kicking out his legs to knock his attacker off balance. He heard a body hit the ground next to him and what sounded suspiciously like a female sound, a grunt. Rolling to his knees, he grabbed his attacker by the arm. A very small arm. It took him a moment to realize that he was looking at Amaline.

"Ammie!" he hissed. "Stop fighting, lass. Look at me! 'Tis Jamison!"

Amaline had been swinging her free arm and her feet, trying to kick him, but when she saw who it was, she immediately came to a halt. Her eyes widened.

"Jamison!" she shrieked.

He pulled her up off the ground. "Aye," he said quickly. "I am here. I'll help ye. Where is Havi?"

Amaline was in tears. "I do not know," she said. She pointed to the gatehouse. "She was at her post the last I saw but… but there are Welsh there trying to open the portcullis!"

Seized with fear, Jamison looked over to the big gatehouse and could, indeed, see that it was swarming with men. He released Amaline.

"I must go help her," he said. "Amaline, listen to me. There are too many men for ye to fight. I want ye go to the keep and stay inside. Bolt the door and dunna let anyone in ye dunna know. Is that clear?"

Amaline shook her head. "I cannot!" she said. "I must fight!"

He shook his head. "I dunna have time tae argue," he said. "If ye stay here, the Welsh will take ye. Get inside the keep and stay there.

Go."

He meant what he said; Amaline could see that. She looked at the wall where men were spilling over. "But… but the wall…."

He spun her around, pointing her towards the keep. "Ye canna stop it," he said, swatting her on the buttocks. "Get tae the keep!"

With a yelp, Amaline did as she was told, rubbing her buttocks as she dashed towards the keep. Hoping that she would, indeed, listen to him, Jamison made his break towards the gatehouse, unsheathing his broadsword as he moved. He knew Havilland was in that mess of men, somewhere, and intended to find her. It was all he could think of, all he could focus on.

As he came upon a mass of fighting, struggling men, he began to swing his sword at everything he recognized as Welsh. He'd been around the Four Crosses soldiers enough to know their manner of dress, and the Welsh were quite different. Heads began to roll as the enormous Highlander plowed his way through the fight at the gatehouse.

Men began to realize there was a devastating element in their midst and the English were evidently not the targets; the Welsh were. But men were still fighting and struggling as the Welsh tried to battle their way up to the second floor of the gatehouse where the great levers for the portcullises were. Already, the battering ram was doing damage on the first portcullis and, somehow, the inner portcullis had been raised about three feet, enough for men to go under it. Jamison ducked under it, too.

The first thing he saw was Tobias, backed up against the wall in a brutal fight with a Welshman. Tobias had been wounded, a nasty wound to his left shoulder, so much so that the arm seemed useless as he struggled to fight with his right hand. Jamison came up behind the Welshman trying to kill Tobias and gored the man in the back, straight through the torso so that his blade came out of the man's chest. Tossing the body aside, he pulled Tobias off of the wall.

"Tobias," he hissed, struggling to catch his breath. "Are ye badly hurt, man?"

Tobias shook his head. "I do not think so," he said, his eyes wide with surprise. "What in the hell are you doing here?"

Jamison waved him off. "A story for another time," he said. "Where is Havilland?"

Tobias pointed to the bailey with his good arm. "In the bailey last I saw her," he said, his tone urgent. "She was fighting a man who was considerably bigger than she was. I couldn't get to her. Find her, Jamie… find her and make sure she is well."

Jamison didn't have to be told twice. He plowed his way out of the gatehouse, ducking below the half-lifted portcullis again and emerging into the bailey where there were several groups of men fighting. He hadn't noticed Havilland when he'd come into the gatehouse and even now, he couldn't see her. His panic started to rise but he fought it. He had to keep a level head if he was going to do her any good at all.

Several long and painful seconds of looking around for her produced no results and it was becoming increasingly difficult for him to maintain his composure. He was starting to move off to the north, towards the great hall, when he caught sight of a man on the ground, half-propped up against the wall. Almost immediately, he recognized the gatehouse sergeant he'd had dealings with. The man was bleeding heavily. He rushed to the man, dropping to a knee.

"Have ye seen Lady Havilland?" he asked. "I was told she was out here, somewhere."

The sergeant pointed towards the kitchens. "That way," he said, weakened. "He took Lady Havilland. I tried to stop him but he gored me. You must help her!"

Jamison could no longer keep his panic in check. "*Who* took her?" he demanded.

The sergeant continued to point weakly towards the kitchen yard. "A Welshman," he said. "Go! Help her! He will kill her!"

Jamison took off at a dead run. Broadsword in hand, he blew into the kitchen yard only to be faced with more fighting and an open postern gate. Men were pouring through it and he turned in the direction of the bailey, bellowing at the top of his lungs.

"Breach!"

It was the battle cry and Four Crosses soldiers began to shift in the direction of the kitchens; Jamison could see them moving. But that wasn't his concern; his concern was finding Havilland. Looking around the kitchen yard in desperation, he didn't see her anywhere. As he ran towards the postern gate to see if she had been taken outside of the walls, he heard a faint scream.

He recognized it.

Havilland!

Jamison propelled himself through the postern gate only to see that the wall in this section was crowded with men trying to enter the gate. It was a narrow passage so only one man at a time could pass through and he shoved men back and out of the way so he could pass. More screams down the path towards the river caught his attention and he bolted down the trail, slipping and sliding in the darkness as the trees covered most of the bright moonlight. Beneath the canopy, it was dark and eerie.

Jamison ran as much as he could without tripping and killing himself, sliding down the hill, hearing more screams. As he neared the river, he heard sounds of fighting. It spurred him forward. As he neared a bend in the path, he caught movement off to his left. Two figures were battling in the darkness, one of them decidedly female. He could hear Havilland grunting as she battled for her life, swarmed upon by a man who was trying to subdue her.

Rage filled Jamison. It was rage like he had never experienced before, something so black and horrific it was as if his soul had been taken over by the devil. Anyone who would touch Havilland so, or worse yet, hurt her, deserved all of that rage and more. He didn't hesitate to bring up his sword but it was difficult to see in the darkness. He wanted very much to gore the man assaulting her but he was gravely concerned he might strike Havilland, instead.

Therefore, he had to get closer so he could see the figures more clearly, but as he approached, there was so much struggling and blurred lines of bodies that he knew he couldn't use his sword. The bodies were too close together and he couldn't chance hitting Havilland. Therefore, he sheathed his sword and marched up on the pair in a necessary move. He had to get that close to discern them in the darkness.

He had to see his target.

But it was still difficult to see. In desperation, he reached out and grabbed someone. He didn't care who it was at that point but he had to separate them. As soon as he grabbed a head, he realized very quickly that he had the man in his grasp. Now, he had a fight on his hands for the man was strong. He didn't take kindly to be grabbed. Fists began to fly in the darkness but that was what Jamison did best; fighting with his fists. He began landing a series of powerful blows, knocking his opponent off balance in the darkness.

Out of the corner of his eye, however, he could see Havilland as she began to run away. She was terrified and rightfully so, but he didn't want her to return to the castle and back into the fray. Therefore, he had to give himself away. As she ran, he bellowed.

"*Havilland!*" he boomed.

Several feet away, and in nearly complete darkness, Havilland came to such an abrupt halt that she tripped and fell to her knees. Having spent the past several hours in battle, and the last several minutes in the fight for her life, she was in battle mode. Everything she did was to preserve her life, including running away when someone challenged her attacker. She was positive it had been another man who wanted to claim her, someone intent to steal her away, but the sound of a familiar voice had her astonished to the bone.

Her heart leapt into her throat.

"Jamison!" she gasped.

There was a good deal of grunting and punching going on in the darkness and realizing that Jamison had returned fueled Havilland with unimaginable joy. It also fueled her with determination. He had come back, God only knew why, but that didn't matter now. Questions would have to wait. At the moment, she had to help him in his fight to save her. Now, she had to save *him.*

Havilland still had a small dagger strapped to her leg, hidden beneath her tunic, but in battling with her abductor she hadn't been able to get a hand free to retrieve it. Now, she had the opportunity and she fumbled with her tunic, yanking the razor-sharp knife from its sheath. Holding the blade offensively, she rushed to Jamison as he battled with the Welshman.

But she had much the same problem as Jamison had in that it was very dark and the men were fighting very closely. But she could see which was one was Jamison, purely from his size, so when the pair swung in her direction again, she leapt onto the Welshman's back and plunged her dagger into the man's back, right at the base of the neck. She did it four times before he finally fell to the ground.

As he went down, she went down with him, leaping from his back, stumbling sideways before regaining her balance. The man lay at her feet, groaning, and she kicked him for good measure.

"I hope you die a slow and painful death, you bastard," she hissed. "I hope you pay in eternity for what you have done!"

Jamison, winded from the fight, could see that the struggle was clearly over. He caught a glint of the dagger in Havilland's hand and imagined she had used it quite effectively. Her victim wasn't moving much and he was certain the man wasn't going to rise again. With the immediate threat over, he took a deep breath and crouched down beside the man who was clearly dying.

"How many men have ye brought?" he asked. "Tell me what I need tae know and I'll end yer life mercifully."

The Welshman gazed up at Jamison, unable to move, but the hatred in his eyes was unmistakable. "You may win this fight but the war is not over," he said haltingly. "There will be more of my kind coming. We will come until we cannot come any longer. This is not finished."

Jamison well understood the mentality of the Welsh. It was very similar to that of the Scots in their fight for independence against the English. In that sense, his people and the Welsh people were quite similar. Therefore, he understood the mentality well.

"But *ye* are finished," he said quietly. "And yer death was in vain. Four Crosses shall not fall this night, not while there is breath in me body."

The Welshman continued to hold his gaze but the man was fading fast. "Mayhap not tonight, but there will be other nights," he muttered. "Remember me when that night comes. Remember Morys Preece when the last Welshman drives his spear into your heart. It will be my spirit behind that spear."

Havilland, who had been listening to the conversation, dropped to her knees beside him. "Morys?" she repeated, shocked. "Your brother is Evon. That is why you were asking for him!"

Morys couldn't move his head but he tried to look at her. "I asked you where Evon was," he said. "Where are you holding him? Is he inside the castle?"

Havilland lifted her eyes to Jamison, who was gazing at her in the darkness. She wasn't sure what to say so Jamison took charge. He did it with the confidence of a man who knew he had won, who knew he had triumphed at the end of a long and hard-fought battle.

"Yer brother is dead," he said. "I had the privilege of watching the last o' his life drain away as I killed him, as I will have the privilege of watching the last o' yer life drain away. Ye canna beat me, little man, and ye canna beat the fierceness of the people at Four Crosses. A lioness lives there and ye tried tae tame her, but she killed ye in the end. I hope that is the last thing ye remember – ye were killed by a woman."

Morys' eyes widened and his mouth worked as if he wanted to say something, but he couldn't. His body wouldn't permit it. As Jamison and Havilland watched, the light left Morys' eyes and drained away. His body relaxed and the life went out of him completely. Such was the death of a rebel, much as it had been in the death of his rebel brother.

It was over.

Havilland's gaze lingered on Morys' body a moment before she looked up at Jamison to see that he was staring at her. As she looked at him, so many things came to mind to say to him, all of them rushing over each other, wanting to be heard. There was so much emotion in her heart and in her soul, that she could hardly contain it.

"You… you came back," she finally said.

He nodded faintly. "I did."

"Why?"

A hint of a smile crossed his lips. "That's a good question," he said. "Mayhap it was because I wanted tae convince ye tae reconsider yer decision. Mayhap it was because a foolish Scotsman found me and told me he was recruiting men tae join the Welsh in their siege against Four Crosses Castle. Mayhap I came back tae take ye as a prize in battle and then ye canna refuse me."

Because he was smiling, she dared to smile in return. Out of that somewhat humorous explanation, she discerned something of the truth.

"You were recruited to fight with the Welsh?" she said, puzzled. "Is that really true?"

He nodded. "We were staying at an inn not far from here when a man came, looking for men tae fight in tonight's attack," he said. "Ye know I couldna return home knowing ye were facing danger. I had tae come back and make sure ye survived."

It was a very touching thing to say and her emotions, struggling to come forth, finally burst the dam of her composure. She knew what she had to say. In looking at him now, she knew that she could never again be parted from him.

"I am so sorry if I was cruel to you," she whispered huskily, the tears forming. "I truly felt I was making the best decision for both of us but I've since realized that I was wrong. It is a miserable existence I have sentenced us to be without one another. Would I rather have you alive and without me? I would. But I have come to the conclusion that I am very selfish, Jamison. I do not want to be without you and I do not want you to be without me. You just referred to me as a lioness… I am *your* lioness. I will always be your lioness. And I cannot live with the thought of living my life without you. It was horrible for me to try and convince you that was for the best and I pray that you can forgive me."

He watched her, struggling with her regrets, and his heart, so broken by their separation, now swelled with joy. He was hoping he hadn't dreamed her words because if he had, it would surely kill him.

"I forgive ye," he murmured. "But what do ye want? Ye know I must return home, Havi. Will ye come with me as me wife or did ye simply say those words tae satisfy yer guilt at having said them?"

She wiped the tears away that were falling. "De Lohr will be here soon," she whispered. "He will take over the castle. I am no longer needed here. But you need me. You need me to fight off those damnable MacKenzies. I will kill every one of them, I swear it."

He grinned, so very touched by her words. "Ever the lioness, aren't ye?"

"If you are The Red Lion, then being your lioness is my destiny."

Those words filled him more than he ever thought they would. *His lioness*. Now, he felt whole. He felt complete. He'd never known that words, simple things, could make such a difference in his life and how he looked at it. A dreaded return home would be a triumphant return home now. With Havilland's love and support, he was the strongest man who had ever lived.

He was invincible.

"I love ye, lass," he said with more feeling than he'd ever shown. "More than all the stars in the heavens, I love ye."

"Still?"

"I never stopped."

Havilland's smile grew, knowing now that all was well between them. Her decision hadn't cost them anything but longing and a little time. The love they had for one another, the devotion, was still there. It was stronger than ever. He would have never come back to Four Crosses has it been otherwise.

"Then we shall face life together," she said, her eyes glimmering at him in the weak light. "Your father's anger, the MacKenzie's vengeance, and everything else life brings us. There will be nothing so great that we cannot surmount it together."

He loved her confidence, her strength. He reached out, touching that sweet, dirty face that he loved so well. "With ye by me side, I can face anything at all."

She kissed his hand as it came near her lips. "As can I."

He stood up, pulling her away from Morys' corpse and into his arms. What he had to say, he would say without a dead body between them.

"Then we look tae the future with hope," he said, holding her as close as he could with all of the layers of tunics and mail in between them. "And any decisions we make, we make together. I'll not let ye make another decision again for me, even if ye feel it's the best one for us both. I'll have a say in it, too."

She grinned, lifting her mouth up to his for a sweet kiss. "Aye, my lord."

He closed his eyes, responding to her gentle kisses. "Say it again."

Her arms went around his neck, her forehead against his. "Aye, my lord."

"Nay," he breathed. "Not that. Tell me ye're me lioness."

"I am your lioness. To the end of the world and beyond."

For the warrior known as The Red Lion, they were the sweetest words he'd ever heard.

EPILOGUE

Year of our Lord 1289 A.D.
Early June
South of Foulis Castle, Scottish Highlands

THIS WAS NOT something Havilland had ever dreamed of.

On a beautiful June day, with the sea breezes blowing in off of the Firth of Moray, she was standing on a rise overlooking a field of undulating sea grass. The breeze was whipping it about, creating swirling patterns, and Havilland stood on the crest of the rise with more than a thousand Highlanders. They were all looking across this gentle field at another line of Highlanders about a quarter of a mile away to the south. They were all lined up on this brilliant morning, waiting and watching.

Havilland stood next to Jamison. Dressed in a tunic, breeches, and her mail coat, she was strapped down with her sword and her usual array of daggers. Her husband was also dressed for battle, although his style of dress resembled hers much more than it resembled the Highlanders he was commanding. But his red hair gleamed in the morning sun, making him a very easy target for the opposition. Havilland had asked him twice to wear his helm but he wouldn't do it. His mother, sweet but firm Ainsley, had asked him as well, but he also denied his mother. He wasn't going to hide who he was beneath a steel bucket.

This battle was, after all, about him.

Word had gotten around that Jamison Munro had returned to the

Highlands and the MacKenzies was more than ready to meet him. They'd sent word to Foulis Castle two nights ago that they would be waiting on the plains surrounding the Burn of Foulis, just to the south of the castle, and they expected Jamison to be there as well. Jamison had anticipated the summons and he was ready for them.

He and his massive army, that is.

It was a sight to behold. Sutherland stood in support of him along with Ross and MacKay. Beaux, Kendrick, and Caspian were back in charge of their own men, having return to the Highlands with Jamison and his wife. On the long trip north, Havilland had become good friends with all three of them. They accepted her and admired Jamison for his choice in a wife.

Agnes MacLennan notwithstanding, Havilland de Llion was quite perfect in their eyes. Not only was she beautiful, but she had a fire in her soul that was reminiscent of the warrior women of the north. They would jest with her and ask her if she wasn't a Scotswoman in disguise.

But the real test came when they finally reached Foulis Castle. Oddly enough, George and Ainsley accepted their son's new wife fairly quickly. The story from Jamison was that he had already married Havilland before he received the news of Georgie's death so there wasn't much he could do about marrying Agnes MacLennan. In fact, George sent word to old Amos MacLennan and offered up Robert instead of Jamison, which Amos gladly accepted. One big Munro son was as good as the next, he said.

With the bargain sealed, George then sent a messenger to retrieve Robert from Castle Questing but it was at Ainsley's insistence that Robert not be told why. She suspected her randy son wouldn't want to marry a fourteen-year-old lass, and especially not one as plain as Agnes, so Robert was returning home to a surprise marriage.

Jamison, Beaux, Kendrick, and Caspian had a good laugh over that fact. Finally, Robert, the trouble-making brother, would get his comeuppance. No more chasing after Eva MacKenzie or any other lass that he fancied. Fear of the wrath of Amos MacLennan would keep him limited to one bed and one bed alone – his own.

But the fact remained that Jamison had come home and, without the marriage to young Agnes, the MacKenzies had him in their sites. There was no avoiding a confrontation with them so when they sent the summons to Jamison, he didn't refuse it. This is what he'd come home for, after all. Now, it was time to face his enemy.

And that's what had brought them to this day. Standing on the rise overlooking the fields of Foulis, he turned to look down both sides of his lines; Sutherland, Ross, MacKay were there with hundreds of men, but the most men came from old Amos MacLennan. Amos had been told that Jamison had killed Connell because the man had tried to murder Robert. An attempt on Robert was as good as an attempt on his daughter, so Amos had said, so Jamison had nearly six hundred MacLennan men at his disposal in spite of the fact that they were kin to the MacKenzie. Evidently, a betrothal to the Munro Clan bore more weight and Jamison now had more men than the MacKenzie.

If they wanted a fight, he would give them one.

"I have never seen a battle like this," Havilland whispered at his side. "What do we do? Do we spend all day staring each other?"

He grinned, looking down at her. He wished she had remained back in the castle with his mother but he knew that had been too much to ask. She was at his side and wouldn't leave.

"Nay," he said, putting an arm around her shoulders and kissing her forehead. "Soon enough, the MacKenzie will send a messenger across the field and I will send one tae meet him. They will discover terms and return tae me. If I dunna like the terms, then we will march across the field and squash them."

Havilland's eyebrows lifted. "Is this how it is always done?"

He shrugged. "Sometimes."

"No laying siege to Foulis?"

He nodded. "That can happen, too," he said. "But a Scotsman's way of fightin' isna the English way. We show our strength in other ways."

"Like facing your enemy across a field and showing them all of your men?"

"Like that."

Havilland was quite baffled by it all. "The only battles I have ever faced have been from the inside of a castle," she said. "I have never faced a battle on a field like this before."

He looked at her. "This will be hand tae hand combat if we fight," he said quietly. "I know ye want tae fight by me side and I love ye for it, but it's as I told ye last night – I will spend all of me time worrying about ye and probably get me head cut off. If it looks as if we are going tae battle, will ye please consider going back tae the castle? It would ease me mind considerably, love."

They'd had this discussion before and she had stubbornly refused. But this time, she looked out over the opposing forces and actually considered his request. Seeing all of those Scots intimidated her although she wouldn't admit it to him. "I do not want to leave your side," she said. "If you fight, I want to fight with you. This is my battle as much as it is yours, Jamie. As your wife, if they threaten you, then they threaten me."

He hugged her and kissed her forehead again. He didn't want to get into that discussion again because it had become quite heated last night. She had ended up in tears. So he let it go, mostly because he already had a bargain with Kendrick, who was positioned the closest to him – if the battle started, then Kendrick was directed to make his way to Lady Munro and bodily remove her from the fighting. It would be a struggle, to be sure, but Jamison wanted her out of the heat of battle. He only hoped that Kendrick would come away with all of his fingers, toes, and eyes. He knew Havilland could fight dirty when provoked.

But he hoped it wouldn't come to that.

So he stood with his wife, waiting for the MacKenzie to send his messenger onto the field. He already had his youngest brother, Hector, waiting to ride to meet him. But the MacKenzie seemed to be hesitating for some reason and he wasn't sure he liked that. He hoped the man wasn't waiting for reinforcements to arrive although his scouts told him that they'd not seen sign of any. So they stood and they waited.

Finally, towards the nooning hour, a rider broke away from the MacKenzies' lines and charged across the field, the horse's mane and tail blowing in the brisk sea wind. Seeing the rider approach, Hector dug his heels into the side of the blonde steed he was riding, galloping across the grass until he and the MacKenzie rider came together somewhere in the middle, near the banks of a small stream that ran through the meadow.

The moment had come, the moment that could decide the tides of the battle. Everyone was watching them with both curiosity and trepidation. Havilland, in a completely un-warrior-like move, slipped her hand into Jamison's.

"What do you think they are talking about?" she asked anxiously.

Jamison was watching the pair in the distance. "I dunna know," he said honestly. "More than likely, the MacKenzie rider is demanding me head."

She gasped. "Is he?"

He grinned, giving her a wink to let her know he was jesting. "Nay," he said. "Dunna worry, love. Even if they asked for it, they'll have tae fight tae get it. And ye'll not let them have it, will ye?"

She shook her head vehemently. "They will have to go through me first," she said, squeezing his hand. "Then what else could they be speaking of?"

He simply shook his head, watching as Hector suddenly turned his horse away from the MacKenzie messenger and thundered his way back to the Munro lines. He headed straight for Jamison.

Young, excitable Hector brought the horse to a halt, kicking up clods of earth and spraying anyone within ten feet of him with it, and that included Havilland. A chunk of moist earth hit her on the corner of the mouth and she spit it out in disgust, glaring at the rash young knight, who smiled apologetically at her. Shaking her head at him, she brushed the dirt off her face and chest as Jamison looked at his brother with reproach.

"Do that again and I'll turn the wife loose on ye," he said. "Now, tell me – what did the messenger say?"

Hector was agitated. "Padraig MacKenzie wants to know if ye'll meet him by the stream," he said. "He wants tae speak wit' ye. It will just be him. He wants ye tae come alone."

That was an unexpected request. "Padraig?" Jamison repeated. "Why?"

Hector shook his head. "The messenger dinna say," he said. "Will ye go?"

Jamison looked out at the line in the distance, pondering the proposal. By this time, Kendrick and Caspian and Beaux had made their way over to him, all of them wanting to know what the messenger had said. When Hector repeated what he had told his brother, the three men looked at Jamison.

"What are ye going tae do?" Kendrick asked. "Padraig is a man of honor, Jamie. He's not like the rest of those brutes."

Jamison's expression was pensive. "Yet he killed Georgie," he said, turning to glance at his friends. "I doubt this is a trap but the fact that he killed Georgie tae lure me home… how much honor can he have?"

Beaux shook his head. "Padraig dinna order the death of Georgie," he said. "It had tae be his da. Somerled MacKenzie was much like Connell – the man had that taste for blood in him. Padraig isna like his da."

That was generally true. Still, Jamison was puzzled and wary. "Then I wonder what he has tae say tae me."

"You will not know unless you speak with him," Havilland said quietly. All of the men looked at her but she was looking at her husband. "Make sure your dirk is close at hand when you hear what the man has to say. You have come this far, Jamie. At least he is willing to talk before striking."

She was absolutely right. It was sage advice from his wife. It was also her approval to put himself in a fairly risky situation but it was the only choice he had. Lifting his hand, he motioned for his horse to be brought forth, the big black beast with the hairy mane and tail. As the animal was brought through the ranks of men, Jamison turned to Havilland and kissed her soft, warm mouth.

"Ye hold the line here," he told her. Then, he looked at his friends around him, men anxiously awaiting his order. "Go back to yer men. If ye see Padraig move against me, ye will unleash the archers. Do ye understand?"

Beaux, Kendrick, and Caspian nodded grimly, but Jamison looked pointedly at Kendrick at that point. "And ye, Ken… ye know what tae do."

He meant in taking Havilland to safety. Kendrick nodded. "I do."

There was nothing more to say. It was difficult not to feel the tension, the apprehension of what was to come, as Jamison mounted his horse. He was doing a fairly good job with ignoring the anxiety until he looked at Havilland's face. She, too, was trying very hard to ignore the tension but he could see the fear in her eyes. He reached out a hand to her.

"Not tae worry, love," he said. "I'll know what he wants soon enough and we'll know what our course of action should be."

She nodded bravely. "Hector and I will make sure the MacLennan archers are ready."

"Good."

"Where is your dirk?"

He squeezed her hand and let it go. "Where Padraig canna see it."

With that, he kicked his horse forward and the animal charged off, kicking up clods of soft earth as it went. Racing through the cool morning air, many thoughts were rolling through his head when he should have been focused on Padraig. Thoughts of Havilland and of their future together. Thoughts of his clan and his brothers and the peaceful future they needed. He was even thinking thoughts of de Lohr and of Four Crosses, of Madeline and Amaline, and of Havilland's desire to return to Wales. So many things rolling through his head when he should have only been thinking about Padraig. Perhaps he was reflecting on a life well-lived and the desire to continue that life. He wanted to see Havilland present him with their first-born son.

But first, he had to get through this day.

He was halfway to the stream dividing the meadow when he saw a rider break out from the MacKenzie lines. Knowing it was Padraig, he slowed his horse and came to a complete halt once he reached the stream. He dismounted, putting the horse between him and the MacKenzie lines to prevent a MacKenzie archer from targeting him. Once off the horse, he stood there and waited for Padraig to arrive.

He wasn't long in waiting. Padraig made his way across the field in good time, slowing his animal down once he reached Jamison. Unlike Jamison, however, he remained mounted. A stocky man with dark hair and a surprisingly gentle expression, Padraig MacKenzie was well-liked in his clan. His opinion was trusted and he had proven himself to be wise and reasonable. When his gaze finally met Jamison's, he nodded his head in acknowledgement.

"Jamison," he greeted. "My thanks for meeting me."

Jamison remained behind his horse. "I suppose ye have something tae say tae me."

Padraig nodded. "Indeed, I do," he said. "The first thing I need tae tell ye is that me da died last week. I am now the MacKenzie."

That drew a reaction out of Jamison. "I dinna know," he said. "I hadna heard. I dunna believe me da has, either. He would have told me."

Padraig shook his head. "No one knows," he said. "I've given orders that the death be kept a secret until I choose tae announce it."

That didn't make much sense to Jamison but he didn't comment on it. "I see," he said simply.

Padraig smiled weakly when he saw that Jamison had nothing more to say to the news. "I think 'tis time for total honesty," he said. "I know me da was out for yer blood because of what ye did tae Connell. If ye want tae know the truth, 'tis me da who killed Georgie. He did it so ye'd return from wherever ye'd gone and face his rage. He also did it tae take

George Munro's heir as ye took his. It was a reckoning."

Nothing the man said surprised Jamison. "I suspected as much," he said. "Is that all ye wanted tae tell me?"

Padraig climbed off of his horse. He took a few steps in Jamison's direction and Jamison found himself mentally calculating how fast he could unsheathe his dirk. He was still quite wary of the man's motives.

"Nay," Padraig said. "I wanted tae ask ye if we canna solve our hostilities in ways that dunna involve men dying and widows weeping. I have no desire tae fight ye, Jamison. I've always believed our clans could live in peace but me da and Connell thought differently. They were entrenched in the old ways, the ways when men had tae fight for their lands and people. But ye and I… we're different. I dunna think ye want a battle, do ye?"

Jamison wasn't particularly surprised to hear this, coming from Padraig. It was difficult not to feel some hope in the matter, the possibility that the MacKenzie's vengeance against him wouldn't lead to bloodshed, so he struggled against having too much faith in what Padraig was saying.

"Nay," he said evenly. "But the fact remains that I killed yer brother when he attacked me brother. I'll not go the rest of me life lookin' over me shoulder for a MacKenzie assassin, Padraig. If we're going tae fight, then let's do it now and get it over with. Let's settle it today."

Padraig shook his head. "I dunna want tae fight ye," he repeated. "And me da's sense of vengeance isna me own. Connell was a brutal, aggressive man. He lived on the scent of blood, just as me da did. Their vengeance is their own; it isna mine. Ye did what ye had tae do tae protect Robbie. I understand that and so do many others in me clan. It's not as if ye went forth with the intention of murderin' Connell. Ye did it tae save yer brother and that's something we'd all have done in the same circumstances. I canna fault ye for that."

Jamison was actually shocked to hear that. That wasn't something he had expected, not in the least. His brow furrowed, showing his surprise and doubt.

"Can I believe such talk?" he asked, incredulous. "Ye brought yer army here today for a reason, Padraig. Ye came for a fight."

Padraig's gaze lingered on him a moment before turning to the line of MacKenzies far back behind him. A group of men stood in the distance, hair blowing in the wind, *brecans* waving like banners. It was a quiet, solemn group.

"Nay, I dinna," he said. "I came tae show ye that each man is willin' tae lay down his arms in a show of peace. In spite of what ye think of the MacKenzies, we dunna like fightin' any more than ye do. We want tae live in peace and the only way tae do that was tae show ye a united clan, each man willin' tae forgive and forget. No one much liked Connell, anyway, and the men that killed Georgie were me da's men. They were paid tae do it."

As Jamison watched, MacKenzie warriors began laying their spears and axes and swords to the ground, putting them upon the soft sea grass. Every man was laying down the weapons he was carrying in an astonishing show of submission.

Jamison was growing increasingly amazed as he watched. He'd never seen anything like it in his life. Was he dreaming all of this? Was it really true that the MacKenzie wanted peace? Although he wanted very much to believe, he couldn't quite bring himself to do it.

"Where are the men who killed Georgie?" he asked. "Unless ye turn them over tae me for punishment, I canna believe ye. What they did was murder, Padraig."

Padraig nodded. "I know," he said. "I had me own men round them up last night. I'll give them tae ye. They are misfits, men me da used tae do dirty deeds the rest of us wouldna. Will ye at least consider a peace between us, Jamison? Ye'll take over yer clan someday and I'd like tae call ye an ally. I dunna want me children tae grow up a-fearin' ye. I want us tae know peace."

So did Jamison. Now that he had a wife and the prayers for children in the future, he very much wanted peace, too. Of all the things he thought that would happen today, this request for harmony was not among them. Coming from a MacKenzie who wanted to change the course of his clan, to turn them from a warring one into one of goodwill, it was almost too good to believe. But believe he did. Jamison knew that Padraig's reputation as a reasonable and wise man was a well-established one. As Kendrick had said, he was a man of honor.

So was Jamison.

"It has tae start somewhere," he said after a moment. "If there is tae be peace, then let it start with us. I am willing."

Padraig smiled, his expression infused with hope. "I was hoping ye would think so," he said. "If ye'll let me, I'll bring the men who killed Georgie tae yer da. He can have them tae punish as he sees fit."

"Me da will appreciate that."

Padraig nodded, glancing back at the line of Munro warriors on the rise in the distance. Then, he cleared his throat softly.

"Me wife…," he began, clearly fumbling for words. "She wanted me tae ask ye… we just had our first son and she wants tae know if ye'll be his godfather. She thinks – she hopes – that it will cement a new peace between us."

It was a great honor that Padraig was giving him and Jamison broke into a smile for the first time since they'd met. Only a man with a sincere interest in peace would make such a serious request. That small gesture, more than anything else Padraig had said, told Jamison that he was, indeed, serious about an alliance.

"It would be me privilege, Padraig," he said. "'Tis quite an unexpected request, I must say. I've never had a godson."

Padraig smiled, also. "My son will be very fortunate tae have ye," he said. "And I hope that we can become more than allies, Jamison. Someday, I hope we can become friends."

Jamison liked that idea. "I'm sure we can."

With that, they went their separate ways, Padraig back to his men to bring forth those who had murdered George the Younger and Jamison back to a very anxious group of friends and warriors who were waiting for the signal to charge. When Jamison told them what Padraig had said and of the peaceful resolution to a volatile situation, there was no escaping the cheer that echoed against the bright blue sky, each man relieved and satisfied in his own way. But none more so than Jamison.

No blood would be shed today.

It was a startling conclusion to a day that Jamison was positive would bring a bloodbath. It was better than he could have ever dreamed. The flight from home, the battles in Wales, the death of George the Younger, and his entire relationship with Havilland had been a struggle revolving around one small incident between Robert Munro and Connell MacKenzie that had changed the course of Jamison's life.

Now, Jamison was coming to understand the incident he thought had ruined his life had, in truth, changed his course for the better. Now, with great hope on the horizon, Jamison and Havilland could do nothing but look ahead and dream of the days to come.

The Red Lion and his lioness had finally found their heaven.

☙ THE END ❧

About Kathryn Le Veque

Medieval Just Got Real.

KATHRYN LE VEQUE is a USA TODAY Bestselling author, an Amazon All-Star author, and a #1 bestselling, award-winning, multi-published author in Medieval Historical Romance and Historical Fiction. She has been featured in the NEW YORK TIMES and on USA TODAY's HEA blog. In March 2015, Kathryn was the featured cover story for the March issue of InD'Tale Magazine, the premier Indie author magazine. She was also a quadruple nominee (a record!) for the prestigious RONE awards for 2015.

Kathryn's Medieval Romance novels have been called 'detailed', 'highly romantic', and 'character-rich'. She crafts great adventures of love, battles, passion, and romance in the High Middle Ages. More than that, she writes for both women AND men – an unusual crossover for a romance author – and Kathryn has many male readers who enjoy her stories because of the male perspective, the action, and the adventure.

On October 29, 2015, Amazon launched Kathryn's Kindle Worlds Fan Fiction site WORLD OF DE WOLFE PACK. Please visit Kindle Worlds for Kathryn Le Veque's World of de Wolfe Pack and find many action-packed adventures written by some of the top authors in their genre using Kathryn's characters from the de Wolfe Pack series. As Kindle World's FIRST Historical Romance fan fiction world, Kathryn Le Veque's World of de Wolfe Pack will contain all of the great story-telling you have come to expect.

Kathryn loves to hear from her readers. Please find Kathryn on Facebook at Kathryn Le Veque, Author, or join her on Twitter @kathrynleveque, and don't forget to visit her website at www.kathrynleveque.com.

Made in the USA
San Bernardino, CA
31 December 2016